RAVES FOR JANET DAILEY
AND *CALD*

"Dailey has written a tale as clearly branded with her imprimatur as the herd on the Triple C Ranch is branded with the Calders' C's. By turns an old-fashioned western and a thoroughly modern romance, this update on the Calder family shows Dailey gamely back on the horse and riding well."
Publishers Weekly

"Entertaining. Fans of the series will find it comforting to return to the Triple C Ranch in Montana to pick up the family saga, which Dailey has done well to keep alive."
Cleveland Plain Dealer

"An epic tale, an intimate romance."
Vero Beach (FL) *Islander*

"Ms. Dailey [has been called] 'queen of the Western romance' and this book proves it."
Dallas Morning News

"One of the writers who pioneered modern romance fiction."
Tulsa World

"A master storyteller of romantic tales, Dailey weaves all the 'musts' together to create the perfect love story."
Leisure magazine

"Dailey is a smooth, experienced romance writer."
Arizona Daily Star

"[Ms. Dailey] . . . has had ample practice
in tugging at heartstrings while creating suspense.
It's a sure fire combination."
Cape Codder

"Janet Dailey's mastery of sweeping romance,
divided by loyalties, and searing passion has made
her one of the bestselling authors of all time."
Lanier County (GA) News

Books by
Janet Dailey

HOMECOMING
ILLUSIONS
CALDER PRIDE

JANET DAILEY

CALDER PRIDE

HarperTorch
An Imprint of HarperCollins*Publishers*

This is a work of fiction. Names, characters, places, and incidents are products of the author's imagination or are used fictitiously and are not to be construed as real. Any resemblance to actual events, locales, organizations, or persons, living or dead, is entirely coincidental.

HARPERTORCH
An Imprint of HarperCollins*Publishers*
10 East 53rd Street
New York, New York 10022-5299

ISBN: 0-06-072723-3

First HarperTorch special paperback printing: April 2004
First HarperTorch paperback printing: October 2000
First HarperCollins hardcover printing: September 1999

Printed in the United States of America

Visit HarperTorch on the World Wide Web at www.harpercollins.com

CALDER PRIDE

Calder Family Tree

Seth Calder ······*married*······ Madeline Chase (Elaine Dunshill—wife of the Earl of Crawford)

Chase (Benteen) Calder ······*married*······ Lorna Pearce

Webb Matthew Calder ······*married*······ Lillian Reisner

Arthur William Calder (died at the age of 3)

(Chase) Benteen Calder ······*married*······ Mary Frances Elizabeth (Maggie) O'Rourke

Tyrone (Ty) Calder ······*married*······ Tara Lee Dyson
then divorced Tara
and married Jessy Niles

Catheen (Cat) Calder ······*married*······ Logan Echohawk

Quint Calder Echohawk

PART 1

Living is never easy
When someone you love has died,
And you have nothing to fall back on
But that iron Calder pride.

ONE

A north breeze swept across the private airstrip and rustled through the grass at its edges. It was Calder grass, growing on Calder land and stretching in all directions farther than the living eye could see.

Directly southwest of the airstrip stood the headquarters of Montana's famed Triple C Ranch, the home of the Calder Cattle Company. For well over a hundred years, the land had tasted the sweat, the blood, and the tears of the Calders.

Too many tears, Chase Calder decided and leaned heavily on his cane. For a moment, his big shoulders bowed under the weight of the thing that hung so heavily on him. But there was no one around to see this brief display of weakness by the Calder family patriarch. He stood alone outside the airstrip's metal hangar.

The drone of a twin-engine aircraft had Chase Calder squaring his shoulders and lifting his gaze to the immense blue sky overhead. His sharp eyes quickly spotted the plane making a straight-in approach to the landing strip. His son Ty was at the controls, and his daughter Cathleen was the plane's only other occupant.

The plane touched down and rolled toward him.

Chase glanced at the heavens, the ache intensifying in his chest.

"Where am I going to find the words, Maggie?" he murmured, talking as he so often did to his late wife.

But there were no words that could dull the pain of the news he carried. Just as there had been none to blunt the knife-stabbing pain he'd felt five years ago when he learned his wife Maggie had died in the plane crash that had so severely injured him.

Chase shifted more of his weight onto the cane, his expression grim as he watched the twin-engine plane taxi to a stop near the hangar. Within seconds of the engines' being shut down, the plane's rear door opened and out stepped his twenty-year-old daughter, Cathleen.

His eyes softened at the sight of her. In many ways, Cat, as the family called her, was the image of his late wife, with her glistening black hair and eyes that were as green as the Calder grass in spring. It was a striking combination, made even more stunning by the mingling of fineness and strength in her face.

Simply dressed in navy slacks and a white silk blouse, Cat came toward him with quick, confident strides. Chase glanced briefly at his son when Ty emerged from the plane, experiencing a familiar surge of pride for this tall and broad-shouldered man of thirty-five who bore the unmistakable stamp of a Calder in every hard-boned line.

But it was Cat who concerned him now, this full-grown woman who was his little girl. Chase straightened to stand squarely on both feet, abandoning his reliance on the cane, needing to be strong for her.

With a smile on her lips that was positively radiant, Cat ran the last few steps and wrapped her arms around him, hugging him tightly. He held her close, reminded again of his daughter's tremendous capacity for emotion, a capacity that could swing to the extremes of laughter, softness, and anger.

"It is so good to be home again, Dad," she declared on a fervent note, then pulled back to arm's length, her green eyes sparkling with happiness. "Where's Jessy?" She glanced beyond him, then tossed a teasing smile over her shoulder when Ty walked up. "Don't tell me Ty's bride-to-be is off somewhere chasing cattle?"

"She's at the house." Chase saw the startled lift of Ty's head and the sudden sharpening of his gaze as he caught the faint scent of trouble in the air.

Cat was oblivious to it. "Wait until you see the sexy nightgown I bought Jessy for her wedding night, Dad. On second thought, maybe you shouldn't." She stepped closer and studiously straightened the collar of his shirt, slanting him a look packed with feminine wiles. "At least, not until I talk you into making this a double wedding. It's ridiculous that Repp and I should wait to get married until after I finish college. That's—"

"Cat." He gripped her wrists to still the movement of her hands, his cane hooked over his arm. She looked up, surprised by the hard tone of his voice. "I have bad news."

"Bad news?" Her eyes made a quick search of his face. "Don't tell me Tara decided to contest the divorce from Ty at the last minute? It's supposed to be final—"

"No, it isn't that. The divorce is final," Chase said. "It's Repp. There was an accident late last night—"

"Dear God, no," she murmured, her eyes widening in alarm. "Is he badly hurt? Where is he? I have to go to him."

She tried to pull free of his hands, but Chase tightened his hold even as Ty gripped her shoulders from behind, bracing her for the rest.

"It's too late, Cat," Chase stated in a firm voice. "Repp was killed instantly."

She stared at him for a long, brittle second, her expression awash with shock, pain, and denial. "It can't be true," she said, in the thinnest of whispers. "It can't be."

"I'm sorry." There were no other words Chase could say.

"No." She said it over and over, her voice growing in strength and volume until she was screaming it. Chase gathered her rigid body into his arms and silently absorbed the pounding of her fists on his chest, waiting through the rage until she finally sagged against him and broke into wild, body-wrenching sobs.

"I'll bring the truck around," Ty said quietly, and Chase nodded.

By the time the luggage was transferred from the plane to the ranch pickup, that first violent shock of grief had subsided, leaving Cat numb with pain. She felt wooden, unable to move on her own, and offered no protest when two pairs of hands helped her into the cab.

She sat between the two men, her head lolling against the seat back, her eyes closed against the horrible ache that moaned through her. Some part of her knew that all the tears in the world wouldn't lessen it. But she didn't bother to wipe away the ones on her pale cheeks.

"How did it happen?" Ty asked.

At his question, her impulse was to cover her ears and shut out her father's reply. A few years ago, a younger Cat would have done that. But she was older now, and wise enough to know that denial was foolish. It changed nothing. So she opened her eyes and listened to her father's answer.

"Neil Anderson's youngest boy, Rollie, was driving on the wrong side of the road. The tire tracks indicate Repp swerved to avoid a head-on, but Anderson's pickup plowed into the driver's side."

"And Rollie?" Ty asked.

"He had a gash to his forehead." The grimness in her father's voice was tangible.

"He'd been drinking, then," Ty muttered in a tone that matched her father's.

"His blood alcohol level was way over the limit. He passed out at the scene."

With a strangled sound of protest, Cat swallowed back a sob. It lodged in her throat until it hurt to breathe. Beside her, Ty muttered a choice expletive and fell silent.

A breeze tunneled through the pickup's opened window, carrying the bawl of a young calf and the fresh scents of spring to Cat, of life reborn. She wanted to scream at the sounds and the smells, at the sunshine that washed the land, but no sound came from her.

The warmth and roughness of her father's hand settled over hers. In his touch there was both comfort and strength. The urge was strong to turn into his arms and cry more tears. But it wasn't what he would have done. Calder men never made a display of their grief; it was something they held inside. Only the very discerning saw the pain that lurked in their eyes.

Never once had she seen her father break down after her mother died, Cat recalled. For the longest time she believed that he had resisted it because to do otherwise would have been a sign of weakness. Now she understood that the pain and grief were too personal, too intimate, reaching beyond anyone else's understanding.

So she wrapped her own pain deep inside and

remained motionless, accepting the comforting weight of her father's hand but seeking nothing more.

The pickup truck pulled up in front of the massive two-story house that four generations of Calders had called home. Long known as simply The Homestead, it stood on a knoll overlooking the cluster of buildings that made up the Triple C headquarters. It was built on a large scale, a silent statement of dominion over the vast, rolling plains that sprawled in all directions.

Through tear-blurred eyes, Cat saw her brother's soon-to-be bride, Jessy Niles, waiting on the front porch. Slim-hipped and long-legged in her typical dress of boots, blue jeans, and white cotton shirt, she had been raised on the Triple C. Her roots went deep into the soil. From the first day the ranch had come into existence, a Niles had worked on it. It was a claim that could be made by several other families, including Repp Taylor and his parents.

Repp. A fresh wave of anguish ripped through Cat at the thought of never seeing him again, of never feeling his arms around her. He had been her first love, her only love. Now he was gone forever, leaving Cat with a gaping emptiness in her life she didn't think she could endure. But of course she would. That's what made it so painful.

"Cat." There was a tug on her hand, followed by her father's gently insistent voice. "Come on. Let's go in the house now."

His hand was at her elbow when Cat stepped from the cab. Jessy came to greet them, her attention centering on Cat, but not before her glance had run to Ty in a quick, warm look of love and relief that he had safely returned to her. Then her hazel eyes were on Cat, direct as always and full of compassion.

Jessy offered no trite words of comfort, but simply curved a hand on Cat's shoulder. "The Taylors send you their sympathies."

"You have seen his parents?" she asked, only now giving a thought to the enormity of their loss.

"I stayed with them for a while this morning."

Cat looked in the direction of their house. "I need to go see them."

"Later," her father stated.

Some distant part of her acknowledged that she was in no fit state to see them now. Without protest, Cat submitted to the guiding pressure of the hand that directed her toward the house. She never noticed when Jessy swung in behind to walk with Ty, each slipping an arm around the other, needing the reassurance of contact, with death striking so close.

It was a quiet group that entered the big house and walked directly to the sprawling living room. Chase paused beside his favorite armchair, his hand falling away from Cat's arm.

"I think we could all use some coffee." He leaned his cane against the chair.

"I'll get it." Jessy took a step toward the kitchen, then hesitated when Cat continued toward the oak staircase.

Chase noticed her movement as well. "Cat?" A look of concern darkened his eyes.

"I'm going to my room." Her voice was flat, drained of all emotion.

As one they watched as she climbed the stairs, holding herself stiffly erect. Her pale cheeks glistened with the wetness of earlier tears, but her eyes were dry now.

When she was nearly to the top, Ty murmured to Jessy, "Maybe you should go with her."

Jessy shook her head. "No. I think she would rather be alone right now."

Jessy sensed Ty's disagreement and understood

its cause. For too long he had regarded his sister as headstrong and impetuous, on the irresponsible side, and more than a little spoiled by an adoring and indulgent father. He didn't realize that, in addition to his mother's beauty and capacity for sudden fury, Cat had also inherited a good deal of Calder steel and that unbendable iron pride of a Calder. And—like a Calder—she wanted to grieve in private.

"I'll check on her later," Chase said firmly, settling the matter.

The sound of an upstairs door closing broke the stillness that had held all three of them motionless. Chase lowered himself into the armchair while Jessy left to bring coffee. Sweeping off his hat, Ty dropped it on an end table and sank onto the couch.

"What about Rollie Anderson?" he asked. "Has he been arrested?"

"I was told charges would be filed as soon as he is sober enough to understand them." A thread of anger edged the clipped reply. It was still there when his father continued, "I understand he has three previous drunk-driving convictions. With a manslaughter charge, it's virtually guaranteed he'll serve time."

"That will make things rough on Neil Anderson and his wife," Ty remarked idly. "Anderson is too old and too crippled with arthritis to keep the place going without help. And they can't afford to pay a hired hand."

The Andersons owned a small farm along the eastern boundary of the Triple C. Most of the time they had barely eked out a living. Rollie Anderson was the youngest of three sons, and the only one still living at home.

"If Anderson is smart, he'll sell the place and retire," Chase stated as Jessy returned to the living room with the coffee.

"Who should retire?" She set a mug of steaming

coffee on the table next to Chase.

"Neil Anderson," Ty answered. "We were just saying it would be best if he sold his farm."

"I wouldn't count on that happening any time soon. That farm means as much to Neil Anderson as the Triple C does to you." As always, Jessy spoke with a man's directness. "He will hang onto it until his last dying breath."

"I have no doubt he will try," Chase agreed as Jessy handed a mug to Ty, then sat on the couch next to him, their legs touching.

"Which brings me to something else I wanted to talk to you about, Ty." Her hand slid onto his knee in easy possession. "Under the circumstances, I think we should postpone our wedding until next week."

"What do you mean—postpone it? Why?" Ty challenged her.

"Because I don't think it would be right for us to get married so soon after Repp's funeral."

"It wouldn't be right if we were having some lavish wedding with acres of guests, but it's only going to be your family and mi—" Ty broke off in midword. "Cat," he said in understanding. "From the moment I picked her up at the airport in Helena, she was full of plans to turn our wedding into a double ceremony." He covered Jessy's hand with his. "You're right. We'll wait a week, but no longer than that."

"No longer." Her slow smile of agreement tunneled into him, touching all the soft places. Ty never ceased to be amazed by the warm ease he felt with Jessy, an ease that produced its own kind of heady glow. This was love, strong, steady, and certain.

Looking back, he knew now that he had never truly loved Tara, his first wife. He had been so dazzled by her dark beauty, he had mistaken infatuation for love and completely ignored the fact that they shared neither the same values nor the same loyalties—until Jessy opened his eyes.

"Later, I want to run into Blue Moon and take a look at the pickup," Chase said. "According to the highway patrol, it was totaled."

"I'll go with you," Ty said, then something—some movement, some whisper of sound, pulled his glance to the side hall that ultimately led to the rear of the house.

A lanky, dark-eyed man with metal-gray hair stood in the hall's shadows two steps back from the arched opening to the living room. Culley O'Rourke had a coyote's stealth, always somewhere around but rarely showing himself. And when he did, he was always silent, like now.

"Hello, Culley." Although the man was his mother's brother, Ty had never felt comfortable enough with Culley to address him as his uncle. He still remembered when Culley's hatred toward the Calders had been all-consuming. Even now, after twenty years, it made him wary of trusting Culley too much.

"I heard the plane." Culley fingered the brim of the battered hat in his hands, his sharp gaze darting between the two men. "Where is Cat? Didn't she come home with you?"

"Yes. She's upstairs in her room." Whatever personal doubts he had about Culley O'Rourke, Ty never doubted that he adored Cat as much as he had once adored Ty's mother.

"I'd like to see her." He looked directly at Chase.

"I don't know if you heard that Repp was—"

Culley cut in before the sentence was finished. "I heard about the boy dying. I'd like to see Cat," he repeated.

"Go ahead." Chase granted the request.

Without another word, Culley crossed the room

on silent feet, skirting the area where they sat and heading straight for the oak staircase. No one had to tell him the location of Cat's room, even though he'd been in the house no more than a dozen times in his life.

He had long ago figured out which of the bedrooms belonged to Cat, and spent many a night watching for a light to shine from its window. He didn't take lightly the vow he had made at the foot of Maggie's grave to look after her daughter and keep her safe from harm.

Unerringly he stopped outside her bedroom, hesitated, then rapped lightly on it and waited. But no sound came from inside. Concern for the girl who was his sister's image overrode any further hesitation. He gave the doorknob a turn, found it wasn't locked and opened it far enough to slip inside.

The bedroom was bright and young-girl feminine with floral-patterned wallpaper in tones of mauve, pink, and green. But Culley didn't notice it or the wide ruffles that ringed its old-fashioned vanity table. His gaze went straight to the dark-haired woman standing at the window. She was motionless, her arms hugging her elbows and her face in profile, her gaze fixed in a sightless stare at the world outside.

He studied her for a long minute, seeing again the strong resemblance to his sister and recalling the time their father had been killed. Maggie's face had been just as deathly pale as Cat's was now, and her green eyes had burned with the same bottomless pain that no amount of tears could ease.

Culley had thought she was unaware of his presence. Then Cat spoke. "Repp is dead. Did they tell you?" she asked in a voice completely devoid of emotion.

"I knew." Culley walked over to her. He longed

to hold her and ease some of her suffering. But he had lived too many years without that kind of contact. Made self-conscious by the sudden wish to offer it now, he kept his hands at his side. "You're hurtin' bad, but in time, it'll get better. I swear it will, Cat."

Time. Cat almost laughed at him, but she didn't. There would have been too much bitterness in the sound, and she knew her uncle had offered the empty platitude out of a sincere desire to console her. She nodded and kept silent.

"I wish there was something I could do," he said after a moment.

She caught the note of anguish in his voice. "Thank you, but there is nothing anyone can do."

As she continued to gaze out the window, she noticed a movement below. Focusing on it, she saw her father and Ty walking to the ranch pickup. They climbed into the cab, with Ty sliding behind the wheel. A moment later, the vehicle reversed away from the house. Cat half expected to see the truck head either toward the barns or toward the Taylor house. Instead it swung onto the road that led to the east gate.

"I wonder where they're going." She frowned.

"Who?" Culley stepped closer to the window.

"Dad and Ty."

He spotted the pickup traveling down the east road. "Probably headed for town. They were talking about seeing how bad the truck was wrecked."

Culley had already seen it. Knowing that Cat was coming home, he had slipped into town early that morning to pick up some chocolate doughnuts and brownies to have on hand in case she came to see him. He had just pulled up to Fedderson's convenience store when the tow truck arrived with the wrecked pickup. His sharp eyes had instantly spotted the Triple C brand stenciled on the vehicle's passenger door. One look at the rest of the smashed and mangled cab told him no one could have survived the crash.

For a fleeting moment, he had thought Chase Calder might finally be dead. Although he was no longer gripped by hatred for the man, Culley would have felt no regret at his passing, only sorrow for the grief it would have caused Cat. But he had quickly learned Repp Taylor had been behind the wheel, the man Cat loved—something Culley had never quite understood, believing as he did that she deserved better.

"The pickup was totaled," he told Cat. "Ain't nothin' left of the cab but a bunch of twisted steel and crumpled metal." A low, horrible moan came from her as she wheeled from the window, eyes tightly closed against the grisly image. Culley realized what he'd done and hurried to rectify it. "It had to have killed him outright, Cat, without ever feeling nothing, without even knowing what hit him. You've got to think of it that way."

"I wish I couldn't think at all." Her voice was little more than a thready whisper.

He lifted a hand to comfort her, then let it fall back to his side, uncertain what to do or what to say. He turned and looked out the window at the dust plume left in the wake of the departing ranch pickup.

TWO

The small town of Blue Moon hugged the edge of the two-lane highway that raced past it. To the rare passing motorist, it was an oasis of buildings plunked in the middle of nowhere, proof that civilization had reached into the heart of this grass desert. That it existed at all was due to the simple fact that Blue Moon was the only town for miles in any direction. In recent years, its population had tripled after Texas-based Dy-Corp began strip-mining coal on the old Stockman place not far from town. Progress had definitely come to Blue Moon. Some thought it was a good thing; some didn't.

But for the first time in half a century, the Triple C Ranch was no longer Blue Moon's biggest customer. That position now belonged to Dy-Corp, with all its employees and their families. Yet a Calder was still regarded with considerable respect by the town's longtime residents.

When the Triple C vehicle pulled up to the combination grocery store and gas station, Emmett Fedderson spotted Chase Calder right away. He broke off his conversation with the former sheriff and went to greet him, out of politeness and respect.

"Chase. Ty." He nodded to the two of them when they climbed out of the truck. "I've been expecting someone from the ranch to come by, but I never figured on it being you. How you been?"

"Fine, Emmett. Just fine." Chase switched his cane to the other side to shake hands with the man. "We thought we'd take a look at the truck."

"It's totaled, I'm afraid. I had Beeker unload both trucks around back so the place wouldn't start looking like a junkyard," he said. "I guess your insurance man will be coming around to check the damage for himself."

"The agent indicated that the adjuster probably wouldn't get out here until sometime next week," Chase told him.

"Figures. They drag their heels about paying off a claim, but you better not be late with a premium. That's the way of it, I guess," Emmett Fedderson declared wearily. "I feel sorry for the Taylors, losing their only boy like that. It sure was one hell of an accident. I was just telling Sheriff Potter about it." He waved a hand in the direction of the old man sitting on the planked bench in front of the store.

At the mention of his name, Potter spoke up. "I told Emmett he ought to park both wrecks out front, right by the highway. Might slow down some of these drivers going hell-for-leather by here."

"It might." Chase looked at the man who had been sheriff since before he was born. No one knew Potter's exact age, but all agreed he had to be nudging ninety if he wasn't there already. Age had shrunk his narrow shoulders and turned his wide hips into bony projections. He looked like a doddering old man, except for his eyes; they were as keen and quick as ever, like his mind. "How you been doing, Sheriff?"

Even though Potter had stepped down several

years ago, the title had stuck. He had been called Sheriff Potter for so long, Chase could no longer remember the man's given name.

"How I been doin'? As little as possible—like always." Potter grinned, showing a full set of yellowed teeth, all his own.

Lazy was a word that had been used more than once to describe Potter while he was in office. He had never denied it, simply replying that a lot could be learned by simply watching and listening. Chase doubted there were any dark secrets that Potter didn't know, including Chase's own.

On a more somber note, Potter added, "I don't reckon I'll make it to the funeral. I'd appreciate it if you'd carry my condolences to the Taylors, Chase, and to that pretty little green-eyed daughter of yours, too. I know she had her cap set to marry that Taylor boy," he said, proving again that very little escaped his notice, despite his age.

"Yes, I'll tell them." But the mention of Repp's death brought him back to the reason they had come to town. He glanced at Ty. "Let's go look at the pickup."

As they headed around back, accompanied by Emmett Fedderson, a navy blue sedan turned off the highway and stopped next to the self-serve gas pumps. Not recognizing the vehicle, Potter checked the license plates and saw the tags of a rental car.

The driver stepped out, a tall man in a dress black Stetson, partially zipped windbreaker, Levi's, and black eelskin boots. His outfit said cowboy—maybe even rancher—but there was something in the stranger's manner that made Potter hesitate to label him as such. His curiosity aroused for no clear reason, he studied the man a little closer, watching as he flipped open the cover to the car's gasoline tank, loosened its cap, then reached for the hose and inserted the nozzle in the tank.

The stranger was as lean as a winter wolf, and he had a way about him that made Potter suspect he could be just as dangerous as one, under the right circumstances. His eyes were busy, looking, seeing, noting everything around him. Not in a furtive way, but alert and cautious as though from long habit.

There was a time when nearly every western man had that way about them, especially the old-timers. Now it was a look Potter generally saw in only two kinds of men. It made him curious which one this stranger was. Not that it was any of his business anymore. Still, he wished he could get a look at the man's face.

The thought led to action. "Nice afternoon," Potter remarked, seeking to strike up a conversation.

The stranger obliged him by strolling over to the slab-seated bench. His hair was dark, neatly clipped. The high cheekbones and slashing jawline made Potter think the stranger might have some Indian blood. But it was his eyes that caught and held Potter's attention. They were an unusual smoke gray, with thick, sooty lashes. He knew at once he had never seen this man's face before.

"You couldn't have ordered a better day than this." An easy smile touched the stranger's mouth, deepening the grooves that flanked it.

The smile did something to the man's rugged good looks, changed them in a way women would like. Potter judged the stranger as somewhere around thirty, which by his measure was young.

"Yeah, it's the kind a day that makes you forget what a long, tough winter it was," Potter said.

"I noticed the range looks in good condition."

The observation was one a cowman would make. Maybe he had that in his background, but Potter still didn't peg him as a rancher.

"It looks almost gentle, don't it?" Potter remarked, watching as the man's gaze traveled over the grass prairie to the west where it rolled into forever. He barely glanced at the immense blue sky that awed most men seeing it for the first time. "But it's a hard land, full of extremes. It can be brutally cold in the winter, and blazing hot in the summer. Why, I've seen it so bone-dry that a body could stand ankle-deep in dust. Then you got the storms that rain lightning and turn the ground into a quagmire that'll suck your boots off. Yep, this land breeds toughness into a man, or it breaks him."

The man nodded as though he understood. "It's a big country, wide open and empty. A man could lose himself out here with no one the wiser."

"I don't know about that. A stranger would get spotted right off," Potter told him. "We don't get that many out here."

"I don't suppose you do." The stranger glanced inside the building, then back to Potter. "Is this your place?"

"No. It belongs to Emmett Fedderson." He pointed to the small sign above the door that listed Emmett as the proprietor. "He's around back with the Calders. There was a nasty head-on collision last night on the highway. It killed one of the Triple C ranch hands outright, but the Anderson boy walked away from it with little more than a scratch. Naturally, he was drunker than a hoot owl."

The stranger's expression never changed, yet Potter felt his interest lift. "Oh? Which one of the Anderson boys was that?" he asked, as if he knew the family.

Which Potter was ready to bet a whole month's pension check that he didn't. Potter gave him a sly look and ran his thumbs under his galluses. "Maybe you oughta show me just who's asking?"

The gray eyes turned cool for a half a second. Then the stranger reached inside his windbreaker, pulled out a wallet-sized leather case, flipped it open and held it out.

Potter looked at it. "Logan Echohawk. Treasury Department." He thought about that for a moment. He'd never had much dealings with the federal boys, though he'd always heard those FBI men were arrogant bastards. The Treasury Department, that was another matter. Just about everybody Potter knew—on both sides of the law—considered Treasury agents incorruptible.

He chortled in satisfaction. "I figured you for one side of the law or the other. You see, I was sheriff here for more years than some men live. Folks always thought I sat around too much doing nothing. But you can learn an awful lot from just looking and watching. You get to know who's just plain rowdy and who's gonna be trouble. Usually you can even figure what's gonna set it off." He realized he was rattling on, something he had done a lot more these last few years. Not many people listened to him, though. But the stranger did. He was listening closely, sifting through the bits and pieces just like Potter himself had done. "It was Neil Anderson's youngest boy Rollie that caused last night's wreck. Which boy are you after?"

"Latham Ray Anderson." He returned the identification to his pocket.

"Lath, huh." Potter tugged on his galluses. If he had been in his favorite chair, he would have rocked back to think about that. "I can't say I've heard his name mentioned in years. That boy had a belly full of anger, though," he recalled. "He hated the farm, and the way his pa made him work like a dog on it. He hated having nothing and naturally hated anyone who did have anything. It didn't surprise me when he joined the Army straight out of school. In fact, I was kinda relieved. Lath had a streak of mean in him that always worried me. Every now and then you run across ones that just seem born with an instinct for violence. Some of the bad ones grow out of it. I was hopin' the Army might knock it out of Lath. I guess they didn't. What did he do?"

"We just want to ask him some questions," the stranger replied. Potter could tell the man wasn't about to divulge any more information than that, ex-sheriff or not.

"He hasn't shown his face around here in years—not since his brother Leroy's funeral about six years back. If he had come around, there's enough people who still remember him that the news would have spread faster than a grass fire." Potter paused and looked up at the man, suddenly tracking his thinking and taking it a step farther. "Course, Lath always did hate the hard life his ma had. I remember the time Lew Michels caught him slipping a bottle of perfume in his pocket. Lath said it was a present for his ma. Lew made him sweep floors to pay for it. About a week later his storefront window got broke. It always seemed an unlikely coincidence to me. But you're right if you're thinking that. With his ma gettin' on in years, Lath might keep in touch with her."

The man smiled, his eyes crinkling at the corners, a mixture of amusement and respect in their gray depths. "Not much gets by you, does it?"

"Looking, listening, and thinking has been a habit too long," Potter declared, liking this stranger more and more. "Don't know how much information you'll get out of them. The Andersons have always been a closemouthed clan. None of them thinks much of the government, or any other kind of authority. It's an attitude you see a lot in folks as poor and proud as they are. It's a combination that can make a body bitter and resentful."

"It can do that." The gasoline pump clicked off. The Treasury agent walked back to the rental car, topped off the tank, and put the nozzle back, then went inside to pay. Within minutes he was back. Again, he paused, his glance running to Potter. "Which way to the sheriff's office?"

"Turn right just past Sally's Place, then straight ahead two blocks. You can't miss it," Potter told him.

The stranger glanced in that direction. "What can you tell me about the current sheriff?"

Potter's expression turned sour, revealing a contempt toward his successor. "Sheriff Blackmore likes the badge and the authority it gives him, and he ain't shy about telling people, either. Too bad his brain isn't as big as his mouth."

The information didn't require a direct response, and the agent offered none, merely nodding. "Thanks," he said. "It's been a pleasure talking to you."

"Hell, the pleasure was all mine," Potter replied and meant it. It was the first time he'd felt useful in years. With sharp regret, he watched the man walk to his car. On impulse he called out, "Say, if you ever get tired of the government rat race and all the political posturing, you might give some thought to moving here. This country could use a man like you."

"I'll keep it in mind." The stranger sketched a wave, then opened the driver's door and ducked inside the car.

Within seconds the car pulled away from the pump island and onto the highway. Potter watched it make the turn past Sally's and head toward the sheriff's office. From around the corner came the crunch of footsteps, signaling the return of Fedderson and the Calders.

When they walked into view, Potter studied the long shadows cast by Chase Calder and his son. He thought of the stranger and knew he wouldn't be awed by the Calders. And he wasn't the kind to crawl into a man's pocket just because there was money in it, like Blackmore. Yup, Potter nodded to himself, this country definitely needed a man like him. Too bad he wouldn't be hanging around.

Logan Echohawk pulled up in front of the squat, brick building and parked the rental car at the curb. His glance was drawn again by the vast and raw plains that stretched away from the town. Stepping from the car, he felt the call of it. He had never been a man who cared much for desks and cities. But in this day and age it was the way of things. Yet always, somewhere deep within him, there ran a touch of the primitive and untamed. Maybe it came from the fraction of Sioux blood in his veins.

He breathed in the smell of wildness that came off the tall grass prairie. In some ways, he could still be called a warrior. But today, he was a hunter, and his quarry was a man. Turning, Logan walked into the one-story building that housed the local sheriff's office.

Twenty minutes later, a deputy escorted Rollie Anderson into the interview room where Logan waited with Sheriff Blackmore, a barrel-chested man in his fifties with a belly that hung over his belt. Even in orange jail garb, Anderson looked like what he was—a big, strapping farm boy with wheat-blond hair, blue eyes, and a sun-browned face that showed a telltale band of white near the hairline where his cap always sat. A wide bandage partially covered one pale eyebrow, and the effects of a bad hangover were evident in the pasty gray undertone to his skin and the dullness of his blue eyes.

His head came up when he saw Logan, his puzzled glance running to the sheriff. Blackmore waved him toward a chair at the scarred metal table.

"Sit down, Anderson," he said. "This is Agent Logan Echohawk from the Treasury Department. He wants to ask you some questions."

"Questions?" Rollie lowered himself into the chair and stared at the identification Logan pushed across the table to him. He wiped a hand across dry lips. "My God, how much more trouble can I get into?"

"Do you have any coffee, Sheriff?" Logan paused, glancing at Rollie. "Would you like a cup?"

"Yeah." He rubbed his forehead above the bandage as a nod from Blackmore sent the deputy out to fetch the coffee. "You wouldn't have any aspirin, would ya?"

"Sorry." Logan took a pack of cigarettes from his pocket and shook one out, offering it to him.

"Thanks." His hand trembled visibly when he carried it to his mouth. Logan lit it for him, then returned the lighter to his pocket along with the cigarettes. "I swear I don't remember anything about the accident. Hell, I don't even remember climbing into the truck to go home. All I did was go to Sally's for a couple beers. I'd been working in the fields all damned week." He puffed on the cigarette and nervously tapped the end of it in the charred ashtray, his eyes sliding to Logan. "They're gonna throw the book at me, aren't they?"

"It doesn't look good."

He stared at the ashtray, shoulders slumping. "Maybe I deserve it. I don't know. But my ma, what's gonna happen to her? My old man's too crippled up to work the farm anymore. Without me, how's she gonna live?"

"Maybe your brother can help?" Logan suggested.

"Lath?" Rollie scoffed at the idea. "He hates that place."

"Maybe there's some other way he can help out. Have you talked to him?"

"No. He called Ma from Texas a few weeks ago, but . . ." He shrugged off the rest.

"Does he know about the accident and you being in jail?"

"Ma might have called him, I don't know." He shrugged again, then tensed. "Wait a minute. You're here about Lath, aren't you?" he said accusingly.

"That's right."

"I should have known." He crumpled the half-smoked cigarette in the ashtray. "You just don't leave a guy alone, do you? How many times does Lath have to tell you that he didn't know those guns were stolen when he bought them?"

"We just want to talk to him. We need a little more information about the man he bought them from."

"Yeah, right. Too bad for you that Lath moves around a lot, isn't it? Sure, he was in Texas a few weeks ago, but he could be in Timbuktu now."

The deputy returned with two Styrofoam cups of acid black coffee. Aware that he had obtained about as much information as he was going to get from Rollie Anderson, Logan talked to him a few minutes longer, then rode with Blackmore out to the Anderson farm to talk to the parents.

A newly leafed cottonwood tree formed a canopy over the mourners gathered at the grave site. For generations, the small cemetery near the river had served as a final resting place for the ranch's dead. Today the remains of Repp Taylor would join them, and the Triple C employees and their families had turned out en masse to pay their last respects to one of their own.

Cat stood bareheaded and tearless behind the Taylors, a single red rose gripped in her hand. Deaf to the words of prayer the minister intoned, Cat stared at the coffin. The spray of flowers was entwined with a ribbon stamped with golden letters that spelled out OUR SON.

There was none that said HUSBAND. The absence of it cut into her. She made no sound; a sharp hitch in her breathing marked the only change.

Control was something she had learned in the last two days, control aided by a numbness that kept all emotion frozen deep inside. *Just get through this day* had become her watchword. Cat was careful not to look beyond it, inwardly knowing the future looked too bleak, too lonely and empty.

Her father's voice rumbled an "Amen" beside her. Realizing the prayer was over, Cat murmured a quick one herself. A pitch pipe sounded a note, and a quartet of male voices began singing "Shall We Gather at the River." Others joined in the familiar hymn. Suddenly the service that had seemed unendurably long was over much too soon, and a quietly weeping Norma Taylor was led from her son's casket.

It was Cat's turn. Numbly she stepped forward and placed the bright red rose, still in tight bud, atop the floral spray. Her fingers lingered an instant on the velvet petals. Then the pressure of her father's hands guided her away from the grave and toward the Taylors. In wordless sympathy she embraced the woman who would have been her mother-in-law.

"We all grieve with you," her father said when Cat drew back.

The woman made a sound that was near to a sob, then lifted her head, her eyes not focusing on either of them. "I can't help thinking about Emma Anderson," she murmured. "How awful this must be for her—with Rollie at fault in the accident and the authorities looking for her oldest boy. I feel so sorry for her."

Fury was a whip that lashed through Cat, spinning her around and driving her from the couple before she gave voice to it. She was still trembling with it when her father finally caught up with her.

"How can she feel sorry for them?" Her voice vibrated with the effort to keep its volume low and her anger controlled. "How can she care what happens to them? Repp is dead, and Rollie Anderson killed him. Has she forgotten that?"

"Of course she hasn't." Chase caught her arm, forcing Cat to stop. "But she also understands how difficult it would be as a parent to know your child is responsible for the death of another. Now it appears that the law is looking for Lath as well—"

"Lath?" She frowned.

"Yes, Rollie's older brother. Evidently he's in some sort of trouble. The sheriff and some government agent were at the farm a couple days ago to see if they knew where Lath is."

"They both belong behind bars for the rest of their lives." Her voice thickened with the pain and anger that had woven itself through every tissue in her body. "Repp is dead because of the Andersons. And I hate them for it."

"Cat, don't. Hate won't bring Repp back. And revenge won't make the pain any easier to bear." Chase spoke from personal knowledge.

Recognizing that, she turned to him, her green

eyes stark with grief. "How did you do it, Daddy? How were you able to go on living after Mother died?"

"It wasn't easy." He had to be truthful. "Many times it still isn't," he admitted, seeing again his daughter's strong resemblance to Maggie. Sometimes that helped. But sometimes it hurt.

Ty and Jessy walked up, accompanied by the portly, cherub-faced Reverend Pattersby. Chase felt his daughter stiffen at the sight of the minister, and knew she was bracing herself for more murmured words of sympathy. Deciding she had heard enough, Chase spoke first, complimenting the man on his service.

"Thank you," Reverend Pattersby replied with a faintly pleased look. "In times of such tragedy, one can only try to offer some small comfort and leave it in the hands of the Almighty to do the rest. I regret that I can't stay longer for the sake of the Taylors. But I'm afraid I have a long drive ahead of me."

"I'm sure the Taylors understand," Chase returned smoothly.

"I hope so," the minister said, then turned to Ty and Jessy. "I must be off now. I'll see the two of you next week."

"Next week?" Cat echoed in surprise, then directed a questioning look at Ty and Jessy. "But the wedding is this Saturday."

"We postponed it a week," Jessy explained calmly.

"When did you decide this?" Frowning now, Cat glanced from one to the other.

"The other day," Ty answered. "We thought it would be best."

"Best for whom?" Cat demanded, anger flickering again in her green eyes.

Ty knew the quickness of his sister's temper and

sought to placate her. "Cat, we have plenty of time."

"Do you?" she shot back. "I can't tell you how many times I heard that—from Repp, from you, from everyone. Wait until you're older, you all said. Wait until you finish school. Wait until you graduate from college. There's plenty of time to get married. But there wasn't, was there?" she challenged. Without giving them a chance to respond, Cat swung back to the wide-eyed minister. "The wedding will be on Saturday—as scheduled."

She walked off. Reverend Pattersby cleared his throat and opened his mouth. Before he could say anything, Ty spoke up, "She's right. We'll be married Saturday afternoon as planned."

THREE

Cat shifted the gift-wrapped present in her arms and knocked lightly at the door to her brother's bedroom, the one he would be sharing with his new bride after today.

"Come in," Jessy called.

Right on the heels of that came her mother's voice. "Ty Calder, if that's you, you can't come in. You know it's bad luck to see the bride before the wedding."

Fixing a smile on her lips, Cat pushed the door open. "Not to worry. It's only me."

Three steps into the room, she stopped to stare at the tall, slender woman standing in front of the room's full-length mirror. Jessy wore a ivory suit with a collarless jacket cut in a classically simple design. Her long taffy-colored hair was pulled back from her face and plaited in a sleek French braid. The style accented the strong bone structure of her face, giving her a look of elegance and grace.

Suddenly Cat didn't have to fake anything, not happiness for the bride or admiration. "Jessy, you look positively stunning."

"She looks like one of those high-fashion models, doesn't she?" Judy Niles declared with undisguised pride.

"She certainly does." Cat walked into the room, marveling at the transformation that had occurred. "Ty won't know what hit him."

"This isn't the real me." Jessy attempted to take a long stride away from the mirror, but the slim-fitting skirt brought her up short. "The real me goes around in Levi's and denim shirts."

"But not on your wedding day," Judy Niles chided gently.

Jessy paused an instant, then smiled warmly and easily, losing the look of nervous tension. "No, definitely not on my wedding day," she agreed, then glanced at Cat, one sandy eyebrow arching slightly. "Although I wish someone would tell me what a bride does when she's ready thirty minutes early?"

"Why don't I bring up some coffee from the kitchen?" her mother suggested.

"Sounds good." Jessy waited until her mother had left the room before she shook her head in mild irony. "Like I need the caffeine to further jangle my nerves. But it gives Mom something to do."

"And you, too, I imagine." Cat held out her gift. "Why don't you open this? It's kind of a wedding present. I know Ty plans on leaving right after the ceremony. If I don't give this to you now, I might not have another chance." She was rattling on too much, trying to cover the forced brightness in her voice. But the glimmer of sympathy in Jessy's eyes told her that she wasn't succeeding.

"Anyway, this is for you."

She pushed the package into Jessy's hands. When she carried it over to the bed to open, Cat followed. In short order, Jessy dispensed with the ribbons and wrapping paper to reveal a slim box that bore the Neiman-Marcus name.

"I wanted to get you something personal and romantic," Cat explained when Jessy opened it. "Something appropriate for a bride. I hope you like it. I hope it looks good."

Jessy pushed aside the tissue paper and lifted out the naughty silk-and-lace nothing that masqueraded as a nightgown. She looked at it, then turned and, without a word, threw it toward the middle of the floor. It floated down to lay in graceful folds.

"It definitely looks good," Jessy declared, eyes sparkling with a wickedly impish light.

After an instant of surprise, Cat burst into laughter. Jessy quickly joined in. Cat suddenly found her eyes filling with tears and the ache she had forced deep inside broke loose, threatening to surface. She turned away, determined not to spoil Jessy's joy. But it was too late; Jessy's quick eyes had already seen the welling tears.

"Cat." There was a wealth of sympathy in that single word.

"I'm all right," she insisted with a sharp toss of her head.

Jessy took a step toward her. "This is why we wanted to postpone the wedding—"

"It isn't the wedding." Cat briskly wiped away the tears on her cheeks and battled to regain control of her emotions.

"Then what?" Jessy asked in a gently prompting way.

Without answering, Cat walked over and picked up the nightie, then stood there in the room's center, looking at the gown. "Did you know that Repp would never make love with me?" she asked in a voice that was too flat and too cool. "Nothing I ever said or did could get him to change his mind. First he said I was too young. Then he thought I should go to college first, saying I might meet someone there. After my first year, he said we should wait until we were married and do it the right way. I suppose because I am a Calder." A bitterness crept into her voice. "I loved him, Jessy, but he put me on a pedestal and wouldn't let me off. I hate him for being so damned honorable, so damned noble. I hate him for leaving me a virgin." Her voice trembled. "I hate him."

"Repp was a fool," Jessy announced.

Cat tipped her head toward the ceiling and expelled a breath that bordered on a laugh, then looked at her brother's soon-to-be wife, a wry smile tugging at a corner of her mouth. "That's what I have always liked about you, Jessy. You are always so honest and straightforward about everything—your opinions, your wants, your needs. You've never been overly concerned about what other people think. For a long time I didn't understand that, especially back when I still thought Ty should stay married to Tara. But you'll be good for him. You'll be good for each other."

"Most of the time, anyway." An answering smile showed briefly on her face before Jessy turned serious again. "Cat—"

"Don't worry about me." She deliberately cut her off.

"Actually, I don't." The ready admission took Cat by surprise.

"You are made of strong stuff, Cathleen Calder. How could you be otherwise when you are Chase and Maggie's daughter? I saw it in you a long time ago. Others haven't, probably because they have been too busy patting you on the head and telling you what a pretty little thing you are."

"I was wrong." Cat thoughtfully studied the tall blonde before her. "You are going to be good for all of us." Without another word, she walked over, tossed the nightie back in its tissue-lined box and clasped both of Jessy's hands. "If I haven't said it before—welcome to the family."

"Thank you," Jessy replied. Her expression softened without ever losing its look of calm, steady composure.

The bedroom door opened, and both turned as Judy Niles walked in carrying a coffee tray. "Sorry I took so long." She deftly used her elbow to push the door closed behind her, jiggling the cups in their saucers. "But your father had drunk the last of the coffee and I had to wait for Audrey to make a fresh pot."

"How is Dad holding up?" Jessy asked with a knowing smile.

"Don't ask." Judy rolled her eyes and crossed the room to set the tray on the long bureau. She poured coffee into three cups. "I swear your father is more nervous than he was when we got married."

"Poor Dad," Jessy murmured in amused sympathy.

"Your brothers aren't any better." Judy Niles brought each of them a cup, then spied the unwrapped gift on the bed. "What's this?"

"A present from Cat."

She lifted the negligee from its box. "This is absolutely beautiful, so feminine and"—she paused and looked at them with the same impish gleam that Cat had seen in Jessy's eyes—"so deliciously naughty."

"Isn't it?" Jessy grinned, and all three of them laughed like a bunch of girls. A knock at the door interrupted the moment.

"Yes, who is it?" Judy asked.

"Chase," came the answer. "Reverend Pattersby has arrived. We can begin whenever the bride is ready."

"I'll be right down."

The ceremony took place in the den, in front of the cavernous fireplace with its sweeping set of longhorns mounted above the stone mantelpiece. It wasn't the painful ordeal that Cat had thought it might be, mostly because she sincerely wanted Ty and Jessy to find the happiness she had been denied.

But there were moments when the tears in her eyes were for herself. Moments that came when Ty slipped a plain gold band on Jessy's finger, when they fed each other wedding cake and Ty licked the icing from Jessy's fingers, and when they scrambled to the can-festooned Range Rover amid a pelting shower of rice.

The worst came, however, after Reverend Pattersby and the Niles family left The Homestead, leaving Cat alone in the suddenly quiet house with her father, with too much time on her hands, and too little to do but think and remember.

FOUR

The first gray of dawn was a long brushstroke on the eastern horizon. Standing at the edge of The Homestead's pillared front porch, Cat watched the sunrise grow and spread. Fully dressed, she had both hands wrapped around a coffee mug, warming herself with the heat from it. Sleep had been elusive, and dream-tortured when it came, finally driving Cat from her bed an hour earlier. She waited now for the sun to rise and listened to the first stirrings of activity in the ranch yard beyond the house.

Sound carried easily in the early morning stillness, bringing to her the murmur of voices, the grating rumble of heavy barn doors sliding open, and the nicker of horses. Here and there, lights came on, drawing her glance to the collection of buildings and the dark figures moving about them. Morning chores had begun. Cat downed the last of her coffee, set the mug on the top step, and struck out across the yard toward the massive barn.

The huge double doors stood open. Light from the overhead fixture in the barn's long corridor spilled outside onto the packed earth. A buckskin mare poked her head over a stall's partition and nickered to Cat when she walked in. She paused in the alleyway, the barn's warmth swirling around her, redolent of sun-cured hay and horse feculence.

Metal pails clattered together in the feed room. Cat turned toward its door as a young, lanky cowboy stepped out, his gloved hands wrapped around the wire handles to five feed buckets. He stopped when he saw her, his head lifting to reveal the freckled face beneath the brim of his cowboy hat and the wheat-colored hair around his ears.

"Good morning, Nick," she greeted one of Repp's closest friends.

"Morning." He bobbed his head, his glance sliding away. "You're up awful early."

"So are you."

"Yeah, well . . . I didn't have much choice." He looked down the alley at the flanking stalls. "It's a workday."

"I'll give you a hand." She reached for the buckets he carried. After a slight hesitation, he surrendered three of them to her.

Two hours later, her hands gripped a pitchfork instead of grain buckets as Cat scooped soiled straw into a wheelbarrow strategically positioned at the stall door. Intent on her task, she paid no attention to the approaching footsteps until a tall figure paused in the stall's doorway, partially blocking her light. She glanced over her shoulder and saw her father standing there.

Cat wasn't the least bit surprised that he had known where to find her. Her presence at the barn so early in the morning was too unusual; word of it would have spread through the ranch grapevine within minutes of her arrival. It was only logical that her father would have been informed about it.

"Good morning." She picked up a pile of horse

manure, balancing it on the fork tines, and carried it to the wheelbarrow, feeling the strain in her arm muscles.

"Good morning." He stepped to one side, giving her room to dump her load. "Audrey has breakfast ready."

Food held no appeal to her, but Cat wasn't about to admit that, not when she could feel the concerned probe of his gaze. "I'll be up as soon as I finish here." She knocked the last of the droppings from the pitchfork and turned back to the stall.

"Nick can take care of that," he countered, an edge of impatience in his voice.

"I know, but I started it, and I'll finish it."

"Cat—" he began, no longer trying to mask his impatience.

"Dad, I need to do this. I need to work so I—" She stopped as her voice started to break on the sob that filled her throat. She tightened her grip on the wooden handle, battling to control her emotions, all the while keeping her back to him. "I need to work."

A long sigh slipped from him, weighted with weariness. "All right," he said, giving in. "As soon as you get this stall cleaned, come up to the house for breakfast."

"I will." The metal tines sliced under another pile of waste.

Unable to dissuade her, Chase walked away, fully aware of the reason for her actions. There was solace to be found in working yourself to the point of exhaustion where you are too tired to think or feel anything. No matter how much he might wish it were otherwise, there was nothing he could say or do to make her pain easier to bear. This was something Cat had to work through herself. He couldn't help her, which was the hardest thing to accept as a parent, and Chase found it more difficult than most.

Outside the barn, he paused and ran his gaze over the ranch compound, his expression grim and tight. Morning dew clung to a spider's web spun across a corral rail. The drops sparkled diamond-bright in the angling sunlight, but Chase took no notice of them.

Turning, he looked down the barn's long alley as Cat came out of the stall and propped the pitchfork against its wooden side. Unaware her actions were observed, she paused and rubbed at the soreness in her arm muscles, her shoulders slumping in weariness. When she noticed him waiting outside the barn, she immediately squared her shoulders and threw off the aching fatigue to stand taller. With lithe, effortless strides, she walked toward him.

"Ready for breakfast now?" Chase asked.

Nodding her answer, Cat fell in step with him and began the walk to The Homestead. Conversation was minimal, all of it small talk to cover a silence that would have been awkward. Halfway to the house, Cat noticed an approaching plume of dust traveling along the road that came from the east gate. "Someone's coming. It must be Ty and Jessy."

Chase swung his gaze to the traveling dust cloud. "It can't be, not from that direction. They stayed at the old Stanton cabin this weekend."

Cat thought it a singularly unromantic choice. She and Repp had always planned to honeymoon in— Pain sliced through her, cutting off the thought with the cruel reminder that Repp was dead. They would never honeymoon in Hawaii. She would never lie beside him in the night, never know the fulfillment of his embrace. Anger came, anger that Repp had denied her so much because of his ridiculous code of honor and his desire to do right in her father's eyes. She wasn't sure she could ever forgive him for that.

Even worse, she wasn't sure she could forgive

herself. Why had she let it happen? Why had she allowed all of them—Repp, her father, everyone—to tell her what she could do and when she could do it? Why had she allowed them to dictate how she would live her life? The injustice of it twisted itself in with the grief and the anger.

"Probably a feed salesman."

"What?" She caught the sound of her father's voice, but his words didn't register.

"I said it's probably a feed salesman," he repeated.

Cat nodded an absent agreement, not altogether sure his assumption was accurate. Even from this distance she could tell the vehicle was a pickup, and from the humped shape of it, an old one, which was hardly the kind a salesman would drive. Still she could summon little curiosity about its occupant.

The old Chevy pickup bounced and rattled along the dirt lane, its scarred sides pocked with rust. The exhaust pipe spewed the telltale smoke of an oil burner. It mixed with the road dust churned up by nearly bald tires.

Neil Anderson was in the driver's seat, his rheumy eyes fixed on the collection of buildings and the imposing house that grew steadily larger in almost direct proportions to his misgivings. Easing up on the accelerator, he fumbled a moment, then finally pulled the faded red kerchief from the pocket of his bib overalls and mopped at the watery discharge from his eyes. It was a simple task made difficult by the arthritis that gnarled his hands and bent his fingers at an odd angle. He hooked an end of the kerchief back in the overalls pocket and stuffed it inside, then turned a gaunt and bony face toward his wife of nearly fifty years.

Emma Anderson bore little resemblance to the stout, buxom bride she had once been. Years of hard living and unending labor had whittled at her until she was wiry and thin. Now, her once-plump cheeks were sunken and hollow, and her fair skin was leathered and seamed with lines like an old worn-out saddle. The gleam in her dark eyes had long ago become a hard thing that too often reminded him of his failure to provide.

Her bland expression reflected none of his doubts about the mission before them. It bothered him that she could sit there like that, her callused hands calmly folded in her lap while he squirmed with uncertainty.

Unable to keep silent about his concern any longer, Neil finally voiced it. "Coming here is a mistake."

"What other choice do we have? You know what that lawyer told us. If we want to help Rollie, this is the only chance we got."

"It's a waste of time," he stated, gruff with his opinion. "He won't listen."

"He'll listen," Emma replied with confidence. "Calder likes to think of himself as a fair man."

"Listening don't mean he'll help," he muttered, then got to the crux of his unease. "I've never needed no man's help before. Tough as it's been for us at times, I've never had to go to any man with my hat in my hand."

Pride. That's what this talk was all about, Emma thought, smiling none too pleasantly. A man's foolish pride. Life might have been easier if her husband hadn't been so stiff-necked with it. She remembered his anger the first time she and Lath had killed and butchered a Calder steer. She also remembered that with hunger gnawing at his belly, he hadn't been too proud to eat it, not that first time or any time since. Course, he never lent a hand to the killing or butchering, which made it all right, she supposed, her lips pursing in sour sarcasm.

"I don't expect you to beg for his help, Neil." If there was any begging to be done, she would do it without hesitation. Rollie, her youngest, was her baby. Where he was concerned, pride be damned. "You just explain the situation to him, tell him what the lawyer told us, and ask if he'll help."

"He won't," he grumbled.

"We'll see." Determination pushed the point of her chin a fraction higher.

He slowed the pickup as they entered the main ranch yard. The swirling road dust dissipated, leaving only the roll of dark smoke trailing from the pickup's exhaust pipe. Emma sat a little straighter and took great interest in her surroundings. In all her years in Montana, this marked her first visit to the headquarters of the Triple C Ranch. She had heard it described often enough, but this was the first she had seen it with her own eyes.

She scanned the sprawling cluster of buildings—a mix of barns, machine sheds, small warehouses, welding shop, gas station, commissary store, and modern houses for the married help. All of it was neat and tidy. She thought of their own big old drafty farmhouse with its leaky roof and sides that badly needed a coat of paint. The farm was not a place she could point to with pride and say, *This is our home.* It was a place of hardship and physical labor with little monetary reward and a future that promised more of the same. She didn't blame Lath for leaving it as soon as he could, rarely returning to visit.

Emma looked, at last, at the two-story house atop the commanding knoll. With its pillared front porch, it stood big and white and grand against the blue Montana sky. Two people approached the porch, an older man and a young, dark-haired woman.

"There's no more need to wonder whether Calder'll be home or not. That's him and his daughter walking up to the house now." Emma nodded at the pair.

"I see 'em," Neil said, a trace of dread in his muttered reply.

Ignoring him, she studied the two, who now waited at the bottom of the porch steps, watching the ancient pickup coming toward them. Both were dressed in typical ranch gear—boots, jeans, and work shirts.

She touched the cotton fabric of the plain house dress she wore, a floral-patterned thing faded from too many washings. She had been right to wear it. She no longer had any doubt about that, although she knew Neil thought they should have worn their Sunday clothes. In Emma's mind, her good navy dress and pillbox hat had been the right thing to wear to meet with Rollie's court-appointed attorney, but not Chase Calder. It wasn't something she could explain, but she was certain of it just the same.

When the pickup clattered to a stop a few yards from the house, Emma raised a quick hand to her hair, checking for any wayward wisps. Her waist-length hair remained her one vanity. Every night she brushed it the standard one hundred strokes, and every morning she plaited it into braids and wound them in a coronet atop her head. Years ago it had lost its glossy chestnut color and turned a polished pewter gray, but that hadn't lessened the care she took of it or the pride she took in it.

She gave the stubborn pickup door a hard push with her shoulder, then climbed out and walked around to the driver's side to help her husband. His arthritis always stiffened him when he sat too long, and with his twisted hands, opening the truck door was difficult for him. Long used to his grunts and grimaces of pain, she paid no attention to them as she assisted him from the cab and kept a bracing arm around him once he stood upright on the ground. She stayed at his side when he hobbled away from the truck toward the porch steps and the waiting Chase Calder and his daughter. She saw, with satisfaction, the way both Calder and his daughter watched her husband, noting the effort it took him to walk and the discomfort it cost him.

"Morning, Calder." Pain had him biting off the words and breathing in jerky gasps. Neil halted and dug his kerchief from his pocket to wipe at his watering eyes.

"Good morning, Neil, Emma." Chase nodded the greeting to each of them in turn, an unspoken question in his eyes that asked what they wanted.

"If you have a few minutes, Mr. Calder, Neil and I would like to talk to you," Emma spoke quietly, resisting the urge to ask to see him in private without his daughter. She had seen the grief that haunted those eyes, and remembered that she had been engaged to the Taylor boy. From all Emma had heard, the girl took after her mother. And the O'Rourkes had never been the forgiving kind.

Chase measured them both with a thoughtful glance, then nodded. "Of course. Come inside." He motioned toward the house, then turned to his daughter. "Ask Audrey to bring us some coffee in the den, will you, Cat?"

She hesitated only a moment, then swung around and climbed the steps, entering the house ahead of them. Emma breathed easier, relieved that he had excluded his daughter.

The interior of the house was as big and grand as the exterior, the large entryway opening into an even larger living room. Emma looked around with interest while Calder shut the front door. She was surprised by nothing she saw. The Homestead was a popular topic of conversation among the locals. Every visitor to the house came away with descriptions of it that were passed around from one wagging tongue to another.

When Calder led them to a set of double doors on their left, Emma knew what she would see before she entered the room. Sure enough, there above the mantelpiece of the massive stone fireplace were the wide, sweeping horns of the legendary longhorn steer that had led the first Calder herds to this land more than a century ago. A framed map hung on the wall directly behind the desk. Roughly drawn and yellowed with age, it outlined the boundaries of the Triple C Ranch, an area of land larger than the state of Rhode Island.

The man who ruled it walked behind the large desk and sat down, waving them toward a pair of leather and brass-studded chairs that faced the desk. "Have a seat."

Neil lowered himself into the first chair while Emma claimed its twin. Neil mopped at his eyes again, then stuffed the kerchief back in his pocket. "I appreciate you taking the time to speak with us," he said with a nervous bob of his head.

"What is it you wanted to talk to me about?" He directed the question to Neil.

"It's about our boy Rollie," Neil began, then paused and threw an uneasy glance her way. "The missus and me met with his lawyer yesterday, a fellow by the name of Barstow. He's young, but he seemed to know what he was talking about. Anyways, the way he explained it is this—there's a hearing coming up. As things stand now, Rollie is facing a manslaughter charge, which means he'll have to serve some time in prison. Barstow wants to plea-bargain the case and get the charges reduced. He says that the judge might suspend the sentence and release Rollie on probation. But to do that, he says we'll need somebody to speak up for him. Not just anybody, but somebody whose name carries some weight."

Chase leaned back in his chair and regarded him steadily. "And you want me to speak up for him."

"Your word means something around here. Folks listen when you talk." He stated it flatly, making no appeal with his voice.

"Rollie is a good boy, Mr. Calder." Emma leaned forward. "A hard worker, too. He's sorry about causing that accident, sorrier than I could ever say. He never meant for it to happen. It's just that with the milking and the plowing and the planting, he'd worked from dawn to dusk all week. He went into town Saturday night like all boys do. He shouldn't have drank so much, but—boys do that, too. Such foolishness is a part of growing up, I guess."

"Forgive me, Mrs. Anderson, but this isn't the first time your son has been arrested for driving under the influence," Chase pointed out.

"I know." She released a convincing sigh of regret. "Liquor is a terrible thing that's messed up many a man. I could name a dozen people right here in this county who have a problem with it. And that night, there must have been at least a half dozen others at Sally's who drank too much. Any one of them could have caused that crash. But it was Rollie. He was the one at fault." Shrewdly, Emma didn't deny his guilt as she lifted her hands in silent appeal for understanding. "But it was an accident, Mr. Calder. My boy never meant for it to happen."

"But a man died just the same." His expression was unchanged and unreadable.

"I know." Emma let her hands fall to her lap, her slim shoulders slumping. "'An eye for an eye,' it says in Exodus. But I ask you, what good is it gonna do to send Rollie to prison? It isn't going to bring that Taylor boy back."

An eyebrow came up, a coolness entering his gaze. "Surely you aren't suggesting your son should go unpunished?"

"No, I'm just saying there's got to be some way to do that besides sending him to prison," Emma replied.

For the first time, his steady gaze shifted from her. He seemed to be looking inward, considering her words. At the same time, she caught the sound of footsteps approaching the den.

Guessing it was that Audrey person bringing the coffee he had requested, Emma rushed to press her advantage. "Rollie's just a plain, hardworking farm boy, a little foolish and wild sometimes, but he's no criminal. And he's needed at home. Neil and me, we're too old to do all the farm work. Crippled with arthritis like he is, Neil can't be bouncing around on a tractor ten and twelve hours a day. Why, he can't even put the milkers on the cows."

"That's enough, Emma." Neil glowered, the redness of embarrassment creeping up his neck as Cat walked in carrying a coffee tray.

Glancing at neither of the Andersons, she set the tray on a side table near the computer workstation. Cat had overheard much of the old woman's previous speech, both the pleading defense of their son and the wheedling declaration of hardship. Privately she was outraged at the very idea of Repp's drunken killer going unpunished.

"You know it's true, Neil." The old woman's voice was soft in its disagreement, a subtle air of meekness about her manner.

Cat placed the two coffee cups with their respective saucers on the desk directly in front of their chairs. When she turned to retrace her steps to the coffee tray, she encountered the old woman's hostile glance. The visual contact lasted little longer than a wink. The effect of it stayed, giving Cat the distinct impression the woman wanted her gone from the room. It turned her stubborn and fueled the anger she already felt. Deliberately she dallied at the coffee tray, making long work out of the task of pouring her father's coffee.

A silence fell. For a moment Cat was afraid it would last until she left the room. Then Emma Anderson spoke again, in that same humble tone as before.

"My husband is a proud man, Mr. Calder. He's worked hard his whole life. It's hard for him to admit he can't do for himself anymore. But the simplest chore is a task for him now. Rollie's had to do most all the work for the last two years. If Rollie goes to prison, I don't know how we'll keep the farm going. We can't afford a hired—"

Her husband broke in again, gruffly indignant, "That is none of his concern, Emma." Abashed by her admission and struggling to conceal it, he threw a hesitant look at Chase. "Like I told you, this was that lawyer Barstow's idea, or we wouldn't have come here today."

"I understand that." Chase nodded smoothly.

"I guess it all comes down to the question that brought us here, then," he spoke with a bluntness that revealed his lingering discomfiture. "Will you speak to the judge and ask him to go light on Rollie?"

"Please, Mr. Calder," Emma pleaded, trying to temper her husband's request. "There's been enough suffering already. We need our boy to home."

"So do the Taylors," Cat stated, her temper flaring. "But their son is dead. He can never come home."

"Stay out of this, Cat." The warning from her father was quick and curt. Cat checked the hot retort and waited, ready to defy him if the need arose.

"My Rollie isn't a bad boy, Mr. Calder," the old woman insisted. "He just made an awful mistake. He deserves a second chance."

Chase gave a slow nod of his head, conceding the point.

"No." Cat's half-strangled cry put her on the receiving end of another sharp look from him.

Then his attention swung once again to the Andersons. "I understand your situation and respect what you're trying to accomplish. In your place, I would probably do the same. But I think you have forgotten that as long as there has been a Calder on this land, a Taylor has stood beside him. On this matter, I stand with them, just as I stood beside them when they buried their son."

Loyalty. Cat wanted to laugh with relief. At the same time she was ashamed that she had forgotten the strong bond that linked her family with the small cadre of families whose ancestors had been trail hands on that first cattle drive and stayed to help her great-grandfather Benteen Calder build the Triple C.

It was a holdover from the West's early days when taking a man's pay meant you "rode for the brand" and fought his fights, standing beside him, right or wrong. It was an old code of living that ran both ways; to attack a man's rider, provoked or not, was the same as attacking the man. Back then, "All for one, and one for all" had not been merely a trite phrase; it had been a hard-and-fast rule. There were still some who abided by that old western code today, and her father was among them.

"I didn't figure you'd speak up for the boy," the

old man said with a slow, sage nod of acceptance.

"But you must." Desperate, Emma couldn't let that be the last word. "If you don't help us, no one will. Don't you see, they'll all take their lead from you."

"I'm sorry, Emma." Pity gentled his voice and his expression.

She seized on it and sought to twist it to her advantage. "No, please, you've got to help us. Please—"

"The man has given us his answer, Emma," her husband broke in, embarrassed to the point of curtness. "There is no more to be said."

"But what will we do?" She bowed her head and squeezed her eyes shut, forcing them to water. Tears had always been a woman's weapon, and Emma doubted that Chase Calder was the kind of man who would be immune to an old woman's tears. They ran down her cheeks when she finally looked up. "Every time I think about our boy getting locked away with a bunch of hardened criminals, it scares me. You know it'll change him. You know he won't be the same as when he went in. I don't want our Rollie turning into some mean, hard man. He did wrong, but he doesn't deserve that to happen."

Calder was wavering. Emma sensed it in the way he was having trouble meeting her eyes. For one brief moment she was certain he was about to relent. Then he dropped his gaze, a long, grim breath coming from him.

"You need to tell the judge that, Emma, not me," he said. "I can't help you."

"You don't mean that," she murmured in dismay, but she saw the hardening of his expression and knew he meant every word of it.

Fury came, black and swift. She shook with the effort to keep it from him, fully aware that to unleash it would kill whatever slim chance remained.

Beside her, Neil overcame the protest of his pain-wracked joints and struggled to his feet. "It's time for us to go home now." He prodded at Emma with a gnarled and twisted hand, urging her to rise, then bobbed his head at Calder in a respectful nod. "Thank you for your time and the coffee. We will trouble you no longer."

"But what is to become of Rollie?" Woodenly Emma rose from the chair, still pressing her case. She had come too close to give up without trying again. "What is to become of us?"

She resisted the pressure of her husband's guiding hand when he attempted to steer her away from the desk. Slightly built though she was, Emma knew he hadn't the strength to force her from the room.

With eyes still weeping, only more from frustration now, she turned her beseeching gaze on Calder. "Without Rollie, how will we make it? The cows got to be milked morning and night. There's hay to put up, fields to cultivate, crops to harvest—and nobody but us to do it. We're too old to be doing that kind of work. We'll lose the place."

He was deaf to her pleas, his expression closed, shutting her out. All hope for her son's freedom was lost. Calder would not help them. Nothing she could say or do would change his mind.

"You have said enough, Emma," Neil muttered near her ear. "Don't shame me further with your talk."

This time Emma didn't resist when he ushered her from the den, her glance falling on Calder's daughter as they passed her. Suddenly everything coalesced. There was one single reason for her failure.

"It was that Calder girl," she declared in a venomous whisper.

"If she hadn't been there, he would have helped us."

"You are fooling yourself, woman." Fumbling he opened the front door with his crippled hands. "If you're wise, you'll forget what happened here today."

"How can I forget when Rollie may go to prison because of her?" She stalked out of the house.

A silence hung in the study, the air still charged with the woman's emotional outpouring. It held Cat motionless until she heard the click of the front door closing. Uneasy and chilled by the encounter, she crossed to the study window and looked out, watching as the couple made their way to the battered pickup truck.

"I should feel sorry for them." But every time she tried to summon some compassion, Cat remembered the look of malevolence the old woman had given her. Even now it made her want to shudder.

"In a tragedy like this, innocent people on both sides suffer from it," her father stated. "We often forget that."

"He killed Repp." She felt again the rage of that loss. "Am I wrong to believe he should be punished for that?"

"According to state law, he committed a crime. And by law, he has to answer for it."

"You didn't answer my question." She turned from the window, impatient with his evasive answer. "Am I wrong?"

"That depends, Cat"—his watchful eyes studied her face, his own expression remained impassive—"on whether you want justice—or vengeance."

It wasn't the kind of reply Cat had expected. Without a ready answer, she had to stop and think, look inward and examine.

"I don't know. Justice, I think," she said at last.

"If you had to think about it, it probably is." His expression gentled, approval gleaming in his eyes. "Blind hate would have had you demanding it."

Hate had definitely been in Emma Anderson's eyes, Cat recalled. "I have a feeling that we just made an enemy."

"It's possible."

"What will happen to them? Will they lose their farm?"

"I would say it's very likely they will," Chase replied.

In the middle of August, the bank issued its first foreclosure notice on the Anderson farm. Cat learned about it from her uncle Culley.

The news wasn't entirely unexpected. The old woman had virtually predicted it when she had pleaded for help.

"It must have been a bitter blow to the Andersons." Cat looked to the south where the land stretched in an undulating sweep of untamed plains.

"Bitter ain't the word for it." Culley snorted a laugh. "I heard the old lady went after Jim Farber with a shotgun when she found out what he was there for. Old Neil Anderson managed to talk some sense into her."

"I wonder what they'll do?"

"It's hard to say. But I wouldn't be worrying about the Andersons." He sat loose and easy in the saddle, his body swaying with the rhythm of his horse's striding walk. "That Emma is a canny woman, sharp as a New York banker where money's concerned. Most folks don't give her enough credit for them keeping the farm as long as they have." He glanced sideways. "I'd wager that Emma knew that foreclosure notice was coming. They sold their herd of dairy cattle two weeks ago, and nobody's been able to figure out what became of the money. The Andersons claim they had to use it to help their son, which strikes me as unlikely, considering Rollie's got himself a public defender for a lawyer. Me, I figure Emma socked that money away knowing they would be needing it. They'll get by just fine. You wait and see."

She said nothing, her attention drifting to some far-off point.

Watching her, Culley could tell she had something else on her mind.

"What are you thinking so hard about?" he asked at last.

A soft laugh feathered from her. "Am I that easy to read?"

"To me, maybe. What's the problem?"

"I wouldn't call it a problem, really. It's just that I've decided I'm not going back to college this fall." The announcement was made with a large measure of calmness and certainty.

Worried that he might say the wrong thing, Culley stopped to think this thing through, searching his mind for the right response. In his heart, he was glad that Cat would not be leaving. But Maggie had set great store on a college education. It was something she would have wanted for her daughter. On the other hand, if Cat didn't want to go, would Maggie have made her?

"What did your father have to say about it?" he asked finally.

"I haven't told him yet."

"You don't figure he's going to like the idea, do you?" Culley guessed.

"That may turn out to be an understatement," Cat replied with a casual wryness.

That settled the issue in Culley's mind; if Chase Calder would oppose her decision, he was for it. The fact that it was what Cat wanted to do only added weight to his reasoning, tipping the scales.

"It's your life. You got to live it as you see fit," Culley stated, hearing his words and liking the sense they made. "You're a grown woman. It ain't his place to be telling you what to do anymore. You can tell him I said so. And if he gives you any trouble, you have him talk to me."

The underlying thread of fierceness in his voice moved Cat. She turned to him with a look of affection. "I love you, Uncle Culley."

He reddened and ducked his head, embarrassed by her simple declaration. "Guess you'll be sticking around here, then," he remarked needlessly, self-conscious and struggling to cover it.

"This is my home." The quiet conviction in her voice had a steely quality.

Her gaze lifted to travel over the wide, rolling plains, cloaked in their summer-tan colors beneath a big, brassy sky. It was a strong land, in some ways a hard land, its vastness stretching the eye farther and farther. Every bit of it, close to six hundred square miles, was Calder range. Born and raised on it, she knew this land in all its tempers—the harsh savagery of its winter blizzards and the warmth of its chinook winds, the awesome violence of its spring thunderstorms and the lush green of its new grass. It was a land and a heritage that she had thought she would share with Repp. But that wasn't to be now. The thought of him was like a pain squeezing her heart again, making it ache.

"If I have to live the rest of my life alone, then I'll do it here." Her head came up when she said that, pride asserting itself, making it less a statement of loneliness and more one of resolve.

Culley knew she was remembering Repp again. He wanted to say something to assure her that things would get better, but he didn't know the words. In the end he decided it was best to get her thinking about something else.

"Do you want me to be there when you tell Calder you aren't going back to college?" he asked.

"Thanks, but I'll handle it." Cat glanced at the sun, gauging the hour by its position in the sky. "It's time I was heading back."

"I'll ride with you part of the way." He reined the bay horse to the left, pointing it toward the headquarters of the Triple C, Cat's home.

Cat made her announcement at dinner that evening after coffee was served. As expected, her decision was not greeted with approval. To her father's credit, he reacted to the news with commendable restraint. It was Ty who erupted. "Good God, Cat, you only have a year left. It's idiotic to quit now."

"Some may think that, but I don't." Cat toyed with her coffee cup, conscious of her father's cool gaze.

"I know these last couple months have been difficult for you," her father began smoothly. "But before you make any hasty decisions, I think we should discuss this."

"There is nothing to discuss," Cat replied. "I have already sent a letter to the dean of admissions, informing her that I won't be returning for classes this fall."

"Without talking to me first?" It was that, more than her decision, that raised his eyebrow. "I think you could have told me about this before you mailed the letter."

"Maybe I should have," she conceded. "But it is my life and my decision to make."

"Cat, you know how much your mother wanted you to have a college education," he reminded her.

"Yes, I do." She was stung by the implication that she was somehow being disloyal to her mother's memory. "But it was never what I wanted."

"Of all the selfish—" Ty hurled his napkin on the table.

"I am not selfish!" Cat came out of her chair. "All my life I have done what somebody else wanted me to do. I was never given a choice about boarding school; I was sent. Out of high school, I was told not to get married, but to go to college first. I didn't even get to choose what university to attend. Before I knew it, I was enrolled in your alma mater." She flung a hand in Ty's direction, giving full rein to her temper. "And heaven forbid that I get married while I'm still in college. I was told that was unthinkable. And being a good little girl, I did what I was told. Well, not any more."

There was an instant of stunned silence in the room. Only Jessy showed no surprise at the vitriol that laced her outburst. The glimmer of approval in her eyes told Cat that she had at least one ally present.

"I still have some of my things there that I'll need to go get," she said. "I plan to leave in a day or so, pack them up and come home."

Chase tried again to talk her out of it, but Cat was adamant in this. In the end, he accepted her decision.

FIVE

The rear of the Blazer was jammed with boxes, framed pictures and assorted odds and ends, the accumulation of three years at the University of Texas. Cat had only one stop to make, the result of a phone call to her friend and sorority sister Kinsey Davis Phelps.

The instant Kinsey had learned of her decision to drop out of college, she had wailed, "Cat, honey, you can't do this! I know you're all broke up about your fiancé dying, but this will be our last year. You've got to come back." After thirty minutes of trying to talk Cat into changing her mind, Kinsey had finally given up. "To tell you the truth, honey, I thought we Phelps were good at digging in our heels, but you Calders have cornered the market on stubborn. But you can't break up the gang like this. Have you told the other girls yet?"

"I haven't had time, and I don't now. I'll get hold of them once I'm back home. Which brings me back to the reason I called you—I'll be pulling into Waco around suppertime. If you're free tonight, we could get together."

Kinsey groaned in regret. "J.J. asked me to spend

the weekend with her in Fort Worth. Daddy's flying me up there this afternoon. Wait a minute," she said with sudden excitement. "We're getting together with Babs and Debby Ann tonight at the White Elephant Saloon, probably go over to Billy Bob's later— You know there's talk that Billy Bob's might be closing," Kinsey had added as an aside. "Why don't you meet us there? Then the whole gang will be together again. If we can't talk you into staying, then we'll have one big blowout of a party to send you on your way back to Montana."

Cat had quickly agreed. It was the one regret she'd had, coming back before fall classes resumed: she wouldn't see any of her college friends. Now that had been handled.

By the time Cat reached the city limits of Fort Worth, the sun had slipped below the horizon, leaving long streaks of red in the sky to form a vivid backdrop for the concrete and glass towers of downtown. She followed the north-south freeway that bisected the city.

But it wasn't the coming reunion with her college friends that occupied her thoughts. It was pieces of her own family's history, the stories that had been passed down about her great-grandfather Chase Benteen Calder. Texas-born, he had been raised on a ranch somewhere south of the city and had fallen in love with the daughter of a local store owner. Fort Worth had been his last stop before heading north with a herd of cattle, his young bride at his side, to build a permanent home in Montana.

Cat was struck by the parallel that Fort Worth was to be her last stop before going to Montana for good. The difference was, she was making the journey alone, without the one she loved. The loss of Repp twisted through her, sharp enough to bring the sting of tears to her ears and blur her vision. Cat almost missed seeing the exit sign for the historic Stockyards District. Hurriedly she switched lanes and took the off-ramp, then turned west on Twenty-eighth Street.

As Cat made the swing onto East Exchange, the Blazer's tires rumbled over the street's old-time paving brick. Directly before her, the famous FORT WORTH STOCK YARDS sign hung above the street. More pickups than cars were parked along the street, and the wooden sidewalks, covered with shed roofs, were crowded with pedestrians, tourists, and locals alike, all garbed in western gear.

By some miracle that Cat didn't question, she found a parking place only two doors from the White Elephant Saloon, her rendezvous point with her sorority sisters. The twang of guitars and the rhythmic pound of piano keys from a honky-tonk band filtered into the street from one of the bars.

Before locking the Blazer, Cat took her credit cards, cash, and identification out of her purse, pushed them all deep in the side pocket of her Wranglers and shoved her purse under the driver's seat, then locked the vehicle and tucked the keys in the other pocket. August's sweltering heat still clung to the air, bringing beads of perspiration to the surface of her skin.

Yet, standing there, surrounded by the flavor of the Old West, Cat felt the infectious spirit of the place swirl around her—something reckless and carefree, something that grabbed the moment and squeezed every drop of enjoyment from it, the devil with tomorrow. It was a feeling that said a night on the town was a time to put aside your woes and celebrate something, anything. Suddenly that was exactly what Cat wanted to do.

"Cat! Cat Calder!" A familiar voice yelled her name. It came from the White Elephant.

Cat turned and saw a long and lanky Kinsey Davis Phelps running to greet her, turning heads as she came, with her model-like mane of long brown hair, lavishly fringed western shirt, skintight jeans, and real lizard-skin boots.

"Honey, when I saw that Blazer go by, jammed with boxes, I knew it was you." Kinsey wrapped her in a girlish hug, then hooked an arm around her and swept her toward the saloon. "Everybody's inside waiting for you, except Debby Ann. She won't be off work for another hour yet. You've lost weight, haven't you?" she said with a quick, assessing look. "Babs is going to kill you. The poor girl has put on another five pounds this summer, and the way she's gobbling down nachos she'll add another five pounds tonight. J.J. has just about convinced her to go to a spa for a week before classes start. Personally, I think she should go for *two* weeks. But you know J.J.—she would never tell Babs that for fear of hurting her feelings."

"While you spare no one's," Cat chided in a laughter-laced voice.

Grinning, Kinsey lifted a shoulder in a careless shrug. "As my daddy always says, the truth only hurts for a little while."

"Maybe, but with you, truth tends to be a blunt instrument. You keep hitting people over the head with it."

"Little ol' me?" Feigning innocence, Kinsey pressed graceful fingers to her throat.

Cat laughed, then forced herself to ask, "So, how is J.J.? Is her wedding still on for Christmas?"

Kinsey stopped and drew Cat aside before they walked into the saloon. "I can't believe I forgot to tell you." She dropped the pitch of her voice to a conspiratorial level. "The wedding's off. It seems Donnie Paul got another girl pregnant, somebody in

Houston, and he's going to marry her instead. J.J. is just devastated. Personally, I think she's well rid of him. Men are not worth half the tears we cry over them—" Kinsey stopped abruptly and cast a guilty look at Cat. "I just put my foot in my mouth again, didn't I? I honestly wasn't thinking about Repp when I said that. I'm sorry, honey."

"I know that. Believe me, if I didn't, I would be pulling that lovely hair of yours out by the roots," Cat replied. This time Cat was the one who took Kinsey's arm and led her inside the crowded saloon. Kinsey directed her toward a rear table where the two girls waited.

Blond and apple cheeked Babs Garvey greeted Cat with a warm hug and an immediate, "You rat, you've lost weight." Behind Babs's back, Kinsey gave Cat an I-told-you-so look. "J.J. has, too. Grief does that to you, I guess."

"I guess," Cat replied with deliberate vagueness, then turned to J.J. Richardson. Freckled and sandy-haired, J.J. was the plain one of the group, average in height, build, and looks. Like Cat, she came from a ranching dynasty, except that her ancestors had discovered a huge pool of oil beneath their West Texas spread. Instead of stepping forward to welcome Cat, J.J. hung back, eyeing her with a mix of hesitation and dread.

Cat guessed at its cause. "Kinsey told me about Donnie Paul."

"Thank God," J.J. murmured and caught Cat's hands in her own, squeezing them tightly.

Kinsey flopped onto one of the chairs, managing to look graceful doing it. "Donnie Paul is a jerk, and J.J. is well rid of him."

"I wish you would quit talking like that, Kinsey," J.J. complained. "When you call him names like that, you make it sound like I have no taste at all in men.

For your information, Donnie Paul is pretty wonderful in a lot of ways."

"Drop that torch you're carrying, honey, and name one," Kinsey challenged her.

"Wellll," J.J. dragged the word out, stalling to give herself time to come up with a convincing answer.

"Look at her—she has to *think*," Cat teased, sitting down and joining the familiar and affectionate baiting.

"No, I don't," J.J. retorted. "You all saw him. You can't deny Donnie Paul has a great body, gorgeous shoulders—"

"Substance." Kinsey waved off her answer and reached for the pitcher of margaritas on the bar table, then filled two salt-rimmed glasses, one for herself and one for Cat. "We want substance, not surface."

"Substance?" J.J. looked blank.

"Substance," Babs chimed in. "You know, the important stuff—"

Kinsey interrupted again, "—like—is he any good in bed?"

When Babs exploded with laughter, Cat forced a smile, on edge as she always was whenever their conversations turned to the subject of sex.

High color rosed J.J.'s cheeks. Briefly she dropped her gaze, then looked up with an embarrassed grin, and admitted, "Actually, Donnie Paul was fabulous in bed."

"Donnie Paul?!" Kinsey hooted in disbelief.

"Yes, Donnie Paul," J.J. asserted, then leaned forward, inviting them closer while she confided, a naughty light dancing in her eyes, "To be honest, guys, he is like the Energizer bunny in bed. He just keeps going and going and going."

Laughter exploded from Cat, joining Babs's gleeful squeal and Kinsey's full-throated roar. The slyly sexual remark was completely out of character for J.J.; it was the surprise of it, even more than the humor in the comment, that had the entire group holding their sides.

"Oh, mercy." Wiping the tears from her eyes, Kinsey sighed in exhaustion. "No wonder you want Donnie Paul back."

"Who wouldn't?" Babs murmured.

"Do you all remember the football jock I dated last spring?" Kinsey asked.

"Chris Harper, the running back?" Cat picked up her glass and took a sip of the tequila-laced drink.

"I thought Harper was the tight end." J.J. frowned.

"No, but he did have great buns." Cat grinned.

"That's the one I'm talking about." Kinsey pointed a finger at Cat. "He was always bragging about what a love machine he was. Believe me, the batteries were not included."

When the second round of laughter died, Babs rubbed her hands together in gleeful anticipation. "Another kiss-and-tell session, what fun!"

"Speak for yourself," J.J. countered. "Because I certainly haven't kissed anyone other than Donnie Paul to talk about."

"You know what this means?" Cat raised her drink glass and waited while the others followed suit.

Before she could offer the toast, Kinsey said, "To the Kappa gang, and our last manhunt together."

"Hear, hear," they all echoed and clinked their glasses together above the margarita pitcher, scattering clumps of damp salt onto the table.

Cat had barely swallowed her drink when Babs nodded to point out someone. "There's one for Kinsey."

"Where? Which one?" Cat turned in her chair, readily joining in the window-shopping game they frequently played, surveying the selection of males present and picking one out for an unattached friend. It was done mostly in jest, although there were always those rare occasions when they spotted a guy who was too good-looking to pass up. At those times, they would push the girl forward, urge her to check him out—sit behind the wheel, so to speak, maybe take him for a test drive.

"The guy in the plaid cowboy shirt and ten-gallon hat just coming back from the rest room," Babs identified her choice.

Kinsey took one look at him and muttered in horror, "Good grief, you take that hat off his head, and he wouldn't be more than five foot four, if that."

"But he could be a great dancer," Cat teased. "You should go find out."

"No thanks." Kinsey shuddered expressively and lifted her glass, taking another quick drink.

"What about the guy playing bass guitar in the band?" J.J. suggested. "He's not bad."

By the time Debby Ann Spring joined them twenty minutes later, the margarita pitcher was empty, and they had exhausted the supply of likely male candidates for their game. "What d'you say we all go to Billy Bob's?" Babs looked around to see their reaction.

"Sounds good to me." Cat stood up, then swayed a little, suddenly light-headed. Shaking it off, she guessed at the cause. "As soon as we get to Billy Bob's, I have to get something to eat. One more margarita on an empty stomach and you'll be picking me up off the floor."

"I'm hungry, too," Babs said as Cat dug the money from her jeans pocket.

"How can you be hungry after eating that whole platter of nachos?" Kinsey argued in reproof. "You all but licked the platter clean and you know it."

"I did not!" Babs stalked alongside her as the

group exited the saloon en masse.

"You did so. I saw your tongue prints on that platter," Kinsey fired back.

"That's a lie!"

"You two, stop bickering for a minute." J.J. called for peace, or at least a temporary truce. "Are we walking or driving to Billy Bob's?"

"It's only two blocks," Cat pointed out. "Let's walk."

For once Kinsey had little to say during the two-block-long walk up Rodeo Plaza to the Texas-sized nightclub, billed as the world's largest honky-tonk. The place was jammed with Friday night revelers, a living sea of cowboy hats, pearl snap shirts, blue denim, and cowboy boots. With J.J. plowing a path for them, they curled past the huge dance floor and finally found an empty table near the back. When the harried cocktail waitress stopped at their table, Cat added a barbecue sandwich to Kinsey's order for a pitcher of margaritas and five glasses.

For a time, the din of thousands of chattering voices, punctuated now and then by an exuberant "Yee-haw," made conversation difficult. With a host of new candidates available to them, the manhunt game was quickly resumed, despite the interruption caused when J.J. dragged them all on the floor to do a line dance.

When the noise and the crowd became old, they left Billy Bob's and ventured back to Exchange Avenue. "Where to next?" Kinsey wanted to know.

"How about the Longhorn?" J.J. suggested.

"Count me out," Debby Ann said. "I'm bushed after working all day. I'm heading home."

"Me, too," Babs echoed.

"Why? What time is it?" Kinsey peered at her watch. "Good grief, girls, it's only eleven o'clock. The shank of the night."

"It may be the shank of your night, but not mine," Debby Ann told her and turned to give Cat a good-bye hug. "I can't believe you're not coming back. It isn't going to be the same without you."

"I'll miss you guys, too," Cat said in all sincerity. Cat felt positively maudlin when the two girls walked away. She knew at once that she'd had too much to drink. She wasn't drunk yet, just enveloped in a warm, fuzzy glow that felt kind of good.

"Come on. Let's go to the Longhorn." Kinsey linked arms with Cat and started down the street.

"Not me." Cat pulled back. "It's time I found myself a hotel and called it a night."

"This isn't right." Kinsey eyed Cat with unexpected poignancy in her expression. "We can't break up like this. Not without a final farewell drink."

Cat hesitated, the same emotions tugging at her. "All right," she said finally. "But only one drink."

"Only one," Kinsey promised and took her by the arm again. "Come on. There's a bar here in the Stockyards Hotel."

Low laughter and lively music played by a country combo greeted them when they entered the comfortably crowded bar. Cat spotted an empty table near the small dance floor where couples two-stepped to an old George Strait tune about a fireman. They trooped over to it and sat down facing the dance floor. When the gum-cracking waitress arrived, they ordered a round of margaritas. The waitress returned with their drinks on her next sashay through her section.

Kinsey picked up her glass, then turned her sad eyes on Cat. "Honey, I can't think of a single toast to offer. I guess there isn't one for good-bye."

Silently they touched glasses above the table's center. For an awkward moment, no one said anything. Then the band struck up a rowdy and fun-filled Cajun song that had Cat tapping her toe to its infectious beat.

"This place is something." She glanced up at the pressed tin ceiling where the blades of a belt-driven fan turned slowly, circulating the smoky air.

J.J. looked around. "I think the decor is what they call 'cowboy baroque.'"

"And you know the old saying," Kinsey said, grinning: "If it ain't baroque, don't fix it."

Cat laughed. "Kinsey, that is bad."

"That's what I like"—Kinsey slapped the table in emphatic approval, then nodded at Cat—"a happy drunk."

"I am not drunk," she corrected, then added with a naughty twinkle in her eyes. "A little tipsy, maybe."

"A *little*?" Kinsey hooted and nudged J.J.

J.J. spoke up, changing the subject, "Hey, did you guys notice the barstools? They're saddles."

"Forget the saddles. Get a load of that guy at the bar." Kinsey pressed a hand to her chest. "Oh, be still, my lascivious heart."

"Which one?" Cat asked before turning to look.

"The tall one on the end. You can't miss him."

"Oh, yes!" J.J. emphatically agreed when she located him. "You know, when my granddaddy really liked someone—I mean, *really* liked him—he used to say, 'He's not only a good man, he's a *man*.' You knew it was the highest compliment he could give, but I never really understood what he meant until now. That guy is a *man*."

It took Cat a second longer to spot the man at the bar. When she did, she went still, her breath catching at the sight of him. For a moment, it was like seeing a ghost. He was tall, a couple of inches over six feet, trimly muscled with wide shoulders and slim hips. The hair showing below the dark brim of his cowboy hat was a deep blue-black.

"He looks like . . . Repp." Cat stared at his face, strong and lean like the rest of him.

"If he does, honey, then your pictures of Repp didn't do him justice," Kinsey murmured dryly.

On a closer look, Cat was forced to agree with Kinsey's assessment. The only things this man had in common with Repp were his height and build, the jet darkness of his hair and the impression of strength in his features. But the physical resemblance was enough to quicken her heartbeat and awaken all the old longings.

"It doesn't look like he's with anyone," J.J. observed. "And he isn't married, either."

"How do you know?" Kinsey challenged her.

"He isn't wearing a ring."

"There's proof for you," Kinsey scoffed.

"He's looking this way, Kinsey. He's looking this way." J.J. pounded on Kinsey's arm, almost squealing the words.

Cat had the distinct feeling he was looking directly at her. For a moment it was as though there was nothing and no one else in the crowded bar except the two of them.

"I think we'll need to draw straws for this one," Kinsey began.

"I'll check him out." A surge of irrational jealousy pushed Cat to her feet. However briefly, the stranger had reminded her of Repp. For that reason alone, she couldn't bear the thought of either Kinsey or J.J. flirting with him.

Never breaking eye contact with the stranger, Cat cut across the dance floor, ignoring the couples who circled it. As she drew closer, she saw that the man looked nothing at all like Repp. His eyes were a smoky gray color with incredibly dark centers that seemed able to bore deep inside and unlock all her secrets. There was a saturnine quality to his face, a leanness accented by high, prominent cheekbones, features that were chiseled in hardness and bronzed by the sun. His mouth was the only soft thing about him. Cat found herself focusing on it as she walked up to him.

Only at the last did she lift her gaze to again meet his. She recognized at once that telltale gleam of a man's interest in a woman.

Men had looked at her that way before. But this was the first time she had ever reacted to it. Cat didn't know if she should blame this quivering excitement she felt on the tequila she had consumed or the fact that she had initially mistaken him for Repp. Whatever the case, she didn't question it further—or the boldness with which she returned his look.

"My friends and I are on a manhunt," she announced, conscious of her pulse tripping all over itself.

Instantly his eyes narrowed with a piercing sharpness. Cat had the sudden impression that he had gone on high alert even though his stance hadn't changed. One booted foot was still propped on the bar's brass foot rail, and an elbow still rested negligently atop the bar's tall counter. Without moving his head, he shot a glance at the table where Kinsey and J.J. sat, then came back to her.

Just as suddenly as the sharpness came to his eyes, it turned to a glinting humor. His mouth quirked in a near-smile. "Someone out there is a very lucky man."

His low-pitched voice was lazy and warm, but it was the absence of a drawled delivery that caught Cat's ear. "You don't live in Texas, do you? Where are you from?"

"The Dakotas, originally."

Her glance went to the glossy black of his hair, its length neatly trimmed. Curious and way beyond being conscious of it, Cat reached up and traced a sharply defined cheekbone with her fingertip.

"Are you part Indian?" she wondered, idly liking the sensation of his warm skin beneath her finger.

"Quarter Sioux."

"With gray eyes?" she murmured idly.

"There are some who claim Crazy Horse had gray eyes."

"Really." Cat found herself once again trapped by his compelling gray eyes.

It was suddenly impossible to look anywhere else but into them. Needs too long repressed began surfacing, leaving Cat little room to question the judgment of her actions. She ached to be held, to feel a man's arms around her.

"Tell me, Dakota," she whispered, feeling oddly breathless, "do you dance?"

"You mean, other than a war dance?" he murmured, a faint glitter of amusement in his eyes.

She laughed with a reckless enjoyment of the moment that she hadn't felt since Repp died. "Or a rain dance, or a sun dance," Cat added, carrying his thought further. "Just a plain and simple dance, that's all I want, Dakota."

But it wasn't really *all* she wanted.

"I think I can manage that." He took the margarita from her and set it on the bar next to his long-necked beer bottle.

Spell or attraction—whichever it was—Cat readily surrendered to it when he shaped his hand to the small of her back and guided her onto the dance floor. The song was a slow one, an old standard that mirrored too closely her feelings, except she had no ribbons that he could take from her hair. It was already down, lying against her shoulders. She closed her ears to the song's words and turned into his arms.

She slid a hand onto the slope of his shoulder and felt the banding of solid muscle beneath the white fabric of his shirt. His arm circled the back of her waist. It was the first time in months that a man's arm had gone around her for a reason other than comfort and sympathy. The warm sensation of it nearly dragged a moan from her throat. Until that moment Cat hadn't realized how much she had craved a man's touch.

He didn't draw her close to him. To Cat, it was like being thirsty and given only a small sip of water. Wanting more, she moved closer, leaning into him and resting her head on his shoulder. The enveloping warmth of his body heat was like a healing fire, restoring awareness to senses that had been numbed by grief's pain. Eyes closed, she began to notice the mix of scents clinging to his skin: the heady fragrance of aftershave, the clean smell of soap, and his own earthy odor, all tinted with traces of bar smoke and liquor's sweetness. She felt the brush of his legs against hers as they moved to the music, her hand clasped in the smoothness of his while she listened to the strong, solid beat of his heart.

His hand tightened their grip on her fingers. He tipped his head down, the warmth of his breath fanning her cheek. "You never told me your name." His low voice rumbled from someplace deep inside him.

"Cat." Her answer was instinctive and honest. Instantly Cat knew she didn't want an exchange of names. Names led to a discussion of backgrounds and family histories. The man was a stranger to her; she wanted to keep it that way. Drawing back, she tilted her head up to look into his smoky gray eyes, then took the truth and twisted it. "Maggie the Cat, that's me."

Amusement glinted in his eyes, giving them a quicksilver gleam. "The one on the hot tin roof?"

For the blink of a second, Cat didn't make the connection. Then she laughed at the irony of her choice. When she had innocently paired her name with her mother's, she hadn't given a thought to the character in the Tennessee Williams play. But she remembered her now—how very sensual she had been—and how very desperate and frustrated, aching to love and be loved, and denied that need. It seemed singularly appropriate.

"That is exactly the one I am," Cat declared in a suddenly reckless mood. "You would have recognized me straight off if I'd been wearing my slip."

"Ah, yes, the famous slip," he said with an easy nod. "I knew something was missing."

"That's it." Her glance drifted down to study the lazy curve of his lips.

His mouth was close, close enough to kiss. She wanted to kiss him. She wanted that and more, much more. She wanted all that the fates had denied her with Repp. Rising on her toes, Cat leaned closer until only a centimeter separated their lips. Her breath mingled with his and shallowed out, the sensitive surfaces of her lips tingling with the nearness of him.

"Should I be looking over my shoulder for Paul Newman?" When he spoke, she felt his lips form every word, though they barely touched hers.

"Silly," Cat whispered. "You are Paul Newman."

"Is that why I have the feeling I'm being seduced?" This time he made deliberate contact, touching her lips in a brushing nuzzle.

"Do you mind?" she murmured, straining closer.

"No. But I'll never understand how Paul Newman managed to resist you the way he did." His husky comment struck a painful chord in her memory, sharply recalling all the times Repp had refused her.

Reeling from it, Cat lost her balance and stumbled against him, her lips grazing his jaw. Drawing back, she tried to cover her shattered composure with a careless toss of her head, only to discover she was fighting tears. Her glance ricocheted off his face as she dipped her head and forced a laugh. "That's what comes from having one too many margaritas," she lied.

"So I've heard." But Logan Echohawk didn't buy that as the reason. In his line of work, being a trained observer was essential; too often a person's reaction told him more than words could. That glimpse of pain in her eyes had been brief, but a glimpse was often all that he ever saw.

When she had first approached him at the bar, it had seemed the typical come-on, less subtle than most with a unique opening gambit, but not that much different from the normal. Truth to tell, he had welcomed the advance—a stranger in a strange town, discovering the loneliness that can be found in the midst of a crowd.

He had noticed her the minute she walked in. An awareness of all that went on around him was vital in his profession; over time, it had become as natural to him as breathing. But he would have noticed her anyway. "Maggie the Cat" was the kind of woman who stood out in a crowd. Part of it was her natural beauty—the sculpted fineness of her features, the glossy blackness of her hair, the slenderness of her build with all its womanly ripe curves, and the unusual green of her eyes. But part of it, too, was the proud tilt of her head, the confident stride of her walk, and something else less definite—something vibrant and volatile, some fiery spark that blazed with life.

Initially, she hadn't struck him as the type who picked up men in bars; she didn't look like the type who needed to. Then she had come up to him, and that impression had undergone an instant revision.

Now, holding her while they swayed to the music, her head nestled against his shoulder, her face hidden from him, he found himself wondering about her again. Something didn't ring true. Something more than just her name.

If he were smart, he'd leave after this dance, call it a night, go over the testimony he would need to give at tomorrow's trial, and forget he had ever met Maggie the Cat. But he kept remembering that glimpse of pain, of utter vulnerability.

When the song ended, he followed her back to the bar. She picked up her margarita glass and turned to him, all smiles and bewitching green eyes.

"So, tell me, Dakota—are you a real cowboy or the urban kind?"

SIX

I've been a real one." He leaned both arms on the bar top and hooked his hands around the Lone Star bottle he'd been nursing for the last hour. "Maybe someday I'll go back to it. It's hard to say." Logan took a swig of the tepid beer and cut a sideways glance at her, an eyebrow arching in question. "And you? Have those boots ever waded through the muck of a calving shed?"

"They have," Cat answered with a trace of smugness, then raised one foot, an audacious twinkle in her eyes. "Want to smell? Heaven knows, once it gets into the leather, you can never get all the odor out."

"I'll take your word for it." He chuckled.

She liked the sound of it, and the warm feeling it gave her. At the same time she wished they were still out on the dance floor. She didn't want to engage in all this small talk; she didn't want to know all these little details about him. It only made it harder to pretend that he was Repp. And that was what she wanted—to be in his arms, close her eyes and imagine it was Repp holding her, that it was his hands touching her, his lips kissing her.

Maybe it was wrong; maybe it was foolish. But it

was what she desperately wanted.

"Is there a problem?"

At his prompting question, Cat realized she was staring intently at her drink. Hurriedly she fixed a quick, bright smile on her face and looked up, forcing herself to meet his sharply probing gaze.

"Someone told me that every tequila bottle has a worm in it. I was just checking to make sure there wasn't one in my drink." She rattled the cubes in her glass and raised it to her lips. She tossed down a long swallow of the watered-down drink. Just for an instant, the room swam, reminding Cat that she'd had enough.

Apparently satisfied with her explanation, he turned at right angles to the bar and cast an idle glance around the room, then paused. "I think your friends are ready to leave."

Cat looked back at their table and saw Kinsey and J.J. standing beside it. Kinsey waved and signaled that she and J.J. were leaving, then mouthed the words *Good hunting*, and winked. Laughing, Cat waved a farewell to them, a little relieved that she didn't have to go through a tearful good-bye scene with them.

When she turned back to the bar, he eyed her curiously. "Aren't you going with them?"

She shook her head. "We came in separate vehicles." She went to set her drink on the countertop and misjudged the distance, nearly tipping it over. "Whoops." She quickly righted it. "That was close."

"I'm not sure you're in any shape to be behind a wheel."

"I think you're right," Cat agreed with a wise nod. "Maybe we should dance instead."

She caught hold of his hand and struck out for the dance floor, in full confidence that he would come along. That certainty briefly annoyed him, but it vanished when she turned into his arms and fitted herself naturally to his length, a hand cupping the back of his head and her face nuzzling the side of his neck.

"This is much better," she murmured on a contented sigh.

At the moment, she felt very much like a cat to him, soft and purring, pressing close and rubbing against him. And he was enjoying every minute of it. That was the problem; to touch was to want more. Always more. And he had spent too many nights alone, without the warmth of a woman next to him. He told himself to stop being a fool and simply accept what was offered.

"Maggie—or whatever—"

"Ssh." She pressed two fingers against his lips. "Please. Don't talk. Let's just dance."

But they were doing more than just dancing. Logan knew it, whether she recognized it or not. Every step, every rocking sway of hips brought them into closer alignment, their bodies seeking and adjusting to the contours of the other.

Try as he might, he couldn't ignore the roundness of her breasts pressed against him, or the evocative stir of her breath against his neck. Giving in to the building ache in his loins, he released her fingers and splayed both hands along her slender back. With a turn of his head, he explored the silken texture of the midnight-black hair near her temple.

The brush of his lips against her hair ignited little tremors of longing. Music swirled somewhere in the background as Cat closed her eyes, memorizing the imprint of his long body against hers—the way she should have done with Repp. Her hands wandered over his arms and upper body, fixing the feel of his muscled shape in her mind while her lips committed to memory the salty flavor of his skin.

But any satisfaction she felt was fleeting, leaving her with a need for more. An impossibility, it seemed, until Cat felt the moist heat of his mouth along her cheek. Hungering for a man's kiss, she turned to seek it, aching to taste the hard, driving passion of unchecked desire. Again, he lifted his head that tantalizing fraction that had their chins touching and their breath co-mingling.

With lids half-shuttered, Cat glanced up and found him watching her. Suddenly she couldn't look anywhere else but into his eyes, drawn by their large black centers ringed by a band of silver.

"Kiss me," she whispered as the fierce ache rose again.

His head tilted, changing angles as he lipped her mouth.

Groaning in frustration, Cat slid her fingers into his coarse black hair and tried to force the contact. The muscles in his neck bunched, resisting the pressure she applied while he rubbed his mouth over her lips. Every quivering breath she drew became a tiny moan.

When he lifted his head again, she found him still watching her through eyes three-quarters lidded. He made no move to come back.

Did he think she was going to beg for his kiss? Cat wondered, suddenly furious at the thought. Asking was one thing, but she would never plead.

"Damn you," she cursed in a hoarse whisper.

A small, quick gleam of satisfaction blazed in his eyes. Then it was forgotten as his mouth came down to claim her lips in a deep, drugging kiss. Instantly, Cat sagged against him and gave up all pretense of moving to the music.

This was what she had missed, this passion that she had wanted for so long and thought she would never know. But here it was, life in all its awesome wildness. She felt it. She felt all of it.

When his mouth rolled off hers, Cat moved to reclaim it in quick aggression. But his head lifted and his fingers closed around her wrists, dragging her arms from around his neck and drawing them down to wedge a space between them.

Slow to surface, her senses still spinning, Cat swayed into him and tried to pull her hands free without success. "No, don't let me go." Her voice was a husky murmur, the words slurring. "Hold me."

"The song is over," he told her and shot a look at the other couples making their way off the dance floor. But Cat took no notice of them.

"I don't care," she declared and arched closer, needing to feel his arms around her again.

For a flicker of an instant, his gray eyes mirrored that same desire, and her heart leaped in response. Then a muscle flexed along his jaw, and it was gone. No, not gone. Controlled, she realized. The same way Repp had. Fury swept her, blinding, hot, raw.

"Damn you." Rage choked her voice. "How can you not want me? What do I have to do?"

Grimness hardened his features. "You need some coffee." He shifted his hold on her, seizing her elbow and turning her toward the bar.

She twisted her arm away and all but stomped her foot. "Don't you tell me what I need!" Cat stormed, suddenly embarrassed and dangerously close to tears. "You aren't my keeper. I don't need a keeper. I—"

"You sure as hell need somebody looking after you," he muttered, jaw clenched, his eyes the hard color of granite. "In case you haven't noticed, you are more than half drunk."

"Maybe I am." She weaved a little, feeling the effects of the margaritas and conscious of the world swimming at the edges of her vision. Pride lifted her chin high. "Maybe I need to be. It's really none of your business though, is it?"

Something sardonic glittered briefly in his eyes. "You're right—drunks aren't normally my business, but there are always exceptions."

"You talk big, but that's all you are is just talk." Cat waved a hand in dismissal of him, then looked him up and down with contempt. "You aren't a man. You just masquerade as one."

"You're going to say that to the wrong man one of these times, lady."

"Lady? Who asked you to treat me like a lady?" she hurled in anger. "I'm not a lady, do you hear?"

"That's right." The thinness of his smile held no humor. "You're Maggie the Cat."

"Yes. Yes, I am." Hot tears suddenly burned in her eyes. "And I want off this damned tin roof!" Fighting the tears, Cat swung away and immediately lost her balance, staggering sideways. His hands caught her, steadied her. She shook them off. "Leave me alone. You didn't want to touch me before, so don't touch me now!"

"You're wrong if you think I didn't want to—"

Cat plunged onto the dance floor rather than listen to his explanation. She had heard them all before. She twisted her way around the dancing couples. On the other side, she found a path through the crowded tables and headed for the door, suddenly anxious to leave. In her haste, she bumped against a chair, caromed off it and stumbled straight into a plaid-shirted cowboy.

"Whoa, there, little darlin'." He hooked an arm around her waist, catching her when she would have careened off.

"Sorry—" Self-conscious, she looked up.

"Oooowhee!" He turned wide-eyed with appreciation at the sight of her upturned face. "Look at the pretty package that just landed in my arms." He grinned like a child on Christmas morning. "Little darlin', I do believe that band is playing our song. What d'ya say we rub bellies?"

"I—"

"She's with me."

When Cat glanced over her shoulder, she found herself looking into familiar gray eyes, discovering a hard glitter of impatience in them. "I am not," she denied hotly.

But the cowboy had already withdrawn his arm, turning Cat loose. "I saw the two of you dancing—if you can call it that," he said. "Had a fight, did you?"

"Something like that."

"We did not." But neither man listened to Cat.

"I envy you the kissin' and makin' up," the cowboy said. "It'll be hot springs tonight—and I ain't talking about Arkansas."

"Now that is a laugh." Sarcasm coated her words. Cat stayed long enough to see gray eyes narrow in temper, then swung on a heel and walked off, the cowboy's laughter following her, masking the sound of a second set of long-striding footsteps.

Cat pushed out the door and stepped into the warm Texas night. The fresh air slammed into her. Everything started to spin, and she grabbed one of the wooden posts that supported the sidewalk's shed roof. She held herself very still and waited for the ground to stop spinning. When it did, she saw a second pair of boots in her line of vision, and a pair of long legs. Her gaze traveled up them, but she already knew who they belonged to.

"Why don't you go back to Dakota and leave me alone?" she demanded, her voice thick with a confusing churn of emotions. "I told you before—I don't need a keeper. I can take care of myself."

"I saw the way you were taking care of that cowboy."

"I could have handled him"— perversely, Cat had to add—"assuming I wanted to."

"I suppose you'd rather be back inside, 'rubbing bellies' with that rodeo Romeo," he mocked.

"What do you care?" she taunted. "You sure as hell weren't interested."

His hand shot out and gripped the post directly above her fingers as he suddenly loomed closer, a ridging of anger in his face. "You just keep digging that spur in, don't you?" he muttered. "For your information, I've made love to a woman in a lot of different places, but never in the middle of a public dance floor. I draw the line there, odd as that may sound to you."

She felt the heat of embarrassment creep into her cheeks and quickly lowered her gaze, looking anywhere but directly at him. He dropped his hand from the post and took a step back, dragging in a deep steadying breath.

"Now," he continued, "I don't know who you're trying to get even with or why—though I can guess. But I suggest you find yourself a telephone, give your boyfriend a call, and patch things up if you can."

"I can't," she flashed, unable to check the tears that filled her eyes.

"Why? Or are you too proud to make the first move?" he challenged.

Cat looked at him for a long, tension-filled second, fighting the words and the pain of them. "No," she said at last. "He's dead."

Stunned by her answer, he drew back. "I'm sorry. I—"

"I don't want your pity." She couldn't take it, not from him. "I don't need anyone's pity."

"Of course you don't."

"What would you know about it?" Hurting, Cat

lashed out. "What would you know about anything?" Her throat tightened, turning her voice hoarsely thick. "Dear God, why am I even talking to you?"

Cat let go of the post and started forward, blindly digging in her pocket for the ignition keys. He stepped into her path. "Where are you going?"

"It so happens I'm leaving—if it's any of your business." She struggled to hold onto her anger. It was the only defense she had. She was suddenly tired—tired of fighting, tired of thinking, and most of all, tired of the loneliness. Catching hold of the key ring, she pulled the keys from her pocket.

"You are in no condition to drive." He took the keys from her before Cat had a chance to protest. "Where are you staying?"

"I don't know. A hotel somewhere. I haven't gotten around to checking into one." Cat wasn't looking forward to searching one out, but she wasn't about to admit that.

"In that case, you might as well get a room here at the Stockyard Hotel." He motioned to a set of double doors a few feet away.

Cat hesitated, then nodded. "Good idea."

This easy acquiescence seemed totally out of character for a woman who had exhibited no signs of being either meek or submissive. Logan's gaze sharpened on her. The fiery sparkle of temper was gone from her eyes. Shadows lurked in them now, darkening and dulling the green of them.

It touched something inside him and made him gentle when he cupped a hand under her elbow and escorted her into the hotel lobby. "The registration desk is over here." He pointed to it.

"Wait." She stopped beside a chair upholstered in unshaved cowhide, her expression a study of concentration when she pushed her hand into a side pocket of her jeans. "I've got my money and credit cards."

"I'll make sure they have a room available." He left her by the chair and crossed to the registration counter.

The mustached clerk nodded a hello. "What can I do for you?"

"The lady would like a room, if you have one." He glanced back as she swayed on unsteady legs and sank down to perch on the chair arm.

"Celebrated a little too much, did she?" the clerk observed.

"A little."

"At least she's got sense enough not to be driving." He pulled out a registration slip. "What's her name?"

"Maggie . . ."

"Smith?" the clerk suggested with a faint smile.

Logan glanced back, but she was still frowning over her money.

"That's good enough."

"And the method of payment?"

"If she doesn't take care of it in the morning, you can bill it to my room."

"Very good, sir."

Scant moments later, Logan walked back to her, room key in hand. "You're all set."

She looked up, with that same furrow of concentration still creasing her forehead. "Don't they need my credit card imprint?"

"Not tonight," he told her. "You can pay for the room in the morning."

"Oh." She seemed momentarily puzzled, the furrow deepening. Then her expression cleared with a dawning thought. "I guess you told them who I am."

It was his turn to frown. "I beg your pardon?"

But she didn't appear to hear his question as she

pushed off the chair arm to stand erect. Swaying suddenly, she reached to grab hold of something and fastened a hand on his arm. Immediately he placed a steadying hand on her waist.

A small, self-conscious laugh bubbled from her. "I stood up too quickly that time, didn't I?"

"It looks that way."

"Where's my room?" Her gaze traveled over the lobby, the first traces of fatigue showing on her face.

"It's this way." Keeping a supportive hand under her elbow, he walked her over to the broad staircase and pressed the room key into her palm, then pointed up the steps and repeated the clerk's directions, "Second floor, turn left at the head of the stairs, third door on the left." She gave a great show of listening intently, then nodded her head once in understanding. "Can you make it all right?" he asked.

"Sure."

He remained at the bottom of the staircase, watching as she started up the steps, keeping one hand on the banister's wood railing and using it to pull herself along. A third of the way up, she paused and turned back to him with a puzzled frown.

"Hey, Dakota, where did you say it was again?" The note of annoyance in her voice was self-directed.

It brought a glint of amusement to his eyes. Obviously, she didn't like this addled, helpless feeling that had resulted from too much alcohol in the system. He stared at her for another long minute, conscious that she stirred something more than amusement in him, something that quickened his senses and his desires. It was more than her undeniable beauty that drew him. Beauty, in his experience, had too often been a shallow thing. But in this woman, there was more than mere beauty; there was a pride and strength of character, an assertion of independence in the way she had rejected his sympathy. Someone weaker would have welcomed it, perhaps even wallowed in it. But not this woman. He had the feeling that weakness was something she despised in anyone, including herself.

All of this went through his mind in that flashing instant between her question and his briefly delayed response. "I'll take you to your room," he said, and knew that he welcomed the excuse to remain in her company a little longer, despite the fact that he also knew she was privately grieving for another man.

He joined her on the stairs and spread his hand across her back to guide her up the steps. In a different way, he was just as conscious of her nearness as he had been on the dance floor.

"I can find it on my own." She gave him a perplexed little frown.

"This way will be quicker."

She looked at the key in her hand and nodded. "True."

Together they started up. She caught her toe on the next step and stumbled against him. He reacted instantly to catch her against him and keep her upright. She dipped her head briefly against him, then tipped it back, a rueful laugh slipping out.

"My legs suddenly feel so rubbery," she admitted, a faintly bemused light flickering in her green eyes.

From other women, such a remark would have been a plea to be carried, but not her. Instead, she gathered herself and started up the stairs again on clearly unsteady legs. He stayed with her for two more steps, then scooped her into his arms.

After a startled gasp, she looped her arms around his neck and murmured, "I probably should object, but I'm too tired and this is too comfortable."

"Good, because I wouldn't pay any attention to you anyway."

As he took the next step, she rested her head on his shoulder.

"I've never been carried before, not since I was a little girl, when my daddy would carry me upstairs and tuck me into bed."

The idea of tucking her into bed was a tantalizing thought, conjuring up images that were far from the innocent ones she recalled. It was a woman's body in his arms, not a child's.

"It makes me feel safe," she murmured. "Safe and protected."

Something strong and fiercely tender surged through him. Logan subtly shifted his grip, gathering her closer. At the same time, he was disturbed by his reaction, and oddly irritated as well. He was a man, pushed by the same lusts as other men. Alcohol had lowered her defenses, but only by the law's definition was she drunk. With her guard down, it wouldn't be that difficult to work his way into her bed, and he knew it. If she had been like other women he had met in bars, none of this would be bothering him. But she wasn't. She was a different breed entirely.

She snuggled closer and nuzzled his neck. "You smell good, do you know that?"

"Probably the aftershave I used," he replied as heat curled through him, triggered by the warmth of her lips against his skin. He saw, with a bedeviling mix of relief and regret, that he was nearly to the top of the stairs.

"I like it," she murmured. "It reminds me of the tall grass plains in summer—with a storm coming."

As far as he was concerned, the storm had already arrived. The charged tension of it licked through his nerve ends and sharpened all his senses, making him aware of the curve of her hips and the firmness of her breasts. It was an easy step to remember the taste of her kiss and the way her body molded itself so naturally to his. Much too easy.

By the time he reached the door to her room, her nuzzling had turned into a provocative nibbling, and his breathing had roughened.

He let her feet sink to the floor, her body sliding over his and making him harder than he already was. Her hands remained around his neck, her face upturned and her lips softly parted in a woman's age-old signal of invitation.

But he didn't trust himself to accept, didn't trust that he would stop with a kiss. "I need the room key."

"I need to be kissed again."

Everything tightened to control the needs that churned inside him. He moved his hands up the sides of her rib cage, intending to unlink the fingers clasped around his neck, but they stopped when his thumbs encountered the underswell of her breasts. He went still for an instant, his teeth gritted against the groan rising in his throat.

But the tempting softness of her lips pulled at him. Dipping his head, he drove his mouth against them. His intention was twofold—to satisfy the rawness of his hungers and to frighten her with the brutality of them. She stiffened under the roughness of his assault, then came back at him with equal fierceness.

A breath away from losing the last vestige of control, he ripped his mouth from hers and pushed her at arm's length. Slower to recover, she stared at him with wide, wondering eyes.

"That's the way it can be, isn't it?" She breathed in amazement.

His fingers itched to grab her—whether to shake some sense into her or drag her back to him, he didn't know. The uncertainty stopped him.

"Give me the damned key." Seizing her wrist, he

took the key from her unresisting fingers, conscious of the trembling in his hands.

He shoved the key in the lock, gave it a savage turn, heard the *snick* of the bolt's release and pushed the door inward, then stepped back. Without a word, she walked past him into the darkened room, leaving the door open and the key in the lock. A light from the street filtered through the edges of the closed drapes, giving him glimpses of her silhouette. He stood in the hallway, watching as she walked to the bed and curled her hand around an iron post.

In his mind, he saw her lying beside him in that bed, the light from the windows playing dimly over her naked body, the blackness of her hair fanned over the pillow in an ebony tangle. He imagined her writhing against the building pressure caused by the caressing stroke of his hands.

To dispel the image and the inherent intimacy of a darkened bedroom, he stepped forward and flipped the wall switch by the door. Light pooled beneath the fringed Victorian lamp on the nightstand. Its diffuse glow spilled through the shade and spread onto the bed in mute invitation.

Cursing under his breath, he pivoted from the sight and jerked the key from the lock. "You left the key in the door."

When he took a step to drop the key on the bedside table, she turned and came toward him, her blouse unbuttoned fully two-thirds of the way down. The muscles in his chest and throat constricted, closing off his breathing as he stared at the lacy white fabric stretched tautly over her breasts.

Woodenly he lifted his hand to give her the key. But she ignored it and reached past him, giving the door a decisive push. It swung shut with a dull thud and a click of the latch. She turned back to him and slid her hands up the front of his shirt to his shoulders, her blouse gaping open a little more.

"I want you to stay." She tilted her head back, black hair swinging to hang down her back.

His hands came up, but they stopped short of touching her and, instead, held the air inches from her body. He dragged his gaze from her breasts up to her face. It lingered fractionally on her lips, still slightly swollen from his previous rough kiss, then traveled up to her eyes. He saw the desire in them—and the faint shadowing of grief that lurked at the edges. It didn't take a great deal of intelligence to figure out that she was using him as a stand-in, a substitute for the man who had died.

"This isn't a good idea," he told her, his voice rumbling the warning.

"Why? Because I suggested it?" Her gaze traveled over his face, exploring the angular line of his jaw, his high, hard cheekbones, and the slant of his forehead. His hat sat low on it. "Don't tell me you're one of those men who doesn't like it when a girl makes the first move?"

Reaching up, she swept his hat off and gave it a toss, then ran her fingers through his coarse black hair, combing away the flatness from the hat and studying the wayward strands that curled onto his forehead.

"Because you aren't thinking clearly," he said with a terseness. "You've had too much to drink tonight."

Cat paused to consider that. "Maybe I have," she admitted. "Lord knows, I've never been this brazen before. Maybe the alcohol has washed away my good sense. But I don't recall appointing you to be my conscience."

"Stop kidding yourself." A thread of anger ran through his voice. "It isn't me you want."

A knifing pain twisted through her at his words.

Cat fought it off with a defiant toss of her head. "Isn't it?" she challenged him.

Since entering the hotel room, she had avoided his gaze. His height, his build, the darkness of his hair—they reminded her of Repp. But she couldn't maintain the pretense when she looked into his gray eyes. Yet that didn't stop the little thrill from tingling through her at the dark light smoldering in them.

"Tonight, you made me feel things I didn't think I would feel again. Want things I didn't think I'd ever want. For the first time in months, I feel alive. If that's wrong . . ." She paused, her voice catching on a tiny sob. Anger was her only defense against the pain. "Why do you men have to be so damned noble? I hate this stupid code of honor that demands certain women be treated differently. Who asked you to do that? It sure as hell wasn't a woman."

In all the anger, he saw the emptiness that ached to be filled. It was something he understood, something he felt himself. His hands settled on her, and he lowered his head to brush his mouth across her lips, tasting her tremulous sigh.

"You'd better know that I don't have any protection with me," he warned in a thick murmur.

"I don't care," she whispered back. "All my life I've been protected. Someone else has always decided what's best for me. But not anymore. Not tonight. Tonight I just want you to love me."

It was a request all too easy to fulfill; he'd been loving her in his mind nearly all night. Discarding reason and caution, he gathered her to him as his mouth came back to devour her lips, swallowing her groan that echoed his own hunger.

She was filled with the taste of him. It turned her greedy and demanding, determined to satisfy this raw ache that seemed only to intensify. She strained even closer, trying to absorb him into her. His arms tightened around her like twin bands of steel binding her to him.

A moment later a hand tugged at the back of her blouse, pulling the material free from her jeans, then slipped under it to spread across her back. She breathed in sharply as little shudders traveled through her. His hand followed the curve of her spine, then glided to the front and cupped a lace-covered breast. Her flesh seemed to swell under his hand.

Wanting more, she arched closer and felt the uncomfortable bunching of her blouse. Desperate to rid herself of it and give him free access, Cat pulled at the blouse. A button slipped loose from its stitched hole and the other popped off. As she shed the blouse, his deft fingers dealt with the front closing of her lacy brassiere. Even before she shrugged it off, his hand was on her breast, his thumb rubbing over her nipple.

Another groan rose in her throat as sensation built upon sensation. And there was more to come. But this time she wouldn't be left aching and unsatisfied. The knowledge increased the need to touch him, a need that quickly grew into an urgency to feel the warmth of his skin beneath her hands. She tugged at his shirt, needing to eliminate the barrier it posed. The pearl snaps gave, one after the other popping apart, and her hands spread over his leanly muscled chest, discovering the incredible heat of his skin and the patch of dark curly hair that tickled her palms with its softness.

When she pressed closer, needing to feel the sensation of skin against skin, a corner of his belt buckle jabbed her stomach. Without conscious direction, her hands moved to do away with this new, irritating obstacle and felt the sudden, inward contraction of his stomach muscles, instantly followed by the quick seizing of her hands.

"Slow down," he muttered against her cheek, his breathing as raw and ragged as her own. "We're rushing this, and there's no need. We have plenty of time."

The cursed phrase screamed through her, but all Cat managed to utter was a single, strangled, "No." She pushed back from him, shaking her head.

He caught her chin in his hand and tipped it up, forcing her to look at him. Desire was a hot, dark glow in his eyes. It snatched at her breath and sent evocative shivers through her.

"You are a wild one, Maggie the Cat," he murmured idly. "But if we keep this up, it'll be over before it's begun. I don't want that. Do you?"

What he seemed to be suggesting sounded infinitely more satisfying. The possibility made her answer soft and breathy. "No."

"All right, then." Approval and something else glittered in his eyes—a something else that dazzled and sent her pulse skittering all over the place.

For the briefest of seconds, Cat questioned what she was doing. She didn't know this man; he was a complete stranger. But her reasons were selfish, she knew; she hadn't felt so alive in months, and she was afraid she never would again. In the back of her mind, Cat was certain this was the way it would have felt with Repp.

"We have all night," he told her. "Let's not hurry one minute of it."

"No," she agreed on a whisper.

The thought was a new one. In the past she had always used heat and an unrelenting pressure in an effort to drive Repp beyond the limits of his control. But this—this had breathtaking possibilities.

"So, tell me . . ." He released her chin and let the flat of his fingers glide over the delicate curve of her cheek before skimming the line of her jaw, following it almost to her lips. "Do you want me to undress you?"

SEVEN

Her legs went weak at the thought of his hands easing her jeans off her hips, of his fingers sliding down her lacy bikini briefs. As heady as that thought was, she knew she would be driven wild with frustration before all her clothes wound up on the floor.

"I'll do it myself." She was too familiar with frustration to voluntarily subject herself to more of it.

"My loss." His warm smile was quick and crooked.

His hands fell away, and he stepped around her to the bed. With one fluid swing of his arm, he threw the bedcovers back, then turned to her and glanced at the lamp. "Off or on?"

Standing there completely topless, her jeans unsnapped and half-unzipped, Cat had no idea why she hesitated over her answer. A darkened room would allow her to pretend she was making love to Repp when the truth was something different. Something she would have to face eventually.

"On," she said and wondered how soon she would regret that.

A flicker of surprise showed in his eyes. Then he

moved away from the lamp, shrugging out of his shirt and hanging it on the corner of the straight-backed chair. Cat walked over to the bed and sat on the edge of it to pull off her boots. She undressed by rote, her mind blank, registering no thought or feeling. It was only when she laid aside the last of her clothes that Cat became aware of her nudity and conscious of his gaze on her. She turned to meet it, her head lifting fractionally, the tilt of it wary and vaguely defensive.

He stood, as naked as she, a heat in his eyes that made the air-conditioned room feel unbelievably warm. Her glance wandered over his lean, hard body with an unconscious boldness. There wasn't an ounce of spare flesh anywhere on him. There was only bronze skin stretched tautly across a complex roping of muscle and sinew. He was stunning to look at, all male and fully aroused.

Suddenly uneasy, Cat shot her glance back to his face and saw that he was watching her. The steady regard of his eyes unnerved her a little. It must have showed in her face.

"It isn't too late to change your mind," he said.

Instantly reassured by his remark, Cat allowed a small smile to curve her mouth, fully aware that with most men, it would have been too late the instant she invited them in the room.

"I guess I am my father's daughter. Once he sets his foot on a path, he never swerves from it."

"He's an unusual man." He moved toward her.

"He is." Cat tried to picture this man facing her father, curious to see how he would measure up to the Calder standard. But it was an image she couldn't summon to mind. Not that it mattered. The two men would never meet.

"You are an unusual woman as well. And a very beautiful one. It should be against the law for anyone to be as beautiful as you are." He knew, even before he kissed her and eased her onto the bed, that she would ruin him for any other woman.

As his hand traveled over her in a roaming caress, he also knew that only once before had he been so determined to take his time and drag out the pleasure.

Then, he had been a boy of seven, living on the reservation with his mother. A few days before Christmas, a church group had distributed gifts to the children in his school. The other kids had torn into theirs, but he hadn't. He had never had a real present before, not one wrapped in bright, shiny paper, tied in ribbons with a big red bow. He had sat for the longest time, simply holding it, now and then touching the slick ribbon and tracing the arcing curve of its bow. Finally he had removed the bow and held it up to the window, watching the play of light and shadow change the color of it from crimson to ruby. Next he had eased the ribbons off the box and looped them around his neck. After that he had taken the paper off, being extra careful not to tear it. After folding it neatly, he had laid the paper aside and stared at the box, content for the moment to simply run his hands over it and wonder what was inside. At last he had lifted the lid very, very slowly and stared at the blue and green parka within—not a hand-me-down from the thrift store like the rest of his clothes, but a brand-new jacket. When he put it on, he had felt warm, warmer than he'd ever felt before or since.

Until now—with the heat of her body burning its impression along the length of him. Her reaching hands urged him closer, but he ignored their demands. He intended to enjoy every inch of her beautiful outer wrappings and prolong that moment of opening the box.

Turning to her, he started at the top, with her

lips, driving them apart and swallowing her needy moan. The soft lamplight spilled over them, but his eyes were closed to the contrast of bronzed skin against ivory flesh. Had he noticed it, it would have merely been one more difference to celebrate.

His mouth rocked off her lips and rolled onto her cheek, then followed its curve to her eyelids and the long sweep of feathery lashes. With his tongue, he traced the delicate inner shell of her ear, drawing an involuntary gasp and shudder from her. His own breathing roughened at the sound of it as he shifted his interest, first to the lobe of her ear, then to the graceful line of her neck. At his touch, chills raced over her skin.

The roundness of her breast filled the cup of his hand, its peak turning hard and pointy under the stimulating brush of his thumb. Drawn by the sensation of it, he began a slow foray toward it with only a few detours along the way to explore the pulsating vein in her throat and nibble at the curve of a delectable shoulder bone.

When he lightly rubbed his lips over the very tip of her breast, her fingers clawed into his hair, her whole body arching to end the teasing contact while faint, mewling sounds of frustration came from the back of her throat. But he refused to be hurried, deliberately drawing out the torture with little nips and nibbles before finally drawing it into his mouth.

A keening sweetness nearly shattered his control as she writhed against him, all motion and demand. He fought the primitive instincts that screamed through his system. With an effort, he ignored the thrust of her hips and the frantic press of her hands. He stroked a hand across the flat of her stomach to the swell of her hip, then down a slender thigh and back along the inside of it.

She shrank from him when his fingertips brushed

the cloud of dark hair on their return journey to the flat of her stomach. He went back to the spot, sliding his fingers through her hair, seeking and finding the hot, moist center of her while she twisted in a desperate effort to elude his fingers.

"Dear heaven, no. Please, don't do this," she moaned in a panic. "I don't want your hand. I want *you!*"

The half plea and half demand went through him like a flame. In the next breath, his needs flared as hot and hungry as hers. Shifting onto her, he positioned her hips to receive him while his mouth reclaimed her lips.

Ready for him, she was wet and tight. Too tight. "Relax," he muttered against her lips when she strained to take him in. "You're too tense."

He heard her half-swallowed sob of frustration and echoed the feeling. At the first small loosening, he worked himself in a little farther, taking it slow and resisting the urge to ram it in. Sweat beaded on his skin from the effort and from the torment of her tight sheathing. With each gentle rock of the hips, he penetrated deeper.

Suddenly she bit off a cry of pain at the same instant that he pushed against an inner barrier. He stiffened in surprise, then levered himself onto his elbows.

"What the—" he began, still trying to wrap his scattered thought around this stunning discovery that she was a virgin.

"No. Don't you dare stop now!" There was a raw fury in her protest, a match to the temper blazing in her eyes as she locked her legs behind him and slammed her hips into him.

The membrane tore. The package was ripped open and he was inside it. Her face was pressed against the side of the pillow, pain twisting it, though not a sound came from her. Anger rose, black and bitter in his throat.

"Why the hell didn't you tell me?" He wrapped her hair in his fist and forced her to look at him.

Tears shimmered in her eyes. "What difference does it make?" Her voice was tight with pain and spite.

"Damn you." With eyes closed, he rested his forehead on hers and muttered in regret, "There was a gentler way."

She was hurting. This time it wasn't the kind of physical ache that led to pleasure. More than that, with the way she so tightly sheathed him, he wasn't sure he had the control to wait until she wanted him again. As he shifted to ease some of his weight from her, he saw the wince and felt the dig of her nails.

"It won't hurt much longer," he told her and concentrated on smoothing the tangles from her long black hair and spreading it over the bed's white sheet. "I imagined you like this—your hair tumbling in an ebony fan about your head, your lips swollen from my kisses, your body naked beneath mine."

"Do we have to talk?" Cat pushed the words through clenched teeth and forced her fingers to uncurl.

She desperately wanted to get this over, but the slightest movement produced a fresh ripple of pain. She fought through it and moved her hips, hoping to urge him to completion, fully aware she had made a mistake. A huge, horrible mistake.

He ignored the inviting thrust of her hips and stroked a hand down her side, then up to her breast. "What's wrong with talking?"

He teased the corner of her lips, then paused with a sudden flash of insight that sent a muscle leaping along his jaw. "Or does talking make it harder for you to pretend I'm the man you loved, the one who died?"

"You bastard," she hissed.

"Scored a bull's-eye, didn't I?" he said with more grimness than satisfaction. Anger gave him the edge he needed to keep his desires in tight check. "What was he like?" He nuzzled her ear, feeling the involuntary shudder that danced over her skin. "Tell me about him."

"No. It's none of your business."

"Can't you remember?" he taunted, forcing her to concentrate on his words rather than the slow, circular grind of his hips.

"Don't be ridiculous. Of course I can," she sputtered in anger, barely registering the new discomfort.

"Then what did he look like?" He nipped at her ear while his fingers toyed with a nipple, teasing it erect. "Was he tall? Short?"

"Tall."

"What color was his hair?" he murmured, nuzzling the hollow behind her ear.

"Dark." Cat was unaware of the moment when her hands slid over his back.

"Like mine?"

"Yes."

"What was it like? Short? Long? Straight? Curly?" Logan persisted, determined to keep her thoughts distracted by his questions.

"Short. Short and thick."

Heat curled through her, slicking her skin with perspiration. Cat was stunned to discover the tearing pain was gone. Its place had been taken by a greedy ache that had her hands clutching at him and her hips moving in instinctual rhythm with his.

"What color were his eyes?"

"Dark. Dark brown." She didn't want to talk anymore.

He lifted his head. "What color are mine?"

She looked into them, dazzled by the molten silver color of them. "Gray."

"Say it again," he murmured the husky demand, his eyes never leaving hers.

"Gray," she whispered again, unable to look away, not even when his mouth covered hers and his tongue delved inside to mate with hers in hot insistence.

Her heart pounded in her ears. Sensation spiraled through her in an ever-tightening circle of need, the pressure building until she was consumed by it. The release, when it came, was glorious, draining her of everything but the small, golden aftershocks that left her trembling.

Slow to surface from them, Cat was only vaguely aware of the moment when he shifted his weight off her and rolled onto his side, drawing her along with him. He brushed the hair back from her face with his hand and pressed a kiss to her temple.

"Are you all right?" The sound of his voice drifted to her.

Cat nodded, not wanting to talk, not wanting to do anything that would dispel this warm and liquid feeling. She felt the moist heat of his lips against her skin again. Then he was untangling his arms from around her, drawing away. The mattress dipped under his weight, and she heard the whisper of his feet touching the floor. A rustle of sheets followed as he gathered the bedcovers and pulled them over her. Cat snuggled into them, eyes closing in utter contentment.

A light flicked on in the bathroom, the glow of it bright against her eyelids. She turned from it as water gushed and splashed in the sink. It was a lulling sound that soothed away the last of the tangles and deepened the feeling of languor.

Drifting in that drowsy state between sleep and wakefulness, she wasn't aware of the exact moment of his return. He stood beside the bed, a damp towel in his hand, studying the small smile that turned up her lip corners, a smile he had put there. Possessiveness rushed through him with a potency that rocked him. Shaken by it, he hesitated a moment longer, his gaze traveling over this woman who was a total mystery to him.

Where she was concerned, he was certain about only one thing—in his arms, she had filled all the empty places in him. For a short fragment of time, he had known what completeness could be. The memory of it tightened everything inside him and made him want again.

When he slipped under the covers, she turned to him, all sleepy-eyed and beautiful. "You're back," she murmured, then pulled in a sharp breath of surprise when she felt the wetness of the towel touch her stomach. "What's that?"

"A towel." He wiped the stickiness of virginal blood and sex from between her legs. He saw the faint wince and guessed, "Sore?"

"A little."

He gave the towel a toss in the direction of the bathroom. For the time being, he satisfied himself with tucking strands of silky black hair behind her ear. "Are you sorry?"

With her fingers, she traced the lean muscle that ran from his chest to his shoulder. "No."

But he had noticed the slight pause between his question and her answer—and the avoidance of his gaze. He wasn't surprised. Like her, he knew there would come a time when they would both regret tonight, but for different reasons.

Reaching past her, he switched off the lamp on the bedside table, then gathered her to him. In the shadows and darkness, he made love to her again.

* * *

Cat rolled over and slung a leg out. The ache of a dozen muscles registered a sharp and instant protest to the movement, pricking her awake. Sleepily she opened her eyes. Nothing looked familiar. For a disoriented moment, she couldn't remember where she was. Then it all came back to her—the last night on the town with her friends, the margaritas she had drunk, the silly manhunt game they played for laughs, and the man she had found, the strength of his arms, the headiness of his kisses, and—

Her eyes snapped open. She remembered it all, every lusty, guilty minute of it.

Wide awake, she sat up. The sudden movement touched off an immediate pounding in her head. She pressed a hand to it. It was the tequila; it always gave her a wretched headache the morning after. For a brief moment, Cat tried to convince herself that she had been too drunk last night to know what she was doing. But she knew better. The alcohol may have clouded her judgment, but it hadn't directed her actions. He hadn't done one single thing that she hadn't wanted him to do. Not one single thing.

There was a stir of movement beside her. Cat froze, every muscle tensing, every nerve end tingling. She stole a wary glance at the man lying next to her. The sheet was down around his hips, baring his torso. She watched his chest rise and fall in a slow, steady rhythm, silent confirmation that he hadn't wakened.

Even in sleep, there was little softness in his face. Every line of his triangular jaw was strongly chiseled, from the high ridge of his cheekbone to the thrust of his chin. Only the thick black lashes and the wayward lock of black hair that strayed onto his forehead gave hints of the boy he had once been.

Cat jerked her gaze from him, furious with herself for even thinking about him as a boy. He was a stranger. A total stranger.

And she was determined to keep it that way. She wanted to know nothing else about him.

And he knew nothing about her—not her name, not where she lived, nothing. Cat drew immediate comfort from that. She had gotten herself into this mess; now she had to get herself out of it, with as few scars as possible.

Impulse pushed her off the bed, the same rash impulse that had caused her to seek him out. With a stealth acquired from all the times she had snuck out as a teenager to meet Repp, she searched out her clothes in the dark, stuffed her socks and underclothes in her boots, dragged on her jeans, and slipped into her blouse, hastily buttoning it.

Carrying her boots, she crossed to the door, carefully turned the knob and opened the door just wide enough to step through, then closed it just as quietly. She never saw the gray eyes that opened to watch her. The hallway was empty and silent. Cat hurried to the staircase and paused long enough to hook her fingers through the bootstraps and adopt a confident stance, then started down the stairs, swinging her boots with forced nonchalance.

When she reached the bottom of the stairs, she saw she had no audience. There was no one in the lobby or at the registration counter. In a half dozen strides, Cat was out the door and hurrying across the bricked street to her Blazer. She dug the keys out of her jeans pocket, unlocked the driver's door and scrambled behind the wheel. She didn't draw an easy breath until she was on the interstate headed north.

On the outskirts of Fort Worth, Cat stopped at the first motel she found, checked into a room and took a long, hot shower. But no amount of soap and water could wash away the guilt she felt. To conceal it, Cat lifted her head higher and climbed back in the Blazer.

Fifteen hundred miles and two days of hard driving later, she turned off the highway and drove through the east gate onto Calder land. Tears welled in her eyes at the sight of the vast, rolling prairie. She pulled to the side of the road and stepped out to gaze at the leagues of endless, bending grass. The wind carried the scent of sun-baked earth, summer-cured grass, and the wildness of the land to her. She drank in a deep breath, filling her lungs with the familiar smells.

She was home. Texas was far behind her—Texas and the memory of a night she was determined to forget. She had made a mistake, but it was a mistake she would never repeat. It was a vow Cat swore to herself, and to Repp's memory.

The unwanted image of level gray eyes flashed in her mind.

Suddenly it hit her—what if she was pregnant? Cat grabbed hold of the driver's door and hung on.

PART 2

Nothing can ever change
The shame that you feel inside,
But you'll raise your son always knowing
He'll grow up with that strong Calder pride.

EIGHT

"What did you say?" The question was riddled with disbelief. Anger would soon follow; of that, Cat was certain.

"You heard me right the first time, Dad." Cat didn't turn from the window. Without looking, she knew the shock that would be in her father's eyes, the same shock that had momentarily robbed his voice of its usual strength. Instead, she kept her gaze fixed on the bare branches of the cottonwood trees along the riverbank, shorn of their leaves by a brisk October wind. "I honestly don't think you want me to say it again."

"What the hell do you mean—you're pregnant?" he demanded with gathering force.

"Exactly what I said."

"Damn it, look at me when I'm talking to you!" He slammed a fist on the desk and came out of his chair. The sound cracked through the room like the explosive *pop* of a whip. Her body jerked a little at the loudness of it. Then Cat pivoted from the window. If there had been a convenient hole in the study, she would gladly have crawled into it. But there was none, so she faced him squarely, never flinching from the hard gaze of his eyes. "You can't walk in here and calmly announce you're going to have a baby without offering some explanations, Cat."

"You aren't going to like them." Her chin came up a fraction of an inch.

Chase probed her cool composure with narrowed eyes. Beneath it lay a crackling tension and a well-contained anxiety. It had him hauling in his temper.

"I don't know why I'm surprised," he said. "I know how much you and Repp—"

"Do your math, Dad," she cut impatiently across his words. "Repp isn't the father. If he was, I would be showing already."

His gaze raked the slimness of her waist and belly, a quick calculation confirming her words and hardening his expression. "Then, just who the hell is?"

Cat showed the first trace of unease. "I don't know."

"What?" The clipped quiet of his voice had an ominous ring.

"I said, I don't know." Cat felt her own anger rising to meet his and fought to quell it as she crossed the room. "He was some guy I met in a bar."

"In a bar?" Chase thundered and swung away to face the wall and the framed map that hung on it, dragging a hand through his hair. "I can't believe I'm hearing this from you." He turned back to confront her. "For God's sake, you're my daughter."

"So it would seem." Fire flashed in her green eyes. "I've been told you were about my age when you got my mother pregnant with Ty."

"Don't go changing the subject, Cat." His expression darkened in warning. "We're talking about a man you picked up in a bar. I presume he had a name."

"I'm sure he did, but we didn't exchange names.

I don't know who he is, where he lives, or what he does. And he knows nothing about me."

"Are you sure about that?" he asked. "There are few places that a Calder isn't known on sight."

"I didn't meet him here."

An eyebrow went up. "Then where? When?"

"Last August in Fort Worth. I stopped there on my way back from Austin to meet some of the girls from my sorority. A kind of impromptu farewell party."

"Was he a friend of theirs?"

"No. I told you he was some cowboy I met in a bar," Cat repeated with growing exasperation.

"He's a cowboy?"

"Yes—no," she hastily corrected herself. "He said he had cowboyed before and that he might go back to it someday. But it was obvious that it wasn't what he did now."

"Why was it obvious?" Chase came around the desk and leaned against the front of it, folding his arms across his middle.

"I don't know." She shrugged in vague confusion. "It was this air of authority he had—confident and self-assured."

That troubled her. Endless times in the last two months Cat had searched her memory for something about the man to dislike—for any detail, no matter how trivial, that would allow her to despise him instead of herself. She hadn't succeeded.

"What did he look like?"

She laughed a little bitterly. "Oh, he was the requisite tall, dark, and handsome."

"Like Repp." It was said calmly, and with certainty.

Her glance cut to him in surprise. "Yes." Honesty forced Cat to add, "Except he had gray eyes."

Chase was pleased with the frankness of her

answer and the strength of character it revealed. Although the opportunity had been there, she had made no excuses for her actions. On the contrary, she had subtly assumed full responsibility for them.

"What else did you talk about?"

"We didn't do that much talking, Dad." A little edge of self-disgust crept into her voice.

"You said you met him at a bar in Fort Worth. Which one? Billy Bob's?"

"Why? What difference could it possibly make?" The instant Cat asked the question, a cold shaft of suspicion pierced her. "You're going to hire someone to look for him, aren't you?"

He didn't deny it. "Your child should have a name."

"My child will be a Calder," she flared. "I can't think of a better name than that."

Chase straightened from the desk and walked around it to once again take his seat. Only then did his level gaze return to her. "Being a Calder is difficult enough without being born a bastard, father unknown."

From the entryway came the sound of the front door closing, followed by the approaching footsteps and the rattling *chink* of spurs. Deaf to all of it, Cat stepped up to the desk, her body rigid with anger.

"Don't you dare look for him, Father." Her voice vibrated with barely contained fury. "If you do, I swear I'll walk out of this house and I won't come back. You'll never see your grandchild. Do you hear? Never!"

Ty paused in the doorway, his glance running from one to the other with a puzzled look. "What are you talking about, Cat? What grandchild?"

She swung half around, throwing him a white-hot glare. "The one I'm having," she snapped. "Father can give you all the sordid details. I'm not up to another inquisition."

She delivered the last as she swept past him out the door, the heels of her boots striking the floor in hard, quick taps. Ty's gaze followed her, then swung back to examine the grim set of his father's features. Frowning, he took off his hat and ventured into the study as the slamming of the front door resounded through the house.

"What Cat just said—" Ty began warily, sensing trouble.

"It's true." A long, disgruntled sigh whispered from him. With a wave of his hand, Chase motioned Ty into a leather-covered chair and related the situation. Ty listened, breaking in now and then with a sharp question of his own. The answers didn't please him any more than they had Chase.

Disturbed and irritated, Ty rubbed a hand over his face and through his hair and sank against the tall chair back. "Damn her," he muttered in a windy rush. "What the hell was going through her mind? Didn't she consider the consequences—" He stopped and shook his head, releasing a humorless laugh. "Cat never considers the consequences, only what she wants at the moment. When the hell is she going to grow up?"

"Give her some slack, Ty," Chase replied in mild censure. "Youth is a time for making mistakes. We've all made our share—and, hopefully, learned from them."

The memories of a few of his own flashed through Ty's mind and took away some of the heat toward his sister. "What are you going to do now?"

"See if I can't find out who the father is. Discreetly, of course," he added when Ty's eyebrows shot up.

"As stubborn as Cat is, if she finds out you're looking for him, she's likely to do what she threatened and walk out."

"She might," Chase agreed with a nod. "Which means I'll have to take steps to make certain she doesn't."

"It won't be easy, unless . . ." Ty paused, a sudden thought occurring to him. "Are you planning to send Cat away to have the baby? If she was gone long enough, you might be able to pass the baby off as Repp's. People around here would accept that and not be so quick to condemn her."

"That's a choice Cat will have to make." Lying went against the grain. As much as Chase wanted to protect his daughter, that was an option he would never suggest to her. "Where's Jessy?"

"They drove the horses out to winter pasture." Ty glanced at the wall clock. "She should be back any time now."

"Let her know what's happened," Chase told him. "I have a feeling Cat could use a woman to talk to now." He paused, his mouth quirking. "Ironic, isn't it? I always thought you and Jessy would give me my first grandchild. Instead, it's Cat."

The sharpness of the wind stung Cat's cheeks as she crossed the ranch yard. The coldness of its breath warned of winter's fast approach and took much of the heat from her anger. Slowing her steps, Cat turned up the collar of her coat and glanced at the leaden clouds overhead. The threat of snow was in them. She wasn't surprised. Winter came early and stayed late in the northern plains. This year she had the feeling it would be the longest winter in her life. Despair came crowding in. Cat pushed it back and struck out for the long building and its attendant small paddocks that doubled as both a first-aid center for the workers and an animal hospital.

A stocky, wide-hipped cowboy sat atop the fence rail of an outside pen at the hospital barn. Recognizing Wyatt Yates, the manager of the horse-breeding operation, Cat angled away from the barn's entrance toward the pen.

"How is Sandstone?" she asked without preamble and stepped onto the bottom rail to look inside the pen. The pregnant sorrel mare stood in the far corner, her head drooping in a dull and listless pose, the injured back leg lifted off the ground.

"No better. Her temperature's higher than it was this morning." Wyatt raised a cigarette to his mouth, his hand cupping it to protect the burning tip from the wind.

"The infection has spread through her system, then," Cat murmured more to herself than to Wyatt. She glanced at the swollen area near the mare's hock, the site of the small cut that had initially seemed so harmless.

Wyatt nodded once, somewhat grimly. "Doc Rivers is coming out to look at her. There isn't going to be any choice, though. We'll have to start pumping some heavy doses of antibiotics into her."

"She could lose the foal." For the first time Cat thought about the new life growing inside her own body.

"More than likely," Wyatt agreed.

At that instant, the instinct surfaced to place a protective hand over her stomach. Cat knew then, with total and absolute certainty, that she wanted to have this baby—not because of any personal moral beliefs, but because she wanted it. In the face of that revelation, all the problems and ensuing scandal of her decision seemed suddenly unimportant.

The veterinarian arrived at the same time that the crew returned from moving the horse herd to its winter pasture. Ty waited at the stables to help unload the half dozen stock horses that would be kept at headquarters through the winter. Cat noticed him, but her attention was quickly claimed by the vet, Andy Rivers. The instant he saw the mare, he skipped the usual pleasantries and went directly into the pen. Cat held the mare's headstall while he examined the horse, plying both Cat and Wyatt Yates with questions. As expected, he administered a large dose of antibiotic, advised them to closely monitor the mare and notify him immediately of any change in her condition, then checked on a calf they were treating for pneumonia.

After he left, Cat tended to the other patients in the hospital. It was nearly suppertime when she finished with the last one. She stopped to look in on the mare, then lingered, postponing the moment when she would have to face her father again.

Jessy joined her, echoing the question Cat had asked earlier, "How is Sandstone?"

"Doc Rivers thinks she'll pull out of it, but she'll probably lose her foal. Even if she carries it to term, as high as her fever has been, he thinks it will be stillborn."

"I guess we'll have to wait and see," Jessy murmured, detecting something more than simple regret in Cat's voice. If Ty hadn't talked to her, she might not have noticed it. "Cat," she began and saw her stiffen, instantly on guard and defensive.

"Ty told you about me, didn't he?" she stated, her eyes never leaving the mare.

"Yes."

Turning, Cat looked but found neither pity nor censure in Jessy's expression. It lessened some of her tension, but she remained wary. "Let me guess—Dad and Ty are hoping you'll be able to pump more information from me about the baby's father."

"They love you. Did you really expect them to

react any other way?" Jessy reasoned gently.

The question surprised a dry laugh from Cat. "Not really, but that doesn't mean I'm going to let them take over and start deciding what's best for me. It's my life and they have no business running it."

"I agree, but you'll never convince them of that."

The unshakable truth of Jessy's statement brought a reluctant smile to Cat's lips. "Probably not," she said on a suddenly weary note. "It was all such a crazy mistake, Jessy. I missed Repp. I wanted to recapture the way it felt when we were together. I wanted to feel the way it should have been for us. I thought I could find Repp in another man's arms. Instead, I lost him. Now, every time I summon Repp's image, I see gray eyes."

The pain of regret was in her voice. Jessy reached out and laid a comforting hand across the back of Cat's glove.

"I'm sorry."

"Thanks." Cat managed a wan smile and turned from the fence.

"What will you do now?"

"Do?" Cat didn't follow the question.

"Ty thought you might want to go away for a while—until after the baby is born."

"I considered it, but it felt too much like cowardice. Besides," Cat paused and lifted her gaze to the sweep of rolling plains beyond the ranch buildings, a warmth entering her eyes, "I want my child to be born here."

"It won't be easy," Jessy warned. "There will be a lot of talk, some of it ugly. Not so much because you're having a child out of wedlock, but because you're a Calder."

Cat smiled wryly. "Calders have always given people a reason to talk—Ty, my father and my grandfather before that, maybe even Benteen Calder for all I know. I'm just carrying on the tradition."

Jessy laughed in spite of herself. "And another chapter gets added to the Calder legend."

"You mean scandal," Cat corrected and pushed from the fence, turning toward the house. "At least the worst is over now that Dad knows. I still have to tell Uncle Culley, though. The rumors will start flying before long, and I don't want him to hear about it from someone else."

"Are you worried what he'll think?" By mutual consent, they started for The Homestead.

"A little," Cat admitted. "He's convinced I can do no wrong."

"That's why he'll understand." Jessy's mouth curved in a small smile that warmed her eyes. "Actually, I'm going to enjoy being an aunt almost as much as I'll enjoy being a mother someday."

Cat seized on the chance to change the subject. "Have you and Ty talked about how many children you want?"

"Are you kidding? I scared him to death." Jessy grinned. "I told him I wanted to fill that house with children."

"Really?" Cat was surprised. For too many years she had watched Jessy on horseback, doing a man's work and doing it better than most. This was a side to her sister-in-law that she hadn't considered before. But she found it amazingly easy to picture this tall, slender blonde with a towheaded child on her lap. "You will make a wonderful mother, Jessy."

"So will you."

"I hope so." Suddenly Cat was awed by the responsibility she was assuming. It turned her sober and thoughtful.

NINE

Stalks of grass poked through the thin layer of snow that covered the eastern Montana plains. The cycle of freeze and thaw had hardened the snow's surface to a glittering crust that sparkled in the morning sunlight as if scattered with millions of mica flakes. The white and gold beauty of the land stood in stark contrast to the dirty slush and mud of the ranch yard, frozen hard as a rock by night and turning greasy slick by day.

The calendars were turned to the first week of December, and already The Homestead wore its holiday finery. Garlands of greenery, strung with twinkle lights, wrapped the pillars of its front porch. More garland draped the front door, drawing attention to the large wreath that hung in the center of it.

Bells on the wreath jingled musically when Cat pushed the front door open and stepped onto the porch. She paused to pull on her gloves, recognizing the sound of her father's footsteps following her outside, the invigorating crispness of the air sharpening all her senses. Her eyes glowed with it when she lifted her gaze to the high blue sky.

"There's a chinook coming." She glanced to the

west where the warm, dry wind always came sweeping off the eastern Rockies. "You can almost feel it in the air."

"We're due for one," her father replied, then said for the fourth time in the last hour, "I wish you would let one of the boys drive you into Blue Moon. I don't like the idea of you going by yourself."

"Dad, I am perfectly capable of driving myself to the doctor for a simple checkup." Cat turned a chiding smile at him. "I'm pregnant, not an invalid. And not very pregnant, at that. See?" She smoothed a hand down the front of her coat, showing him that there was almost no bulge to her abdomen. "If I ever get too big to fit behind the wheel, I promise I'll take you up on your offer, but not until then."

Truthfully she couldn't imagine anything that would be more miserable and awkward than being driven by one of the ranch hands. Not one critical word had been said to her, but the sudden silences had proved to be more condemning. The silences, the quickly averted glances, the new and cool politeness and the low, murmured exchanges behind her back, no matter how much she had expected it, still hurt.

The fall from grace had been a long one. Cat had been the ranch's darling; the staff had taken pride in her beauty and intelligence and spoiled her every bit as much as her parents had. On the occasions when she had lost her temper, they had shaken their heads, clicked their tongues, and smiled at what a little firebrand she was. They could have forgiven her anything but this.

In a land where the old codes lingered, respect was important for a woman. For a Calder, it was vital. And Cat had lost theirs. Somehow she had to get it back—if not for her own sake, then for the child yet to be born.

Turning, she raised on her toes and planted a kiss on her father's cheek. "Stop worrying about me. I'll be fine." The air's cold temperature turned her breath into a frosty vapor. "See you later."

When she crossed to the porch steps, the red wool muffler slipped off her shoulder. Cat slung it back over and reached for the hand rail.

"Watch where you're going," her father warned. "There might be ice on those steps."

"Yes, Dad." The wooden planks were desert-dry under her feet. Cat skipped down them and struck out for the Blazer.

"And be careful on those roads," he called after her. "As muddy as they are, they'll be slick. I don't want you ending up in a ditch halfway between here and town."

"Neither do I." She reached for the door handle, then paused, catching the distinctive drone of airplane engines. Shielding her eyes with a gloved hand, she scanned the sky and quickly spotted the twin-engine aircraft. She watched it a moment, long enough to realize it was lining up to land at their airstrip. "Are you expecting company, Dad?"

"Phil Silverton is flying one of his associates in. He's bringing some paperwork that has to be signed right away. You know how lawyers are," he said with a grin, "they always make even the simplest thing sound like a life-or-death situation."

"That's why they charge the big bucks." Cat grinned back, then glanced at the plane as it turned on its final approach. "If you want, I can pick them up for you. I have time, and it shouldn't take more than a few minutes."

"There's no need," he said. "Ty's already at the strip waiting for them."

"He is?" She looked in the direction of the hangar, suddenly puzzled that neither of them had mentioned any of this at breakfast. Suspicion rose, sparking a wary anger. "Dad, you didn't hire an investigator to—"

"Do you honestly think I would tell you if I did?" A trace of amusement showed in an expression that was otherwise unreadable.

"No, but . . ." Uncertainty had her voice trailing off, leaving the thought and the sentence only half-formed.

"Drive careful." He waved and headed back inside.

Cat threw another glance toward the airstrip, then climbed into the Blazer and set out for town, her thoughts troubled by a man with blue-black hair and gray eyes.

Flames crackled and crawled over the split logs loosely stacked in the study's massive stone fireplace. Ty stood near it, an elbow resting on the mantelpiece while he idly rubbed a forefinger across the blunt ends of his mustache, his body angled toward the man seated in front of the desk. Dressed in a dark suit and striped tie, Ed Talbot looked more like an accountant than the ex-cop and crack investigator that he was.

"I'm afraid I haven't been much help." Ed Talbot flipped his report closed. "Other than the motel bill in Roanoke, no other charges have turned up on your daughter's credit card. The desk clerk says she checked in around five in the morning and checked out an hour or so later. Her friends claim they last saw her around midnight at Booger Red's Saloon, but nobody there remembers her."

"Nobody?" Ty questioned that.

"Nobody," the investigator repeated, then

recalled with a tired smile. "According to half the people who worked there, only two memorable things happened in August—a cocktail waitress got mugged in the parking lot after her shift ended, and a treasury agent spent two nights next door at the Stockyards Hotel." He paused and looked across the desk at Chase. "I'm sorry, but there was too little to go on and the trail was too cold by the time we got on it. If you have any new information, I'll be glad to see where it might lead."

"No, we have nothing new at all." None of Chase's inner frustration showed on his strong-lined face. Like Ty's, it was masked. "You have been very thorough, Mr. Talbot."

"I'm paid to be." The investigator recognized the note of dismissal and returned his copy of the report to the briefcase at his feet. "I'm only sorry the results weren't what you had hoped."

"We knew it was a long shot going in." He gestured to Ty. "My son will drive you back to your plane."

After they left, Chase gathered up the report and carried it to the fireplace. Page by page, he fed it to the flames, letting each one burn to white-hot char before adding the next. When Ty returned, Chase was stirring the blackened and brittle sheets with a poker, crumbling them into bits of ash.

Ty dropped his hat on a chair seat and glanced at the pile of black ash atop the glowing logs. "You burned Talbot's report." It was what he would have done. Only a fool waves his hat at a wild bull.

"I didn't want Cat to accidentally come across it."

"What now?" Ty leaned against the side of the desk, hooking a leg over the corner of it.

"Now"—Chase returned the poker to its stand—"we have to accept the fact that we may never know the identity of her baby's father."

"As usual, Cat has gotten her way in this," Ty muttered, an irritation sifting through his nerves.

"She's going to have a rough time of it, Ty. There isn't much we can do about that," Chase stated. "But when the baby comes, others will follow our lead. The child will be a Calder. A Calder born and bred, and I want him—or her—accorded the respect of one."

Love was a word that didn't come easily to Chase Calder's lips. Ty had learned that about his father and understood that he was expecting him to treat the child with more affection and pride than might be customary under ordinary circumstances.

"The baby will give me a chance to hone my fathering skills for the time when Jessy and I have our own family." A smile gentled his rawboned features.

"You'll be a good father-figure to him. A child needs one," Chase added, his glance straying to the fire and the ashen remains of the investigator's report.

Every single parking place within a block of the Blue Moon Clinic was already taken by the time Cat arrived. She wasn't surprised. Dr. Daniel Brown came to the clinic only once a week, and his day was always crammed with patients to be seen. Cat parked across the street from the sheriff's office and walked the block and a half to the one-story building that housed the clinic.

The December-brisk air had rosed her cheeks, giving her a healthy glow as she entered the small anteroom that doubled as a reception area and waiting room. Chairs lined three walls, nearly every one of them occupied. Heads lifted automatically to glance at the new arrival, then froze to regard her with narrow-eyed speculation.

Ignoring the not-so-subtle elbow nudging that went on, Cat turned to the wall-mounted coat rack, pulled off her gloves and the red knit cap on her head and stuffed them all in the pockets of her black wool coat, then unwrapped the red muffler from around her neck, shaking her hair loose, and shrugged out of her coat. Shoving the scarf in a sleeve, she hung the coat on a vacant hook and crossed to the reception counter, tensely conscious of the many eyes inspecting the bulky cable knit sweater she wore in hopes of determining how much was sweater and how much was baby.

The strong scent of cinnamon wafted from the crystal bowl of dried flower petals and seeds on the counter, but no amount of potpourri could mask completely the clinic's antiseptic odors. "Good morning, Sara," Cat greeted the nurse on the other side of the counter, Sara Battles, a gray-haired widow with a sharp nose and a life-soured mouth.

The woman raked her with a disapproving glance and shoved a clipboard toward her. "Sign in," she said and proceeded to flip through a pile of folders.

Cat picked up the pen and added her name to the list, noticing five signatures ahead of hers that hadn't been crossed off yet. "How long do you think it will be?"

"We'll get to you when we get to you, Miss Calder, and not before." The woman was by nature a rude and snippish sort. Today she seemed to take an inordinate pleasure in informing Cat of that fact.

More sensitive than usual to such remarks, Cat took instant offense. "I don't recall asking you to take me ahead of anyone else, Mrs. Battles," she replied.

"It wouldn't do you any good if you did." Sara

Battles snatched a folder from the pile and bustled off toward the examination rooms.

Cat turned, catching a few smugly amused looks before they were smoothed away. Two people nodded to her, but the rest ignored her. With her temper still simmering just below the surface, she walked over to the low table in the middle of the room. A spindly, artificial Christmas tree stood atop, strung with bubble lights, beaded garland, tinsel and a scattering of red and gold plastic balls. Ragged and well-thumbed magazines were strewn around the base of it like the discarded wrappings of presents on Christmas morning. Cat picked up one of the magazines less tattered than the others and sought out a chair along the wall, smiling a stiff acknowledgment to her seatmate, then doggedly leafed through the year-old periodical.

During the interminable wait for her name to be called, the silence in the waiting room was loud; any conversing that took place was done in whispers.

The connecting door between the waiting area and the series of examination rooms swung open. The gray-haired nurse stepped out to announce in a sharply ringing voice, "We are ready for you now, Miss Calder."

Leaving the magazine on the chair, Cat crossed to the door. Before it swung shut behind her, she heard the rush of murmurs that marked her departure. With her usual impersonal coolness, Sara directed Cat to one of the rooms and instructed her to change into one of the gowns.

Almost an hour later Cat lay on the table, her head turned to watch the fluctuating pattern of wavy lines on the ultrasound's monitor while Dr. Daniel Brown—Dr. Dan, as he was affectionately known by all his patients—slowly moved the hand-held apparatus over her abdomen. Sara Battles stood off to the side, remaining in the room as ethical practice dictated.

"The little guy is waving at you. See?" Dr. Dan pointed to a small movement on the screen, then winced in regret. "That was a revealing slip of the tongue, wasn't it? I hope you wanted to know it's a boy."

"Yes," Cat whispered through a fierce lump of tenderness and stared at the shadowy image on the screen. The image of her baby. Her son.

Later, after the examination was over, Cat dressed in a haze, still wrapped in that warm and wondrous feeling, unaware of the glow in her eyes or the smile on her face. She paid no attention to the sudden silence that marked her return to the clinic's waiting area. In her mind, she hummed a lullaby while she donned her winter coat, cap, and gloves. Lastly, she tossed one end of the red muffler over her shoulder and walked outside into the December sunshine.

A son. The word sang through her, turning the morning into something glorious and beautiful, a moment to be remembered. Still smiling, Cat set out for the Blazer.

Four feet from the clinic, she was brought up short by an acid voice behind her. "Look at you with your head up like you were somebody special, and you, no better than a common tramp without an ounce of shame."

Bristling instantly, Cat whirled to find herself face to face with Emma Anderson, her thin body hunched in a faded brown coat that had seen better days, an old scarf tied around her, a mittened hand clutched around a pill bottle, her face pinched mean with hate.

With an effort, Cat channeled her anger into an icy sarcasm. "And a very good morning to you, too, Mrs. Anderson."

"Go ahead and carry on like some high and mighty princess. It won't do you no good. Folks know what you are now." Her narrow lips curled in contempt. "You had 'em fooled for a while, carrying on the way you did over the Taylor boy, and making sure my boy went to prison for it."

"I am not responsible for your son going to prison," Cat flashed.

"You as good as turned the key to lock him in," the woman declared. "He was a good boy, but that didn't matter to you. There was no forgiveness in your heart, not a grain of mercy. You wanted him punished. You didn't care that it meant we'd lose everything we owned, that we'd wind up old and poor, living on the dole. Well, 'as ye sow, so shall ye reap.' And you're gonna be reaping your rightful harvest. Folks around here will have no mercy on a trollop like you."

"I don't have to listen to this." With her jaws clenched in fury, Cat spun on her heel and made to walk away.

"That's right, run away." Emma Anderson came after her. "We don't want your kind around here, spreading your legs to any and every man that comes along."

Cat swung back, hotly indignant. "That is a lie!"

The woman sneered at that. "You think people can't remember the way you threw yourself at the Taylor boy, rubbing yourself all over him even when you were out in public. And he wasn't the first, I'll wager. Which is why your pa always kept you on such a short rope around here—and it's probably why he sent you off to boarding school the minute he saw you were going to turn into a wild little Jezebel just like your mother."

"How dare you talk about my mother like that?!" Cat demanded, white with rage. "You aren't fit to even mention her name."

"The O'Rourkes are trash. They always have been, and they always will be. Blood tells, and you're an O'Rourke through and through."

Culley appeared beside her, coming up from behind in that soundless way he had. "Shut your mouth, old woman." His voice was low and thick with threat.

Emma reared her head back, focusing on him like a snake about to strike. "You can't scare me into shutting up, Culley O'Rourke."

"I ain't trying to scare you, old woman. I'm telling you not to be talking bad about my sister or Cat," he warned, then paused, his expression taking on a sly and crafty look. "If I hear that you been blackening their names, I may have to do me some talking of my own about those *two* jailbirds you raised."

The woman went white for an instant, a look of alarm leaping into her eyes. Something flat and ugly took its place. "Lath and Rollie are good boys. It's the law that done 'em wrong," she stated and struck out across the snow, her boots crunching through the snow's brittle crust.

Cat watched her. "I have never come so close to hitting anyone in my whole life," she muttered and buried her fisted hands deep in her pockets.

"You can forget about her. She won't be spreading any more lies about you. If she does, she knows I'll be telling some tales of my own," Culley made it a vow. "And mine will be true."

"It doesn't matter." Cat pulled her gaze from the woman and started out once again to retrace her steps to the Blazer. "She was only saying what others are thinking. I just never realized the talk had gotten that bad—to where they think I'm—"

"You ain't that kind of girl, and we both know it," he cut in and fell in step with her, his hat pulled low on his grizzled head, his hands shoved in the pockets of his sheepskin-lined denim jacket, and his shoulders hunched against the nipping wind. "Some folks just got dirty minds. When something like this happens, they just let them go wild. One person says something, then somebody adds to it, and the next guy starts swearing it's the gospel truth. That's how rumors start and lies get spread."

"I know," she said on a gusty breath that billowed in front of her like a cloud. "It's just so unfair." Cat felt the sting of tears, which only made her angry all over again.

"Humans ain't the kindest creatures on this earth," Culley pronounced. "Some take real delight in kickin' a fella when he's down, and the rest just scatter like a herd does when a pack of coyotes attack a lamed cow."

"There's a cheerful thought," she murmured dryly.

"Sorry, but . . ." He paused, struggling to get his tongue around the right words. "When Maggie—that is, your ma—found herself in this same fix, she went off to California where all this kind of talk couldn't reach her. Maybe that's what you should do."

It was the same suggestion he had made when Cat first told him she was expecting a child. Her answer was the same now as it had been then. "I can't do it, Uncle Culley. This is my home. I won't leave, especially not now. If I did, it would be the same as admitting that everything they've said about me is true. And I won't do that. I can't."

Culley walked with his head bowed for several strides, thinking about her answer. "If you're determined to stay, then you'd better learn to guard your feelings. You're too quick to let people see that their talk gets to you. You can't let them rile you like that old woman did back there at the clinic. You need to be more like your father. Calder is a master at not revealing what he's thinking or feeling. Ty's good at it, too," he said with a decisive nod. "That's the way you have to be, Cat."

Coming from Culley, that was saying something. For years the only good thing he'd say about Chase Calder was that he loved Maggie, maybe as much as Culley had loved his sister.

"I'll try, Uncle Culley," Cat said a little wearily. "I'll honestly try."

"You've got to do more than try," he told her. "Or they'll make your life hell."

"I'm beginning to see that." But she refused to be daunted by it. Resolute in her decision, she lifted her chin a little higher in a gesture that was typical of her, and pulled a hand from her pocket to link arms with her uncle. "I'm glad you came into town today. Somehow you always manage to be around when I need you."

"I remembered you had a doctor's appointment this morning, and I'd heard some of the talk going round."

"So you decided to show up in case you needed to come to my defense, which—as it turns out—you did." She thought back to the confrontation with Emma Anderson and recalled the comment he had made that had brought a quick end to it. "How did you find out the Andersons have another son in prison?"

He had a sly and knowing look on his face again. "I run into old Sheriff Potter a couple weeks back, and he hinted as much to me. Then last week I saw one of the deputies in Fedderson's and asked him about it. He's the one who told me Lath was doing time down in Texas."

"What did he do?"

"It was something about illegal weapons, either buying or selling. I didn't get the straight of it."

"I see," Cat murmured.

"I figured it could be useful information," Culley explained. "That old lady was a Hatton before she married Anderson. The Hattons always were a grudge-holding sort."

Cat nodded absently, finding it all suddenly depressing. Determined to throw off this gloomy talk, she turned to her uncle with a quick, bright smile. "I haven't told you the news—I'm going to have a boy."

It would have been better if it had been a girl, Culley thought. Folks around here would give a boy a rougher time of it. He started to say so, but Cat looked too happy so he said nothing.

TEN

On the last Sunday before Christmas, upward of two hundred people from all four corners of the ranch converged on the headquarters. The annual party for the workers and their families was a holiday tradition on the Triple C. As always, it was held in the one-hundred-year-old barn with its long, wide alleyway that had once garaged the buggies, wagons, hayracks, and plows used in the ranch's early days. And, as always for the occasion, the huge barn was transformed into a festive hall, complete with strings of lights hanging from its massive oak beams, a Christmas tree decorated with paper chains, popcorn strings, snowflakes, and ornaments made by the ranch children, both past and present, and a large piñata—a custom brought to the ranch by those first Texans who had made the Triple C their home.

Since early morning, large salamanders had blown their heat through the cavernous alleyway, taking much of the chill from the air. The assemblage of people did the rest. Now children ran about in heavy sweaters and sweatshirts, and the roar of the portable heaters was drowned by the chatter of voices, the laughter of children, and Christmas carols that came over the tape deck's speakers.

Ty came back from the groaning buffet tables carrying a plate mounded with turkey, ham, candied sweet potatoes, sage dressing with gravy, cranberry sauce, and green beans. Jessy got up from the seat she had saved for him, took one look at the food piled on his plate, and shook her head in amusement.

"If you manage to eat all that, Ty, you won't need a pillow to fill out that Santa suit," she said, ribbing him about his new role at the Christmas party as she had done ever since Chase had announced he was relinquishing it.

"Watch it, or I'll have a Mrs. Claus outfit made for you," he warned, a lazy gleam shining in his eyes.

"In that case, I promise to be a good girl, Santa," Jessy countered with mock contriteness, then slipped in a final gibe, "but you'd better practice your ho-ho-hos."

"And you'd better get in line before all the food is gone." He gestured toward the buffet tables with his fork.

"I'm not worried. I saw how much food Tucker fixed. Right now," she paused and craned her neck to scan the far end of the barn, "I think I'll give Mom a hand. She's trying to get the kids corralled so we can get the Christmas program under way."

"Good luck." Ty picked up his knife and fork to slice off a bite of ham.

"We'll need it, as always," Jessy replied.

The children's Christmas program was a tradition at the employee party, and long one of its highlights. This year Judy Niles had received the dubious honor of being named coordinator of the event. Naturally, she had roped Jessy into helping.

Truthfully, Jessy hadn't minded, although she

still squirmed when she recalled some of her own less-than-shining moments as a participant—such as the time she had beaten up on Tommy Summers after he had razzed her one too many times about being a "sweet little angel." She had ended up with a black eye—plus tattered wings and a crooked halo.

After an initial sweep of the area failed to turn up her mother, Jessy sought out her father. Stumpy Niles was leaning his squatly built frame against one of the stalls, busy finishing off a large slice of pumpkin pie with whipped cream.

"I can't find Mom. Have you seen her?" Jessy turned to survey the throng of milling mothers and excited children.

"Gabriel—alias Ricky Goodman—refuses to put on his costume," Stumpy explained between bites. "He insists only girl angels wear robes. Your mom took him off to have a private talk and see what they could negotiate."

"A private talk? Here?" Jessy raised an eyebrow in skepticism.

He smiled in agreement, then nodded to a spot across the way. "Some kids are over there snickering outside the stall where they're keeping the sheep." He scooped up the last bite of cream-smeared pie. "I figure that's where she took him."

Jessy looked across the way and spotted four young girls huddled outside one of the stalls, giggling behind their hands. "I think I'll let Mom straighten Gabriel out on her own while I get the heavenly choir organized. Have you seen Cat? She promised to help me."

"She was over at the dessert table, giving Tucker a hand dishing up the pie."

Catching a telltale glimpse of the bright red sweater Cat had been wearing earlier, Jessy nodded. "I see her."

"She should have had more sense than to wear that color."

Jessy whipped her head around, stunned by the unusually caustic comment from her father. "What do you mean? It's Christmas red."

"Some might call it scarlet," he said with dry censure.

"Dad, you are wrong about Cat," she said, suddenly impatient with him and with the quickness of others to look harshly on her. Jessy knew there had been talk about Cat.

Stumpy turned a cool eye on her. "You mean she ain't pregnant?"

"Of course she is, but—"

"Then I'm not wrong."

"It wasn't the way you think, Dad. I can't believe you can be so quick to condemn her for what happened."

He looked off into the middle distance. "I don't know if I can explain it, but it boils down to this—she's a Calder." He held up a hand to stave off her protest. "I know you're going to say that it isn't right or fair—that it isn't modern thinking. But that's the way it is here."

The truth of his words was inescapable. Jessy recognized it and said nothing as he moved away. Perhaps elsewhere in the country, such strict moral conduct was no longer expected. But it was in this remote stretch of country called the Triple C.

"Miz Jessy." A small hand tugged at the hem of her sweater. Jessy glanced down into the earnestly serious face of six-year-old Beth Ramsey. "Miz Niles says she needs you to get the heavenly choir together."

"Tell her Cat and I will be right there."

"Okay." The girl started to leave, then turned back with a swing of her long, beribboned braids.

"Miz Jessy, how come nobody's got the part of Round John?"

"Round John?" Jessy repeated with a puzzled frown. "Who is Round John?"

Beth rolled her eyes and sighed with weighty exasperation. "You know—the guy in the song—Round John Virgin."

Laughter bubbled up. Jessy swallowed it back and struggled to keep a straight face. "Beth, I think you should go ask Mrs. Niles that question," she said and watched the girl head off across the way. Then, grinning to herself, Jessy went to get Cat.

The Christmas program came off with the usual cases of stage fright, flubbed lines, and missed cues. Santa Ty arrived and led everyone in the singing of "Silent Night," then supervised the breaking of the piñata. While the children scrambled after the candy and trinkets, Cat hurried Santa out a side door into the sharp cold of a biting north wind.

"You were a terrific Santa. The kids loved you," Cat told him as she ducked around a corner to the sheltered side of the barn.

"They would have loved anybody in a red suit," he muttered, then swore, "Damn, this beard itches." He pulled it off and scratched at his cheeks, never checking the long strides that carried him swiftly along the length of the barn to the opposite end. His pace forced Cat into a running walk, which she welcomed, as cold as it was outside.

"Where did you leave your things?" she asked through numbing lips, her breath billowing in a cloud about her face.

"In the feed room." Ty had the hat and wig off by the time they reached its outside door. He tossed them to Cat when she followed him inside. She closed the door behind her, breathing in the room's enveloping warmth and the sweet smell of oats and corn. "I still think Dad makes a better Santa," Ty said.

"Only because he has had more practice." She laid the hat, beard, and wig in the suit's storage box, which had been left atop a grain barrel. "You need to work on your ho-ho-hos, develop a lower register in your voice before next year."

A wide smile split his face. "Everybody's an expert."

"Naturally." Cat grinned back, then cast an assessing glance over him. "Do you need any help getting out of that?"

"I can manage." He pulled out one of the three pillows that gave the necessary roundness to his flat belly. "Go back to the party, but stay away from the punch. Somebody spiked it."

"So what else is new?" Cat mocked wryly. "Someone does that every year."

"Yes, but this year you have a little one to think about." His glance flicked to her stomach, concern and gentleness mixing in his expression.

Cat smiled softly in return, instinctively sliding a caressing hand over her belly, conscious of the slight flutter of movement within. "I think about him all the time," she told Ty, then crossed to the feed room's inner door that opened onto the barn's wide alley.

When Cat stepped through the doorway, she found herself in the midst of a dozen cowboys, mostly single men, grouped together. A couple of Repp's friends nodded to her. Cat smiled in response and cut through their circle in blithe unconcern, intent on locating her father.

An arm snaked out, hooking her waist and swinging her around. Her upraised hands collided with the wide chest of the ranch's would-be Romeo, Dick Ballard. Her arms stiffened in surprised resistance.

"Hey, fellas, look what I caught me," he called over his shoulder. "Didn't I tell you I'd get lucky standing under this mistletoe?"

Cat shot a quick look overhead and saw nothing but the Christmas lights strung across a massive beam. "There isn't any mistletoe."

"It's on my hat, sweetie. It's on my hat," he informed her with a cocky grin.

A year ago Cat would have laughed and planted a loud, smacking kiss on his lips, and everyone would have thought her a good sport. In the flash of an instant, Cat knew such an action would be held up to an entirely different light this year.

Thinking fast, she reached up and flipped off his hat. "Sorry, the mistletoe seems to be gone. Nice try, Ballard."

A few of his friends chuckled in approval, but Ballard wasn't amused. His expression darkened, a redness creeping under his tan.

His arms immediately tightened around her. "That's what you think, sweetie," he muttered and came at her openmouthed.

Cat twisted her head down and away. His mouth landed in her hair as she strained against his hold, struggling to get free. Binding her with one arm, he trapped her chin in his hand and forced her head up. Cat instantly clamped her fingers over his mouth and pushed his face away.

"Let her go, Ballard." Ty's barked order had his hand shifting from her chin to her arm.

"Don't go getting all riled up, Ty. All I want is a little kiss," he declared, his glance then sliding down to Cat. "And everybody knows she's free with them."

"I'm not as free as you think I am," she snapped in a fury of temper.

Ty took one long stride forward, but before he

could intervene, Chase stepped into the circle. An instant hush fell over the barn, electric undercurrents charging the air.

"How long have you been on the Triple C payroll, Ballard?" he asked with an iron coolness, his gaze locking on the cowboy, never once straying to Cat.

"About five years," he replied with the belligerence of a man convinced he was about to be fired.

"Around here, Ballard," her father began evenly, "it is always a woman's prerogative to say no. And it is always a man's obligation to accept it. It's time you learned that."

Without a word of anger or threat, he had switched everyone's focus from Cat's conduct to Ballard's. Sensing the shift in attitude, the cowboy reddened visibly and released Cat, stepping back and bobbing his head in apology. "My mistake," he said to her.

A moment ago her temper and sense of outrage would have had Cat responding with sharpness. But she knew at once that it wasn't what her father would do.

Copying the levelness of his tone, she said, "We all make mistakes, Dick. Heaven knows I have." Reaching down, she picked up his hat and handed it to him, conscious that people had begun turning away, losing interest in them.

Dick fingered the sprig of mistletoe on his hat band. "I guess this wasn't such a good idea."

"I wouldn't blame the mistletoe," Cat said quietly.

"I guess not." He looked at her with a new measure of respect, then donned his hat and nodded to her, grinning with a ghost of his former cockiness before moving away to rejoin his compatriots.

When she walked over to her father, Cat saw the

approval in his eyes, though he said nothing to her. It was Ty who asked, "Are you okay, Cat?"

"Of course."

Still grim-lipped, he eyed the cowboy. "I've never liked Ballard that well."

Cat glanced after the cowboy. "You can't fire a man for thinking the way he did about me, Ty. If you did, you might find yourself without anybody on the payroll."

"I'm glad you realize that." Her father wore a quietly pleased look.

"I do." She realized that and much more.

With his words alone, her father had totally changed the way others would remember the incident. If they talked about it at all, it would be to discuss his clear and simple statement of the treatment he expected women to be accorded in order for their opposite number to be regarded as a man. It was a measure of the respect his men had for their boss that it was important to them to be seen as such by him.

Noble had always seemed a pretentious word to Cat, certainly not one to be applied to her father. He was strong, quietly confident, hard at times and loving at others, a leader of men definitely, but more than that, a man of the land who lived by old codes. Nobler codes.

For the first time in her life, Cat took pride in that. Her uncle Culley had been right—she would do well to emulate her father. In some corner of her mind, she understood that it was the only way to regain the respect she had lost.

She saw that it wasn't enough to simply *be* a Calder; she would have to *act* like one. Which meant she would have to work longer and harder than anyone else, without complaint—woman or not, pregnant or not; that her conduct would have to be above reproach at all times; and that she would have to curb her emotions, especially her lightning-quick temper, and use her head, as her father had done only moments ago.

But knowing what to do and doing it were two very different things. Very little had ever been demanded of her. When Cat considered what she was demanding of herself, the enormity of the task before her was almost overwhelming. She immediately blocked it from her mind before it paralyzed her.

That evening, after the Christmas party had wound down to a close, instead of returning to The Homestead and leaving the cleanup to others, Cat remained behind and helped. The following morning, she was the first one at the barn. By the time the others arrived, she had already begun removing the ornaments from the tree and storing them in their boxes.

It was a small thing, insignificant in many ways. But it was a first step.

The second week of January, the winter's first blizzard buried the Triple C under eighteen inches of snow. Howling winds piled it into man-sized drifts, obliterating the landscape and creating a wild, storm-tossed ocean of towering white waves that, in places, curled back on themselves. Snow-blocked roads, downed utility lines, frozen water pipes, stranded livestock—emergency situations came at them from every direction.

Cat pitched in wherever she could help, doing whatever needed to be done. When the backup gasoline-driven generator at the South Branch camp went out, she hauled a new one to them, following behind Jim Trumbo on the ranch's road grader, one of several pieces of heavy equipment used to maintain the miles of roads that interlaced the Triple C. On her return trip to headquarters, she carried spools of electric cable for the ranch's full-time electrician Mike Garvey and his assistant. As soon as the weather cleared sufficiently to take to the sky, she climbed into one of the single-engine Cessnas and took part in the air search to locate the scattered pockets of stranded livestock. Later, she made endless trips on the tractor, hauling bales from the hay shed to the airstrip, where others waited to load them in planes. When she wasn't doing that, Cat was at the first-aid center, working with Art Trumbo's wife, Amy, a registered nurse, treating everything from frostbite and muscle sprains to the not-so-uncommon cold. In addition, she did stints at the cookhouse, serving coffee and late meals to the road and utility crews as well as the working ranch hands. With everyone working equally long hours, no one noticed the amount of time Cat put in, and she did nothing to draw attention to it.

When calving season arrived, it was a time of round-the-clock work in invariably miserable conditions. Cat spent her share of hours in the calving sheds, tramping through the muck and the mire, making sure there was always fresh coffee for the men, now and then pitching in to pull a calf, and taking over the care of the orphaned ones.

Through it all, Cat used her spare time to turn a corner of her bedroom into a nursery. Her old baby crib and changing table were hauled down from the attic. With each trip to town, she brought home a few more items for the baby until she had a supply of little undershirts, socks, sleepsuits, and newborn outfits along with the requisite bibs, rattles, teething rings, baby powder, diapers, and assorted baby items, all of it augmented by purchases Jessy had made.

Morning after morning Cat examined her relatively small melon-sized belly in the mirror and worried when it failed to reach the elephantine girth she thought it should have. Dr. Dan assured her that she was simply one of those rare women who didn't get big, and for her not to worry, both she and the baby were fine. Then he encouraged her again to get plenty of exercise.

April rolled around, that changeable time of year when the seasons mixed, with winter's snow one day and spring's sunny warmth the next—the month when the horses were traditionally brought in from winter range. When her father objected to Cat going on the gather, she reminded him of the doctor's advice to exercise. In the end, he relented, and Cat went along, although she found herself assigned mainly to pasture gates.

But her father wasn't so easily persuaded when spring roundup time came. The temper Cat had struggled to contain over these last months threatened to erupt in the face of his calm adamancy that she wasn't going. It glittered in her eyes as she came to an abrupt stop and swung to face him, her gloved hands clenched in rigid fists at her sides.

"Dad, you are being ridiculous." Her voice vibrated with the effort to keep her anger in check. She waved an impatient hand at Jessy, busy scraping her boots across the mud brush by the front door. "Would you forbid Jessy to go if she was the one who was pregnant?"

"No, her father replied evenly. "I would expect Ty to do that."

Cat turned on her brother when he joined them on the porch. "I suppose you agree with him."

He hesitated, his gaze traveling past her to their father, then back to her. "You shouldn't be taking unnecessary risks, Cat."

She propped her hands on her hips and looked from one to the other. "I can't believe I'm hearing this. Jessy, talk to them," she appealed to her sister-in-law. "Explain that I'm not some fragile thing that needs to be wrapped in cotton."

"I'm afraid it wouldn't do any good, Cat." Amusement gleamed in her hazel eyes. "Men don't want to believe that."

"This is positively archaic," Cat muttered and took her turn at the cast-iron boot scraper when Jessy finished. "I have been riding all along. The exercise is good for me. Dr. Dan—"

"You've used that argument before," her father broke in smoothly. "It won't work this time. You are too close to term."

"My due date is almost two weeks away." Which was stretching the truth a bit. It was more like nine days. "Practically every woman on this ranch has told me the first baby usually comes late. I am not about to sit around twiddling my thumbs for the next two weeks—or more. I'll go crazy."

"Just the same, you need to start taking it easy," her father stated.

"Wait a minute—this is my body and my child. I think I know better than you what I am capable of doing," Cat declared, angry now and not trying to hide it. "I am not going to do anything that would endanger me or my baby. I have no intention of tearing off across the countryside after some steer. And I am not about to work the branding fires where I might get kicked—"

"That's right, you won't. Because you are staying home," Chase stated.

Too furious to speak, Cat glared at him, but her anger left no mark on him. She recalled all her fine resolutions to control her feelings as he did. Pride and self-will surfaced, cooling her temper in an instant.

"I have no wish to defy you, Father, but I am going on the roundup," she informed him, matching his direct tone. "Short of locking me in my room, you can't stop me. And I wouldn't advise you to try that, unless you want to see me crawling out of a second-story window."

The change from blazing anger to cool control was so swift and so complete that it momentarily stunned Chase. But only a flicker of it showed in his eyes. For a long second, he studied this woman before him, clad in boots and hat and a cowboy's long black duster, splattered with mud. Her dark hair was drawn loosely back from a face devoid of makeup. But her rough man's clothing couldn't disguise the womanliness of her or her natural beauty.

In so many ways, Cat was the image of her mother, but not in this. Maggie would have continued to storm and rage at him, and—more than likely—searched for something to throw at him. Now the smoothness of her expression and the steadiness of her gaze showed Chase that Cat was his daughter as well. She was a Calder. This was not a challenge; it was a statement of her intentions, issued as a Calder would do it.

Chase hadn't thought it possible to love his daughter more than he already did. He saw now, he was wrong. The knowledge of it roughened his voice when he spoke, "If anything happened to you out there, Cat—" He left the rest of it unsaid.

"I understand." And it showed in the soft curve of her lips and the sudden warmth in her eyes. "But I could as easily fall down the stairs as off a horse."

There was no more discussion. She was going.

ELEVEN

The bawl of calves and the bellow of cows filled the wide hollow in the plains where encircling riders kept the herd bunched. The cattle were a cross of Hereford and Angus with enough longhorn thrown in to create a colorful patchwork of rust, black, roan, and brindle. At the far end of the hollow, ground crews waited by branding fires while other riders, working in pairs, walked their horses into the herd and separated the unbranded calves, their ropes snaking out swift and sure to ensnare hind legs and drag them gently to the fire.

Roundups on the ranch had been conducted in this manner for more than a hundred years. The cowboys of the Triple C wouldn't have it any other way, showing the same disdain for holding pens and squeeze chutes that they did for rattlesnakes and politicians, insisting that the old way was faster and less stressful on man and beast. It was the same reason they gave for sleeping on the hard ground under a big, open sky—unless it rained. Then they grumbled, hunched their shoulders, and cursed the mud that sucked at the feet of anything that walked.

But the only clouds visible this morning were puffy

white ones—the innocent kind that intensified the turquoise blue of the sky. Chase automatically scanned them and, just as automatically, brought his gaze back to the slight-built rider on the herd's edge, one of the group that kept the cattle bunched for the roping teams. Cat seemed to be fine. She sat relaxed and easy in the saddle, yet fully balanced, ready to turn back any animal that tried to break from the herd. Her black duster was tied behind the saddle, not needed on this warm spring morning. The flannel shirt she wore, of green and black plaid, hung loose, drawing no attention to the small, round belly it covered.

Reassured once more, Chase shifted his weight in the saddle, seeking a more comfortable position, the leather creaking a little, his teeth clenched against the sharp and almost constant arthritic pain in his back and hips, resulting from the injuries he suffered in the plane crash that had taken Maggie's life. He knew he was lucky even to be able to sit a horse. But two hours in the saddle and he was more stove up than a man half again his age. Judging by the grinding ache, he had almost reached that limit.

He gathered up the chestnut's reins, thinking to ride back to the motorized cookshack, have some coffee, and stretch the kinks out of his back and legs. The drowsing chestnut, a veteran of countless roundups, heaved a weary sigh of resignation and lifted its head, then paused and swiveled its ears in the direction of an approaching rider. Chase saw him as well and let his hands settle back on the saddle horn when he recognized his son. Ty cantered his horse the last few yards up the sloping side of the grassy bowl and reined in alongside Chase.

"How's Cat?" Ty pushed his hat back and rested a forearm on his saddle horn while his gaze skimmed the other riders, circling the herd until finally locating his sister.

"She seems to be fine."

Ty watched her a moment. "The boys aren't too happy about her being here."

"Neither am I," Chase replied, then added somewhat grudgingly, "At the same time, I have to admire her for what she's doing."

Ty nodded with equal reluctance. "She set out to pull her own weight and prove how tough she is, and she's certainly doing that. Although why she is, I don't know."

"Because toughness is a quality men respect out here, and Cat knows that."

"Not in women."

"In women, too," Chase stated, with a decisive nod. "We just don't want them to be less of a woman because of it. That makes for a fine line to walk."

"A very fine line," Ty agreed dryly.

Chase smiled at that. "We have always expected more from women—set higher standards for them than we ourselves are willing to meet. It isn't fair, but it's a fact."

"I guess you're right." A freshly branded calf, sporting a shiny new ear tag, ran toward the herd, bawling for its mother. Idly Ty observed the reunion. "Arch tells me we've got about twenty head of Shamrock cattle in our gather."

"Sounds like O'Rourke is up to his old tricks of wintering his cows on Calder grass," Chase remarked in a voice arid with disapproval.

"Probably couldn't afford the hay to feed them," Ty guessed. "I swear I don't know how he makes a living off that ranch."

"He doesn't need much, just enough to pay property taxes and put food on his table. He certainly doesn't spend anything on keeping the place up." Which was another strike against him, in Chase's book.

"That's true enough." Straightening in the saddle, Ty cast a searching glance toward the cookshack. "I'm surprised he hasn't shown up here yet, as close an eye as he keeps on Cat."

"More than likely he'll ride in around noon—in time to eat."

Ty nodded at that. "I told Arch to cut the Shamrock stock out and throw them back across his fence as soon as this bunch gets branded." Automatically, his gaze swung northward in the direction of his uncle's ranch, then lingered on the pair of riders trotting toward them. "We have company."

Turning in his saddle, Chase studied the lead rider, a short, wiry man with a narrow face and a full mustache as dark as his hair was white. "Looks like Dode Hensen." He could think of only one reason his neighbor to the north would be paying them a visit. In the years since he'd had his run-in with the owner of the Circle Six Ranch, the two men hadn't exchanged two dozen words. This was definitely not a social call.

That thought was confirmed moments later when Dode Hensen rode up to the lip of the grassy bowl and reined in a few yards from them.

"Calder." He gave Chase a brisk nod of greeting, his eyes cool, a wad of chewing tobacco making a bulge in his leathered cheek.

"Hensen." Chase nodded back. "What can we do for you?"

"I'm missing a couple cows. Registered Angus. Thought they might have gotten mixed in with your stuff," he said, then added, by way of explanation in the event Chase thought it may have been deliberate, "Snow drifted kinda high a time or two this winter. Gets packed hard enough and it's like a bridge over a fence."

"That's been known to happen," Chase agreed.

"As far as I know, Mr. Hensen," Ty put in, "we haven't come across any stock carrying the Circle Six, but you're welcome to cut the herd and look for yourself."

"Obliged." He flicked a hand toward his companion, a boy who looked to be in his late teens. "Junior, take a ride down there and see if my cows are there."

The boy bobbed his head in quick acknowledgment, then touched a spur to his horse and rode down the slope toward the herd. Ty went with him. Dode Hensen continued to sit his horse, his gaze following the boy. Chase let the silence ride. If there was to be any talking done, he had decided Hensen would start it. But it was clear the man had something on his mind.

Below, the teenager quietly walked his stocky gray gelding into the herd. Hensen turned his head and spat a stream of yellow juice into the grass, his gaze never leaving the rider.

"Don't want you thinking, Calder, that I threw my cows on your grass," he said after a long minute.

"That was a long time ago, Hensen," Chase replied. "A different time, different circumstance."

"Gotten older, that's for damned sure." He shifted in his saddle as if to ease a stiffening ache in his bones. "That's MacGruder's youngest boy down there."

"He's got his stamp." Chase took in the boy's big, muscled chest, dark hair, and blunted, pugnacious features.

"Same as your son's got yours," Hensen observed, shifting the tobacco wad in his cheek. "My daughter married herself a lawyer over in Billings a few years back. Got herself a couple kids now. Ma's been agitating to sell out, move closer so she can spend more time in town, with the grandkids. Don't know what I'd do with myself in town, though."

"It's a hard decision," Chase agreed.

"Don't reckon it's one I have to make just yet." He turned and spat again. "Got a few more years of work left in this body."

Chase nodded, then made a neighborly gesture. "The coffeepot at the cookshack is always full, if you got time for a cup."

"Another time, maybe." The old man gathered up the reins to his horse as the MacGruder boy left the herd and rode back toward them. "Don't look like my cows is in your gather. Reckon I'll check with O'Rourke, see if they strayed onto the Shamrock. Can't afford to lose registered stock."

"Luck to you," Chase said, fully aware that on a small ranch like the Circle Six, the loss of two cows and their offspring could mean the difference between a good year and a poor one.

"Hope I don't need it." The rancher backed his horse a few steps, then swung it away from the bowl and waited for the boy to come alongside him.

Together they set off, heading toward O'Rourke's place. Chase watched them a moment, then turned his horse toward the cookshack and rode over to get himself a cup of coffee and a much-needed break from the saddle.

At noontime, the clang of the cook's triangle rang like a clarion above the din of lowing cattle and creaking saddle leather, a welcome sound to Cat. She was more tired from the morning's work than she wanted to admit, tired enough that she didn't argue when Ty ordered her to eat with the first shift of riders.

Cat walked her horse to the picket line and dismounted, careful to keep her face expressionless and hide her fatigue, but there was nothing she could do about the smudges under her eyes. A line had already formed at the washbasins. Cat joined it to wait her turn and unconsciously pressed both hands to the small of her back, arching a little in effort to ease the dull and persistent ache that seemed to be centered there. The action pushed out her small, rounded belly, making its shape clearly visible beneath the loose shirt she wore.

Arch Goodman noticed it as he wiped his wet hands on a towel. His eyes narrowed on her in blatant disapproval. "This is no place for a woman in your condition. You belong t'home."

Her newly acquired control allowed her to smile in a chiding manner. "And deprive my son of the chance to claim he went on his first roundup before he was even born?" Cat spread a hand over her belly, the gesture at once loving and protective. "I don't think so, Arch."

Startled by her response, he blinked. There was a warm glint in his eye when he turned away, a glint that silently hinted he rather liked that idea.

"Good answer," Jessy murmured near her ear, coming up to join her in line. "It's the kind of brag they like to make about a Calder."

"It will be a true one," Cat responded in the same soft undertone that wouldn't reach beyond her sister-in-law's hearing.

A space cleared at one of the washbasins. Cat walked over to it, rolled back the sleeves of her shirt and washed her hands, then splashed water on her face. But the refreshing wetness failed to chase away that dull, heavy feeling that plagued her.

Jessy stepped up to the basin next to hers and ran a critical eye over Cat, noting the faint shadows under her eyes. "Are you okay?"

"Sure." But her quick smile wasn't totally convincing.

When she left the grub line, Cat glanced without interest at the food piled on her plate. For most of her pregnancy, she had been ravenous, devouring everything in sight. It was a surprise to discover she wasn't the least bit hungry. She blamed it on the tiredness she felt, and wondered if she had the strength to get through the rest of the day, troubled that she might have started something she couldn't finish.

Cat squared her shoulders, trying to throw off the weariness, and glanced around, looking for some quiet, out-of-the way place to sit. Her father called to her and motioned to the vacant campstool beside him. She hesitated, reluctant to come under the scrutiny of his too-sharp eyes. Just then a slim, narrow-shouldered cowboy stepped from behind one of the stock trailers, his hat pulled low on his forehead, half hiding his face. A wash of relief swept through her when she recognized Culley. Quickly she signaled to her father that she would be joining her uncle, then walked over to him.

"Hi. Did you just get here?"

"A few minutes ago." Culley turned over a five-gallon bucket and motioned for her to sit down. Cat readily accepted the makeshift seat while he squatted beside her. "Thought you'd be back at The Homestead," he said.

She shook her head and poked her fork into the potatoes on her plate. "The doctor said I should get plenty of exercise. It's supposed to make it easier when my time comes."

Culley supposed that was true. He didn't know too much about woman things, and he wasn't comfortable talking about them. He changed the subject. "They took old man Anderson to the hospital yesterday."

Cat looked up in surprise. "What happened?"

"Fedderson says he had a stroke. They don't know if he's gonna make it."

"I'm sorry to hear that." An instant image of Emma Anderson flashed in her mind, along with the memory of the vicious slurs the woman had hurled. Determined to block it, Cat took a quick bite of potato, but it lodged somewhere in her throat.

"Fedderson said Anderson's been wandering around town like a lost soul all spring. I guess he didn't know what to do with himself without fields to plow and crops to plant."

"She'll probably blame me for that, too." Cat returned the fork to her plate, leaving it lie there.

Culley gave her a worried look. "I didn't mean to upset you. I—"

"It's okay. Really," she insisted.

"Aren't you going to eat that?" he asked when she set the plate aside.

"I'm not hungry. I had too big a breakfast, I guess," she lied, then turned to him with a masking smile. "I don't suppose you'd mind getting me a cup of coffee, would you?"

"Course not." Straightening, he went to fetch it.

Alone, Cat sagged back against the stock trailer, letting her weary muscles relax. The baby kicked, drawing a wince from her that was quickly followed by a smile. She rubbed a soothing hand over her protruding stomach, seeking to quiet the active infant within. It was good simply to sit and feel the wind on her face, spiced with the smells of men, horses, food, and the rawness of the land.

Culley came back with her coffee. Thanking him, Cat took the metal mug and sipped at the scalding hot drink, not talking, knowing Culley wouldn't mind. He had never been a man given to idle conversation. Nursing his own cup of coffee, he leaned a narrow shoulder against a corner of the trailer, content with her company.

After a time the men began wandering back to the picket line, their noon meal eaten, their coffee drunk, and their cigarettes smoked. Cat lingered, taking advantage of every minute of respite she could. Across the way, her father rose somewhat stiffly from his campstool and headed toward the picket area. Cat noticed the way he favored his right leg, and guessed his hip was bothering him again.

When he drew level with her, he paused, studying her with probing eyes. "Are you going back out?"

She nodded. "In a minute. After I make a nature call."

"I'll be heading back to The Homestead around five o'clock. You can ride with me," he told her, then his gaze sliced to Culley. "We'll be cutting out your cattle."

A small movement of his head was Culley's only acknowledgment. After her father moved out of sight, Culley pushed away from the trailer and murmured to Cat, "I'd better be getting my horse."

He sloped off, disappearing behind one of the stock trailers where he had left his horse tied. With his departure, Cat summoned the energy and got to her feet, automatically pressing a hand against the nagging pain in her lower back. She carried her plate and coffee cup over to the wreck pan, then went behind the stock trailer, letting its bulk screen her and afford some privacy while she relieved herself.

She had barely taken two steps toward the picket line when the first sharp and twisting pain sliced through her, driving Cat to her knees, stealing both her breath and her voice. She grabbed one of the stock trailer slats and hung on, stunned by the powerful force of the contraction. Her mind kept saying the baby wasn't due for another week, but her body told her differently.

After an eternity of seconds, the pain subsided, leaving her shaken and gulping in air. With one hand on her belly, Cat pulled herself upright and stood for a minute, fighting through the initial waves of panic to gather her composure, organize her thoughts.

A little laugh slipped from her, partly from fear and partly from joy. She was going to have her baby.

Our baby, a voice corrected as a face swam in her mind's eye, gray eyes shining above high, hard cheekbones.

Cat shook away the image, blocking it out as she had done hundreds of times in the last months. "*My* baby. This is *my* son." Her hand moved protectively over her stomach, asserting possession.

She didn't know how long she stood there, mentally adjusting to the idea that the baby was coming now, not next week. She felt no compunction to hurry, to sound the alarm, confident she had plenty of time and more concerned that she appear calm and poised when she faced the others, especially the ranch hands.

She thought through the steps she needed to take—send Tucker out to the herd to inform her father, drive back to the house and pick up her bag, phone Dr. Dan—and the second pain stabbed through her, impossibly stronger than the last, drawing an involuntary cry of surprise and agony from her before Cat could bite it off.

This was too soon. There was supposed to be more time between contractions. Even as some rational part of her mind registered those thoughts, she felt the wet gush of her water breaking. Dear God, the baby was coming *now*!

Still caught in the throes of the contraction and struggling to breathe through it, she heard hoofbeats pound out the familiar cadence of a trotting horse. Someone called her name, but she couldn't respond, not with this knife blade brutally twisting inside her womb.

She clutched at the side of the trailer, half-doubled over with the pain, teeth clenched, grinding. An uncertain hand touched her.

Through half-closed eyes, Cat saw a pair of worn and dusty boots, then her uncle's thin and worried face peering at her from beneath his hat brim.

"Cat, what's wrong? Is it—" He broke off the question, a kind of panic and frozen helplessness in his eyes.

She nodded, the pain beginning to dull now, at last allowing her to focus on something else. "Get Jessy," she said, panting, aware it was no longer her father she needed; it was a woman. "Quick!"

White-faced, Culley needed no second urging. He bolted from her and sprang into the saddle, sawing at the reins to wheel his horse away from the trailer before sinking in the spurs. The startled gelding leaped into a gallop. Continually jabbed by spurs and lashed by the reins, the horse never slackened its headlong place.

Heads turned as Culley charged the herd, but he took no notice, his eyes frantically searching and locating the distinctive tawny yellow of Jessy's hair. He rode straight to her, mindless of the cattle scattering before him and the curses of the riders trying to hold them.

"Culley, what the hell are you doing—" Jessy took one look at his white and wild face and her anger vanished. She knew. "It's Cat."

His head jerked in a nod, his horse wheeling and turning beneath him. "The baby's coming. You got to help her."

Although Jessy didn't share his degree of alarm, she did recognize that action needed to be taken. Standing in her stirrups, she waved and shouted to her father-in-law, "It's Cat. She's started."

He lifted a hand in acknowledgment. She saw Ty was with him. As one, the two men turned their horses toward the noon camp. Jessy did the same, letting her mount break into a gallop to keep up with O'Rourke.

All four riders converged on the camp about the same time. Culley led them behind the stock trailer where he had left Cat. She was sitting on the ground, half-propped against a tire, her body arching in agony, a fist jammed in her mouth to choke back a scream, her legs spraddled, and her face contorted with pain, sweat plastering loose strands of hair to her face.

Jessy peeled out of the saddle and threw the reins at Culley. "Take the horses and get them out of here." She hurried to Cat's side, kneeling down and taking hold of her hand, wincing a little as Cat's fingers instantly dug into it. "Easy now," she murmured. "Remember to breathe."

Cat threw her a grateful look, a glimmer of fear mixing with the pain in her green eyes. Chase saw it as he awkwardly knelt beside her, overriding the protest of his stiffened joints.

"Damn it. Cat, why didn't you listen to me? I told you a roundup was no place for you." Irritation and concern warred as he watched the look of pain slowly diminish and her teeth loosen their grip on the fist in her mouth, her muscles relaxing.

"That was a dandy." Cat blew out a breath and gave him a weak smile.

Chase was unimpressed by her show of bravery. "Come on. Let's get you in the truck and to the hospital. Ty, give me a hand." He tunneled an arm under her to help her to her feet.

"It's no use." Cat shook her head, a smile still edging the corners of her mouth. "Your grandson isn't going to wait for a hospital."

"Are you sure?" Jessy studied her closely.

"Oh, I am very sure," Cat said with a decisive nod of her chin. "The contractions are coming much too fast. This little guy is in a big hurry." She stroked a hand over her stomach.

"Then we'll get you to the house," Chase replied, not to be put off.

"We won't make it, Dad. And I'm not going to have my son born in the cab of a pickup somewhere between here and there." On that, Cat was adamant.

"I'll be damned if he's going to be born out here," he snapped.

A breathless little laugh bubbled from her, a mix of anxiety and humor. "Don't you see, Dad? This is good. This is perfect—your grandson born out here, underneath a Calder sky."

"She's out of her head," he muttered to Jessy. "The baby isn't going to come that fast."

The words were barely out of his mouth when another contraction ripped through her, arching her like a bow and making a believer out of Chase.

Grabbing onto the side of the trailer, Chase hauled himself upright and started barking orders. "O'Rourke, tell Tucker to put water on to boil, and we'll need whatever he has in the way of towels or cloths. And tell him they damned well better be clean. While you're at it, grab some blankets and bedrolls. Ty, get on the radio and call Amy Trumbo. Tell her to get here as fast as she can. We may need her. If not, the baby will. Then come over to the cookshack and give me a hand with the table Tucker uses for the wash-basins. We'll need to rig up some sort of shade, too."

After he left and the pain subsided, Cat sagged back against the tire again, the contractions sapping her strength, each time leaving her feeling a little more weak, a little more exhausted. Compassion was in Jessy's eyes as she smoothed away the damp strands of hair from Cat's face.

"Scared?" she asked.

"A little." Cat didn't mind admitting that to Jessy.

"So am I," Jessy replied. "I have handled the birthing of hundreds of calves in my time, but this will be my first baby."

Cat smiled at that, as she was meant to do, and worked to regulate her breathing. "Mine, too."

"I think it's time we got some of these clothes off and saw how you're doing. What d'you say we start with the boots?"

As she started to move away, Cat clutched at her arm. "First you have to get me a rope or a piggin' string, something I can bite on to keep from screaming."

"Don't be ridiculous, Cat." Jessy frowned at the request, her voice sharp with disapproval. "You go right ahead and do all the screaming, yelling, and cussing you want."

"No!" Temper blazed in her eyes, along with a wildness, and her grip tightened on Jessy's arm. "I am not going to scream with all these men to hear me. I am not!"

"That's crazy," Jessy declared in exasperation. "Over half of all the men here are married with children running around. They've heard their wives in labor."

"But I'm not them," Cat replied forcefully. "If you aren't going to find me something, I'll do it myself."

When she started to clamber to her feet, Jessy pushed her back against the tire and pulled a large bandanna from her jacket pocket.

"Here, tie some knots in this and use it. At least it's clean, which is more than can be said for a rope or a piggin' string."

Twenty minutes later, a pickup roared toward the noon camp, bouncing along the tracks of pressed-down grass made earlier by the trucks hauling the stock trailers to the site. The ranch nurse, Amy Trumbo, was behind the wheel. She would later explain that four-year-old Buddy Martin had come down with the measles. She had been on her way to the north camp to check on him when the call came over the radio about Cat.

By the time Amy arrived, they had rigged up a makeshift tent, using blankets for side screens and stretching a piece of canvas over it for a roof, anchoring one side to the stock trailer and the other to a pair of tent poles. Jessy had washed the table down with a bottle of alcohol from Tucker's first-aid kit, and Cat had forsaken her plaid shirt and maternity denims in favor of one of Tucker's clean white shirts, size extra-large, which hung almost to her knees. An extra set of clean dishcloths from the cookshack covered the bedroll that had been called into use as a mattress, and two more bedrolls served as propping pillows. It was a considerably more sterile environment than Amy had expected under the circumstances.

She shooed Ty out, telling him, "Your turn will come when Jessy has hers. If we need you, we'll holler." She glanced at Chase and saw that he wasn't about to leave his daughter's side. She said nothing and set about examining Cat.

When she finished, she raised an eyebrow. "I was going to suggest taking you to the Goodmans' house, but you're right. I don't think you would make it. It won't be long now."

"I hope not," Cat murmured, already drenched with sweat.

Amy laughed. "Consider yourself lucky, girl. I was fourteen hours in labor with my first one, and seventeen with my second—and last—baby."

At the moment, that was an ordeal Cat didn't want to even think about. Her own was enough as another contraction bore down on her, spiraling through her insides with white-hot savagery. Her teeth sank into the cloth knots. Wadded and saliva-wet material clogged her mouth, smothering the groaning cry the pain ripped from her throat. She grabbed hold of her father's hand and squeezed with all her might.

Away from the birthing site, Culley hovered in the shadowed edges next to the cookshack, his gaze glued to the trailer area while he chewed on the already raw cuticle of a thumbnail. The second shift of riders were in camp, finishing up their noon meal in a rare silence, their glances straying constantly to the trailer.

When Ty came around from behind the trailer and paused to light a cigarette, Art Trumbo grinned knowingly. "Amy chased you out, didn't she? She was quick enough to tell me how useless I was in the delivery room when our kids were born," he remarked, then asked with studied casualness. "How's your sister doin'?"

"Fine." Ty took another quick puff on his cigarette and struck out toward the cookshack. "Did you boys leave any coffee in the pot?"

"There should be a cup or two," Art told him, then tossed another knowing grin to the others. "Now the three p's begin."

"The three p's?" one of the bachelors questioned.

"Yeah, puffin', pacin', and pourin'," Art explained. "When you aren't pacing back and forth puffing on a cigarette, you're pouring yourself another cup of coffee."

There were a few smiles and, here and there, a nod of agreement, then a tense silence again settled over the camp, all ears tuned to the muffled sounds coming from behind the trailer. A rider reined in his horse close to camp, asked the status, and received a shrug for an answer. He carried it back to the herd.

"I thought there was supposed to be a lot of yellin'." Nineteen-year-old Perry Summers glanced uncertainly at the older married riders.

"Usually is." Art Trumbo nodded.

"I hope to tell you." Tiny Yates rose to his feet, shaking the dregs from his coffee cup. "When Buddy was born, Pammie yelled and screamed and cussed me eight ways to Sunday the whole time. Why, she called me names I never knew she knew. Somewhere she come up with a whole new vocabulary when little Ellen was born. And her screams gained a couple octaves."

"Sure is quiet," Perry murmured in a worried way.

Ty echoed that sentiment. The difference was he knew the effort his sister was making to throttle any outcries. He had seen her face twisted white with agony, seen the knotted bandanna her teeth ground against and the way her head thrashed from side to side. He had seen it, and he cursed her for it. But that was Cat—always dramatic. She had changed in a lot of ways these last few months, but not in that.

Irritated and more worried about his sister than he cared to admit, Ty took a long drag on his cigarette, eyes squinting against the smoke. Soundlessly O'Rourke appeared beside him, a forefinger crossing over the chewed and bloody base of his thumb.

"Cat ain't gonna die, is she?" Anxiety riddled his voice.

"Of course not," Ty snapped with impatience, the question grating nerves that were already raw.

But his answer didn't ease any of Culley's fears. "They'd tell us if anything was going wrong, wouldn't they? They'd let us know?"

Ty wasn't sure about that, and it showed in his eyes.

Suddenly there was a new tenor to the murmurs coming from behind the trailer, a note of urgency entering them. Everyone in camp caught it and went instantly still, gripped by a tension they couldn't have explained.

The full-blown wail of a baby broke it, drawing smiles that were quickly hidden by hurriedly adopted expressions of nonchalance. Art Trumbo tugged on his gloves and proclaimed to no one in particular, "My Amy knows about as much as any doctor does."

"When do you figure Grandpa Calder's gonna be passing out the cigars?" Tiny Yates wanted to know.

None of their talk was of any interest to Culley. He moved away, taking a circuitous route around the motorized chuckwagon toward the makeshift tent behind the stock trailer. The bawling infant may have reassured the others, but he had only one concern, and that was Cat.

Moments earlier, Cat had been certain she hadn't an ounce of strength left in her body. But her baby's strident cries brought a fresh surge of energy to her. She pushed onto her elbows, eager to see her child, impatient to hold this wondrous squalling miracle that was her son.

"Would you just look at how long his arms and legs are," Cat marveled softly as the baby waved and kicked and stretched, fending off Amy's efforts to bundle his newly washed body in a towel.

"He's gangly as a colt," Jessy agreed and readjusted the bedrolls behind Cat, propping her in a half-sitting position.

With both arms, Cat took the swaddled infant from Amy and gathered him to her. He stopped crying at once and looked directly at her with round and darkly blue eyes. She gazed at the reddened face, the wet mop of glistening black hair.

"You are so beautiful," Cat whispered, completely losing her heart to him.

A shaft of sunlight fell across the baby's face, the

brightness startling both of them. Cat quickly shielded his eyes from the glare of it and looked up. Culley stared at her, one hand still holding aside the draped blanket. She saw the deepening look of worry in his eyes, and guessed that she looked a sight, with her hair all wild and disheveled, still damp with sweat. But she was beyond caring about her appearance; her cup was too full with the joy she felt over her beautiful new son.

"Uncle Culley, come see my baby," Cat invited.

He hesitated, then moved closer, his gaze never ceasing its study of her. "Are you okay?"

"Oh, yes," she replied with unmistakable fervor, glancing up at him, green eyes shining.

Culley looked at the delicate pallor of her skin, the smile on her lips, and the radiance of her face. When he had first seen her, so ghostly pale with her hair all snarled in clumps, he had thought she was at death's door. Now she reminded him of the picture of the Madonna in his mother's Bible.

"Isn't he beautiful, Uncle Culley?" She gazed adoringly at the bundle in her arms.

In his thinking, babies were something women were to fuss over, not men. But he peered dutifully at the infant. "Kinda red, isn't he?"

She laughed softly. "All babies are when they're first born."

"Oh." He searched for something good to say. "He don't look like a Calder."

To Culley's surprise, Chase remarked, "With all that dark hair, I have a feeling he's going to take after his mother."

"Have you decided on a name for the little guy yet?" Amy asked curiously.

Cat nodded. "Since he will be part of the fifth generation of Calders on the Triple C, I'm going to call him Quint. Quint Benteen Calder."

The baby waved a tiny fist in the air.

PART 3

Trouble comes from nowhere.
Now you will have to decide
If the son should know of the father
At the loss of that fierce Calder pride.

TWELVE

A pickup carrying the Triple C logo on its doors swung off the highway, splashed through a puddle left by a recent spring rain, and rolled to a stop in front of Sally's Place. Behind the wheel, Chase switched off the engine while Cat opened the passenger door, then turned back to the boy seated between them.

Four days away from his fifth birthday, Quint Calder had that slender, coltish look of a boy trying to grow into his long arms and legs. Beneath a battered and much-worn straw cowboy hat, his hair gleamed blue-black in the sunlight. There was already a hint of high cheekbones showing in the softness of his face. Head bent, a furrow of concentration marring the smoothness of his forehead, Quint worked to unfasten his seat belt.

"Let me get that for you." Cat reached to help him.

"I can do it myself, Mom," he asserted quite calmly.

"Of course." Cat drew her hands back, exchanging an amused glance with her father.

Quint's remark was typical of a boy seeking to establish his independence. But in other ways, her son was far from typical. Rowdy and boisterous he was not. By nature, he was serious and quiet, a trait that many mistook for shyness. But there wasn't a bashful bone in his body. On the contrary, Quint was absolutely fearless, a fact that had caused Cat many an anxious moment. He was slow to anger, but when sufficiently provoked, he had a temper to rival hers, although Cat could count on one hand the number of times Quint had displayed it. He was a thinker and a doer rather than a talker. The ranch hands called him "little man."

As always, when Quint succeeded in unbuckling his seat belt, he didn't look to Cat for praise. In his way of thinking, such a simple task wasn't worthy of it. Aware of it, Cat swung out of the truck and held the door open for him, while Chase climbed stiffly out the other side.

Quint scooted forward in the seat, stood, then paused and reached down to pick up the cane lying on the floor. "Here's your cane, Grandpa." Matter-of-factly he passed it to him.

"Thanks." Chase took it.

Turning, Quint headed out the passenger side, the tail of his shirt hanging out of his jeans. Noticing it, Cat stopped him at the door. "Let's tuck your shirt in." With a deftness that came from long practice, she proceeded to push the material inside his jeans.

"What d'we got to do in town, Mom?"

"I have some shopping to do first, then—"

"Are you shopping for my birthday present?" Quint wanted to know, excitement sparkling in his gray eyes, gray eyes that never failed to remind Cat of another pair of eyes equally gray. It was a sight she still found a little disconcerting.

"No, I have already bought your present." Smiling, she gave his hat brim a playful tug, pulling it down onto his forehead.

He quickly righted it and jumped to the ground. "What did you get me?"

"You don't really want me to tell you, do you?"

"No. Surprises are better," Quint stated with adultlike certainty, then walked to the front of the truck where Chase waited for them. "Are you going shoppin' with us, Grandpa?"

"Nope. I'm gonna have a cup of coffee and visit with Sally." He nodded toward the building that housed the combination restaurant and bar. "Would you like to join me? Maybe have a soda or some hot chocolate?"

The suggestion of hot chocolate had Quint's eyes lighting up, but he turned first to Cat. "Is it okay if I go with Grandpa?"

"Sure. Just behave yourself and mind your manners," Cat told him.

"I will," he promised solemnly, then trotted forward and automatically took his grandfather's outstretched hand.

At this early hour of the afternoon the lunch crowd had already left and the coffee drinkers had yet to arrive, leaving the restaurant virtually empty of patrons. Chase and Quint had their pick of tables; Chase chose one near the counter and sat down, hooking his cane onto the back of a white-painted chair.

Quint crawled onto another one and peered around the empty restaurant. "Where's Miss Sally?"

"Back in the kitchen, I imagine," Chase guessed from the clank and clatter of silverware and dishes coming from the direction of the batwing doors. "She'll be out directly."

Quint nodded in sober understanding and sat back to wait. It was a short one, as the proprietress, Sally Brogan, pushed through the swinging doors into the restaurant proper. Age had thickened her waistline and turned her once copper-red hair a snowy white, a color that intensified the serene blue of her eyes.

Sally stopped in surprise when she saw the pair at the table. A look of pleasure leaped into her eyes, a look that became hungry as she ran her gaze over Chase. She had been in love with him more years than she cared to count. Once she had believed she had a chance with him. Since Maggie's death, however, she had seen even less of him than before. She had finally come to accept that he would never offer her more than his friendship.

"I didn't realize I had customers." Approaching the table, Sally smiled a warm welcome. "Have you been here long?"

"Just sat down," Chase told her.

"This can't be Quint." She turned to the boy. "You are growing as fast as the spring grass."

"Kids do that, Miss Sally," he explained.

Her smile deepened in amusement. "I guess they do at that."

"Quint has a birthday coming up this Thursday," Chase informed her.

"A birthday? How exciting. How old will you be?"

"Five."

"Have you decided what you want for your birthday?" Sally asked.

Quint contemplated that for a long minute, then sighed. "I guess I got just about everything a boy could want."

Sally laughed in amazement. "I'll bet your mom was happy to hear that."

"I guess." He shrugged the answer, then volunteered, "Mom went shopping. Grandpa and me decided to come visit you. He's gonna have some coffee, but I want hot chocolate."

"Would you like a marshmallow with that hot chocolate?"

"Please." A rare smile curved his mouth. "Can I drink it at the counter if I'm careful not to spill?"

"Of course you can."

"Thanks." Still beaming, Quint scrambled off his chair, raced over to the counter and hauled himself onto one of the stools.

Sally had set his hot chocolate, topped with two fat marshmallows, before him, then brought two cups of coffee to the table and sat down with Chase. "He's quite the boy," she remarked.

"Sometimes it seems like he's four going on fifteen. He's definitely not the harum-scarum type." Chase studied his grandson with pride.

"I should say not," Sally agreed.

"So, what's been happening in Blue Moon?" Chase sipped at his coffee.

"Sheriff Blackmore had triple bypass surgery on Monday. He took sick over the weekend, I guess. They rushed him to the hospital in Miles City."

"How's he doing?"

"They say he came through the operation in fine shape, but it'll be a while before he's back on the job."

"Who's filling in for him? Jim Atchison?"

"No, Jim resigned last November and took a job on the police force in Lewiston. The new man they hired to replace him this past winter has taken over for Blackmore. I don't think Don Hubble liked that very much. But Don is one man that, I swear, doesn't know 'come here' from 'sic 'em.'"

"I know what you mean."

"How's Jessy?"

Chase smiled, recalling, "I never knew a woman could be so sick—and so happy about it at the same time. She's wanted a baby for a long time."

"When's it due?"

"Early December."

Quint hopped off his stool and walked back to the table. "I'm all finished, Grandpa."

"Pull up a chair and join us, then." Chase nodded.

"Okay." Quint climbed onto the chair he had previously vacated, and settled back to listen with spongelike attention to their talk.

Leaving the Michels dry goods and hardware store, Cat walked back to the pickup, deposited the sacks of party favors on the floor of the cab and headed over to Fedderson's. A semi trailer rig barreled past her on the highway, its diesel engine at a full-throated roar. Dust swirled in its wake. Cat turned her face away from it and blinked to clear her eyes of its stinging particles.

Distracted by the dust cloud, she was slow to notice the man idling outside the entrance to the gas station and grocery store, his hand cupped around a cigarette, his back propped against the building, one leg bent. His hair was a dirty blond color, worn long and pulled back in a ponytail. The blue marks of a tattoo adorned a forearm that bulged with muscle, like the rest of him.

But it was the coldness of his eyes that had Cat averting her gaze and walking straight toward the door. He pushed away from the wall and turned, planting his bulk close to her path. "Don't tell me that you don't remember me, Miss High and Mighty Cat Calder?" he taunted. "I figured I'd run into you one fine day, but I didn't think it would take almost a year."

She stopped, her gaze snapping back to him, taking in with a rush his broad, blunted features and ruddy complexion. With an effort, Cat managed to conceal her surprise as recognition flashed in her mind.

"Rollie Anderson. I heard you were home." But little remained of the big, strapping farm boy she remembered except the husky shell. Somewhere in the last five, almost six years, he had lost that fresh-faced innocence, the ready grin and boisterous humor. There was a new hardness about him now, tinged with something sullen and cold.

"I didn't come home to much, did I?" His mouth twisted in an unpleasant smile. "My mother says I have you to thank for that."

"She's wrong, of course, but I don't expect you to believe me. It's too easy to blame someone else, and the Calders have always been handy for that," Cat replied without heat.

He looked at her for a long second. "It was an accident. I never set out to hurt anybody."

"Repp died just the same." But it was the image of a man with smoke gray eyes that lived in her mind, not her fiancé's face. It was a secret she kept to herself.

With the cigarette pinched between his thumb and forefinger, he took a last drag on it, his eyes squinting at her through the smoke. "I heard how much you mourned him," he said with a knowing smirk. "Where's your kid?"

Stiffening, Cat raised the angle of her chin fractionally higher.

"With his grandfather."

The squeal and hiss of air brakes pulled his attention from her. Glancing around, Cat saw a bus slowing to make the turn off the highway into Fedderson's. With the diesel engine throttled down to a growl, the bus swung into the station. When she turned back, Rollie Anderson wore a look of expectancy.

"See you around." He moved off toward the bus, obviously meeting someone.

Idly curious, Cat lingered a moment. The bus door *swooshed* open, and a man in a jeans jacket and cowboy hat clumped down the steps, a grin splitting his face as he grabbed for Rollie's hand. The edges of his hair showed blond beneath his hat, and his face had the same broad, blunt features, but etched with more lines.

"Damn, but it's good to see you, Lath." Rollie's voice was gruff with pleasure as he hugged the man to him in a rough, back-pounding embrace. "It's been too damn long since you were home."

Lath was his older brother's name, Cat remembered, and took a closer look at the man, who stood a good inch shorter than Rollie.

"Hell, if I'd come back any sooner, the old man would have worked me to death on that hellhole of a place he called a farm," Lath declared in a voice liberally tinged with a Texas drawl. "Believe me, little brother, there are a lot easier ways to make money." The bus driver swung down behind him and walked to the vehicle's baggage compartment, opening it up and dragging out a green duffel bag. Cat turned away and crossed the last few feet to the store's entrance. Behind her, Lath asked, "Where's Mom? I figured she would be here."

"She's had her fill of town. She never did cotton to it, and no one cottoned to her. She's back at the trailer, cooking you up a feast," Rollie replied and added something else, but the jangle of bells triggered by Cat pushing the door open drowned out his words.

Inside, she nodded a greeting to the bored-looking woman at the cash register and went straight to the post office window in a rear corner of the store's expanded grocery section. After collecting two packages destined for the ranch, Cat paused in the fresh produce section to inspect the shipment of ripe red strawberries, one of Quint's favorite treats. As she reached for a shopping basket, the bells above the outside door jingled again.

On the heels of its musical clatter came Lath's drawling voice, in midsentence, "—is thirsty business. A six-pack ought to hold me till I get home." Rollie mumbled something in response, but Lath Anderson made no attempt to lower his voice or hide the sharp edge to it. "What do you mean, we don't have credit here? Since when?"

Cat slipped the packages in the shopping basket and glanced toward the front of the store, catching a glimpse of the two brothers but unable to hear Rollie's murmured reply. The body language of his turned-aside head and hunched shoulders hinted of embarrassment. A second later, Emmett Fedderson plodded into view, looking wary and nervous.

Lath spotted him at almost the same time. "Emmett, you're just the man I wanted to see," he declared and draped an arm around the old man's shoulder in pseudo-friendliness. "Rollie just told me some news that really hurt me. He said you cut off Ma's credit after Pa died. I gotta tell you, I don't take kindly to that. No, sir, I don't take kindly to that at all."

"The bill got too big." Emmett attempted to ease away from the younger and bigger man, but Lath tightened his grip, his fingers applying pressure to keep him close. "I didn't like doing it, but it got to be more than I could carry, business being what it is and all."

Cat turned back to the strawberries, selected a quart and looked for another, still listening to the run of conversation, uneasy without being sure why.

"Business is something I understand, Emmett," Lath told him. "A man running a business has got a lot of hidden costs and worries that most people don't even think about, more things than just an unpaid bill or two. Things like shoplifting and vandalism, fires and robberies—why, I guess you'd even have to worry about a runaway vehicle crashing into the front of your store. Yup, a fella's got to think about all those possibilities, don't he?"

"I guess," Emmett agreed uncertainly.

"Well, I should hope to shout you do. And while you're thinking about all those things that could go wrong, there's something else you should think about, too, Emmett."

"What's that?" Stress threaded his voice, giving it a small waver.

"I'd like you to consider opening Ma's credit again, seeing how both Rollie and me are back to look after her."

"But the bill—"

"Now, Emmett, you just think about it for a few days," Lath broke in. "You're a smart man. I know you'll do the right thing."

There was a slight pause. "I see you got a customer at the pumps, so I won't keep you from your business. Enjoyed the talk, Emmett. I surely did."

In the silence that followed came the scuffle of heavy, plodding feet, then the jangle of bells. The threat—if that's what she had heard—turned Cat vaguely angry. Yet a dozen other constructions could be placed on his words, all of them innocent. She picked up the second quart of strawberries without checking closely for bruised fruit.

Impelled by a sudden, inexplicable need to be out of this place, Cat moved away from the strawberries, striking out for the cash register. Too late, she realized the narrow aisle led her directly past the store's refrigerated liquor section. Halfway to it, she paused just as Lath Anderson stepped into view, his attention momentarily on the selection of beer brands. She had two choices: continue on or turn around. To Cat, that wasn't any choice at all; she continued on, her head up and her gaze coolly averted, determined to make no eye contact with either brother.

She knew the moment Lath Anderson noticed her. The rake of his glance was almost a physical thing, touching her even as she heard the low whistle of his indrawn breath.

"Aren't you a looker." He shifted, moving into her path, leaving only a narrow gap between himself and the refrigerated case. "Damn, Rollie, why the hell didn't you tell me Blue Moon had beauties like this living here? I would have come back sooner."

"Excuse me, please." Changing course, Cat made to go around him, but his arm shot out, barring her way. Halting, she at last looked at him. His cocky grin had a reckless charm to it that might have been captivating if it hadn't been for the wolfish gleam in his pale brown eyes. She returned it with a wintry directness. "Would you let me by?"

"The sight of you seems to have knocked my manners clear out of me." His grin widened. "I guess you'll just have to give me a minute to recover my wits."

"I don't think so," Cat murmured dryly and made a half turn away before his hand caught her arm.

"Don't go running off without telling me your name, honey."

She looked down at the hand on her arm, then up at his face. Rollie stood uneasily behind him. "Lath, for God's sake, that's Calder's daughter," he muttered in near warning.

Lath's eyes widened in mute surprise, then centered on her with new and wicked interest. "Cathleen Calder," he murmured, remembering. "You always were a gorgeous little kid. Mom wrote that you got a kid of your own now, but it seems to be a kinda mystery who the father is. Turned a little wild, did you?"

Cat answered him with silence and a long, cool look. Briefly she toyed with the thought of attempting to twist free of his restraining hand. It was something she once would have done without hesitation. Wiser now, Cat recognized it was the sort of reaction a man like Lath Anderson would welcome. Still, some instinctive tensing of muscles must have given away that initial thought, and his fingers tightened their grip in response to it.

"She's giving me the silent treatment, Rollie." He directed the words over his shoulder, his pale brown eyes glittering with some new light. "I don't know why it surprises me. You Calders never did have much to say to an Anderson—unless it was something against us. You never took the time to get to know us. We're really right friendly folk."

"In that case, you should be all too happy to let me by," she countered smoothly.

He clicked his tongue in mock reproof as he moved closer, his other hand reaching out to slide up her arm in a stroking caress. "And I was just thinking we should get better acquainted."

It took every ounce of will to keep from flinching away from his touch. She channeled the revulsion she felt into her eyes. "Do you miss prison that much, Mr. Anderson?"

Shock flickered in his eyes. "What?"

"Don't tell me you've forgotten that sexual assault is a felony?" she asked.

His eyes narrowed, a hotly brilliant light burning

in them. Behind him, Rollie muttered, "Jeezus, Lath. Grab the beer and let's go. Ma'll be wondering where we are."

He stepped back, a shrewd slyness in the quick smile he sent her, his hands falling away. "I'll be seeing you again, honey," he said with a wink.

Cat squeezed past him, his low laugh burning in her ears. Her glance swept over Rollie Anderson, but there was no sympathy visible anywhere in his hard expression, not that she had expected to find any.

At the cash register, she wasted little time paying for the strawberries. As she crossed to the door, a patrol car, bearing the sheriff's insignia, pulled up to the store. Cat walked outside, half-irritated that it had not arrived earlier.

A man stepped out of the patrol car, tall and leanly muscled, the tan of his uniform pointing up the bronze of his skin, the blue-black ends of his hair visible beneath the brim of his western hat. Cat gave him a polite but dismissive nod, then faltered, her shocked glance racing back to the high, hard cheekbones and a pair of smoke-gray eyes that momentarily mirrored her own surprise. Then pleasure warmed them, and a smile crooked his mouth in that familiar way Cat remembered all too well.

Frozen in place, she was unable to move or think, only feel the crazy rocketing of her pulse and the enveloping heat of that night.

Memories she had blocked for almost six years came rushing back, vivid and sharp as yesterday, replete with all the churning hunger and need.

An interval of three feet separated them, every inch in it electrified. His low voice broke the silence, the sound of it stroking her like a caress.

"I wondered if I would ever see you again."

"How—why—" Shaken by the memories and feelings he had awakened, Cat paused a beat to regroup.

Automatically she shifted the packages in her arms, holding them in front of her, using them as a barrier to break the force of his presence. "What are you doing here?" Even to her own ears, her voice sounded remarkably calm and level, considering the chaos going on inside.

He stood before her, exhibiting that same quiet competence and latent strength, his steady gaze absorbing every nuance of her expression. "There was an opening in the sheriff's office. I took it." His smile lengthened a little. "It's a far cry from Fort Worth."

She looked at the badge he wore, and the name below it—Logan Echohawk. How had he found out she was here? Did he know about Quint? These and a hundred other questions raced through her mind, bringing Cat to the edge of panic. She had rebuilt her life, her reputation; people had begun to respect her again. Now—fear licked through her.

"Fort Worth was a long time ago." She was deliberately curt, determined to have him know that she wanted nothing further to do with him. "Good day."

She walked off, resisting the urge to run, conscious of his gaze following her. The faint jingle of bells reached her, and the tingling sensation of being watched left her. Cat dragged in a shaky breath of relief, but even as she did, she knew this wouldn't be her last encounter with him. Blue Moon was too small and the area too sparsely populated.

With an effort, Logan dragged his gaze away from her, still struggling with the riptide of feelings the sight of her had unleashed, each one as potent and fresh as it had been that night. The desire was there to go after her, but he didn't—just as he hadn't stopped her that night in Fort Worth when she slipped out of the hotel room.

Instead he swung his attention to the two men

coming out of the store, his gaze centering on the shorter of the two brothers, watching the flare of recognition and the instant thinning of his lips.

"I see the bus got in a few minutes early. And here I planned to be on hand to meet you when you got off, Lath."

Ignoring that, Lath swaggered two steps closer. "Well, well, well, if it isn't Agent Echohawk." His glance flicked to the deputy's badge pinned to his shirtfront. "My mistake, it isn't Agent anymore, is it? Looks like you took a couple steps down."

"I decided I wanted a bit more peace and quiet in my life." His smile was as cool and unrevealing as his level gaze.

Lath grinned. "Yeah, I heard you got shot up pretty bad last year. I don't wonder that you decided to take early retirement. There's nothing like taking a couple of bullets to make you lose your stomach for the wild side of the street."

"You're free to think that if you want, but I wouldn't take any bets on it." Humor slid into the hard angles of his face, a humor that held some acid and some iron. He glanced at the plastic sack Lath carried, marking the telltale bulge of a six-pack. "I hope you're planning on drinking that beer after you get home. There's a law against driving under the influence."

"Rollie and me wouldn't think of driving and drinking," Lath declared with a great show of innocence. "We're reformed citizens. We won't be breaking out any beer until we get home."

"See that you don't," Logan said and walked past them into the store.

The woman at the cash register looked up and brightened visibly. "Hi, Logan."

"Mary." He responded with an absent nod and crossed to the tobacco counter. "How's business?"

"Tuesdays are always slow," she said with a shrug. "If you're looking for Emmett, he's over in the garage, probably jawing with Bill Ruskin."

"No, just stopped by to pick up some pipe tobacco." He carried a tin of it to the register, his glance straying out the glass storefront to the two men climbing into an old pickup. "Did those two give you any trouble?" he asked, but his thoughts were already traveling along another track.

"Not really." She rang up the purchase. "The older one ragged Emmett a bit for cutting off his mother's credit, asked him to reconsider opening it, but that's about all."

"The brunette who was in here earlier, who is she?" He handed her a ten-dollar bill and waited for his change.

"The brunette?" Her frown disappeared with the dawn of understanding. "Oh, you mean Cat Calder."

"Cat," he repeated, thinking that it hadn't been that far from the truth when she called herself Maggie the Cat.

"Cathleen, actually, but everyone calls her Cat. Her father owns the Triple C," she said, then laughed at herself. "Look at me explaining that to you, like you haven't been here long enough to have heard all about the Calders and their ranch."

"Hard not to," Logan agreed. The ranch was the largest in the state, practically a country all by itself. In a community as small as this, the ranch and its owners were popular topics of conversation. Truthfully, he hadn't paid a lot of attention to it beyond garnering the simple facts that Calder was a widower with a son and a daughter. It had never crossed his mind that the daughter might be the woman who had haunted him all these years. He tried to remember some of the things that had been said about her, then pushed such thoughts away.

"Thanks." He pocketed the change the clerk handed him, and gathered up the tobacco can to head for the door.

"Take care of yourself, Logan," the woman called after him.

He answered with a wave. Outside the store, he paused, lifted his hat and settled it back lower on his forehead, brim tilted down. Shaking his head, he laughed at himself with a kind of twisted humor. "You do know how to pick 'em, Logan."

As simply as that, he put aside any hopes he might have had in Cat Calder's direction, and walked back to his patrol car. Experience had left him with few illusions about his place in today's world. Lawmen of every kind were treated as a breed apart, hated by a lawless few, needed by the respectable many, and welcomed in the home of almost none.

Cat had looked at his uniform and walked away. If he had any doubts, she had removed them. Sending no more glances to locate her whereabouts, Logan slid behind the wheel, turned the key and reversed away from the store, then swung north onto the highway, needing the release speed could give him.

THIRTEEN

A mile north of Blue Moon, Lath dug a cold can of beer from the plastic sack and popped the top on it, the sound sharp and distinctive in the truck cab. Rollie threw him a startled look, then darted an anxious glance at the rearview mirror, scanning the road behind them.

"Jeezus, Lath, are you crazy?" he blurted. "What if Echohawk comes along and pulls us over?"

Undeterred, Lath chuckled and chugged down another long swallow. "I thought prison might have changed you, but you're still the cautious one, always careful not to get into trouble." His sidelong glance glittered with amusement.

Rollie's mouth tightened at the jibe. "Lord knows, you got into enough trouble for both of us."

"Yeah, the old man was always on me for settin' such a bad example." He nodded at the memory. "Like workin' himself from dawn to dusk on that farm with nothing more to show for it than a bunch of calluses and aching bones was a better one." He took another swig of beer, then drained the can, crumpled it, and tossed it out the window, then reached in the sack for another one. "Do you want one?"

"No." Rollie shot another look at the rearview mirror.

Lath noted it and laughed derisively. "Quit worrying about Echohawk. He won't be following us. His kind counts on intimidating you." He snapped the tab on a second can.

"I wouldn't be too sure of that." Another check of the rearview mirror showed an empty road behind them.

After taking a short sip, Lath held the can in his lap and stared thoughtfully into the middle distance. "I swear you coulda knocked me over with a toothpick when you told me Echohawk was here. I wonder what made him pick a godforsaken part of the country like this?" he mused. "Nothin' ever happens here. Maybe that's what he was counting on—handling nothin' more serious than an occasional drunk, a rustled cow, or some domestic dispute."

This prompted Rollie to recall, with a curious frown, "Back at Fedderson's you said something about Echohawk getting shot up?"

"It was about a year or a year and a half ago. Echohawk and some of his ATF buddies got into an old-time shoot-out with a paramilitary group down in southwest Texas. He got hit in the leg and took another bullet in the chest. It punctured a lung. It was touch-and-go for a while, I heard. I know of a few boys who were pulling against him." Lath paused, turning thoughtful again. "He must have decided to call it quits after that. Probably figured he had used up all his luck." He grinned suddenly. "It just could be that he has. Yes, sir, it just could be."

Rollie didn't like the sound of that. He started to ask what Lath meant by it, then decided it was better if he didn't know. Ahead the highway began its climb into the broken country, leaving the flatness of the prairie behind it. A scattering of pine trees marched along the stony footslopes of this Rocky Mountain outlier, joined here and there by clumps of aspen.

Uneasy with the silence that had fallen, Rollie sought to break it and direct his brother's thoughts away from any scheming he might be doing. "I told you, didn't I, about meeting up with Buck Haskell while I was in prison."

Lath responded with a disinterested nod. "You mentioned he took you under his wing, so to speak."

"Yeah, he said he was paying back a debt he owed the family."

"A debt? How's that?"

"You're gonna like this one, Lath," Rollie said with a stretching smile. "It seems the old man got drunk one night, and Buck knocked him over the head and rolled him, took every dime he had."

"He rolled the old man?" Lath barked out a laugh. "When the hell was this?"

"Before he married Ma, I guess."

"If that don't beat all," Lath murmured, still grinning at the thought. "As tight as he was with a nickel, don't you know he must have been crazy mad when he came to?"

"Every time I think about how dead set he was against drinking, it makes me smile."

"By God, we owe Buck one," Lath declared.

"That's what I told him."

"Haskell must be getting up there in age now."

"Must be." Rollie shrugged and negotiated the curve in the road. "He told me he was born just a few days before Chase Calder."

"I just realized, you two had something in common," Lath remarked. "You both wound up in prison thanks to Chase Calder. I gotta tell ya, Rollie, I never thought you got a fair deal. Maybe you did have too much to drink, but it was still an accident.

You're sure as hell no criminal. They shouldn't have sent you there."

There was little about those years that Rollie wanted to remember. He moved his big shoulders, trying to throw off the thought of them. "Prison wasn't so bad."

Lath gave him a knowing look, then faced the front again and offered a succinct comment, "Shi-it."

After an instant of silence, Rollie broke into a somewhat sheepish laugh. Lath joined him. In that moment of laughter, a thousand unspoken experiences were shared, everything from the humiliation of a strip search to the ominous and echoing clang of lockup. Rollie felt closer to his older brother than he ever had in his life.

A lodgepole gate marked the entrance to the former S Bar Three Ranch. The long cross-member that had once connected the two posts hung drunkenly against the farthest one. Catching sight of it, Rollie slowed the truck to make the turn onto the rutted track that wound away from it, curling back into a crease in the broken hills.

This time Rollie's glance at the rearview mirror was an automatic one, born out of driving habit. Shock froze the half smile on his face when he saw the reflected image of a vehicle rounding the curve behind him, the familiar light bar of a patrol car on its roof.

He threw a look over his shoulder, needing to confirm it with his own eyes. "Jeezus, it's Echohawk. I told you he'd follow us."

Lath wheeled around in the seat to look, his eyes agleam as if it were some kind of game. "I figured him wrong. That's one for him."

He checked to see how close they were to the gate, and looked back to measure the distance to the approaching patrol car, then squared around in the seat. "We'll make it."

Sure enough, the patrol car was still a quarter mile distant when Rollie swung the pickup onto the rut-riddled lane. Grinning widely in secret triumph, Lath turned sideways and waved at the vehicle, silently watching to make sure Echohawk drove past the gate. When he did, Lath laughed softly and settled back in the passenger seat, lifting the can of beer to his mouth. Rollie eyed him warily, unable to remember a time when his older brother hadn't enjoyed flirting with danger. It was clear he hadn't changed in that.

The dirt track snaked a three-mile long path into the rugged foothills and culminated at the site of the old ranchstead. After years of standing empty, scoured by the elements, the buildings stood on the verge of collapse, their rotting boards weather-bleached an ancient gray. There was a huge hole in the barn roof, and one side of the house had caved in. The stumps of old posts marked the former location of a corral. Near it, repairs had been made to an old lean-to, and a milk cow grazed inside an electric fence beyond it.

In the midst of all this decay and neglect stood a mobile home, its base skirted with bales of straw to block the tunneling of winter's cold. The area around it had been shorn of weeds, giving the chickens a place to scratch and peck. One flew out of the pickup's path, squawking a protest.

"I know it doesn't look like much," Rollie said, seeing the place through his brother's eyes. "But I got the trailer cheap, and Littleton is renting us the land for practically nothing. Ma's got her milk cow and chickens, and the ground behind the barn was pretty fertile, so I plowed that up so she could plant some vegetables."

"As long as Ma's happy, I wouldn't care if it was a hog lot." Lath reached over and pushed the horn on the steering wheel. The blare of it scattered more chickens as the pickup rolled to a stop just yards from the front steps. "We need to pick up some guinea hens. As much as I hate their racket, they're the best damn watchdogs a body could have. If anybody comes sneakin' around, they'll let you know about it."

The door to the house trailer popped open, and out stepped Emma Anderson, an apron tied around the plain housedress she wore. Her long gray hair was wound in its habitual coronet of braids atop her head. A smile of welcome rearranged the lines that seamed her thin face.

"Lath. I mighta known it was you making all that noise," she declared with mock sternness before descending the steps.

"Hey, Ma. How's my best girl?" Long, loping strides carried him to her. He promptly picked her up and spun her around, laughing at the protest she made.

"Latham Ray Anderson, you put me down this instant," she scolded, but for all the sharpness of her voice, the sparkle in her dark eyes was that of a young girl.

Seeing it, he laughed again and gave her a big smack on the cheek, then set her down. A little breathless, she pulled primly at the dress his hands had hitched up, and raised a smoothing hand to her hair.

"You are such a scamp," she admonished, then succumbed to the upswell of affection and clasped his face between rough and liver-spotted hands. "It is so good to have you home, Lath. Why didn't you come sooner?"

"Now, Ma, you know I was on parole and couldn't

leave until now," he chided gently, capturing her hands and pressing a kiss against them. "But that's all over with and I'm as free as the wind."

"That wind better not be blowin' anywhere but right here," she informed him, then stepped back and waved a hand toward the pickup. "Now, you go get your things and bring 'em in the house while I see to dinner. From the looks of you, you haven't had a decent meal in months."

Turning, she grabbed onto the handrail and climbed the wooden steps to the door, without directing a single word to Rollie. He wasn't surprised by that; he had always known Lath occupied a special corner of her heart. The years he'd been away had only solidified it.

Inside the house trailer, Rollie helped himself to a cup of coffee and sat down at the old Formica-topped table. After stowing his gear in a back bedroom, Lath sauntered into the trailer's compact kitchen and dining area. Emma stood at the range top, laying pieces of batter-dipped chicken in an iron skillet, the hot oil sizzling and popping in the stillness of the room.

"Is that fried chicken you're fixing?" Lath stopped to grab a can of beer out of the refrigerator.

"Yes, and it's fresh chicken, too," Emma replied. "I killed and dressed it myself this morning."

"There's only one thing I know that would taste better than your fried chicken and that would be a big juicy steak." He crossed to the table and pulled out a chair.

"A steak." She paused in her task, considering the word, then shook her head and laid another piece of chicken in the skillet. "I can't recall the last time I had fresh beef to put on the table. Not since we lost the farm, that's for sure."

"Guess we'll have to do something to change

that." Lath leaned back in the chair, hooking an arm over a corner of it as he grinned at Rollie. "Seems to me, Calder owes us a beef or two for all the hardness he showed this family."

"They owe us a lot more than that," Emma snapped, making no secret of the ill will she bore them.

Rollie stared at the black surface of his coffee, aware he should have seen this coming. It wouldn't be the first time his family had butchered a Calder steer. And from the sounds of it, it wouldn't be the last.

The late spring sun sat well up in the western sky, lengthening the hours of daylight into early evening. With tackle box and fly rod in hand, Ty waited at the bottom of the steps to take advantage of the light and get in some fishing. Jessy was beside him, a little pale after her day's bout with nausea, yet lit with an inner glow that gave a radiance to her face. The Homestead's galleried front porch echoed with the thud of cowboy boots as Quint ran to join them, a child-sized fly rod clutched in his hand.

At the top of the steps, Chase smiled at his grandson's haste, but a more sober look entered his eyes when his glance shifted to a trailing Cat. These last two days he hadn't been able to shake the feeling that something was bothering her. She seemed unusually quiet, preoccupied with her own thoughts. Lately, her smiles had seemed a little too stiff to him, her laughter a little too forced, and her silences too frequent.

"Wait a minute. Don't I get a hug?" Her call stopped Quint.

Chase watched as she crouched down and held

her arms open. Quint ran into them, and she hugged him close. For an unguarded moment, her eyes were tightly closed and a look of near desperation pulled at her face, strengthening Chase's closely held suspicions.

Quint pulled back, forcing her arms to loosen. "You can come fishing with us, too, Mom."

"I know, but it's been a while since I've seen Uncle Culley," she said, her hands busily adjusting the lay of his denim jacket and straightening its collar, finding reasons to touch him. "I think I should go visit him. You have fun, now, and mind your Uncle Ty."

"I will," he promised and off he went, clattering down the steps.

Rising to her feet, Cat watched the trio set off toward the river. She stood there for a long minute, and Chase observed the troubled light that stole into her eyes.

"I guess I'd better be going, too." When she turned, the light was gone. But Chase was certain it hadn't been a trick of the sun.

"What's wrong, Cat?"

"Wrong?" Alarm flickered briefly in her eyes before she managed to laugh off his question. "Nothing's wrong. Whatever gave you that idea?"

"Something's bothering you," he insisted.

"I don't know what it would be," she countered with a very convincing shrug, "other than wondering if I have everything ready for Quint's birthday party tomorrow. With so many children coming, there's bound to be something I overlooked. I just hope it isn't something important." Without giving him a chance to question her further, Cat moved to the steps. "I should be back in time to tuck Quint into bed."

"Drive careful," Chase admonished.

"Always," Cat replied, instantly picturing in her mind the uniformed officer she had faced three days ago. Quint's father now had a name—Logan Echohawk. Again she was gripped by a terrible sense of foreboding.

It was an hour's drive from the Triple C headquarters to the Shamrock Ranch. Far from being relaxed by it, Cat was wound in an even tighter ball of nerves by the time she reached the ranch lane.

When she pulled into the ranch yard itself, Cat was stunned to see a Chevy truck parked near the house. Culley never had visitors. Briefly she wondered if he had bought a new pickup, then she saw the old one by the barn.

Puzzled, Cat headed for the house. A few feet from the screen door, she caught the muffled voices coming from within, one she recognized definitely as Culley's. She climbed the steps to the covered front porch and went inside.

The instant the door swung shut behind her, all conversation in the house ceased. "Who's that?" Culley barked from the kitchen, his voice sharp with suspicion.

"It's me, Uncle Culley." She crossed to the kitchen doorway, her glance going first to her uncle, seated at one end of the table facing the door, then to the man next to him.

Smoke-gray eyes locked with hers, holding her completely motionless. Gone was the uniform of Logan Echohawk. He was dressed once again in the clothes of the man she had called Dakota.

Cat stiffened, blocking the swift rise of memories. She had locked the door to the past; she had no desire to open it.

"I didn't figure on you coming over here tonight, Cat," Culley said. "I was just sitting here talking to Logan. I guess you haven't had a chance to meet—"

She cut him off. "I know who Mr. Echohawk is."

"Hello, Cat." He pushed the coffee cup away and leaned back in his chair with negligent ease, tipping his head back in a way that forcibly reminded her of Quint.

"What are you doing here?" Cat demanded, nerves taut.

"I had some business to discuss with your uncle."

In her mind, there was only one kind of business a law officer could have. "What do you want with him? Uncle Culley hasn't done anything wrong." She was instantly furious and on the defensive. "I know people around here may have said some things about him, but they aren't true. He's never hurt anybody—"

"I don't think you understand," Logan interrupted smoothly.

The strain on her nerves was too much. She broke under it, her control shattering, unleashing a temper she had long held in check. "No, you don't understand! I want you to leave my uncle alone. If you have any questions for him, you can talk to his lawyer. But you stay away for him!"

"Cat, you've got this wrong." Culley frowned at her.

"It's okay, Culley," Logan told him, casually rising to his feet. "We'll iron out the details another time. Thanks for the coffee."

His calmness infuriated Cat even more. She trembled with anger and a dozen other emotions she refused to acknowledge. He walked from the room at an unhurried pace, his wide shoulders briefly filling the doorway.

"What the hell was that all about?" Culley wanted to know.

The door hinge creaked. He was leaving. But he planned to come back. He had indicated as much in his parting remark to Culley. She couldn't let that happen. She was too afraid of the questions he might ask—and the answers he might get. Answers that could turn her world upside down.

She caught up with him halfway to his truck. He swept her with one cool, swift glance and continued without a check in his stride. "If you've come to apologize, consider it accepted." The golden glow of the setting sun washed over his profile, deepening the bronze cast of his skin and accenting all its bold angles.

"I didn't come to apologize," Cat informed him, the heat still in her voice. "I came to tell you I meant what I said inside. Don't you come around here again and bother my uncle. You stay away from him and you stay away from my family."

His steps slowed. "Is that a threat?"

"Take it any way you want. Just stay away from them."

He came to a stop, angling his body toward her, his eyes coolly critical. "I was told the Calders are arrogant and high handed, quick to use their weight to crush any opposition."

"Not quick to use it, but ready to," Cat replied, a defiant tilt to her chin.

He moved perceptibly closer. "I'll tell you this once—and only once—don't try it with me." The coldness in his gray eyes told her as clearly as his words that he wasn't the kind of a man to back down. A little shiver of gladness danced through her, which she quickly checked. "Do we understand each other?"

"Perfectly. As long as you stay away from me and my family, we'll get along fine."

"Believe me," he said in an equally caustic voice, "beyond acquiring grazing rights from your uncle, I have no interest in your family or you."

"Grazing rights?" Cat blinked in surprise.

"It so happens that is what O'Rourke and I were discussing when you arrived."

"But . . . what would you want with the grazing rights on Shamrock?"

"The same thing any other rancher would want."

"But you're—"

"—a deputy sheriff," he supplied the title. "Currently I'm also serving as acting sheriff while Blackmore is recovering from surgery. It's a job with a steady income. Nowadays, small ranches aren't all that profitable."

Somewhere along the line, the anger had left him, but the growling need that replaced it was just as strong. Almost reluctantly he watched the play of expressions over her face, his glance drawn to her lips, the memory of their taste and texture returning to tempt him all over again.

"You're thinking about buying a ranch here." Cat recalled he had mentioned getting into ranching again on that long-ago night in Fort Worth.

"I already have."

"What?" She looked at him.

"I bought the Circle Six." A dry smile edged his mouth. "I guess that makes us neighbors, doesn't it?"

"No." Cat swung away, struck by the certain eventuality that one day he would meet up with Quint.

"It's a pity you can't pick your neighbors, isn't it?" Logan said mockingly. Her hair gleamed a glossy black in the sun's waning light. To his regret, he remembered the silken feel of it tangled in his hands.

She turned back to him in obvious agitation. "You had hundreds of places you could have gone. Why did you come here? Why?"

"I wasn't searching for you, if that's what you

think. Sorry, but you weren't that unforgettable."

Had she thought that? Cat realized she must have, because it stung to know she had played no part in his decision. "Then why did you come here?"

"Because I happen to like it."

"But it isn't always like this," she argued. "The winters here can be brutal."

"You forget I'm originally from the Dakotas. The winters here aren't that much different."

Frustration pushed at her. "What do I have to do to make you leave?"

His smile turned lazy and taunting. "What are you offering? A repeat performance of our night in Fort Worth?"

Furious, she struck out at him, her hand arcing toward a lean cheek. He blocked it, his fingers clamping around her slender wrist. With a jerk, he pulled her against him, molding her to his length. The contact with his flatly muscled body snatched at her breath and stirred alive all the old needs that had once driven Cat into his arms. His head tipped toward her, his face filling her vision, the moist heat of his breath warming her lips. She felt hot, the closeness of him leaving her in no doubt that he was as aroused as she was. Could she use that?

The question had barely crossed her mind when Logan killed that hope. "Pleasurable as it would be to take you again, Cat, it wouldn't work," he murmured, his gaze traveling over her face. "I'm here to stay. Get used to it."

That was impossible, and Cat knew it. "I'll buy your ranch. Whatever you had to pay for it, I'll give you more," she offered in desperation, for the first time truly thankful for the trust fund her mother had established.

He chuckled. It wasn't a pleasant sound. "Money and pressure—I was told those were two ways the

Calders dealt with a problem. I can't be bought, Cat. And don't try pressuring me, because I'll push back. Hard."

He released her with a short, abrupt shove and walked away. A camp jay swooped across his path, aiming for a thickly needled pine tree. With a sharp cry of alarm, it suddenly veered from its path. Alerted by its call, Logan snapped a glance at the site. A dark figure lurked in the tree's deep shadows.

The discovery of the man was a cold shock to his senses, proof of how completely he had been absorbed by Cat. That it was only O'Rourke mattered little. The man had gotten behind him, unseen and unheard. No one knew better than Logan the potential danger of such a lapse in his guard. The skin along the back of his neck crawled from the thought of it. Yanking open the door to his truck, Logan cursed her, and he cursed himself.

Culley waited until the pickup had started down the lane before he soundlessly moved out of the tree's shadows. His gaze followed the departing truck with quiet speculation, his mind turning over the things Logan had said against the Calders.

He came up behind Cat, catching her unaware. "Are you okay?"

She turned with a start, then relaxed visibly. "Uncle Culley. I didn't hear you come out."

He could have told her the front door squeaked, but the back door didn't. Instead he asked, "What was that all about with Echohawk?"

"Nothing." She stared after the truck, absently massaging her right wrist.

Culley took note of the action, his eyes narrowing. "Did he hurt you?"

"No, I—" She threw off that question and came straight to the point. "He said he was here to lease Shamrock grazing rights. Is that true?"

"We were talking about it." Culley nodded. "Running stock is young man's work. I'm getting too old for it."

"I don't want you to sell him those rights, Uncle Culley. Not for any price." She wore a determined look that he knew well.

"What'd he do to you?"

"Nothing."

He didn't buy that. "It's plain enough you got something against him. You lit into him from the moment you walked in the door. You must have had a run-in with him before. I don't think it was around here." Culley didn't mention the comment he'd overheard about Fort Worth. That was for Cat to tell him.

She released a long, tension-filled sigh, her head dipping a little. "Logan Echohawk is Quint's father." There was no one else she would have trusted with that knowledge.

"The eyes," he murmured. "I should have seen it."

"What will happen when he sees Quint? Will he notice the similarities? Will he care that he has a son? Will he demand a father's rights, or will he use Quint to get his hands on the Calder fortune?"

Culley tipped his chin to one side in a denying fashion. "I got the impression he doesn't think too much of the Calders."

"Nobody does when they're on the outside looking in," Cat replied with heavy cynicism.

"Logan didn't strike me as the kind who talks outa both sides of his mouth."

"Maybe he isn't. He certainly seems determined to stay here," she said, then sighed again. "I don't know what to do, Uncle Culley. I feel like there's a sword hanging over my head, and the rope holding it is fraying."

Advice had never been his strong suit. But he had a willing ear. "Sometimes just talking it all out makes it all clearer."

Cat shook her head. "I don't see how."

"Well . . . what's the worst that could happen?"

"That's easy." Wryness tugged at her mouth. "For my father to find out who he is. Dad would insist that I marry him, as if that would somehow legitimize Quint's birth."

"And you don't want to marry him," Culley guessed.

"Repp is the only man I ever wanted to marry. With him gone—I couldn't love anyone else." Even as she said that, she went hot with the memory of how readily her body had reacted to Logan. It was an animal thing. It had nothing to do with her heart.

"Marrying him would give the kid a father, though."

"Quint doesn't need one. He has Ty and my father. He couldn't have better role models."

Not to Culley's way of thinking, but he refrained from saying that. "It strikes me if that's the worst that can happen, you don't have much of a problem. If Calder tries to make you marry him, you can just take the kid and leave, come over here and stay with me until you can make him see reason."

"I hate to think of that," she murmured. "Quint won't understand all the quarreling and shouting, people making him a battleground. The Triple C is his home, his heritage. I want him to grow up there, loving it as much as I do. There has to be some way I can protect him from all this, but I don't know how."

"It would be confusing to a kid," Culley agreed absently, distracted by other thoughts her remarks had triggered.

She glanced to the west where the sun sat half below the horizon in a golden fire. "If I'm going to be home in time to tuck him into bed, I'd better be going.

"Are you sure? I got some cookies in the house."

"Maybe another time." She reached for his hand and watched him turn self-conscious. Touching always came awkward to him. "I'm sorry for unloading all my troubles on you tonight. I guess I needed someone to talk to, and there isn't anyone else I can trust as I do you."

"If you need me, you let me know."

"I will," Cat promised, her smile warming. "I honestly don't know what I'd do if you weren't here, Uncle Culley."

It was the same thought that was on his mind, but he said nothing as she brushed a kiss across his cheek, then walked away with a quick wave. He stood there while she climbed into the Blazer and drove out of the yard.

After she was out of sight, he waited there a little longer, then crossed the ranch yard to the pole corral. A halter with an attached lead rope hung on a near post. Culley gathered it up and slipped between the corral rails. A scrawny bay gelding snorted in quick suspicion and turned his head to eye him warily. The horse waited until Culley was almost to him, then flung up his head in a halfhearted attempt to elude capture.

Culley grabbed a handful of scraggly mane. "Whoa there, you old buzzard bait." The horse stopped, snorting again, and Culley slipped the halter on with practiced ease. "You and me's got us some nighthawking to do. It's for sure I ain't gonna be around forever to look after Cat."

The jaw strap buckled, he led the horse to the barn. Five minutes later, he rode out and headed west, into the crimson fire of the setting sun. Having seldom ventured onto the Circle Six during his night wanderings, it took Culley some time to make his way across the rugged hills and locate the ranch yard. He rounded a thinly wooded shoulder of land and spied the yard light. He reined in, then swung the surefooted bay up the slope and circled around to find a vantage point.

An outcropping of rock near the crest of the hill offered both concealment and an unobstructed view of the ranch yard. Culley hobbled the bay in a grassy hollow on the other side of the hill, removed the binoculars from a saddlebag, and climbed to the outcropping.

The yard light's far-reaching glow touched on the front of a shed barn and made dark, distinctive shapes of the horses dozing in an adjacent corral. From memory, Culley knew that a set of stock pens for sorting and loading cattle stood somewhere in the night-thick shadows south of the barn. He skipped over the storage building and machine shop and focused the binoculars on the single-story house.

Logan's pickup was parked alongside the patrol car next to the house. The presence of the two vehicles confirmed that Logan was at the ranch. Light gushed from a kitchen window, illuminating a section of the front porch that ran the length of the house. Culley's angle gave him a limited view of the kitchen, but he could detect no movement within.

After watching it for a long run of minutes, he surveyed the rest of the house through the glasses, but no other light showed. Puzzled, Culley lowered the binoculars, then raised them again to scan the shadowed recesses of the porch. A pinpoint of light flared briefly, then vanished. Culley zeroed in on it and discovered the black shape of a figure seated just beyond the glow of the lighted kitchen window.

Logan sat idly in the sturdy rocker, his fingers loosely gripping the bowl of the pipe clamped between his teeth. He puffed on it, but tonight he found no pleasure in the sharp tang of smoke on his tongue. His restless gaze wandered over the ranch yard, probing the shadows from long habit. He had lived too long with the need for such vigilance to ever abandon it completely, even here on the ranch that was his haven from the pressures of dark alleys and human treachery.

The evening hour was his time to relax and regain some of his faith in human nature. But there was no ease in the winy air for him tonight. Somewhere to the south lay the headquarters of the Triple C Ranch, a fact that had never mattered much to him when he bought the Circle Six. But that was before he had learned Cat lived there.

Crowded by the thought, Logan pushed out of the rocker, setting it swaying. He crossed to the edge of the porch and knocked the hot ash from his pipe. It fell in a scattering of sparks that died seconds after touching the ground. But the fiery ache in his loins wasn't so easily put out.

FOURTEEN

"Mom, wait for me!" Quint's voice carried across the quiet of the Sunday afternoon.

Halting, Cat turned, a bouquet of spring's first wildflowers clutched in her hand. She smiled when she saw Quint running toward her, a hand clamped over his new straw Stetson, a birthday present from Cat and currently his most prized possession. Out of breath, he skidded to a stop beside her.

"I didn't think you'd hear me," he declared.

Cat raised an eyebrow. "And I thought you were taking a nap."

"I woke up." He looked at the flowers in her hand. "Are you going to the cemetery?"

She inadvertently tightened her grip on the delicate flower stems. To Quint, her visits to Repp's grave site were a common occurrence. Only she knew that twinges of guilt prompted this one.

"Can I come with you?" His request eliminated any chance of privacy, but Cat found it impossible to refuse him. "Of course you can."

Automatically he reached for her hand, and they set out together, angling across the ranch yard toward the small cemetery. "Mom, do I have to take naps on roundup?" Quint asked after they had traveled several yards.

She hid a smile. "I guess you don't think you should."

"The guys would tease me." The very glumness of his voice revealed the humiliation he would feel.

"They might," Cat agreed with a straight face. "Maybe if you went to bed earlier at night, you wouldn't need to take a nap."

"Thanks, Mom." He looked up, a smile bursting across his usually solemn face.

"You're welcome." Idly, she wished all of life's problems were so easily solved.

Her visits to the cemetery followed a never-changing pattern. She always stopped first at her mother's grave. After a moment of silent prayer, she left a spray of wildflowers at the base of the granite marker, then made her way to the Taylor plot.

Kneeling, Cat laid the remaining flowers on Repp's grave and automatically traced the letters of his name, etched into the smoothly polished surface of his red granite marker, the old ache for what might have been rising up in her throat.

"Was he my dad?"

Quint's question had the impact of a body blow. Cat turned with a sharp and silent indrawn breath, her glance racing to his quietly serious expression. Never once had Quint ever shown the slightest curiosity about his father or, to her knowledge, even wondered about his existence.

"What made you ask that?" Cat stalled, trying to decide what she should tell him.

His slender shoulders rose and fell in a diffident shrug, a look of uncertainty entering his gray eyes. His response forcibly reminded Cat that children were much more sensitive and observant than adults realized. His question had been forthright, but her response hadn't been, and Quint knew it.

Determined to repair the damage, Cat captured his hand and drew him to her, gathering him into the loose circle of her arms. "Repp wasn't your father, Quint, although I know he would have liked to be," she told him truthfully. "You're just the kind of son he would have wanted. I know he would have been the proudest dad to take you on roundup with him. And he wouldn't have let the men tease you about taking a nap, either. He would have told them to keep quiet, that a person deserves to rest after they've worked hard. There's no doubt he would have loved you a lot. And you would have loved him, Quint."

He listened with solemn care, but Cat couldn't tell what he was thinking. Nerves raveling, she braced herself for direct questions about his father. But it soon became apparent that she had been granted a reprieve. But for how long?

Monday marked the first day of spring roundup on the Triple C. By tradition, the north range was the starting point. It was a fact known to any and all, and one that Lath Anderson counted on as the four-wheel-drive truck traveled along a dirt back road, its lights out. Clouds shrouded the moon, turning the night pitch black. A high-powered rifle rattled in the gun rack behind his head. The case with the infrared night scope lay on the seat beside him.

"This is crazy." Rollie crouched over the wheel, peering into the blackness ahead of them. "I can't see where I'm going."

"Just keep aiming for that butte straight ahead." Lath pointed to the landmark, discernible only by the faint star-glitter that outlined it.

"What butte?" Rollie grumbled. "I don't see why the hell I can't turn the headlights on. As of yesterday, the whole crew is over on the north range. You said yourself they wouldn't finish up there until Thursday at the earliest."

"Just the same, there's no point in advertising ourselves." He leaned forward, expectantly scanning the blackness ahead of them. "Slow down. We should be coming up to the gate."

"How can you tell?" Rollie muttered, dryly sarcastic, and reduced speed.

Lath chuckled. "You're worse than a bitchy old woman. Next you're gonna be wantin' to stop somewhere and ask for directions."

"Very funny."

"You know, what we really need is a couple pairs of night-vision goggles," Lath mused idly, all the while closely watching the side of the road. "I had me some once. Man, they were wild."

"What we need is some light."

The slow-moving clouds rolled past a corner of the moon. The sliver of light gave shape and form to the surrounding landscape, glinting on the metal of a fence gate. Lath hee-heed a laugh and punched Rollie's shoulder.

"'Ask and ye shall receive,' brother. That's all you gotta do," he declared.

But Rollie didn't think God had any part in their night's venture. He swung the truck off the road and stopped in front of the gate. Lath hopped out, unlatched the gate, and dragged it open, waving Rollie through. As soon as the truck cleared the gateposts, Lath left the gate standing open and scrambled back into the cab.

"Head for the base of that bluff over there," Lath told him, pointing to their right. "There's always a bunch of cattle bedded down in that grassy gulch."

"How do you know?" With more of the moon shining down to light the way, Rollie set out toward the spot.

"Because I been scouting this while you've been off playing in the coal pit every day," he added the last on a note of derision. "Ma wants some beef for the table, and I aim to see that she gets it—and take a few pokes at the Calders while I'm at it."

The roughness of the uneven ground made for slow going. After what seemed an eternity to Rollie, they arrived at the bluff and maneuvered the truck into position to block the gulch, formed by an outreaching foot of the high bluff.

Somewhere around a half dozen cows with young calves lumbered to their feet, snuffing in alarm. Two stood their ground to eye the intruders warily while the rest trotted to the back of the gulch.

"Was I right or what, little brother?" Lath lifted the rifle from the window rack, attached the night scope, then loaded the ammunition.

"I don't see any steers." Rollie judged, mainly by the calves mothering up with grown cows.

"No, but if it's the same bunch, there's a couple of heifers that'll make good eatin'." He climbed out of the truck and leaned atop the hood, using it for a stand. Rollie moved out of the line of fire, coming around to the passenger side while Lath put his eye to the scope and scanned the choice of targets. "This is better than a shooting gallery."

He picked out a cow, took aim and squeezed the trigger, the sharp report echoing off the bluff walls. A dark shape crumbled to the ground as a calf bawled. Confusion reigned, the bunched cattle rushing about in panic, seeking escape. There was none.

Lath fired again, then again. Rollie saw a second animal stumble to its knees. For an instant, he was too stunned to react. The rifle cracked again, breaking that grip of surprise.

"What the hell are you doing, Lath?" Another cow crashed to the ground while the second one struggled to rise. "We haven't got room in the back of that truck for more than one carcass, not with that winch back there. Have you gone crazy?"

Lath never took his cheek away from the rifle. "What's the fun of stealing one of Calder's beeves if he don't find out about it?"

Buzzards glided in lazy circles along the thermals rising from the bluff. More were on the ground, some too gorged from their feast of dead flesh to do more than flap their wings and lumber out of the riders' way while others roosted in the trees.

Flies swarmed over the bloated carcasses, the hum of their beating wings a steady drone that filled the grim scene. The heat of the noonday sun intensified the stench of rotting flesh. Ty's horse snorted and tossed its head, not liking anything about this place.

Neither did Ty as he stared at the carnage before him, a cold anger welling. "You said they'd been shot?" he fired the question at the middle-aged cowboy Mike Summers.

"I didn't check all of them, but I'd say so," Mike replied stiffly. "We saw the buzzards circling, then found that calf, hobbling on three legs, half-dead with fever—hell, he was so weak, Shane and me walked right up to him. That's when we saw the bullet hole. We figured the buzzards were waiting for him to die. Then we smelled this." He nodded at the bodies of the slain cattle, frozen in death and partially mutilated by scavenging vultures and coyotes. "It was deliberate, Ty. There ain't much doubt of that. I wish to hell I could get my hands on the bastard that did this."

"We will," Ty stated in a hard, flat voice. "First, we'll need to file a report. Ride back to camp and call the sheriff's office on the mobile phone. Get him out here."

"Right away." Mike backed his horse a few paces, then wheeled it around and pointed it toward camp. The horse broke into a canter on its own, eager to be away from the place that smelled so strongly of death.

Ty's horse made a swing to follow, but Ty checked the movement and surveyed the area a minute longer, then rode over to the shade of some scrub willows where the two injured calves were being held.

Around noontime, Chase rode out from camp at Broken Butte to look over the first batch of cattle that had been brought in. Quint followed, astride a short-coupled bay mare renowned on the ranch for her ability to mollycoddle the greenest rider, hence earning the name Molly. Having ridden since the age of two, Quint was far from green, but neither was he an old hand, especially in the occasionally explosive arena of roundup.

When Chase halted his sturdy buckskin gelding a short distance from the small herd, Quint reined the mare around to come alongside him. The tractable Molly obeyed and stopped of her own accord abreast of the buckskin.

Copying his grandfather's pose, Quint folded both hands over the saddle horn and surveyed the scene. A cow and her calf attempted to break from the bunch, only to be turned back by the day-herder.

"They're a bit snuffy," Quint observed, quick to use one of the terms he'd picked up from the older hands.

"A bit," Chase agreed with a touch of drollness.

Hoofbeats drummed somewhere behind them. Frowning, Chase swiveled in the saddle, his gaze narrowing at the sight of a horse and rider galloping into camp. His haste clearly signaled trouble of some sort.

"Come on, Quint," he said to the boy. "Let's see what's up." He swung the buckskin around and lifted it into a canter. Quint followed suit, pounding his heels against the mare's sides, urging her to close the gap with the buckskin. They arrived in camp at the same time as the approaching rider.

Chase took one look at the grim expression on Mike Summers' face and demanded, "What happened?"

"We got about a dozen head of dead cattle and a couple wounded calves. Ty sent me back to notify the sheriff, says we'll need to make a report." The horse shifted restlessly beneath him, the bridle bit clanking against its chewing teeth.

"Wounded? How?"

"Looks like they been shot." Repressed anger laced the terseness of his reply.

Chase's own lips thinned. "Where is this?"

"Over at the bottom of the bluff, where those buzzards are congregating." Mike motioned to the northeast. "Not far from Three Mile Gate." With that information passed along, he rode over to use the mobile phone in the truck to call the sheriff's office.

Off to the northeast, some three miles distant, circling buzzards made black dots in the sky. Chase studied them with hard eyes. His fingers tightened on the reins, and the buckskin shifted, gathering itself in anticipation of a signal to move forward. But Chase glanced at his grandson, who had never seen death. Young as Quint was, he would be doing him no favor to shield him completely from it.

"Are you and Molly up to a long ride?" Affection gentled the grimness of his expression.

"Sure." Quint had heard the exchange between Chase and Mike Summers, and now wore the avid look of a boy about to embark on a kind of adventure.

"Let's go." But Chase regretted the hard lesson Quint would learn.

As he pointed the buckskin toward the distant bluff, Mike yelled from the truck, "They're sending someone out. Tell Ty to keep watch for a patrol car."

Chase nodded and touched his spurs to the buckskin. The horse set out at a jogging trot, and Chase didn't increase the pace. He had a fair idea of what they would find when they reached the site, and he wasn't in any hurry to see it.

There was no hope for one of the calves, Ty discovered. The bullet had shattered the right shoulder socket. The outlook wasn't so grim for the second calf. A bullet had gouged a deep crease across the top of its neck, but had failed to sever its spinal cord. The danger now was from the infection that had already spread through the animal's system.

Shane Goodman was at work, doing what he could with water and his kerchief to break the hard scab and crusted blood caked over the wound. Ty stepped in to help him, a muscle coming to life in his jaw at the sight of the pus that seeped through the first cracks. It was slow work, but the fever-drained calf was beyond caring.

After the wound had been cleaned and the raw, inflamed flesh exposed, Ty walked to his ground-hitched horse and rummaged through his saddlebag for the tube of antiseptic salve to slather on the wound and protect it from flies. Over the cantle, he spotted the approaching riders. Even at a distance, there was no mistaking his father. And he had Quint with him.

Ty swore under his breath and turned, tossing the tube to the cowboy with the calf. "Here. I'll be back."

He gathered up the trailing reins, looped them over the sorrel's neck, and stepped into the saddle. With a touch of the spur, he sent the horse forward and rode out to intercept them. A fresh breeze swirled off the grass, but its clean scent couldn't erase the death stench that had been burned into him.

Chase greeted him with the message, "The sheriff's office has a car on the way."

"Good." Ty nodded briskly. "We've got one calf we might be able to save, but we'll need a trailer for him. He's too weak and too sick to make it on his own."

"And the other one?"

Ty shook his head. "We'll have to put him down," he said, aware of young ears listening intently.

Chase nodded his acceptance of the verdict and looked beyond him toward the bluff area, gathering the reins in an obvious signal that he intended to look the situation over himself. Ty swung his horse half a step to the side, blocking his path, and glanced pointedly at Quint, then back to his father.

"It's bad," he said.

Chase lifted his head, then nodded and turned to his grandson. "I have a job for you, Quint. We need someone to keep a lookout for the sheriff's car and direct him back here. This is very important, now. Do you think you can do that?"

"Sure." Bright-eyed and eager, Quint sat straighter in the saddle.

"Come with me." A hundred yards away, the rough, rolling ground lifted to a high swell. Chase rode to the top of it and waited for Quint to draw alongside of him. "Do you see that gate by the road?"

"Uh-huh." Quint nodded, his gaze fixing on it.

"I want you to ride down there and wait at the gate. When you see a police car coming down the road, I want you to wave your hat so he'll know where to stop. Okay?"

"Okay."

"I'll be over by that bluff. When the officer gets here, you'll need to show him where we are."

"I will." Quint booted the mare forward, clicking his tongue in encouragement.

Chase waited atop the rise until Quint reached the gate, then rode back to rejoin Ty. "How bad is it?" he asked when he reined in.

"Bad. From the looks of it, they were killed a couple days ago," Ty told him. "The buzzards and coyotes have already been at work on them."

"Are you sure it's not the work of scavengers?" Chase questioned, then raised another possibility. "There's been some cattle mutilations reported over in the Dakotas."

"I'd bet on the coyotes here."

"Let's go look." He lifted the reins. Side by side, they rode to the scene of the slaughter.

A rooster tail of dust plumed behind the fast-traveling patrol car as it sped along the isolated dirt road that traversed an outflung section of the Triple C Ranch. Just ahead the road made a wide, sweeping curve to swing around a hill. Slowing the car to make the turn, Logan checked the crudely drawn map on his clipboard and located the curve in a road that ran otherwise arrow-straight. He glanced one last time at the directions scribbled in the right-hand margin of the map, then laid the clipboard on the passenger seat.

It couldn't be much farther. Leaning forward, Logan peered upward through the top half of the windshield, scanning the sky. Off to the west, buzzards drifted on rising air currents. Rounding the hill, the road straightened again. He brought his gaze back to it and the fence line that crowded close to it. Slowing again, he watched for the gate.

Logan saw the rider first—a small boy on a full-grown horse, waving his hat in sweeping arcs over his head.

Given a choice, Logan would have steered clear of the Triple C and anything that had to do with the Calders. But duty hadn't allowed him that luxury. When the call came in, he had been the only one available. All the rest of the deputies had been either off duty, too far away, or tied up on other calls.

Seeing that the pasture gate was shut, Logan stopped the car on the road and stepped out, automatically adjusting the holstered gun on his hip. The boy had his hat back on his head, the overhanging brim shadowing a face that couldn't have been more than five or six years old.

"Afternoon." Logan touched his hat in greeting.

"Afternoon, sir." The boy sat as tall as he could in the saddle, his shoulders squared with adultlike importance. "I waved my hat so you'd know where to stop."

"Good thing you did," Logan acknowledged. "I

might have driven past the gate before I saw it."

The dozing mare flicked a curious ear at him as Logan approached the gate. When he went to unlatch the gate, his glance fell on a set of tire tracks. Close to a dozen cattle had been reported killed, a number that represented a sizable loss to any outfit, and one that couldn't be taken lightly. Logan crouched down to study the tracks.

"Whatcha looking at?" the boy asked, the saddle creaking as he leaned forward, trying to see.

"Some tire tracks." Logan straightened and turned his thoughtful gaze on the boy. "You don't know whether anybody's come through this gate in the last couple days?"

"No. Is it important?"

"It could be."

"I'm supposed to take you over to that bluff where my grandpa is. That's where the dead cows are."

"Mind if I swing up behind and ride with you?"

The boy shrugged. "Molly won't care, but what about your car? Are you just going to leave it there?"

Logan nodded. "Until I know something more about those tire tracks. Just give me a minute to radio in and let them know the situation here." He went back to the patrol car, made the call and returned.

Grabbing hold of the saddle horn, he swung up behind the cantle and settled into a semi-comfortable position on the leather skirt.

"We're all set," he told the boy.

"Let's go, Molly." He clicked to the mare.

"Is Molly your horse's name?" Logan guessed as the mare broke into a shuffling trot.

"Yup."

"I guess we never got around to introducing ourselves. My name's Logan. What's yours?"

"Quint."

"Pleased to meet you, Quint."

"Yes, sir." He clicked to the mare again and slapped his heels against her sides, urging her to a quicker gait.

"No, let's keep it slow," Logan told him.

"Can't you ride?" the boy asked on a note of astonishment, then quickly added, "Molly's a good horse. If she feels you slippin', she'll stop right away."

"I can ride," Logan assured him with an amused smile. "But I'd like to do a bit of looking around on the way, if that's all right with you?"

"Sure." There were those small, slender shoulders lifting in another shrug. "Whatcha lookin' for?"

"To see if a vehicle might have been driven through here in the last day or so." He surveyed the wild roll of land between the gate and the distant bluff face.

He saw nothing to arouse his suspicion and turned his attention to the pickup and stock trailer parked some distance from the bluff.

Two riders looked on while a pair of cowboys gently steered a wobbly calf toward the trailer's ramp. Logan centered his gaze on the mounted men. Both looked to have been cut from the same cloth, big-boned and taller than the average rider, dark-haired and dark-eyed with broad, rugged features. Logan had heard the Calders described often enough that he knew he was looking at father and son.

When the mare shuffled to a halt near the trailer, Logan slid off its rump, then stepped forward to nod to the boy. "Obliged for the ride, Quint," he said and turned to the two riders.

The older one swung out of the saddle with the unhurried deliberation of his age. "I'm Chase Calder." He stretched out a hand in greeting.

"Logan Echohawk, acting sheriff in Blackmore's absence." He took Calder's hand and returned the firmness of its grip.

Chase frowned, puzzlement flickering in his dark eyes. "Have we met before?" he asked curiously.

Logan shook his head. "I would have remembered."

"You look familiar," he said in explanation, then waved a hand toward his son. "This is my son, Ty, and you've already met my grandson."

"Yes, Quint was kind enough to give me a ride," he replied, then nodded to Ty and came to the point. "You reported some cattle killed. I'm curious if any of your men might have gone through that gate recently?"

"Not in the last week," Ty answered. "Spring roundup started Monday. We worked the north range first, and shifted operations here late yesterday afternoon, using the South Gate. Why?"

"I noticed a set of tire tracks. Double-check with your men and make sure none of them have used that gate in the last week or ten days." With a turn of his head, Logan glanced toward the bluff face and the circling buzzards. "Are the dead cattle over there?"

"Yes. Six cows and four calves." Ty took a closer look at the officer, his interest aroused by his businesslike attitude and obvious competence. Ty couldn't imagine any of the other deputies—or even Blackmore, for that matter—noticing the tire tracks and wondering about them.

As crimes went, dead cattle usually didn't rate very high with the sheriff's office. Ty had instructed Mike to call simply to make their deaths a matter of record. With a touch of cynicism, he wondered whether Echohawk wanted the position of sheriff to become a permanent one and sought to enlist the support of the Calders.

"Could I have the loan of a horse?" Logan asked, turning back.

"Take mine." Chase offered the reins to his buckskin.

Taking the reins, he led the horse a few steps forward and stepped smoothly into the saddle, his long legs eliminating the need to shorten the stirrups. He put the buckskin on the bit, then swung his attention back to Chase. "Don't let anyone use that gate until I can take an impression of those tire prints."

Chase nodded. "I'll see that the word's passed."

"I'll ride along." Ty nudged his horse forward with a squeeze of his legs. When Quint started to rein his horse around to accompany them, Ty stopped him. "No, you stay here, Quint."

Disappointment dragged down the corners of his mouth, but he made no protest. Logan noticed the boy's wistful look and gave him a smiling nod of farewell, adult to adult. He had a glimpse of the boy's expression brightening before the buckskin carried him past the bay mare.

A breeze stirred through the tall green grass, bending it before the two riders. The afternoon stillness was broken by the creak of saddle leather and the muffled two-beat thud of trotting horses. Under other circumstances, Logan would have enjoyed the warmth of the sun on his back and the feel of a responsive horse beneath him. But the job demanded a different awareness of his surroundings, the kind that searched out and absorbed every detail.

His keen eyes noticed the narrow band of bent grass that marked the previous passage of several riders, a fact he filed away with a glimmer of irritation. A coyote paused near the mouth of the wide gully and boldly watched their approach, then trotted off when they drew too near, its sides bulging with the fullness of its stomach. Logan caught the first putrid whiff of rotting flesh, the rankness of it confirming his half-formed suspicion that the killings were at least a couple of days old.

He reined in short of the entrance and studied the scene before him. A pair of buzzards stood guard over one of the carcasses. They briefly glared their defiance, then pecked at the dead cow, determined to get another bite before they were driven off. Nearly all the dead cattle were crowded against the back of the gully, suggesting they had been trapped there. Logan took note of the width of the gully's mouth, then glanced once again at the faint trail left by the first riders.

"How many of you have ridden in there?"

"Four altogether," Ty replied.

"Did anybody get down to take a closer look?"

"Mike did. After he and Shane Goodman came across the wounded calf, he wanted to see if these had been shot, too. Why?"

"I was wondering—just in case I run across any footprints." Logan resumed his visual search of the area. "I don't suppose any of your men recall hearing any gunshots in the last, say, two or three nights?"

"Not to my knowledge, but it would be unlikely. This is a remote section of the ranch. You might check with Culley O'Rourke over at Shamrock Ranch. He's been known to go riding at night. He might have heard something."

"Thanks. I'll do that," he said, then added, "Stay behind me. I don't want to sort through any more tracks than necessary."

He started the buckskin forward, its steps mincing and uneasy. Ty swung in behind him. Single file, they entered the gulch at a walk and hugged the outer edges of it, their nostrils instinctively pinching against death's rank and rising odor. At their approach, the buzzards hopped off the carcasses, then lumbered into flight with an ungainly flapping of wings. The flies showed no such concern for their presence, the thrum of their wings setting up a steady and solid buzz in the background.

At the head of the gulch, Logan reined in and inspected the scene from a different angle. His searching gaze picked out a large patch of dark-stained grass that remained flattened. It had the look of dried blood, but there were no dead animals in its vicinity. He walked the buckskin toward it and drew rein when he was still short of it, his gaze scouring the area. Flies blackened a twisted pile of shriveled entrails.

Studying it, he said over his shoulder, "When you finish your gather here, I think you're going to come up a cow short."

Ty drew up level with him for a closer look. "You think they butchered one?"

"Looks that way," Logan swung the buckskin away to finish his walk-through of the site.

Twenty minutes later, he had learned as much as he could from horseback. At the mouth of the gulch, he swung out of the saddle and wrapped the buckskin's reins around the branch of a low bush. "This may take a while," he told Ty. "If I find anything, I'll get back to you."

He set out on foot, this time to comb the entire area for evidence, a time-consuming task made worse by the swarming flies and fetid odors. A part of him questioned the necessity of such a thorough search, but there was something about the wanton slaughter that made him uneasy. Experience had taught him to trust his instincts.

The afternoon sun stretched its burning light across the rough plains when Logan rode back from the patrol car, empty evidence bags and latex gloves tucked in a saddle pouch. Idly he noted the stock trailer's closed endgate and the four men gathered beside it, their glances swinging to him. The pickup's passenger door stood open, revealing the sleeping figure of a boy curled on its seat. The child's innocence tugged at a corner of his mouth.

At the mouth of the gulch, Logan reined in the buckskin again and stepped effortlessly to the ground. After tangling the reins in the branches of a low-growing bush and removing his gear from the saddlebag, he headed into the gulch.

The fast drumming of hooves pulled his glance to the west where a rider approached at a gallop, bypassing the trailer to make straight for the gulch. Halfway between the two, the rider pulled up with a suddenness that swung the horse sideways, giving a full view of the rider in profile.

It was Cat. Recognition jolted through him like a flash of lightning, pinning him to the spot. A man's clothes couldn't alter the shape of the woman's body within them. With jaws clamped tight, he stared across the intervening space. For a moment, the air had that charged and sulky feel of storm-thick clouds weighted with thunder.

Restlessly tossing its head, Cat's horse danced in place, revealing the indecision of its rider. A voice lifted, pulling her attention from him to the small group of men by the stock trailer. She threw him a last look, then swung away and cantered her horse to them, a single black braid hanging down the center of her back.

Regret knifed through him, slicing the tension that had held Logan motionless. He bit back a savage oath, angered to discover that even though she wasn't for him, he still wanted her. The need was a deep ache that wouldn't be reasoned away.

Nerves raw, Cat was out of the saddle the instant her horse came to a stop. Her glance flew to her father, quickly noting the look of indulgent humor in his eyes—not censure or accusation, nothing that suggested any of her fears had been realized.

"Quint," she began, then her searching glance saw him, curled up asleep in the truck. She smiled in relief.

"I caught him nodding off in the saddle," Chase explained. "I managed to convince him that Molly needed a break. He dropped off to sleep about ten minutes ago. Too much excitement, I guess."

"They told me back at camp about the cattle." Her glance strayed to the gulch, but it wasn't relief she felt when she discovered Logan was nowhere in sight. "When I saw your buckskin, I thought that's where you were."

"No, I loaned him to the new man that's taken over for Blackmore. Echohawk's his name. Seems to know his job, too."

"You can bet Blackmore wouldn't have spent more than ten minutes in there, as bad as those rotting carcasses smell," Ty put in.

Cat listened to the exchange with only half an ear. Her thoughts were still on Logan, wondering how it was possible that a father wouldn't instinctively recognize his own son—unless—"Did Quint see—" she began impulsively, then paused, unsure how to word the question without arousing suspicion.

"We kept him away from the gulch," Ty said, as if that answered her question. "The scavengers had already been at work. It wasn't something he should see at his age."

She took that to mean Logan hadn't met Quint yet. Tension raveled through her all over again. "I think I should take Quint and go back to the house. You can get by without me, can't you?" she asked Ty.

"Sure." He gestured in the direction of Shane

Goodman, lounging against the trailer's slatted sides, a cigarette cupped in his hand. "Shane was just going to head back there with the wounded calf. You can ride with him. That will give Quint a chance to sleep a little longer."

"I'm ready when you are," she told Shane, eager to leave.

"Let's go." He pushed away from the trailer, taking a quick, last drag on his cigarette before crushing it under his heel.

Surrendering her horse's reins to Ty, Cat climbed into the truck cab and gently eased Quint onto her lap. He stirred once fitfully, then snuggled against her, something he seldom did at the advanced age of five. Smiling, she slipped off her hat and laid it on the seat next to him while Shane climbed into the driver's side and started the engine. Once the brake was disengaged, the truck rolled forward. The trailer hitch squealed as he swung the wheel toward the west.

Cat frowned. "I thought we were going back to the ranch."

"We are."

"But Three Mile Gate is just over there. Why are you going this way?"

"We can't use that gate. That Echohawk fella found some tire prints there," he explained. "He thinks they might have been left by whoever killed those cows. The guy's sharp."

That's what worried her. Logan was neither blind or stupid. And he wouldn't be pushed.

Five miles from the Triple C headquarters, Quint pushed up and looked around with heavy eyes. "Where are we going?"

"Home. I thought I'd get back early and give Jessy a hand with supper." Cat gathered him onto her lap. He leaned his head against her shoulder, too groggy with sleep to remember he was too old to be held.

He scrubbed a hand over his face, then stared out the window, silent for a long run of minutes. His head swiveled against her shoulder as he turned to glance at Shane. Seeing the cowboy behind the wheel seemed to jog his memory.

"Did Shane tell you some cows got killed?"

"Yes, he did."

Again there was a lengthy pause. "I never got to see them. I think dead animals must look awful."

"Not always." Her response seemed to reassure him in some way.

"Grandpa gave me a job to do."

"He did?" She smiled, moved by the importance he attached to that.

"Uh-huh," he confirmed with a vigorous nod of his head. "I waited at the gate all by myself so the sheriff would know where to come."

Stunned by his answer, Cat struggled not to show it. "You did? And all by yourself, too?"

"Yup."

"What did you think of him?" Unconsciously she tightened the circle of her arms, gathering him closer to her.

"He was okay." His slim shoulders lifted in an awkward shrug. "I gave him a ride on Molly."

"I'll bet he appreciated that." An oddly poignant picture of the two of them riding the docile mare flashed in her mind. Cat knew she should have been relieved that neither of them had felt any connection to the other. After all, she wanted father and son to remain strangers to each other. So why this twinge of regret? She shied from the possible answer to that.

Instead she focused on the positive. It was becoming increasingly obvious that she was the only one who saw Quint's resemblance to Logan. No one else had noticed it. Certainly Culley hadn't until she pointed it out to him.

Perhaps her secret was safe after all. It was ironic that she had been afraid all this time without cause. Logan was no threat to her whatsoever.

FIFTEEN

Evening spread its thickening darkness across the high plains, blurring the dips and swells of the rolling terrain. Night's first pale stars glittered dimly in the empurpled sky while below, twin headlight beams raced ahead of the speeding patrol car. Behind the wheel, Logan fixed his hard gaze on the halo of light in the near distance. He had been told the headquarters of the Triple C Ranch resembled a small town. It definitely threw the light of one.

He watched it grow brighter, his foot heavy, the speedometer hovering at seventy. Weariness pulled at him, adding its strain to his restless, irritable mood. He was conscious of the day's grit on him and the hunger that gnawed at his empty stomach, reminders that what he wanted most was a hot shower, a cold drink, and a filling meal, not necessarily in that order. But all that would come later; he had a stop to make first.

It was the job that brought him to the Triple C. Nothing else. Naturally Cat would be there, he had no doubt. That knowledge hardened his features, turning them into an impenetrable mask.

The patrol car topped the last rising swell of land,

and the lights of the sprawling headquarters broke brilliantly through the deepening cloak of nightfall. Logan slowed the car and swung it toward the white-pillared front of the big house that rose head and shoulders above the rest of the buildings. It was a rangeland mansion, not as grand or elaborate as others he'd had cause to enter, but a mansion nevertheless.

Parking in front of it, Logan switched off the headlights and killed the engine, then stepped out, a high tension threading its way through his muscles. His gaze lifted to the two-story house and the fanlike gushes of light that spilled from its windows, giving its solidness a look of warmth and welcome.

He crossed to the front steps, impatience lengthening his stride. There was no bell to ring at the front door. He lifted the heavy brass knocker and brought it down solidly three times. The hard clanging shattered the evening's hush and grated on nerves already made raw with tension and fatigue.

There was a warning turn of the knob before the door swung open and light flooded the porch. A tall, slender blonde stood in the opening, her classically strong features composed in an expression of warm interest tinged with curiosity.

Before he could utter a word, her glance flicked to his uniform and a smile lifted the edges of her wide mouth. "You must be Sheriff Echohawk." She extended a hand in greeting. "I'm Ty's wife, Jessy."

"A pleasure, Mrs. Calder." He had long ago found formality was best. It subtly established a boundary that the average person preferred.

"I expect you're here on business." Releasing his hand, she backed away to admit him. "Please come in."

"Thank you." He stepped inside and automatically removed his hat, combing a hand through his hair to lift its flatness.

In that same fractional second, he scanned the interior area, visually fixing the layout in his mind from habit. There, across the wide sprawl of the living room, stood Cat, poised at the bottom of the stairs, her shoulders bared by a pale blue sundress that softly draped her body. She lifted her head, showing him a pride that was like steel. He stared at her, knowing a hunger for which no word existed.

Then Jessy Calder spoke, and Logan clamped off his feelings and switched his attention back to the blonde. "Ty and Dad Calder are in the den." She walked toward a set of double doors, indicating he should follow.

Chase Calder sat behind a huge desk, still every inch the range lord, yet shorn of some of life's vigor now. Ty lounged beside the room's massive fireplace, a shoulder braced against its stone face, a forefinger rubbing across his mustache in a thoughtful pose. He came erect when Logan walked into the room.

"Echohawk, good to see you." Chase rocked back in his chair, but didn't rise. "Ty and I were just talking about the dead cattle, and wondering what you might have learned?"

"One thing is certain, Mr. Calder. Somebody out there doesn't like you very much," Logan stated with an abruptness that was perhaps not politically wise.

Chase gave him an amused look, a metal-hard irony at the corners of his mouth. "The Triple C has always been a big target for people with stones in their hands. A lot of things have changed, but that hasn't."

"And probably never will," Logan agreed with an answering glint of wryness. "I could be wrong, but this reads like more than a simple case of malicious mischief."

"What did you find today?" Ty asked.

"A half dozen bullets that I dug out of the carcasses, the print of a bootheel near that pile of entrails, and only one shell casing, which tells me the rest were picked up. I also found a blood trail in the grass that ran about ten yards before it disappeared. It looks to me like they butchered one of the cows, then used a winch to drag it to their vehicle and load it up."

No sound marked Cat's entrance into the room, but Logan knew the minute she appeared in the doorway. It was an animal awareness he had of her. But he allowed no break in his talk to betray the fact her presence was in any way unsettling. "At this point, it's only supposition. All the signs point to that, but I can't say it as a hard and fast fact."

"You said *they*," Cat broke in, walking the rest of the way into the room.

"This is my daughter, Cat," Chase began.

"We've met," Logan acknowledged her with a curt nod, his expression falsely passive.

"Yes," Cat confirmed with an aura of confidence and smooth self-assurance. "Sheriff Echohawk was at the Shamrock the other night when I went to visit Uncle Culley. It turns out that he's our new neighbor. He bought the Circle Six."

Chase raised an eyebrow in mild surprise. "I'd heard Henson had sold out. Welcome to the area."

"Thanks."

"Cat had a good point," Ty interposed, bringing the conversation back to their previous topic. "By *they*, are you saying you believe there was more than one person involved?"

"If a cow was butchered and the carcass removed, as I suspect, it's logical that—even with the aid of a winch—it would take at least two people to handle it."

Chase idly rocked in his chair, studying Logan with thoughtful eyes. "You sound convinced that's the way it happened."

"Like I said before, the signs seem to point that way," he replied. "And it would be easy enough for a truck to block the entrance to the gully and trap the cattle inside. We'll have a better idea about whether I'm right when you finish your gather."

"But to kill all those cattle and butcher only one, that makes no sense," Ty said with a troubled shake of his head.

"Maybe they did it for the joy of killing, maybe to cover up the fact they had butchered a beef. Or maybe, they wanted to make certain you found out what they did. If you came up a cow short in your gather, you might not think much about it. But no one can ignore nearly a dozen dead animals."

"You're saying it was a calling card of sorts." Chase studied him with narrowed eyes.

"I'm saying they wanted to throw it in your face," Logan replied smoothly. "Any ideas on who might hate you that much? A former employee, maybe?"

"I can't think of anyone. Ty?" Chase deferred the question to his son.

"Offhand, no."

"Check your records. Make me a list of anyone you have fired in the last year." He was conscious of Cat filling his side vision, but he kept his attention centered on the two men. The stiff control he placed on himself made him abrupt.

"The list will be a short one," Ty replied. "We don't have much turnover on the Triple C. Most of our hands were born and raised right here on the ranch."

"Then that will make my job an easy one." Logan paused, and that pause accented the rest of his words, giving them weight. "This wasn't a random act. They weren't just driving around, saw the cattle, and decided to shoot a few. This had to have been planned by someone familiar with the area. If it's someone with a grudge against you—as I suspect—maybe slaughtering some of your cattle will satisfy them. But I wouldn't count on it. This kind of thing can feed on itself and escalate. I'd have your men keep a lookout for anything unusual and anyone with no business being around."

"We'll get the word out tonight." Chase looked to his son, silently passing the chore to him.

Satisfied, Logan said, "Get that employee list to me as soon as you can. And if you think of anyone whose toes you might have stepped on, inadvertently or otherwise, add their names to it."

"Of course," Ty said.

"If there's nothing else you can add, I'll be going," Logan said and proceeded to take his leave of the two men.

In silence, Cat looked on, aware of Logan Echohawk as she had been of few men in her life. He stood with a balanced straightness, as though ready to whip into action at the first hint of danger. For the first time, she realized that he had a capacity for violence, sharply controlled, but present just the same. In profile, his bronzed and angular features were chiseled in unsentimental lines, vaguely tinged by a distant bitterness. She briefly wondered at that, then pushed that curiosity aside. She had other, more important matters on her mind.

During those initial moments after he first arrived, the old fear had rushed back that he had learned the truth about Quint. It had driven her to the den where Cat discovered again that her fear was groundless. He didn't know, and there was no reason to believe he ever would. She had overreacted before. She was determined to correct that now.

When he turned to leave, Cat said calmly, "I'll see you out."

His eyes briefly locked with hers, setting off a small tingle along her nerve ends. It was, Cat thought, the dangerous gray color that made his glance feel like a jolt of electricity.

"That isn't necessary," he told her, his voice cool in its rejection.

Cat didn't answer, instead simply turned and headed for the door, asserting her will through action. The accompanying sound of his footsteps was an echo to her own. She continued through the door and onto the porch, then paused near a white column and gazed into the night. Moonlight sprayed its frost-glow over the ranch buildings and silvered the vast sweep of prairie beyond them. Familiar as it was to her, the scene pulled at her, stirring up again the deep attachment she had to this land that was her home.

Drawing level with her, Logan halted and faced the front, for a moment looking into the night as she did. Then he angled his head toward her, and she felt the force of his gaze tunneling into her.

"There is obviously something you wanted to say before I leave." The challenging dryness of his voice held a faintly sardonic note.

She squared around to face him, coolly composed and serious. "Anyone who knows me well will tell you that I tend to be too impulsive and quick-tempered, traits that I have worked hard to control. But recent events have shown that I haven't succeeded all that well," she said. "The things I said to you the other night at my uncle's—I was out of line. What you do or don't do, who you see or don't see, is really none of my concern. I had no business talking to you the way I did."

"You don't apologize very often, do you?" A whisper of her perfume reached him, emanating from the smooth curve of her neck and conjuring up unsettling images of sultry nights and satin sheets.

"Probably not as often as I should," she admitted, then asked, slightly defensive, "Why?"

"Because you don't do it very well." Logan turned a sidelong glance on her and felt the instant play of electricity between them. "It's all that pride you wrap yourself in, like armor."

"And you don't, I suppose," she murmured with some heat.

Something that passed for amusement slanted the line of his mouth. "We weren't talking about me."

Cat chose to ignore that. "I should explain that I never expected to see you again. In fact, I hoped I never would. That night in Fort Worth was a mistake, one that I have tried very hard to forget—"

"It seems you were no better at it than I was," he observed.

She continued as if he hadn't spoken. "As far as my family is concerned, they think you are a complete stranger. I prefer that they never find out otherwise. Unfortunately, I can no longer control that."

"Am I supposed to take an oath of silence now?" he mocked, then turned serious. "If I did, would you believe me?"

Cat hesitated, stung by how vulnerable she was. "I would want to," she said at last, lifting her chin a notch.

"It goes against your grain for someone else to hold your reputation in their hands, doesn't it?" Logan observed and watched her eyes turn stormy. He didn't fault her for that. Pride and honor were two things he understood. Sometimes they were all a man had, especially when he lost his faith in things like the goodness of his fellow man.

"Naturally, it does," she replied, very cool and controlled again.

He could feel the invisible barriers she threw up

to keep him at a distance. It rankled. Logan had little respect for barriers; he had battered in too many of them in his job. The impulse was there to do it again.

"I'm curious about something." Almost leisurely Logan swung toward her, his glance skimming the bareness of her shoulders and the shadowed hollow of her throat before rising to the green of her eyes. "Are you still mourning your dead boyfriend?"

Resentment flared, turning her voice frigid. "That is none of your business."

"I never said it was." His mouth crooked. "I thought it was supposed to be 'until death do you part,' and here you are still sleeping with a ghost."

"I happen to love him," she insisted stiffly.

"He's dead, Cat. That's why you were so eager to crawl into bed with me. Remember?" he taunted.

"I told you that was a mistake I would like to forget."

"It's impossible, isn't it?"

"You have no idea how impossible it is." She looked away, pain thickening her voice and bringing the bright sheen of tears to her eyes.

Angered by the sight of them, Logan cupped a hand to her face, his thumb capturing her chin and turning it back toward him. "Who are you crying for, Cat? You or him?" he challenged.

"Certainly not for you," she lashed out in sudden anger. "Never for you."

Logan had known that, but hearing it snapped the last thin thread of control. Roughly he hauled her to him, his fingers twisting into her hair and forcing her head back. His mouth came down hard to crush her lips. This time he took what she wouldn't willingly give him, and liked the fight she gave him, finding it offered its own kind of stimulation.

He kept up the pressure until her struggles lessened and her body softened against him. Lifting his head, he looked with savage satisfaction at the aching need that darkened the green of her eyes. In the very next instant, Logan understood the emptiness of his victory. The moistness of tears shimmered at the edges of her eyes. He hadn't driven out the memory of her lost love. It was a bitter discovery that stopped him cold.

"You can stop worrying, Cat." Anger tightened his voice, giving it a raw and husky edge. "A lot of men might brag about bedding you, but I'm not one of them."

She gave him a startled look that revealed her surprise and told him, more clearly than words, the low opinion she had of him. Swinging away, he went down the steps at a swift pace, more irritable than before.

From his favorite watchpost, hunkered down in a small pocket of ground some distance from The Homestead, Culley saw it all. Although he had been too far away to hear their talk, it had been impossible to mistake the charged tension between them when they faced each other, their bodies taut and motionless like a stag and a doe during mating season.

A car door slammed with a metallic thud, and an engine turned over with a rumbling growl of power. Headlights flashed on, cutting through the darkness. Briefly their twin beams swept over Cat as the patrol car made a reversing turn away from the house before it took off, its fast-spinning tires spraying gravel.

As always, Culley focused on Cat. She stood with one slender hand resting on a pillar and the other pressed to her stomach, her head turned in the direction of the departing vehicle. After it disappeared, she appeared to take a moment to gather herself, then turned and went inside.

Culley rocked back on his haunches and considered all that he had seen, both tonight and over the last few days. The ululating call of a coyote drifted across the plains, a plaintive and primitive sound. Lifting his head, Culley listened to it, glanced again at the house, then stole off, making his way back to the place where he had left his horse tethered.

An hour after leaving the Triple C headquarters, Logan pulled into Blue Moon. Light pooled beneath the canopy at Fedderson's, illuminating the gas pumps. More light poured through the store's plate-glass windows. Logan noted that, but his brooding gaze centered on the lighted neon sign at Sally's Place and the half dozen pickup and utility vehicles parked in front of it.

Faced with easily an hour's worth of paperwork before he could call it a day, Logan swung the patrol car into an empty parking slot, radioed his twenty, and stepped out. As much as his empty stomach wanted food, he wanted the distraction of people around him to get his mind off Cat. She was becoming like a drug that he knew was no good for him, yet each encounter with her left him wanting more. It was an addiction he was determined to conquer.

The jukebox blared a honky-tonk song amid the crack of billiard balls and laughing, raucous voices. Logan paused inside the door and scanned the inhabitants of the café-bar, conscious of the second looks the uniform brought him and the instant muting of loud talk. Most times such things amused him, but today wasn't one of those times.

As he finished his sweep of the bar area where the bulk of the customers were gathered, his glance was stopped by a pair of brashly arrogant eyes staring back at him. Lath Anderson grinned with insolence and lifted his long-necked bottle of beer in a mocking salute. His younger brother, Rollie, gave him a sharp nudge, his own glance skipping off Logan. Still grinning, Lath swung away.

Logan felt again that fiddling along his nerves that warned of impending trouble. He started toward the men's room to wash up, then, pushed by a testiness, Logan altered his course to pass by the two brothers.

Observing his approach in the back bar's mirror, Lath swiveled around on his stool when he drew close. "Workin' kinda late, aren't you, Echohawk? Or are you pullin' the evening shift this week?"

Logan halted. "Does it matter?"

"Guess not." Lath shrugged one shoulder, still wearing his cocky grin.

"Have you found yourself a job yet?"

"Tell you the truth, that's been a bit of a problem for me. No one seems to be doin' any hirin' right now."

"I heard Dy-Corp had some openings," Logan remarked, then turned his glance on the younger one. "Isn't that true, Rollie?"

"I couldn't say." His attention remained on the bottle in front of him.

"You're still working there, aren't you?"

"Yeah." Rollie picked up the bottle by its neck and took a quick swig from it.

"He's always been the hardworking one of this family. Ain't ya, little brother?" Lath tossed the question to him, without taking his hard and glinting eyes off Logan. "Me, I'm just the no-account one."

"With no desire to change," Logan observed, and threw another glance at Rollie, now eyeing them both uneasily. "You're running in some poor company, Rollie."

"He's my brother."

"I guess a man can't choose his family," he said.

He sent a glance at Lath, then continued to the men's room, washed away the worst of the day's grime and returned, this time skirting the bar area and heading for a table on the café side of the room. Taking off his hat, he dropped it on an empty chair and sat down next to it, reaching for the plastic-covered menu, propped between the sugar jar and napkin holder.

Sally Brogan came to the table, carrying a pot of coffee and a glass of water. She set the glass before him, righted the cup on the table and filled it with steaming coffee. "You look like you could use this," she said, her quick eyes picking up the hints of fatigue etched into his face.

"About a gallon of it," Logan admitted, reaching for the cup, drawn by the steam's rich coffee aroma.

"I heard there was some trouble out at the Triple C today. Nothing serious, I hope," Sally remarked, fishing for specifics.

Logan shook his head. "Just some cattle killed."

"How?"

"They were shot."

She clucked her tongue in a small sound of dismay and sighed. "I don't understand people nowadays, shooting at something just because they feel like it—with no respect at all for someone's property."

Such people had always been around, but Logan didn't bother to point that out to her. "How about a steak, medium, and a baked potato with all the trimmings."

"Anything else?"

"Don't think so." A burst of laughter from the

bar area drew his attention. Idly he ran his glance over the crowd, noting that the Anderson brothers had moved to the pool table. "Busy night."

"It's Friday," Sally replied as if that explained everything, then looked in the direction of the noise and blaring music, her expression colored by something thoughtful and a little sad. "We used to fill up mostly with cowboys from the surrounding ranches. They were a wild and rowdy group out for fun and a good time. They never had much money to spend. Cowboying still doesn't pay that much. It's one of those jobs you do because it's in your blood. The crowd we get now mostly came here chasing the high dollar Dy-Corp pays at the strip mine. In some ways, they're just as loud and crazy as the cowboys were, but it's an angry loud, I've noticed."

"A little homegrown philosophy, Sally?" Logan chided lightly.

She smiled at herself. "Age does that to you, I guess. Or maybe I notice it more because I'm not as happy in my work as I used to be."

"There's been talk you might be selling out."

"I've been here thirty years. Maybe it's time to call it quits."

"Thirty years. I guess you know about everyone around here."

"Sooner or later, they all come in here."

On impulse, he asked, "You don't, by any chance, know who might have a winch mounted in their truck?"

"You mean besides Emmett?"

"Emmett Fedderson." He wanted to make sure they were talking about the same person.

"Yes. Off the top of my head, he's the only one that comes to mind. But you might ask him. I may have the monopoly on food, but he has it on gas."

"I'll do that. Thanks."

"No problem." She started toward the kitchen. "I'll have DeeDee get your food right out."

Logan nodded and took a sip of his coffee, then settled back in the chair and waited for the caffeine to kick in and revive him. As relaxed as he looked, he never lost that sense of alertness. He had lived the life of a lawman too long for it to ever leave him completely. His eyes kept moving, noting the comings and goings around him.

Across the way, Lath chalked the end of his cue stick, leaned over the table, and took aim on the white cue ball. He drew the stick back and shot it forward, sending the ball crashing into the triangular grouping of colored balls. Amidst the clatter and rumble of balls spinning across the felt-covered slate, Lath straightened and walked around to a side pocket, picked up the chalk again, and rubbed it on the tip while he studied the table. Rollie stepped to the side, out of his way, both hands clamped around his own pool cue.

"Do you think he suspects us?" he asked in a voice audible only to his brother.

"If he does, it's only 'cause you're acting so damned guilty."

Lath knocked the twelve ball in a corner pocket. Straightening, he threw a glance at Rollie, a smile forming. "Relax, will ya? He hasn't got a single clue that'll lead him back to us. He can suspect till he's blue in the face, but without proof, he can't touch us."

"I know that," Rollie mumbled, uneasy and vaguely sullen, his glance sliding across the room.

"Then whatcha worried about, huh?" Lath changed his stance, maneuvering for a shot at another ball. "Have some faith, little brother. Didn't I say they wouldn't find those cattle till today? Didn't I?"

"Yeah, it's all coming down just like you said it

would, but just what the hell did we accomplish?" Rollie challenged him. "Sure, we butchered a beef and killed some cows, but so what? Calder's got insurance to cover a loss like that. Ma's right. We didn't hurt Calder at all."

The blue-chalked tip of the cue stick hovered a fraction of an inch from the white ball while Lath let the words sink in. Grimness plucked at a corner of his mouth. "Not this time, we didn't. But we will, I promise you that. I just got to figure out the right way to do it."

"Do what?" Rollie asked, catching something in Lath's voice that had his eyes narrowing.

"When I got it figured, I'll tell you." He tapped the stick against the cue ball. It rolled forward, struck the edge of the striped fourteen ball and sent it spinning toward the far side pocket, where it grazed the bumper and caromed away from the hole. Lath swore good-naturedly at the miss, and stepped back from the table. "Your turn, little brother."

As Rollie moved up to survey the table, the door opened and Emmett Fedderson plodded into the café-bar, dressed in his habitual rust orange jumpsuit, a billed cap covering his nearly bald head. He paused to catch his breath and mop the sweat from his face with a soiled handkerchief.

"There's another one that needs to be hurt," Lath remarked and lifted his beer bottle, taking another swig from it. "Only he'll be easy to do."

Gathering himself, Emmett turned toward the crowd at the bar and yelled above the music and noise, "I'm fixing to close up. Any of you need gas to get home on, you better get it now."

"I'll take you up on that, Emmett." Lath flashed a sudden grin, a peculiar gleam in his eyes. He shoved his cue stick at Rollie. "Hang onto this, little brother. And don't be cheatin' while I'm gone."

Rollie took the stick and watched as Lath sauntered over to Fedderson and held the door open for him, then followed him outside.

Rollie had a moment's pity for the old man, but it was quickly gone. He propped Lath's stick against the table and took aim on a solid-colored ball poised on the edge of a corner pocket.

Outside the restaurant, Lath waved a hand toward an old pickup sporting a new primer coat the color of rust. "Hop in, Emmett. I'll give you a lift to the station and save those legs of yours a few steps."

Emmett didn't trust him, and it showed in the look he gave him. But the day had been a long one, and his tired body was feeling it. He nodded and said gruffly, "Obliged for it."

It took him a minute to haul his bulk into the cab, then collapsed hard on the seat, wheezing a little from the effort. Even that little bit of exertion had sweat beading on his face. He dragged the soiled kerchief from his pocket and wiped it over his mouth.

A low chuckle came from the driver's side. Emmett saw Lath watching him. The light from the restaurant windows shone through the windshield, partially illuminating his face, giving Emmett a glimpse of lips curled back in a laughing grin and of eyes that had an animal sheen to them. For a dry-mouthed instant, he had the eerie feeling that he was riding with Lucifer himself.

"You're getting old, Emmett," Lath turned the ignition key. The engine coughed a couple times, then caught with a reluctant rumble.

"Tell me somebody who ain't," he garumphed, facing the front again, uneasy and determined to conceal it. "You sure ain't getting any younger yourself."

"Now that's a dyed-in-the-wool fact for sure, Emmett." He reversed the pickup away from the restaurant and aimed it toward the lighted canopy over the gas pumps. "The difference is—I got a long life ahead of me."

"I wouldn't be too sure of that, if I were you."

"Emmett," Lath said and clicked his tongue in mock reproach. "You ain't so old that you forgot, only the good die young?"

He laughed again, and something in his laughter made Emmett's skin crawl. It started him thinking about old Mrs. Anderson's overdue account and Lath's constant prodding for it to be reopened. He stole a sideways glance at Lath, certain it was a subject he'd bring up again. It was just a matter of how soon. Irritated by the prospect, he shot a look at the gas gauge, illuminated by the dash lights. Its arrow hovered near the full mark.

"It don't look to me like you need any gas." He flicked an accusing finger toward the gauge.

"You can't pay any attention to that. Rollie tells me it was broke when he bought the truck." The pickup rolled to a stop beside the pump island. Lath shifted the gear stick into Park and switched off the engine, glancing sideways at Emmett as he did so. "I honestly can't tell you whether I'll be charging ten or twenty dollars' worth of gas."

"You won't be charging anything. I told you before, you haven't got an account with me, not till you pay what you owe." Emmett spoke with force to combat the scared, crawly feeling in his stomach.

"I'm sorry to hear that, Emmett. I'm truly sorry. You don't leave a fella much choice."

"What do you mean by that?" Emmett frowned, half turned in his seat, the passenger door pushed partway open.

"Mean?" Lath feigned a look of innocence. "I meant just what I said. A man's gotta do what a man's gotta do. You understand that, don't you?"

Emmett searched through that answer word by lazily drawled word, seeking something that would justify this growing uneasiness. But he could find no concrete threat in any of them, not separately or together. He climbed out of the pickup and shut the door. "It's cash or no gas," he said through the window.

"You called it, Emmett. No gas." Lath started up the truck and drove off, the sound of his cackling laughter floating above the engine noise and sending a shiver down Emmett's back.

He tried to shake it off, but it clung to him, echoing in his mind all while he went about shutting down the gasoline pumps and locking up for the night.

There was no smile on Lath Anderson's face when he walked back into the restaurant. His glance swept coolly over Logan without lingering. It might have been accidental that he looked in his direction at all, but Logan didn't think so. Lath Anderson was the kind that always liked to know where the law was.

"More coffee?" Sally paused beside his table, coffeepot in hand.

"Please." Logan nodded and dragged his attention back to the steak on his plate, slicing off his second bite. "Does Lath Anderson come in here much?"

"He's been in a few times." Tilting the pot, Sally poured coffee into his cup. "Why?"

"Just curious."

Sally smiled at that. "No law officer is ever 'just curious,' but that's okay. I won't ask you to explain."

"I'm not sure I could."

"I know what you mean." Her smile faded. "Even as a boy, Lath never caused any trouble, but you always had the feeling he could."

"Everyone has the capacity to cause trouble."

"You're probably right." She breathed in deeply and let it out in a sigh. "If there's anything else you need, just holler."

"I will."

After the first few bites, the edge was off his hunger, and the meal became no different than a thousand others that he'd eaten alone, without conversation to liven it. He listened to the laughter from the bar area, and the constant run of talk, holding himself away from it as he had always done—except that night when Cat had walked over to him and pulled him into it.

Annoyed that he had allowed the thought of her to cross his mind, Logan washed the last bite of food down with a swallow of coffee, rose from his chair, dropped some tip money on the table, then gathered up his hat and the check and walked over to the cash register.

With the pool game over, Lath sat at the bar and stared at Logan's reflection in the back mirror, tracking him as he paid for his check and crossed to the door. After it swung shut behind him, Lath took a long pull on his beer, then set it back on the bar counter, idly turning it in semicircles.

"I don't get it," he murmured. "That guy's got too much smarts to be in this out-of-the-way place."

"What guy?" Rollie glanced over his shoulder.

"Echohawk."

He squared back around to the bar and shrugged. "Maybe he just likes it here."

"Maybe. Then again, maybe he's lost his nerve."

"He doesn't act like he's lost it."

"No," Lath conceded. "But I'd sure like to know."

"Personally, I hope I never have to find out." Rollie tipped the bottle to his mouth.

Lath chortled and slapped him on the back, gripping his shoulder and giving it a shake. "By God, little brother, you're smarter than I thought you were."

Both pleased and a little embarrassed, Rollie said, "Hell, I am your brother."

They both laughed.

It was late when Logan finally finished up all the paperwork and made the long drive to his ranch. He bypassed the house and drove straight to the barn. Tired as he was, he still had the horses to feed. Leaving the lights on, he climbed out of the patrol car and headed toward the barn's wide door.

"I already throwed 'em some hay." The voice came out of the deep shadows near the barn.

Whirling in a crouch, Logan had the holster flap loose and his hand on the gun butt before the voice registered as a familiar one. Even then the high alertness didn't leave him, his gaze raking the shadows, seeking the source of it.

"Step out where I can see you." That same tension gave his voice the hardness of command.

Culley O'Rourke separated himself from the shadows without the slightest sound. "Sorry. I didn't mean to startle you, Logan."

"What the hell are you doing here, O'Rourke?" He straightened slowly, gripped by an anger that came from being caught completely off guard.

"Just waiting around for you to come."

"It's usually my enemies who wait in the shadows, O'Rourke."

"I reckon that's so." He nodded, then lifted his hand, motioning toward the corral. "Like I said, I noticed your horses hadn't been fed, so I went ahead and threw 'em some hay."

"Thanks." Logan made an effort to rein in his anger. "I had to work late finishing up some paperwork."

"I know." Culley studied him with a bright-eyed watchfulness. "I saw you with the kid today."

"The kid." For a puzzled instant, Logan didn't know who he meant. Then he remembered Calder's young grandson. "How did you see me? Where were you?"

"Up on the bluff."

"What were you doing up there? That's not Shamrock land."

There was a small lift of his thin shoulders that seemed to shrug aside the question. "You can see for miles from atop that bluff."

"What do you know about those dead cattle?"

"About as much as you do."

"And what's that?"

"From what I could tell, they looked like somebody used them for target practice."

"How were you able to determine that? Did you go down there?"

"Didn't have to. I got me a pair of field glasses. I watched you dig a bullet out of one of the carcasses."

"I understand you do a bit of wandering at night. You haven't heard anything that might have been gunfire the last few nights, have you?"

"Who's to say they were shot at night?"

"Good point." Logan smiled, some of the tension finally easing. "At the same time, I can't imagine anyone doing it in broad daylight."

"I don't remember hearing gunshots," Culley said, at last answering the question. "But if the wind was blowing just right, it probably would have carried to the north range."

"Is that where you were?"

"There, or somewhere on the Shamrock or else around The Homestead."

"Where's The Homestead?"

"That's the name they gave Calder's house." O'Rourke paused and cocked his head to the side, eyeing Logan with open curiosity. "What made you become a cop?"

"A psychiatrist could give you a long answer to that." A smile half tilted his mouth. "But some people are just born warriors."

That was a new concept to Culley, one he had to think about. A warrior: he liked the sound of it. It conjured up images of a man willing to fight to protect those in his care. "You got any family?"

Logan shook his head, the smile fading. "Not anymore."

"My dad wasn't much, but he was there. That's sayin' something nowadays, when a man sows his seed and never gives a damn about the baby that grows from it. There was a time when folks held a man accountable. Now they figure a man's happiness comes ahead of his responsibility, and look to the government to take care of the kid. But the government can't raise a boy to be a man."

"I suppose not." Logan had never cared much for politics. "Do you have any ideas about who might have killed those cattle?"

"I haven't given it any thought."

"How about someone who might be carrying a grudge against the Calders?"

Culley exhaled a laugh. "The list would be as long as your arm. Practically everyone around here has come up against the Calders at one time or another—and come out the worse for it."

Detecting a bite of bitterness, Logan probed, "Even you?"

There was a long pause while O'Rourke studied

him with close scrutiny. "Let's just say, I didn't shed no tears when I saw those buzzards feasting on Calder beef. It seemed a kind a' poetic justice."

"For what?"

"The dozen head he shot."

"Your cattle?"

"Some were mine, some were MacGruder's, and a couple carried the Circle Six brand."

"When was this?"

"Close to forty years ago. Long before your time." The clipped answer indicated his reluctance to discuss it further.

Logan didn't let that stop him. "What happened?"

"There was a drought. Our wells had dried up and the grass grazed to the ground. And Calder had that north range without a cow on it and water in the river. We drove our herds onto it. We couldn't afford hay, so it was either that or watch them starve to death. Calder met us, told us to turn back. When we didn't, he told his men to start shootin' our cattle. They did." The bitterness of the memory was in his voice and his expression. "I know we were in the wrong, but I still remember how those cows fell." He dragged in a cleansing breath. "It's hard land, and it breeds hard men to hard ways. The Calders are about as hard as they come."

"And your sister married a Calder," Logan remarked, idly wondering at that.

"Yup." O'Rourke dropped his gaze to the ground, the brim of his hat casting his face in shadows. "He loved her. I'll say that much for him."

"Sometimes that's all that needs to be said."

"I guess." He looked up, again observing him in that closely watchful way. "What did you think of the boy?"

Logan frowned, puzzled that O'Rourke would

be asking about Calder's grandson again. "He seemed like a good kid. I didn't really pay that much attention. Why do you ask?"

"'Cause next time maybe you should."

"Why's that?" His pager beeped. Logan checked it and smothered a sigh of irritation. "Excuse me." He walked to the patrol car, slid behind the wheel, switched on the radio and called in. "This is Echohawk. What's the problem?"

There was an initial squawk and a crackle, followed by the excited voice of Deputy Rouch. "There's a fire at Fedderson's. Hubble just called from the scene and said the gas pumps are engulfed in flames."

"Has the foam truck been called in?"

"I don't know," the deputy replied uncertainly. "I never asked."

"Find out," Logan replied. "I'm on my way."

"Ten-four." Rouch at last responded with the radio codes he was so fond of spouting.

"Did he say Fedderson's was on fire?" O'Rourke stepped up to the driver's side when Logan started the engine.

"Yep." Reversing away from the barn, he peeled out of the yard, driving with one hand and buckling his seat belt with the other.

When he hit the highway, he turned on the siren and raced toward Blue Moon. His thoughts traveled along a dozen different tangents, and he found himself wondering again why O'Rourke had asked him about Calder's grandson. But the answer to that would have to come at another time.

SIXTEEN

Daylight brought a steady stream of locals to view the damage of the previous night's fire. It was the most exciting thing that had happened in Blue Moon in years. They stared at the blackened metal shells of the gasoline pumps, the charred tires propped beside them, the fire-scorched concrete around them, and the globs of melted plastic, and listened intently to accounts of those who had been on the scene. All speculated on the disaster that might have occurred if the underground tanks had blown, while others wondered where they were going to buy gas for their vehicles.

The constant flow of people brought business, more business than Sally Brogan had ever had at her restaurant. By four o'clock Saturday afternoon, she was down to one package of buns, a dozen eggs, and two pounds of hamburger, and was completely out of lettuce—and the evening crowd had yet to arrive. Left with no choice, she made a quick trip to Fedderson's store and came out with an armload of groceries.

She was halfway back to the restaurant when a pickup pulled off the highway and parked in front of it. Sally didn't have to see the Triple C brand emblazoned on its doors to recognize Chase behind the wheel. Jessy and Cat were with him, along with young Quint.

"Honestly, Chase, don't tell me you came to gawk at Emmett's burned pumps, too?" Sally walked up to him when he climbed out of the truck.

"Actually, I thought it was time I took these two young ladies out to dinner." But his glance was already sliding past her to the station area. "I did hear there was a fire. It doesn't look like there's much damage."

"It was confined to the island. The gasoline pumps are a total loss. Unfortunately, it may be as much as a week before he can get new ones installed." Sally glanced that way as well, the paper sacks rattling in her arms.

Jessy came around the truck, followed by Cat and her son. "Let me give you hand with those sacks, Sally," Jessy offered, reaching out.

"No, thanks. Right now I have them wedged together. If you took one, I'd probably drop the rest." She turned her smile on the tall blonde. "You're looking well. How are you feeling?"

"Wonderful," Jessy replied, beaming with happiness.

"Where was the fire, Grandpa?" Quint caught hold of Chase's hand, claiming his attention. "Can we go see?"

"We will in a minute," he promised.

"Don't worry, Quint," Sally told him. "Your grandpa wants to see it as much as you do. It seems we never quite outgrow our fascination with fire and its aftermath, no matter how old we get." Sally's astute observation drew a smile from Cat and a quick, admitting chuckle from her father. With a smile of her own, Sally started toward her restaurant. "I'll see you inside."

"Let me get the door for you." Jessy went after her.

Cat fell in step with her father and Quint when they headed across the graveled parking lot toward Fedderson's. Wooden barricades blocked off the fire-damaged pump island and kept the handful of onlookers well away from the site.

A couple of Dy-Corp workers stood at the far end of the restaurant parking lot, watching a man inside the barricades as he inspected the burned area inch by inch. Hearing footsteps behind them, they glanced around and nodded a silent greeting.

The taller of the two said, without preamble, "Guess you heard about the fire last night. The fire marshal just got here a little while ago. That's him going over it now."

But it was the lean and rangy man behind the barricades, standing beside Emmett Fedderson, who claimed Cat's attention. He was out of uniform, dressed in boot-cut jeans, a white western shirt, and a lacquered straw Stetson, looking much as he had the very first time she'd seen him. Her pulse skittered, the memory of last night's hard kiss surfacing abruptly, and the air temperature seemed to rise a good ten degrees.

"Is arson suspected?" her father asked, stopping to talk to the two men.

But Quint kept walking toward the barricades. Cat hurriedly caught him by the shoulders, drawing him to a halt. "This is close enough, Quint."

He stopped reluctantly. But any hope that she might escape Logan's notice vanished as his gray eyes cut to her. She made a point of ignoring him, although she couldn't ignore the vivid and unsettling effect of his presence.

"How come it's all black over there?" Quint wanted to know.

"The fire did that." A lazy breeze carried the smell of smoke and burned rubber. "Remember how black it is inside the fireplace?"

"Uh-huh." Quint nodded.

"It's the same thing."

"You mean, it's like soot?" He tilted his head back to look up at her, and Cat found herself glancing into another pair of equally gray eyes.

"Very much like it, yes."

Quint squared around and stared at the fire scene for a long minute. "What's he doing?" He pointed to the balding man behind the barricades as Jessy rejoined them.

"He's trying to figure out how the fire got started," Cat replied.

"How can he do that?"

"Now that's a hard question." She glanced at Jessy, uncertain how to answer it in terms Quint could understand.

"I think he went to a school to learn that," Jessy put in.

"Will I learn that when I go to school?" Quint asked, clearly intrigued by the possibility.

"Probably not right away," Jessy answered with more than a trace of amusement.

Cat smiled in response to it, but it was an absent movement of her lips as she cast an oblique glance at Logan. She hated this achy need she felt whenever he was around. Last night she had fought it as much as she had fought him; in the end, she had surrendered to both.

It shamed her to realize that she now thought of Logan in that same heated way she had once thought about Repp. The memory of Repp was just that—a memory. The thought of him no longer stirred up any of the old quiver of longings. It shook her faith in her own judgment and somehow cheapened the love she had felt for Repp. But she would not let go of her loyalty to him. She absolutely would not.

A pickup truck turned off the highway, skirted the wooden barricades, and pulled up alongside the building. There was the metallic slam of doors, one an echo of the first as Norma Fedderson stepped from the store and hollered at her husband that he had a phone call.

"Maybe that's the insurance adjuster," he said to Logan and hustled off to take the call.

Logan managed a belated nod and snapped his gaze away from Cat and back to the fire marshal, half-irritated by his absorption with her. From the instant he saw her standing there, the sight of her had been like a potent whiskey racing through his bloodstream. Thirsty again, he looked back to take a second drink.

A silver concho belt cinched the waist of an emerald dress that matched and deepened the green of her eyes and turned her hair a more shining black. A playful wind teased at the hem of the dress's full skirt, then molded the fabric to her and showed each ripely curved line of her body, a body he remembered in intimate detail.

There was a coolness to her expression now, but he knew the fire that lay just beneath it, the fire of both her anger and her passion. He had aroused both, and he could do it again. She knew it as well, and hated him for it.

The scuff of sauntering footsteps sounded behind him. Logan turned with an impatient swing of his shoulders, expecting to see Emmett Fedderson. His piercing glance collided with the mocking eyes of Lath Anderson.

"Heard there was some excitement here last night," he remarked with seeming idleness.

"A little." Recognizing the sudden shortness of

his temper, Logan turned back, his glance running again to Cat.

Lath saw it. "That Cat Calder is quite a looker, isn't she?"

"Keep your mouth off her, Anderson."

"Now, there's a picture," he said with a marveling shake of his head. "Tell you the truth, about the only thing better than having my mouth on her, would be having hers on me. Just thinking about it is enough to make me hard."

Lath glanced sideways to gauge the effect of his words, and shock ripped through him. Echohawk's eyes were on him, cold and wicked like the black muzzles of a shotgun ringed with gray steel.

"One more word, Anderson, and you'll find yourself spread-eagled on the ground eating concrete." The tightly murmured words held a warning note of thinly repressed fury.

"Hey." Backing up a step, Lath held up his hands in mock surrender and laughed to cover the fear churning through him. "How was I to know you had ideas in that direction yourself?"

"You're wrong about that." The reply was snapped out, giving lie to the denial.

"If you say so." Lath shrugged, relieved when those cold eyes were directed elsewhere, and fully aware jealousy didn't get any greener than what he had just witnessed. He looked to where the man was poking around in a pile of ash next to a charred gas pump. "Anybody know how the fire got started?"

"With a match."

"You mean it was deliberately set?" He feigned surprise, and saw Echohawk wasn't convinced. Confident again, he didn't care.

"Where were you last night between midnight and one o'clock?"

"Me? You surely don't think I had anything to do with starting this fire, do you?"

Logan gave him a level look, his temper once more under control. "According to Emmett, the two of you had words last night after he refused to reopen your family's charge account with him. He said it wasn't the first time you'd argued over it."

"He said that?!" He whirled around as Emmett came out of the store, saw him and hesitated. "Am I glad to see you, Emmett. The sheriff here just told me something real distressing. He claims that you said we argued over my ma's account with you. Now, you got to come here and set the record straight."

Emmett shuffled wearily to them, his expression hard and bitter and careful. "What I said was a fact, Lath, and you know it. You was upset 'cause I wouldn't reopen that account."

"Sure, it grieved me, but I never said one cross word to you about it, did I?" he challenged.

"Well . . . no," Emmett gave in, grudgingly. "But you was mad. I could see it in your eyes. And I remember the way you said 'no gas.' Well, I don't have any gas now."

Lath shook his head in a gesture of sad bewilderment. "It hurts me, Emmett, that you think I would have done this. Why, you've known me since I was a little shaver."

"And I didn't dare turn my back on you then, either, or you would have had a half dozen candy bars stuffed inside your pants."

"Now, Emmett, I never took nothing that wasn't paid for."

"You're damned right you didn't, 'cause I always charged 'em to your ma's account," Emmett countered, a dark flush of anger purpling his face.

"This fire's got him all upset, Sheriff," Lath declared. "All I ever did was to ask him politely to consider reopening my ma's account. Emmett's never been anything but a fair and honest man, so I know after he's had time to think about it, he'll admit what I'm saying is true. Isn't that right, Emmett?" He clamped a hand on the man's shoulder, giving it a small shake.

"He was polite enough with his words," Emmett conceded sourly.

Before he could say more, Lath threw a bright grin at Logan. "See? I knew he'd clear things up for me."

"You still haven't said where you were last night."

"Sally closes up at midnight. Me and Rollie left a little before that. So I'd say we were either on our way home or else in bed." His expression never changed. "Anything else you'd like to ask?"

"Not right now."

"If you think of anything, you know where to find me," he said with a wink, then walked off.

Watching him head into the store, Emmett grumbled, "I still think he's the one who started it."

"You could be right," Logan agreed. "But suspicions are no good without proof."

"And you can bet money Lath knows that, too."

Across the way, Chase Calder said something to Cat. She nodded and turned, touching the shoulder of the young boy beside her. He caught hold of her hand, then reached out to take the outstretched hand of Jessy Calder. Logan watched as the two women lifted the boy off the ground and swung him between them. His giggle of delight drifted across the intervening space.

"I'm kinda surprised to see Calder in town when the Triple C is in the middle of roundup," Emmett remarked. "Course, I don't imagine Chase takes an active role in it anymore. Ty sees to it now, I guess."

"I got that impression." Logan nodded absently, his glance tracking Cat all the way to the restaurant entrance.

"That's right. You were out there yesterday, weren't you?" Emmett recalled. "Trouble comes in bunches, they say. My place gets set on fire and Calder gets his cattle killed. I guess you haven't had much time to investigate that."

"Not much." The comment prompted a question he had planned to ask. "Do you know anybody around here that has a truck with a winch mounted in it?"

"Well, there's the one I got, parked around back. We hardly use it anymore since we got the tow truck. And Jim Bradley over at the Lone Tree Ranch has one. Old Gaylord Archibald used to have one, but I think I heard he'd sold it to somebody over at Wolf Point. Farleys had one, but they blew the motor in it. The cost of fixing it was more than the whole thing was worth. I'm pretty sure they ended up junking it." He paused, then shook his head. "I can't think of anybody else. Why'd you want to know?"

"Just curious. Do you mind if I go take a look at yours?"

"Course not. Like I said, it's parked around back in that old shed behind the store."

"Where are the keys?"

Emmett cast a furtive look around them, then lowered his voice. "You don't need one. That padlock on the shed door has been broke for years."

Logan shot him a look, a sudden hunch forming. "And the keys to the truck?"

He blinked once, twice, then ducked his head and mumbled a little sheepishly, "On a hook inside the door."

"I think you'd better come with me."

"Why?" A note of anxiety crept into Emmett's

voice. "You don't think somebody stole my truck, do you?"

Logan ignored the question and called to the fire marshal, "Frank, we're going around back for a few minutes." The man waved an acknowledgment, and Logan started toward the corner of the building. "When's the last time you were in the shed, Emmett?"

"Probably a week." Emmett hobbled after him, puffing a little at the swift pace he set. "It's mostly for storage."

The shed sat off by itself, about twenty yards from the store. Built of wood, its white painted boards chipped and coated with prairie dust, it had the look of an old two-car garage. Rusted wheel rims and old tires were piled along one side of it, half-hidden by the tall weeds and wild grasses that grew around the shed.

Following a narrow path through the weeds, Emmett went around to a side door that appeared to be secured by a large steel padlock. He gave it a downward yank, and it sprang apart. Unhooking it, he pushed the door open and stepped inside, flipping on a wall switch. Three bare light bulbs flashed on, illuminating dusty stacks of boxes, spare engine parts, an assortment of hubcaps, and the truck in question.

A weighty sigh of relief spilled from Emmett. "There it is. You had me thinking it wouldn't be."

"See if the keys are still hanging up." Logan surveyed the windowless interior. Heat hung heavy in the airless shed, musty with the smell of dust and mildew.

Turning, Emmett took two shuffling steps to the right and ran his hand along a stud, then looked down, checking the concrete floor at his feet. "They're gone," he said in a dumbfounded voice. "That don't make any sense. The truck's still here."

Still playing his hunch, Logan walked over to the

truck and glanced through the passenger window. A set of keys dangled from the windshield wiper lever, the silver shine of them somehow taunting.

"They're in the truck, Emmett."

"The hell you say," he murmured, momentarily stunned. Recovering, he hustled to the truck, his body pitched forward with his degree of haste. "They belong on the damned wall. Who—"

"Leave them where they are, Emmett. And don't touch anything else." Crouching down, Logan examined the right front tire, studying the tread pattern and the bits of dirt and gravel lodged between them.

"Don't touch it? Why?" He stopped a good three feet from the vehicle.

"I think your truck might have been—borrowed, shall we say?" he suggested with an ironic lift to his mouth.

"Borrowed? You mean, somebody took it without asking first?"

"It's possible."

Straightening, Logan began a slow, inspecting walk around the truck, taking special note of the long stalks of grass trapped between the running board and the truck body. At last he came to the rear of the truck and stopped. "What do you use this canvas tarp for, Emmett?"

"What tarp?"

"This one." He motioned for Emmett to come over and take a look.

"I don't keep any tarps in that truck. Never had any reason to," he muttered. Confusion creased his face when he saw the stained and rumpled canvas on the floor of the truck bed. "Why, that looks like one of those paint tarps we used a few years back when we enlarged the store and repainted the walls. I had a half dozen of 'em stacked over here in the corner. I wonder who put it in the truck, and how did it get all that grease on it?"

"I don't think that's grease, Emmett."

"What else could it be?" he scoffed.

"Blood." Logan saw the color drain from the old man's face and added, "Cow's blood. I haven't looked, but I'd be willing to bet we'll also find strands of cow hair on that winch cable."

"You mean . . . you think somebody butchered a beef and used my truck to haul it away?"

"That's exactly what I think." His mouth curved, but the smile didn't reach his eyes.

"Calder—those cattle of his that got killed—"

"You're quick, Emmett."

"And they used my truck to do it." His expression fell halfway between astonishment and outrage.

"And they didn't make any attempt to conceal their use of it. On the contrary, they've flaunted it," Logan murmured thoughtfully, recalling the grisly scene of the slaughtered cattle.

"It's that damned Lath Anderson." Emmett all but spat the name. "It's just the kind of dirty stunt that arrogant bastard would pull."

"You think he did it to implicate you?" Logan arched an eyebrow in skepticism.

"He did it to sign his name to the deed, the same way he slashed those pump hoses and rolled my own tires to the island, drenched 'em in my gas, and set the whole thing on fire."

Logan couldn't deny the two incidents bore similar signatures. Still he shook his head. "But what's the connection between you and Calder?"

"It's obvious," Emmett declared. "He's trying to get even with both of us. Me for closing his ma's account and Calder for sending Rollie to prison."

A puzzled line creased his forehead. "How did Calder do that?"

"He didn't, really, but that's not the way old Emma Anderson tells it. Rollie caused the accident that killed Repp Taylor. Repp worked for Calder and was fixing to marry his daughter. Rollie was stinking drunk at the time. Emma went to Calder and pleaded with him to speak up for her son and ask the judge to go light on him. Calder must have refused. Rollie got slapped with the maximum sentence and the Andersons ended up losing their farm. She puts the blame for all of it at Calder's door."

Logan considered that. "That sounds like a slim reason to me."

"You wanta talk about slim, what about me?" Emmett turned indignant. "I've been carrying that Anderson account on my books for better than ten years while they been paying me ten dollars one month, maybe fifty the next, then only five. Every once in a while I'll see a hundred dollars, but with them always charging, they never made a dent in the balance. After they lost the farm, the dang thing doubled. What was I supposed to do? It was business, damn it. I had to cut her off."

"I can see that."

"Yeah, but you're thinking there's more to it than what I'm saying, but I'm telling you there isn't," Emmett insisted on a defensive note. "And I'd bet it's the same for Calder, but you'll have to ask him that."

"I plan on it," Logan said with a nod. "First, though, I need to use your phone and get Berton out here. We'll need to bag up that tarp and send it off to the lab for analysis to see whether this is cow blood. I'll want that cable checked for any hair follicles and the truck dusted for prints. The boldness of this whole thing makes me believe they wore gloves, but there's always the chance they slipped up somewhere. We'll need to compare the tread pattern on these tires with the photo of the ones I found at the Triple C, too."

"Are you going to arrest them?" Hope blossomed in his weathered face.

"Not unless we can lift a matching print," Logan told him. "Without that, it's your shed, your truck and your canvas tarp. Which reminds me, Emmett, do you own a rifle?"

"A rifle? Sure, I got a Winchester thirty-thirty to home. I haven't used it in years, though. You don't think—" He got a stricken look. "Oh my God, what if they used my rifle?"

"As soon as I get Berton over here, we'll go by your place and see if it's still there." He wasn't ready to eliminate Emmett. He had learned long ago not to be quick about closing doors.

As if sensing that, Emmett fell silent and followed him outside, then turned to close the door and slip the padlock back in place. Watching him, Logan smiled wryly. "If I were you, Emmett, I'd get a padlock that works. I'd hate to have someone 'borrow' your truck again."

"I'll be doing that." Sincerity was heavy in his voice.

Leaving the shed area, Logan struck out for the store to make his call to Berton. Emmett plodded along after him. As they rounded the building, Lath was just pulling away from the store. He stopped and poked his head out the driver's side window, a broad, taunting grin on his face.

"I wondered where you'd taken off to. Never guessed you were having a big powwow behind the store, Echohawk." Laughing, he pulled his head back inside the cab, gunned the motor, honked, and took off, the tires squealing as he turned onto the highway.

"It's him, I tell you," Emmett said in low anger.

"He knows just what we found back there, and he's laughing, knowing we can't prove a thing."

Logan could believe that about Lath. Problem was, acts of petty revenge just didn't strike him as Lath's style. He had always pegged him as a man without scruples, motivated mainly by greed. He didn't see where Anderson profited from killing a bunch of cattle and torching some gas pumps.

SEVENTEEN

After Logan made the phone call to his deputy Berton Rouch, he drove Emmett to his home. The Winchester was in the closet. Judging by the dirty barrel, it hadn't been fired—or cleaned—in years. Besides a shotgun he kept at the store and a handgun he had in the drawer of his nightstand, Emmett insisted he had no other guns.

Logan drove a very relieved Emmett back to the combination grocery store and gas station, arriving a few minutes after Berton Rouch, a round, beetle-browed man, completely devoid of humor, pulled in. Together, Logan and Berton bagged the canvas tarp for later shipment to the lab, unrolled a five-foot section of cable, lopped it off with a hacksaw, bagged it as well, then photographed the tires for comparisons and collected the floor mats inside the truck cab to have them checked for blood. When it came time to dust for prints, Logan left the job to Berton. The man was infuriatingly slow but always thorough.

Leaving the airless shed, Logan walked back to the store and conferred briefly with the fire marshal. Beyond confirming the cause was arson and the gasoline from the pumps themselves had likely been the accelerant, Frank Truedell could offer little else. After promising to fax Logan a copy of his report, he climbed in his car and left.

Logan paused beside the barricades. The acrid smell of smoke was keen and strong, tainting the clean air that drifted off the prairie. With a small lift of his head, he swung his glance to the restaurant parking lot, his thoughts coming back to the things Fedderson had said about Calder and the Andersons. His glance touched the pickup that carried the Triple C brand on its doors, its presence confirming the Calders were inside, Cat included. But there was no avoiding that.

His bronze features took on a remote cast as he struck out toward the restaurant. A dozen yards from the building, Logan heard the grating creak of metal rubbing against metal and noticed the slow back-and-forth sway of the chains suspending a wooden swing from the restaurant's porch roof. Drawing closer, he saw the boy sitting on the swing, one hand loosely holding a supporting chain. It was Calder's grandson.

Unbidden, O'Rourke's suggestion came back to him that he should take a closer look at the boy. There was a lean kinking of muscle along his jaw as Logan rejected that idea out of hand. The boy was a Calder; there was nothing more he needed to know about him.

Head down, he made for the steps, intent only on going inside and asking his questions of Chase Calder. His boot touched the first tread and a young voice reached out to him, adultlike in its greeting.

"Evening, Sheriff." There was a child's hope for recognition in the look young Quint Calder gave him.

Logan hesitated, but it wasn't in him to show the

boy the rough side of his temper. Stifling his irritation, he nodded. "Evening, Quint."

There was a little leap of pleasure in the boy's eyes that Logan had remembered his name. It was a small thing, Logan knew, but it gave the boy a sense of importance. And his reaction to it gentled something inside Logan and gave a softening warmth to the line of his mouth.

"Out here getting some air, are you?" Logan paused on the top step and glanced over his shoulder to see the view the boy had.

"My mom said I could come out here as long as I stayed on the porch."

Logan turned back. "That's good advice. There's a lot of traffic at this time of day. It might be hard for someone in a truck to see a boy your size."

"Yeah." Quint shifted sideways in the swing, scooting ahead a bit and letting one coltish leg dangle. "Did ya find who shot our cattle?"

"Not yet. I was just going inside to talk to your grandfather about it. I guess your dad's still out with the roundup," Logan said and sensed an immediate withdrawing of the boy.

"I don't got a dad." Something flickered across the gray surfaces of his eyes, dulling the shine of them.

Logan drew his head back in surprise, his gaze instantly narrowing on the boy. "What do you mean?" The thoughtless question was out before Logan considered the wound it could inflict. He cursed himself for not remembering sooner his own fatherless childhood, even as the ramifications of Quint's statement began registering.

"I don't have a dad," Quint repeated with a downward tip of his head, his slender shoulders lifting in a helpless shrug. "I don't know why. I guess I never ever had one."

If Quint wasn't the son of Ty and Jessy Calder, then—"Your mother's name is Cat, isn't it?" Logan took a step toward the boy, something hard and savage twisting through him at the thought of Cat lying in the arms of another man. He recognized it as jealousy, which made it all the more galling.

Quint shot him a quick, hesitant look and nodded that she was.

Something in the tilt of his head, his quietly serious expression had Logan taking a closer look at him. His straw cowboy hat sat on the back of his head, showing Logan the shock of black hair beneath it.

The slanting sunlight was full on his face, exposing the thinness of it and the outline of strong bones beneath boyish-soft skin. But it was the pewter gray color of the boy's eyes that had another thought streaking through Logan.

"How old are you, Quint?" He had to work to sound casual and keep the demand out of his voice.

"Five." He held up his left hand, spreading his fingers and thumb wide.

"When's your birthday?"

"I just had one last week."

And it would be six years ago in August that he had been with Cat. Mathematically, it worked. It was a real possibility that this was his son. The thought dazzled and stunned him.

Logan refused to let the idea take root, not until he could either confirm or disprove it. He knew of only two ways to do that. One would be infinitely quicker.

"Five is a good age to be, Quint," he said and moved toward the restaurant door.

When he opened it, Quint hopped off the swing and hurried after him, slipping inside before the door closed. Logan paused to take off his hat, his glance cruising the room. Quint ran to the table. "The sheriff's here."

Cat didn't need to be told that. She had seen Logan the instant he entered the restaurant. His gaze locked on her and never wavered as he came toward their table. She felt the quick, uneven thudding of her heart and the sudden shallowing of her breathing, his presence again causing a definite disturbance.

His expression was unreadable when he stopped by her chair. "I would like to have a word with you in private, Cat."

He knew. The suspicion briefly rattled her, but she covered it from long practice, her lips curving in a show of amusement. "That's a bit difficult here, don't you think?"

"What's this about, Echohawk?" Chase eyed him with a sharp frown.

Logan gave no sign that he'd heard him. "Would it be all right to use your office, Sally?" he asked without looking at the gray-haired woman seated at the table.

"Of course," she murmured with obvious hesitancy.

He nodded his thanks, then lifted a hand, palm up, in the direction of the rear office. "After you."

Rising, Cat turned and stepped ahead of him, wisdom convincing her this was a discussion better held in private. In one step, he was beside her, and she felt the intimate pressure of his guiding hand low on her back, directing her toward the hallway. The touch of it was much too familiar and warm, a sensation she didn't want right now, when she needed all her wits about her.

But he didn't take his hand away until they reached the door marked PRIVATE. He turned the knob and gave it a push inward, again letting Cat precede him. Walking over to the desk, she resisted the urge to twist her fingers together and kept them at her side in a pose of calmness.

When he pushed the door shut, the dimensions of the room seemed to shrink. Cat fought off the feeling of claustrophobia and made a slow turn to face him, her glance traveling up his wide, flat chest to the unexpected gunmetal gray of his eyes. Tension licked along her nerve ends.

"What is it you wanted to discuss?" she asked, conscious of the mad drumming of her heart and confident none of this inner agitation showed in her expression.

"I just realized a few minutes ago that Quint is your son." He watched her face. "Who is his father, Cat?"

She managed a laugh, albeit a shaky one. "Is this part of your investigation into the slaughter of our cattle?"

"It has nothing to do with it, and you know it." There was something lazy and dangerous in the way he looked at her.

Trapped, she searched for a way out. "Does it matter? Does it really matter to you, Logan?" The edginess of desperation crept into her voice.

"It matters."

"Because of Quint—or because of all that Calder money he represents?" Her anger came out, hot and tinged with bitterness.

"Then he is my son."

"I never said that."

"No. But a DNA test can prove it. Or had you overlooked that detail?"

"Damn you." Her hands were still at her sides, but they were fisted now.

There was no warning knock before the door swung open, and Chase stepped through and stopped, one hand still gripping the knob, his hard glance divided between Cat and Logan.

"What's going on here?" He spoke with the conviction of a man accustomed to having his questions answered and his orders obeyed. "What do you want with my daughter?"

"This is between Cat and myself." Logan spared him a brief glance, then centered his attention back on her.

"Anything that concerns my daughter concerns me," Chase stated.

"I can't argue with that." Amusement curled the corners of his mouth as he looked at her. "Do you want him to stay, Cat?"

"Yes," she rushed, then just as quickly changed it. "No!" She caught back a sob of frustration and swung away, cursing again, "Damn you, Logan."

Releasing the door, Chase moved to her side, an arm protectively circling her as he glared at Logan. "Just what the hell is going on here? What is this all about? Exactly what is it you think Cat has done?"

"I'm not here in any official capacity, Mr. Calder. My business with your daughter is strictly personal."

"Personal?" He was taken aback by that. "What's he talking about, Cat?"

She closed her eyes for a long second. "Logan is Quint's father."

In the thick silence that followed her announcement, Chase stared at the man before him, then slowly ran his gaze over the office. It was in this very room that he himself had first learned he had a son. Chase remembered the shock of it and the ensuing rush of emotion. Oddly it didn't seem that long ago.

"We'll finish this discussion at the ranch," he stated quietly.

"Dad—" Cat began.

But he heard the beginnings of an argument in her tone. "At the ranch, Cat."

"There is nothing to discuss," she protested.

"You're wrong," Chase replied. "There is a great deal to discuss." His gaze swung to Logan. "I'll ride with you. Cat can follow with Jessy and Quint."

"That's fine with me," Logan stated.

"Well, it's not fine with me!" Cat blazed, now in full temper. "This is my life and my child. I am not some schoolgirl anymore to be told where to go and when. No one decides my life but me."

"That wasn't my intention," Chase told her.

"Really? It sounded very much like it to me."

"Maybe it would be best if Cat rode with me," Logan suggested. "We do need to talk. Assuming"—he paused, a mocking arch to his eyebrow—"that's agreeable with you."

At the moment, nothing was agreeable with her. But she knew that they needed to talk. Riding back to the ranch with him appeared to be the only opportunity.

"I think that's an excellent suggestion," she said at last.

Cat lifted her chin a little, in her trademark gesture of pride, and returned Logan's look of long appraisal. Observing them, Chase felt the raw and wild currents that surged between these two strong and proud and self-willed young people. It stirred him, and made him remember what youth was like—the fire and the flash of it—and what had been taken from him when Maggie died.

Thinking of Maggie, he felt old and tired and alone. But there were decisions to be made, and he knew what they would be. He also knew Cat would fight him every inch of the way.

Turning from them, Chase said, "I'll get Jessy and Quint, and we'll be on our way."

* * *

The sun rode low in the western sky, prolonging the hours of daylight into early evening and pouring its rays through the windshield of the speeding pickup. Reaching up, Logan lowered the visor to block the sun's blinding glare. Cat turned her head from it and stared out the opened side window. The inrushing air whipped at the ends of her long black hair, blowing strands around in a corkscrew of motion.

A charged silence filled the cab of the pickup, broken only by the roar of the wind and monotonous whine of wheels. Logan deliberately let the pressure of it build, well aware that silence was a highly effective interrogation tool. He slowed to make the turn at the ranch's east gate, the road surface changing from pavement to gravel.

On either side of the road, the wide-flung plains rolled in uneven dips and swells, capped by a gigantic sky.

"What is it you want, Logan?" Cat scraped a stray lock of hair from her cheek.

His glance observed her action, then skimmed her profile. "What any father would want: some time with his son."

"He doesn't need you."

"I was raised without a father, Cat." He rested one hand on the top of the steering wheel, his gaze fixed on the road ahead, his eyes narrowed slightly against the sun's brightness. "I asked my mother about him once. But she couldn't tell me his name. It turned out that she had been with a number of men, some she knew and some she didn't. I never asked about him again, but I always wondered." He waited a beat, then added, "So does Quint."

"He has never asked about you."

"Maybe he hasn't, but he's wondered about me."

"You don't know that," Cat insisted curtly.

His mouth quirked in a humorless way. "When I

asked Quint where his father was today, do you know what he told me?"

"No." Resentment turned her stiff.

"He said he didn't have a father, that he guessed he had never had one. He didn't know why."

This revelation gave Cat pause and made her uncomfortable. But she couldn't allow doubt to set in and weaken her resolve. "His answer is hardly surprising, considering the subject has never come up before," she said with deliberate indifference.

"He'll have to be told about me, Cat."

"Why?" she challenged. "It would only confuse him. He doesn't know you. You're a total stranger to him. Quint won't understand any of it."

"He'll understand even less why you don't tell him."

Fully aware that her attitude was indefensible, Cat went on the attack. "Look around you, Logan. This is Quint's backyard, as far as the eye can see in any direction. This is his legacy, his home, his future. He's a Calder, with all the power, influence, and position that the name implies. I've given him that. And you want to take it from him, turn him into Quint Echohawk." The scorn in her voice was rampant and cutting.

"I wonder if you would be quite so contemptuous if his last name was Taylor?" The look in his gray eyes was hard with mockery. "That was your dead lover's last name, wasn't it?"

Shock gave way to fury and guilt. Cat lashed out, the throb of both in her voice. "God, I hate you." She turned her head to hide the tears that stung her eyes. "Why did you have to come here at all? We were happy. Content. Then you showed up and ruined it all."

"That wasn't my intention."

"But that's what you've done. You've totally disrupted our lives, torn them apart. And you don't really care. How can you do that?" she protested. "Haven't I been punished enough? I loved Repp. Do you have any idea what it's been like to live with the shame and the guilt of that night with you? Or how hard it was to face my family and Repp's parents when I learned I was with child because of that night?"

"If I had known you were pregnant—"

"But I didn't want you to know." Anger blazed in her green eyes. "Don't you understand that I didn't want you in my life? And I don't now!"

"What you or I might want doesn't enter into it," Logan replied. "Quint is the only thing that matters now."

"Yes." Her voice grew firm with decision. "And if you truly wanted what was best for him, you'd walk away."

"I'm not convinced that would be best for him." The peaked roof of the Calder home jutted above the skyline, the structure's towering proportions making it visible for miles in the flat and empty landscape. Its size was a statement of its owner's dominion over the surrounding plains, a dominion that implied power, wealth, and prestige, something that Cat had known all her life and none of which he could offer their son. But Logan had only to remember the hole in his own life to know that he could give Quint the one thing no one else could—a father.

"No, you would rather divide him," Cat retorted, the sting of accusation in her voice. "You would always make him wonder if he belongs with you or here on the ranch with me. There will always be a conflict of loyalties and identity."

"Not if we handle it right."

She gave him a long, measuring look, then settled back in the seat, a sudden calm taking over her. "It will be handled right, I can promise you that." Something glinted in her eyes while complacency curved the line of her lips.

She sounded much too confident. It put Logan instantly on guard. It was obvious she objected to granting him visitation rights. But exactly what form the opposition would take, Logan couldn't guess. Her ensuing silence made it clear she had no intention of telling him—yet.

Minutes later, he pulled into the ranch yard and parked in front of The Homestead. Chase swung the ranch pickup alongside him. The instant his grandfather switched the engine off, Quint scrambled out the passenger side of the truck and ran up to Cat.

"We followed you all the way home, Mom."

"I know." She smiled. It faded a little when she saw the curious glance he darted at Logan, but he didn't ask what he was doing here. Cat was suddenly very thankful that Quint was not a naturally inquisitive child, always wanting to know the how and why of things.

Watching them, Logan studied the picture they made together. Her love for the boy was evident in the warm look in her eyes, the easy smile they shared and the loving and familiar way she touched him. Nothing in her manner or tone of voice conveyed to Quint any of the tension or the turmoil of the moment, leaving Logan in no doubt that she would go to any lengths to protect Quint.

But the picture of mother and son stayed in his mind, even after they went inside and Cat sent Quint off with Jessy to get ready for bed, promising him she would be up later to tuck him in.

He followed Chase into the spacious den. Cat paused inside the wide doorway and swung back to close both doors, all grace and motion, her skirt swirling softly about her legs. When she turned back,

Logan saw the battle light in her eyes and the sparkle of confidence. His glance drifted to her lips, laying softly together with just a hint of smugness in their line. But it was their taste he was remembering.

"Brandy?" Chase asked as he splashed some amber-colored liquor in a snifter for himself.

"No thanks," Logan walked over to one of the high-backed chairs facing the desk and folded his long frame into it.

"You don't drink much, do you?" Chase put the stopper back in the crystal decanter.

"Only a beer now and then." Logan didn't bother to add that his mother had been an alcoholic. He couldn't remember a day when she hadn't been drunk or nursing a hangover. As a result, he had fought shy of hard liquor, even as a youth.

Brandy snifter in hand, Chase crossed to the desk with a stiffness of gait that spoke of arthritic and aching joints. He lowered himself into the arm chair behind it, then glanced at both Cat and Logan, idly swirling the liquor in his glass. "Were the two of you able to come to any decision on your way here?"

"There was no decision to make," Cat declared airily, coming to stand near a corner of the desk, her body angling slightly toward Logan.

"Cat has indicated an unwillingness to grant visitation rights," Logan replied evenly.

"Why should I?" Again her voice held that note of breezy unconcern.

"Because I am his father."

"As far as I'm concerned, you're not."

Logan came out of his chair with a rush, at last realizing her game. He stopped a foot away, towering over her in his anger. She tossed her head back, meeting the hardness of his gaze with cool defiance.

"Wait a minute," Chase broke in sharply. "You

said very clearly at Sally's that Logan was Quint's father."

"I should have said he *claims* to be Quint's father," she corrected smoothly. "If he wants to prove otherwise, he'll have to take me to court."

"Are you prepared to perjure yourself?" Chase demanded, disbelief and anger warring in his voice.

"It wouldn't be perjury, merely a lapse of memory." Her lips curved in a taunting smile. "Regrettably, I had too much to drink that night. I don't remember anything about it too clearly, certainly not the man who ultimately took advantage of my weakened condition."

"As I recall, you were the aggressor that night." Logan's voice vibrated with the control he placed on his anger.

It was not the sort of information she wanted her father to hear. She came back quickly to cover it. "And I have no memory of that at all."

"Cat, you're not using your head," her father put in. "Don't you realize how costly a court fight will be?"

"I know. But fortunately money won't be a problem for me, although it could put a strain on your wallet, couldn't it, Logan?" she challenged. "It's quite possible you'll have to finance it. In fact, you may even have to find a better-paying job somewhere else," she murmured with honeyed sarcasm. "Because I promise you, my attorneys will come up with so many cross-petitions and postponements that it will be years before you see the inside of a courtroom."

"You're determined to get me out of here, aren't you?" Logan's eyes were cold with anger.

"Yes, I want you gone—far away from me and from Quint. It's what I've wanted all along," she shot back.

"That's enough!" Her father's voice cut hard

across them. "Answer me one question, Cat. Is he the father of your child or not?"

"I told you—" she began, all cool and arrogant, her eyes still on Logan.

His hand slammed the desk as he rose from his chair. "Don't give me any of your carefully rehearsed speeches for the judge. I want the truth!"

"Yes, he's Quint's father—for all the good it does him," she addressed the last to Logan.

Chase straightened to his full height, his dark gaze boring into her. "Your mother and I did a good job of spoiling you." It was one of the rare times he had ever mentioned her mother. The surprise of it drew Cat's glance, but it was his look of disgust that held it. "But I never guessed you had grown so selfish that you can't bear to share your son's love with his own father."

She paled a little at his harsh censure. "But he's my son—"

"And if you truly wanted what was best for Quint, you would marry this man and give your son a name and two parents," he stated, his mouth coming together in a tight, white line.

"An excellent suggestion," Logan murmured, and the sound of his low voice was like an intimate caress sliding over her skin, stimulating her senses and her much-too-vivid memory of that night. She didn't want to remember the strength of those hands, the gentleness of them or—most of all—the raw and heady sensations she had felt under their touch.

Cat turned from the memory, and from Logan, worried now that her father actually meant what he said. "My son has a name—the best one of all. He's a Calder."

"He's illegitimate, a bastard. Maybe that isn't the harsh stigma it once was. But as long as he stays around here, that's the way he'll be defined when he becomes a man—the Calder bastard. People may not say it to his face, but I guarantee they'll say it behind his back." His words carried an unmistakable ring of truth.

Cat tried to deny them. "You're wrong."

"I wish I were." His shoulders slumped a little with the heavy sigh that claimed him. "One thing I do know—if you marry Logan, the circumstances of Quint's birth will be forgotten."

"But—" She looked at Logan. His eyes had gone from stone-gray to smoke, disturbing in their intensity, tripping her pulse. "—I don't love him."

"There you go again, Cat," Logan taunted softly, "thinking of yourself first."

"You must have felt something for him once," her father pointed out. "Or you wouldn't have a child upstairs now." She opened her mouth to protest that, but he stopped her with an upraised hand. "And don't give me that nonsense about being drunk. You may have been drinking, but something tells me you weren't so drunk that you didn't know what you were doing—or who you were with, although I don't doubt that you might have tried to convince yourself otherwise, both then and now."

She went hot under the shrewdness of her father's gaze. "This entire conversation is ridiculous."

"I'm not so sure about that anymore." He eyed both of them thoughtfully. "Your mother and I had a lot less going for us than the two of you."

"But you loved her," Cat argued.

He shook his head. "At the time I married her, we hadn't seen each other in sixteen years. She was a stranger. I couldn't be sure what my feelings were. I only knew how much she had hated me. Still, it worked out for us. There's no reason it can't for you two." He sat back down. "We'll keep the ceremony simple, just the minister and Jessy and me for witnesses—"

Cat broke in angrily, "I am not going to marry him."

He glanced from her to Logan, a questioning arch to one eyebrow. "What are your feelings?"

"I'd marry the devil himself if it meant having my son with me," Logan answered simply, holding Cat's gaze in silent challenge.

"Then you'd better go find the devil, because I'm not marrying you," she flared. "The whole idea is so preposterous I can't believe you would even consider it, Dad."

"Unlike you, I'm thinking of Quint," her father fired right back. "Marriage is, after all, a partnership that requires mutual respect, tolerance, and a shared goal. If there is affection as well, then it's all the better."

"If you believe that, then why haven't you married Sally Brogan?" She spoke curtly because inside she was shaking. "I'll tell you why—because no one can take my mother's place in your heart or your life. Can't you see that I feel the same?"

"Is that the reason, or are you afraid?" Logan's half-tilted smile mocked even as his eyes burned into hers.

Stung, Cat retorted, "Certainly not of you."

"No, not of me," he agreed. "You're afraid of a lot of things, but I don't happen to be one of them."

The conversation was taking a turn she didn't like. "I'm not listening to any more of this." Turning with an impatient swing of her shoulders, Cat started toward the door. "There isn't going to be any wedding, shotgun or otherwise. And that's final."

Her father's hard voice came after her. "You will marry him, or I will seek custody of Quint myself."

She wheeled around, her heart catapulting into her throat. "What does that mean?"

"Precisely what I said—I'll take Quint away from you myself," he replied.

"On what grounds?" Cat demanded.

"Does it matter?" her father countered. "I can claim anything—that you are an unfit parent or emotionally unstable, whatever I choose. Then it's simply a matter of bringing in a bunch of expert witnesses to back it up."

"But it wouldn't be true," she protested.

"I never said it would be," he reminded her. "I only said I would do it. And there isn't a judge in this whole state that doesn't owe me something. I would win, Cat. We both know it."

"How could you do that to me? You're my father."

Regret clouded his eyes. "I don't want to do it, Cat. But if that's what it will take to force you to do the right thing for your son, I'll do it."

"No." The small cry was wrenched from her.

"You're going too far, Calder," Logan declared, a telling roughness in his voice.

Chase flicked a dark glance at his daughter. "Tell me a better one."

Cat stared at Logan, stunned that he would come to her defense. He turned to her, an unexpected gentleness in his eyes. She felt inexplicably safe.

"One year of marriage is hardly a life sentence," he told her. "If it doesn't work at the end of it, we'll part company—maybe not as friends, but certainly not as enemies."

"Take it, Cat," her father warned. "You know that I will do exactly what I said."

"A year," she whispered.

Logan held out his hand to seal the bargain. The instant she placed her hand in his and felt the warm, solid grip of his fingers, Cat wondered what she had done.

PART 4

How could he betray you
And force you to be his bride?
You have given your word to do it,
Though it tests that stiff Calder pride.

EIGHTEEN

Silence reigned for a moment. The solid and heavy pound of her heartbeat sounded loud in it. Pulling her hand back, Cat looked up into Logan's hard, virile face. The gentleness was gone from his eyes; something else was in them now. Confused and uneasy, nerves jumping, Cat retreated a step.

"I promised Quint I would be up to see him before he went to sleep. If you'll excuse me." The polite phrase came automatically.

Without waiting for a response, Cat walked from the room, fighting the panic that kept pushing her to run. At the bottom of the oak staircase, she paused, still tasting the fear of her father's threat, still confused by the way Logan had sided with her against her father, and still numbed by the agreement she made.

As every thought led her back to Quint, she climbed the stairs. When she reached his bedroom, Jessy was just coming out. She saw Cat and smiled. "He fell asleep while I was reading to him."

"Oh." Cat had a moment's regret, then decided it was just as well. Quint was much too observant for his years, and she had too many emotions tangling together too close to the surface. "I'll just look in on him."

When she reached for the doorknob, Jessy laid a detaining hand on her arm, her head tilting to one side as her hazel eyes closely examined Cat's face. "Cat, are you all right?"

"I will be." She had to, for Quint's sake.

"What went on down there? What's this all about?" Jessy persisted.

"Quint." With that, Cat opened the door and slipped into the thickly shadowed bedroom.

The deep purple color of a fast-falling twilight darkened the room's windows. A small night-light on the bureau threw a feeble glow into the room, its dim light touching the boy sprawled in sleep in the twin bed.

On silent feet, Cat crossed to the bed and paused a moment simply to look at him. Love welled, the fiercely protective and tender kind that knew no bounds. Giving in to the need to touch him, Cat rearranged the lay of the sheet over him and lightly smoothed the sleek strands of black hair from his forehead, then bent and brushed a kiss on the softness of his cheek.

"Good night," she whispered, her voice breaking a little.

There had never been any real choice to make; Cat saw that now. As much as she had loved Repp, she loved her son more. As dramatic as it sounded, she knew it would kill her to lose him. She recalled Logan's remark that he would marry the devil himself if it meant having his son. It was a sentiment she understood totally. By her own mouth she had condemned herself to it.

But only for a year, she reminded herself. Only for a year.

Cat lingered a moment longer by Quint's bed,

then left the room as quietly as she had entered it, pulling the door almost closed behind her. In the hallway, she heard the murmur of voices below, easily picking out Logan's and her father's, both talking in calm, level tones. Frowning, she strained to catch what they were saying, but their words were indistinct. Suddenly furious, she went to find out.

Logan was on his way out of the study when she reached the bottom of the steps. He paused to wait when he saw her coming toward him. Cat wasted no time confronting him with her suspicions.

"What other decisions did you and my father make about my future while I was gone?"

"None."

"Really?" she said with arching skepticism. "Then what exactly were you talking about all this time?"

He ran an unamused glance over her, his expression unfathomable. "I had a few questions to ask your father, strictly official, concerning the cattle killings."

"Oh." His answer stole all the wind from her anger. To cover it, she lifted her chin slightly. "What kind of questions? Has there been some new development?"

Answering that meant telling her about Lath Anderson's possible connection to the case, which would inevitably lead to a discussion of the accident. And Logan wasn't about to mention Repp Taylor's name. "It's a bit involved. You'll have to ask your father." He lifted the hat he carried, motioning with it toward the door. "I was just leaving. Care to see me out?"

"Of course," she murmured, clearly distracted by her own weighty thoughts when she fell in beside him.

His glance traveled over her face, noting the troubled green of her eyes. "Your father invited me to dinner tomorrow. I thought that would be a good time to tell Quint about me—and our wedding plans," he said when they reached the front door.

Logan expected an argument from her as she turned and placed her shoulders against the massive door. "Why did you do it?"

Puzzled by the question, Logan frowned. "Do what?"

"Stand up for me against my father."

His expression smoothed, a glint of something appearing in his eyes. "He was wrong when he threatened to take Quint away from you. Just as you were wrong when you tried to deny me the right to be with him."

Cat shook her head. "That still doesn't explain why you spoke up for me."

"I didn't. I spoke up for what was right," he told her. "You'll find I'm that way, Cat."

Something told her it had nothing to do with the badge he wore. But it was something to be filed away and considered later. There was another very important concern that needed to be settled between them.

"This marriage of ours," she began, a battle tilt to her chin, "it's to be a business arrangement. I won't share your bed."

His head dipped slightly in acknowledgment, a coolness in his eyes. "That's your decision."

His easy acceptance didn't bring the sense of relief Cat had expected. If anything, she felt more on edge.

"Anything else?" He laid a hand on the heavy brass doorknob, signaling his intention to leave.

"Not at the moment." She moved away from the door.

"In that case, I'll see you tomorrow." He slipped on his hat and walked out.

Alone in the entryway, Cat turned from the door, then hesitated, her thoughts and emotions all ajumble. Too restless to sleep, too agitated to sit and too confused to think, she scraped the hair back from her face and sighed, the night stretching long before her.

She took a step toward the living room as her father came out of the den. On another occasion, Cat would have noticed the slight slump to his broad shoulders and the extra lines in his face, but the sight of him this time brought sharply back the memory of his betrayal. Never in her life would she have believed that her own father would turn against her. But he had. The pain of that went deep, turning her suddenly bitter and angry.

"Cat—"

"I have no desire to talk to you, not after what you did." Over the years, she had learned to conceal her feelings. She made no attempt to do so now.

Sadness clouded his eyes, at odds with the half smile that quirked his mouth. "Then maybe you can finally appreciate the pain you so carelessly inflicted with your threat. I hoped to show you how unreasonable you were. It seems I've proved my point."

She felt the slap of his words and reacted in kind. "Is that your excuse?" Contempt was in her voice.

"No, but it is my reason. I have no intention of apologizing for it, if that's what you expect."

"I don't expect anything from you, not anymore."

"I see you're still too proud to admit when you're wrong."

"Pride has nothing to do with it."

"Doesn't it?"

"No." But even to Cat, the denial rang false.

He sighed his disappointment. "You had no right to refuse to let Logan see his son. No one does until he proves to be unfit as a father. I had hoped you would have the guts to admit it."

She half turned from him, feeling broken and battered. "It was wrong. But Quint is a Calder. I didn't want him to lose that."

"Regardless of his name, he's still a Calder."

Her head moved from side to side in denial of that. "It isn't the same, Dad."

"In the ways that count, it is. He will always be a Calder by blood. That's the way people will regard him now. And with your marriage to Logan, he'll no longer be known as my illegitimate grandson."

"You make that sound like it's some horrible cross he has to bear," Cat retorted, angry again.

"I'm well aware that for your generation, having a child out of wedlock has become so commonplace you attach no importance to it at all. But you'll never convince me that it is either right or good for the child—regardless of how socially acceptable such a practice is."

"I'm marrying Logan, aren't I?" she shot back.

"You could do a lot worse than him, Cat."

She turned on him. "How can you possibly know that? The man is a stranger. You know absolutely nothing about him—not his family, his background, where's he from, what he's done, or why he came to Blue Moon. You have to admit Blue Moon is on the road from nowhere to nothing."

He looked at her for a long moment without answering. "There was a time in this country when you didn't ask a man questions about his background or his past. Who he'd been or what he'd done before didn't count. You made your judgments about him based on the way he was around you. During the few times I've been around Logan, he's shown himself to be intelligent, thorough in his work, a man with a strong sense of family, and one who won't be pushed around. Those are admirable qualities, Cat. Now, if you have firsthand knowledge of something against his favor, I'd like to hear about it."

Unable to come up with anything, Cat hugged her arms about her, trying to close out his words. "He wants to tell Quint tomorrow that he's his father."

"It sounds reasonable to me."

"Maybe." Her shoulders lifted in an uncertain shrug. "I've never talked to him about his father. I'm not sure how Quint will take the news."

"That will depend on your attitude, Cat," he told her. "Quint's going to look to you. If you hold yourself aloof from Logan or show hostility toward him, Quint will pick up on that and, more than likely, echo it." He paused to separate and give weight to his next words. "You have the power to turn Quint against his father. Remember, that will leave just as deep a scar on Quint as it will on Logan. If a boy can't look up to his father, chances are he won't look up at all."

Sobered by his words, Cat found she had a great deal more to think about than she had first believed.

Shortly after breakfast the next morning, Tiny Yates stopped by The Homestead with the news that one of the mares had foaled. To Quint, this was monumental news, infinitely more pressing than making his bed. The instant Cat gave her permission, he bolted from the house and headed straight for the broodmare barn. Cat was almost grateful for his absence. All through breakfast it had been a strain to act as though everything was normal, that nothing out of the ordinary was about to occur.

A hundred times Cat wondered whether she ought to prepare Quint for the news. But she didn't know what to say, just as she didn't know how she was going to tell him that Logan was his father. It was almost a relief that all Quint wanted to talk about was the foal.

"He already stood up." Quint sat atop the manger, gazing with rapt attention at the reddish brown foal lying in the straw, its slim sides rising and falling in sleep. "His legs were real wobbly, but they'll get stronger. You can't see his face now, but he's got a white stripe just like Sierra's," he said, referring to the mare nosing at the fresh hay in the manger.

"He's a beautiful foal."

"Tiny says he's gonna be the best-lookin' one of this year's batch."

"He might be," Cat agreed, nerves churning in her stomach. "I think it's time for us to go. He needs his rest and you need to get cleaned up before dinner."

"But it isn't time for dinner yet."

"Not yet," she admitted. "But I bet by the time you get cleaned up and help set the table, it will be a lot closer than you think."

"I'm not really dirty. All I gotta do is wash my hands and—"

"Wrong." Forcing a laugh, she scooped him off the stall and set him down in the alleyway, accidentally knocking his cowboy hat askew.

Issuing a heavy sigh of resignation, Quint pushed his hat squarely on his head and started for the door at a plodding walk. Two seconds later, a new thought struck him. "I'll have time to tell Grandpa about the new foal before I clean up, won't I?"

"I think that can be arranged," Cat agreed, smiling as he broke into a run.

At a slower pace, she followed him outside into the bright sunlight of late morning. The ranch yard was without its usual bustle of activity with so many hands off on roundup. The sleeping quiet of it was like a still picture of a ranch scene with its grouping of buildings, fences, the spring-green of the prairie grass beyond them and the tall blue sky arching into infinity. Quint was the little boy running through it, bound for the big white house on the knoll.

Intent on her gangly son, Cat didn't notice the moving dust cloud along the east road, but the wind brought the thrum of an engine to her. Her heart skittered against her ribs when she recognized Logan's pickup truck bearing down on the house. Quint saw it, too, and stopped to wait for her.

"It's the sheriff." His questioning look asked what he was doing here.

"Grandpa invited him to have dinner with us today." The tension that had lived in the background since last night now leaped to the front.

Quint frowned in his quietly serious way. "But it isn't dinnertime yet."

"It's okay." But it felt far from okay as the pickup rolled to a stop near the house and Logan stepped out, dressed in jeans and a camel tan jacket. "Let's go meet him, shall we?"

Cat didn't wait for his agreement, striding toward Logan with a false eagerness, conscious of the power she had over this meeting and determined to be fair about it. She saw the sudden sharpening of Logan's gaze. Guessing at the question, she gave a quick, small shake of her head, signaling that she hadn't said anything to Quint about him.

"Hello, Logan." She tried to sound breezy and friendly.

"Cat." He touched his hat to her, then shifted his focus to Quint, flashing him a smile. The potency of it momentarily stunned her. It was something she had forgotten about him. "Hello, Quint. How've you been?"

"Fine." Quint's single-word answer seemed to hang there, leaving nothing to follow it.

Cat leaped into the void. "We were just on our way to the house to clean up for dinner. We've been down at the barn looking at a new foal."

"It just got borned today," Quint was quick to add.

"Boy or girl?" Logan directed his question at Quint.

"A boy. Do you want to see him?"

"I sure would," Logan replied, then glanced at Cat, the remnants of that smile creasing the corners of his eyes, "but maybe we should wait until after dinner."

"Okay. I gotta go tell Grandpa about the colt," Quint said and took off for the house.

As easily as that, Cat found herself alone in Logan's company. Edgy and too proud to show it, she slipped the ends of her fingers into the pockets of her jeans and started toward the house. Logan joined her.

"You're early," she commented, for a moment irritated by that.

"Nerves, I guess," he said, his eyes tracking Quint.

"You?" Cat looked at him in surprise.

His sidelong glance held a measure of challenge. "Does it come as such a shock that I have feelings?"

"Not exactly." To her, he always seemed so strong and self-contained that she had never thought of him as being in any way vulnerable.

"The desire for a child is as old as life on this planet. Seeing him stirs emotions I didn't know I had. I expect you've known that a lot longer than I have."

"Yes." She hadn't thought he could feel the kind of love she did for Quint. She needed to revise her thinking, and the prospect didn't sit too well.

"You haven't told Quint anything about me?" The inflection of his voice made it a question.

"I didn't have a chance. He's been so excited about the colt that—" Cat stopped in midsentence and sighed. "Truthfully, I couldn't think of a good way to tell him."

"I doubt there is one."

Later, Quint provided an opening for them when they went to the broodmare barn after dinner. He hung halfway over the top of the stall, the toes of his boots hooked on a lower board and his elbows pressed against the top rail to hold him in place. Logan and Cat stood on either side of him.

As before, he was intent on the foal, watching while it nursed, braced on legs not quite steady, its whisk broom of a tail swishing briskly.

"That colt's like me," Quint announced in his matter-of-fact way.

"How's that?" Logan eyed him curiously.

"'Cause he's got a mom to look after him, but no dad."

Cat paled, her glance shooting over Quint to lock with Logan's. "That isn't true, Quint," she rushed guiltily. "You do have a dad. I should have told you about him before."

He glanced back at her, his eyes roundly interested. "Where is he?"

"Here," Logan said quietly, and Quint turned his way, his brows drawing together in a sharp, questioning frown. "I'm Logan Echohawk, your father. Your mother and I planned to tell you that today."

"You're my dad?" he repeated with an element of doubt.

"That's right." Logan nodded, a new warmth in

his eyes. "We kinda look like each other. You have my hair and eyes, and you're long and skinny, just like I was at your age."

Straightening, Quint swung a leg over the stall partition, straddling it to face Logan. He wore a look of concentration as he studied Logan's hair, eyes, and face. The silence stretched into seconds before he finally tipped his head to one side and asked, "Where have you been?"

Of all the questions Cat had thought he might ask, this one was unexpected. There was a quality in it of a child searching for a lost parent and finally finding him. It moved her and confirmed the need for Quint to be united with his father.

"I was working for the government a long way from here," Logan replied.

Quint digested that information, then asked, "Were you a sheriff then, too?"

"I was a kind of sheriff, yes."

"Did Mom know where you were?"

"No, I didn't tell her."

"'Cause it was dangerous?" he asked in a half-hopeful voice.

"It could have been," Logan conceded. "After I came here, the first time I saw you, I thought your uncle Ty was your daddy. Then I talked to your mother and she set me straight."

"Are you going to leave again?"

"No, I'm here for good."

"Does that mean you're going to live with us?"

Logan nodded. "After your mother and I get married."

Quint turned to Cat. "When will that be?"

"In a couple of days."

"Oh." A rustling of straw distracted him. Quint turned to watch the colt's uncoordinated attempt to explore its new surroundings. The mare nickered to it, summoning it back to her side. "What does a dad do?"

"What do you and your mom do together?" Logan countered.

His slender shoulders lifted in a high shrug. "Sometimes we go riding. When it's warm enough, we go swimming in the river. And we go to the cemetery a lot."

Logan's glance flicked to Cat. There was a heat in it that burned. But his voice was remarkably calm and level when he asked, with seemingly casual interest, "What do you do at the cemetery?"

"We visit my grandma's grave and Repp's, sometimes Nana Ruth's, too. Sometimes we put flowers on them, and sometimes we just look," Quint replied, then frowned curiously. "My mom loved Repp. Does she love you?"

"Honestly, Quint." Cat managed a stilted laugh, an uncomfortable warmth staining her cheeks. "I have never known you to ask so many questions. As for me loving Logan, I will love your father forever for giving me you." She thought she had dodged Quint's question quite handily while still being truthful. "I think that's enough for a while. Molly's out in the corral. I'll bet your dad would like to see your horse."

Quint shook his head. "He's already seen her. We rode Molly together." He unstraddled the board and jumped to the concrete alleyway. "I'd rather go down to the river. Uncle Ty takes me fishing sometimes. He says fly-fishing is an art."

"Your uncle is right." Logan strolled along with him when Quint moved toward the sunshine that streamed through the open barn door. Cat was slow to follow, but neither appeared to notice. Being ignored was a new experience for her, one she didn't particularly like.

Quint released a long sigh. "I'm not very good at fly-fishing."

"I've heard it takes a lot of practice."

"Can you fly-fish?"

"About as well as you can."

"It must take a lot of practice," Quint concluded as they passed into the bright light of afternoon. He walked a few paces, absorbed in his own thoughts. At last, he tipped his head back. "If you're my dad, how come we don't have the same name?"

"Because your mother and I weren't married when you were born," Logan explained. "After the wedding, we'll have yours legally changed to Quint Echohawk."

"Echohawk," Quint repeated. "That sounds like an Indian name. Are you an Indian?"

"My mother was half-Sioux."

"Does that mean I'm an Indian?"

"You're part Sioux."

"Do you live in a tepee?" Quint's eyes got big at the thought.

"I'm afraid not." A wry smile slanted Logan's mouth. "I live in a house the same as you do."

"That's too bad." Quint kicked at a rock. "I think I would like living in a tepee."

The remark was nothing more than a little boy's idle fantasy. Cat knew that, yet it hurt to see how quickly he embraced the things from Logan's world.

Convincing herself that the two of them needed time alone to get acquainted, she angled toward the house. "You guys have fun," she called. "I'll see you later."

Quint stopped, staring at her with a stricken look. "Aren't you coming with us to the river, Mom?"

"No, I thought I'd help Jessy with the dinner dishes."

"But we want you to come with us," Quint protested in a half-fretful tone.

"Yes, we'd both like you to come," Logan added his voice to the request.

Cat resisted their appeal with a smile and a small lift of her chin. "You don't need me along."

A quicksilver gleam of amusement glittered in Logan's eyes. "I think we may have ignored your mother, Quint," he said in a low aside to him. "Women don't like to be ignored."

"It isn't that at all," Cat insisted, flushing at his infuriatingly astute observation. "I just don't happen to be dressed for the river." She touched the white slacks she wore, using them as an excuse.

"We won't go where it's muddy, Mom."

"We forgot to use the magic word, Quint," Logan said. "*Please* will you come with us?"

"Yes, please, Mom."

Quint's heartfelt pleas were more than she could ignore. "All right, if it's that important to you, I'll come."

All smiles, Quint grabbed her hand and kept a tight hold on it all the way to the sloping bank of the river. They paused on the high side of the slope, shaded by the patulous branches of a towering cottonwood tree. Overhead, saw-toothed leaves clattered together, stirred by a soft wind.

"Is this where you swim?" Logan asked.

Quint responded with a vigorous nod. "And sometimes we just wade. It feels good when it's hot, doesn't it, Mom?"

"It sure does, but the water is a little cool now."

"It'll feel good when summer comes, though." Logan stood in a relaxed stance, one knee bent and his thumbs hooked in the back pockets of his jeans.

"And when you look over there," Quint pointed across the river, "all that as far as you can see, and even farther, belongs to my grandpa. It's been Calder land for years and years and years."

"That's a long time," Logan acknowledged. "But don't forget, your Sioux ancestors roamed this land long before the first Calder ever set foot on it."

"They did?"

"That's right. The Sioux as well as the Crow and Blackfoot people, along with some Arapaho and Cheyenne."

"Gosh," Quint murmured, plainly impressed. He asked more questions, a child's kind, about feathered warbonnets, moccasins, and tom-toms.

All the stories Cat had told him about the long cattle drives, the stampedes, and wild prairie fires paled against the colorful and exotic images of war paint and buffalo hunts. She thought of the life she had worked so hard to build for him. Then Logan came along, sharp and lethal as an arrow from a bow, and changed it. Possibly forever.

"Mom, can I go down by the water and look for more rocks?" Quint asked, then explained to Logan, "Sometimes you find some really neat rocks here. I got a whole collection of them."

"You'll have to show them to me sometime," he replied.

"Okay. Can I, Mom?"

"May I," she said, automatically correcting his grammar. "Go ahead, but just be careful so you don't fall in."

"I can swim," he countered in mild exasperation.

"You can't if you hit your head and knock yourself out."

He turned to Logan and lifted his hands in a helpless gesture. "Mom worries a lot."

"Your mother is a wise woman," Logan said, but Quint gave no indication that he heard him as he scrambled down the slope. "He's quite a boy, Cat." Logan's glance went to her, his eyes warm with approval. "You've done a good job of raising him."

She was pleased by his compliment, and the discovery annoyed her. "I suppose I should regard that as high praise, considering how selfish and spoiled you think I am."

His eyes narrowed slightly. "You left out proud and pigheaded."

"My mistake."

He let out a sigh, his head turning toward the river. "No, it's mine. I thought we had come to a truce. I should have known better."

Stung to find herself in the wrong, Cat said in her own defense, "None of this is easy for me, Logan."

"Do you think it's any easier for me?"

"Probably not," she conceded with great reluctance, well aware there was danger in caring about his feelings, in fulfilling his needs and wants.

Somewhere among the masking trunks of the tree-lined river bank, there was the idle stomp of a hoof, followed by a rolling, outblown breath. Logan swung in the direction of it.

At the water's edge, Quint heard it, too, and looked up, raised a hand in a saluting wave. "Hi, Uncle Culley," he said and immediately went back to his rock collecting.

Culley walked his horse from among the trees, slouching in the saddle, his hat pulled low on his forehead. Beneath the brim, his glance snaked from Cat to Logan and back. He reined in near her, hesitated a moment, then swung out of the saddle, his legs bowing a little when he stepped to the ground.

"Afternoon, O'Rourke." Logan nodded to him, his eyes studying him in a watchful way.

Culley nodded back, then centered on Cat. "You okay?"

The simple concern in his eyes made it easy for her to smile. "I'm fine."

His glance skipped to Quint, then over to Logan. "I guess he knows."

"Yes." Cat glanced at Logan and missed the glimmer of satisfaction that showed so briefly in Culley's expression. Logan didn't.

"What happens now?" Culley fiddled with the reins, sliding them back and forth between his fingers.

"We're getting married as soon as it can be arranged." Saying the words brought back the clutching of her stomach and the swift rush of nerves. She had been railroaded into this agreement, both by her father and by Logan. She could fight it, even now. But she had given her word, and a Calder didn't give his word, then try to back out of it. Honor bound her to the agreement she had made, no matter how much she regretted it. But that didn't mean she had to pretend to like it.

"Are you okay with that?" Culley eyed her with a sidelong look.

"I agreed to it."

Culley dipped his head. "I guess it's all but done, then."

"Yes."

"Hey, Mom!" Quint shouted, waving a hand to summon her. "Come look at this."

Logan watched as Cat made her way down the sloping bank to Quint's side. There was something half-angry and half-possessive in the way he looked at her, Culley noted. It was the look of a man seeing a desirable woman and resisting the lusting urges rising up in him. It worried Culley a little.

"I guess she and the kid will be livin' with you now," Culley ventured.

Logan's glance jerked to Culley, his expression once again wearing that cool, impartial look of a cop. "After the wedding, they will."

Culley's gaze bored into him, green and icy hot. "She's been hurt a lot in this life. I'd like to think she'll be safe with you."

Logan had the distinct impression that if she wasn't, he'd find himself coming to blows with the old man. "She'll be safe."

"She better be." It was a warning, clear and simple. "She's all I got left in this world." Drawing the reins up, he turned to his horse and looped them over its neck.

"We'll see you at the wedding," Logan said.

Culley threw a look at The Homestead and gave what passed for a shrug, then slipped a toe into the stirrup and stepped into the saddle, without a single creak of rubbing leather. The horse instantly moved out at a soft-footed walk.

NINETEEN

The guineas set up a racket when the pickup came rattling up the rutted and weed-choked lane. Pulling into the ranch yard of the old Simpson place, Rollie swung the wheel toward the house trailer, his face grimy and streaked with black coal dust from his day's work in the strip mine. In his idle sweep of the yard, his glance briefly touched on the wiry, thin figure of his mother, coming from the direction of the old barn, the vegetable basket under her arm mounded with fresh lettuce.

"You're late." The sharpness of her voice turned the observation into a criticism when he climbed out of the truck.

"I had to stop for gas." Rollie gave his ponytail a quick flip, lifting it off his sweaty neck and letting it fall back, a gesture of his discomfort with her reproach.

"Fedderson got his new pumps installed, did he?" She continued toward the trailer.

Rollie nodded. "They finished hooking them up early this afternoon. Nearly every vehicle in town was there waiting to get gassed up." He looked around. "Where's Lath?"

"He's been messing around all day fixing up that old root cellar. I expect he's still at it," she said. "Leastways, come canning time, I'll have a place to store all our vegetables."

The root cellar was more like a cave that had been dug out of the hillside. The instant Emma had learned of its existence, she had insisted that the house trailer be positioned near it.

"I hope he shored up that one beam." Rollie glanced toward the cellar's entrance, its framework slanted to match the slope of the hill. Its warped and weathered wooden door lay open at a crooked angle, a visible reminder that it needed new hinges as well as boards. "I heard a bunch of hammering earlier, so I expect he has. I wouldn't worry about Lath. He knows what he's doing." Something in her voice insinuated that Rollie didn't.

Rollie smothered the flare of resentment and bowed his head, accepting that he would never be equal to his brother in her eyes.

"Hey, Rollie!" Lath waved to him from the cellar's tunnellike opening. "Come take a look at this. Not you, Ma," he added when she started toward him as well. "This isn't something you should know about."

Without questioning his decision, Emma resumed her course to the trailer steps. His curiosity heightened, Rollie headed for the root cellar as Lath ducked back inside it.

An electric work light hung from one of the overhead beams, and it lit all but the corners of the earthen cellar. Sidestepping the extension cord that ran to it, Rollie walked a few feet inside and stopped in surprise. On all three sides there were nothing but shelves, stacked three high, strung with cobwebs and coated with a decade's accumulation of dirt.

"Lath?" He turned in a complete circle, his

searching glance ransacking every dark corner. But there was no sign of his brother. "Lath, where the hell are you?"

The musty smell of bare earth and stale air pressed in around him. The silence of the place was suddenly eerie. The skin along the back of his neck crawled with it.

"Damn it, Lath," he swore, angry now. "I don't know what kind of trick this is—"

"No trick, little brother," was the muffled reply. "Just a hidden door."

The short shelving on the back wall moved, one side swinging open. A grinning Lath poked his head out, a flashlight in hand.

"Care to come into my parlor?" he invited. "Watch the corners of those shelves, though. I need to make them narrower."

Rollie had to squeeze through the opening, made tight by the jutting shelves. On the other side was near-total darkness. The play of Lath's flashlight beam ran over dirt walls that confined an area of roughly four by five feet.

"I didn't know this was here," Rollie murmured.

"It wasn't. I took out the shelving that was in this area, used some of the old boards from the barn to create a false wall, then covered it with part of the old shelves. Clever, huh?"

"It's clever all right, but what's it for?"

"I needed someplace to stash the shipment of automatic rifles I've got to pick up."

"Rifles?"

"That's right, little brother. Rifles." Lath clamped a hand on his shoulder and steered him toward the narrow doorway. "You don't think I've just been sitting on my hands while you've been working all day?"

Crowded by Lath, Rollie pushed his way through

the opening, then turned on him. "You aren't selling guns again, are you?" It was an accusation rather than a question.

"Now, I know what you're thinking, little brother." Lath held up his hands in a placating gesture. "But I made the mistake of selling to somebody I didn't know once. I'm not about to repeat that. I'm buying from a guy I've known for years and I'm selling to one I've known even longer. Neither one of 'em can afford to turn informant."

"Just make sure you leave me the hell out of it," Rollie warned.

"Whatever you say. But I will need you to drive me into Blue Moon tonight. I finally talked that Kershner fella into sellin' me his van with only three hundred dollars down."

"Only three hundred dollars? Damn it, Lath, I haven't got three hundred to spare, not if I'm gonna make the trailer payment on time."

Lath drew back his head in feigned surprise. "Did I ask you for the money, little brother?"

"You didn't have to," Rollie answered in disgust. "You've been bumming money off me ever since you came back."

"And you're such an easy touch, you keep forkin' it over." He grinned and sauntered over to a rusty metal canister sitting by a shelving post on the cellar's dirt floor. Squatting beside it, he wiped his mouth on the sleeve of his T-shirt, pried off the metal lid, then reached inside and pulled out a thick wad of bills. Rollie's mouth dropped open when he saw the amount of money still left in the can.

"How much is in there?" he breathed the words.

"Close to ten thousand. I got a can with another twenty thousand buried at the southeast corner of the barn." Lath paused in his counting of the money and grinned up at him. "You don't think I spent all that time in prison without some seed money waitin' for me when I got out."

"You mean . . . you have nearly thirty thousand dollars?" Rollie had trouble absorbing that.

"And this gun deal comin' up is gonna net me another five." He raised an eyebrow in open mockery. "Do you still want me to leave you out of the deal?"

Almost woodenly, Rollie walked over to the can, needing to touch the bills and make sure they were genuine. "You made all this from selling guns," he murmured, awestruck.

"Nope. This is only what I managed to save. I did me some livin' with the rest."

Rollie frowned. "If you had all this, why didn't you send Ma some when she was needin' it?"

"I couldn't get to it, not without taking the risk of those Treasury boys following me and seizing it like they did just about everything else I had. 'Sides, even if I had, we both know she would have plowed the money back into the damned farm. This way's better."

"Jeezus, we're rich," Rollie murmured, lovingly fingering the bills. "I can quit my job—"

"Not so fast, little brother." Lath pulled the canister away from him and stuffed the excess bills back inside, pocketing the rest. "You gotta keep that job. One of us has to be makin' an income people can see. That was another mistake I made the last time, flashing more money than I could account for. This time, I'm gonna look poor, live poor, and drive poor, and let people think I'm spongin' off my hard-workin' little brother. In a year, maybe two, I'll have enough that we can blow this place, buy us some new identities, and show Ma the good life."

Seeing all the money turned Rollie into a believer. He watched Lath shove the canister into the black shadows under a shelf. "You aren't going to leave that there, are you?"

"It's okay for now. Later I'll be buryin' it right inside the cellar door." He laid an arm across Rollie's shoulders in a confiding gesture. "I'm tellin' ya that so you'll have it for Ma in case I run into any trouble. Okay?"

"Okay." He was suddenly and deeply moved by the trust Lath was showing in him. He had been the little brother and called the little brother for so long that he'd always felt inadequate. Now, Lath trusted him, and he felt somehow bigger, stronger, more competent.

"I knew I could count on you." Lath slapped his back. "Come on. Let's go get cleaned up. We're both about as rank as an old man's dirty laundry."

It wasn't until he was out of the shower that Rollie remembered the news he'd heard in town. He padded into the kitchen, a towel wrapped around his hips and water still dripping from his long hair. His mother was at the sink, peeling potatoes to add to the roast in the oven. Lath sat on the kitchen counter, a beer in his hand, watching her.

"I forgot to tell you—I saw Reverend Pattersby in at Fedderson's getting gas. You'll never guess where he was going."

"To hell?" Lath grinned.

Emma pressed a hand to her mouth, smothering a girlish titter. "Lath, you're awful."

"No, it was better than that. He was heading out to the Triple C. Echohawk's marrying Cat Calder, and Pattersby's performing the ceremony."

Lath pushed off the counter, surprise digging a deep furrow across his forehead. "Echohawk is marrying the Calder girl?"

"That's what Pattersby said."

"I never heard any talk about him seeing her," he mused aloud.

"He's marrying a tramp, that's what he's doing." At the sink, the paring knife flashed with new fury, sending strips of potato peelings flying into the air. "Her and that little bastard of hers."

Rollie had saved the juiciest tidbit for last. "There's some that are speculating Echohawk is the kid's father."

"Wouldn't that be interesting." Lath arched an eyebrow, then took a thoughtful swig of beer and gazed off into the middle distance.

"It'd be just like Calder to hold a shotgun wedding."

A short, heavy breath of disgust came from the sink area. "A wedding won't change the fact that she isn't fit to be called a mother, Calder or no," Emma declared, her thin body stiff with outrage. "If there was any justice in this world, she woulda known the pain of somebody takin' her son from her long before now."

Rollie scoffed, "Come on, Ma. She's a Calder. Such a thing will never happen."

"I wouldn't be too sure about that, little brother." A hint of slyness crept into Lath's smile. "I wouldn't be too sure about that at all."

"What do you mean?" Rollie asked, with an interest he wouldn't have had a week ago.

Still smiling, Lath kept his own counsel and tipped the bottle to his mouth, downing another long swallow of beer.

Cat stood motionless in front of the tall cheval mirror, her fingers clasped around a pearl necklace. A tap at her bedroom door broke across her thoughts. Looking into the mirror once more, she raised the strand of pearls to her neck and checked to make certain her expression revealed none of the wild jittering of her nerves, then called, "Come in."

The mirror reflected her brother's image when the door opened. "Is Reverend Pattersby here? I thought I heard a car drive up."

"He's downstairs." Ty came up behind her, his dark eyes meeting the green of hers in the mirror.

"I'm almost ready." She fumbled with the clasp, then gave up before her already thin nerves snapped. "Would you fasten this for me? I seem to be all thumbs."

"Sure." He took the two ends from her, the work-roughened backs of his fingers brushing against the skin of her neck while Cat held the weight of her long hair up and away from it. "These are Mother's pearls, aren't they?"

"Yes." She touched the front of them. "I always planned to wear them on my wedding day."

She didn't bother to add that she had always thought she would be marrying Repp. The memory of it clouded her eyes for a moment before she pushed it away and ran an assessing glance over her reflection. The dress she had chosen to wear was made of crepe de chine. The muted shades of teal and lavender draped and floated around her slender, curved figure. The design was simple and elegantly understated, but the effect was much more romantic than she would have liked. Given a choice, Cat would have grabbed something out of the closet and called it good enough. But the dress, like the ceremony, was for Quint's benefit.

"Cat." Ty's hands shifted to the rounded points of her shoulders. "It isn't too late to change your mind. If you do, I'll stand with you."

She thought about it for all of two seconds, then gave a small, sideways shake of her head. "No. I've agreed to this."

When she would have moved away from him, his hands tightened to stop her. "Cat, there is only one thing worse than making a mistake, and that's refusing to admit it. Ask me. I know."

Turning to face him, Cat struggled to show him a calmness she didn't feel. "I promise you this, Ty. If I discover this is an awful mistake, you'll be the first one I'll tell."

"You'd better." Despite the serious gleam in his eyes, his mouth quirked in a smile that disappeared under a corner of his mustache. "That's what big brothers are for, you know."

"I'm counting on that." From the hallway came the clatter of feet running up the stairs, a familiar sound that was distinctively Quint's own. "It sounds like Dad has sent up reinforcements to hurry me along."

This time Ty didn't try to hold her when Cat moved away from him. A second later, Quint pushed the door open and said, in a loud stage whisper, "Mom, everybody's waiting for you."

Seeing him clad in his dress pants, white shirt, and clip-on tie, his hair slicked in a neat side part, Cat knew her choice of dress had been right. Five years old or not, she didn't underestimate his powers of observation. If she had chosen less than her best, he would have noticed and wondered.

"Go tell them I'm coming," she said.

"Okay." Off he dashed with the message, leaving the bedroom door ajar.

Turning, Cat ran smoothing hands over the bodice of her dress, her nerves all raw and edgy again. She inhaled a quick, steadying breath. "Shall we?" she murmured, her glance ricocheting off Ty as she moved toward the door.

The ceremony was to take place in the den. There would be no flowers, no glow of candlelight, no horde of guests, no bridal bouquet, no wedding march, no veil for the groom to lift, no cake to cut, no pelting rice on the newlyweds. The lack of all that should have made it easier. It didn't.

As she approached the set of double doors, Cat fought the urge to slow her steps. Entering the room, her glance went first to Quint, noting the look of pleasure that leaped into his eyes when he saw her. But it was the sight of Logan standing next to her father that halted her.

He was dressed in a dark suit, impeccably tailored to fit his wide shoulders without a wrinkle. The dark color of it pointed up the blackness of his hair and intensified the smoke-gray of his eyes. The suit changed his image, gave power and polish to his lean and chiseled features. The result was dangerously gorgeous.

Cat recalled Logan's mentioning to Quint that he had worked for the government, a world where a suit and tie were common dress for a man. She was reminded again of how little she knew about him.

Ty shifted closer to her, touching her arm and murmuring in concern, "Cat."

She walked forward with a falsely confident step, conscious of Logan's eyes on her all the way. Deliberately ignoring him, Cat fixed her gaze on the minister.

After a brief exchange of greetings, Reverend Pattersby inquired, with an avidly interested glance at each of them, "Shall we begin?"

"Please." Never in her life had Cat been so eager to get something over with as she was this. Anything to end this uneven thudding of her heart.

The minister opened his book, intoning the familiar words, "Dearly beloved . . ."

Facing him, with Logan standing close enough that their arms brushed, Cat knew why a bride normally carried a bouquet. It gave her something to do with her hands.

The problem was eliminated a moment later as her father stepped forward, asserting his right to give her in marriage and placing her hand in Logan's. The warm, solid strength of Logan's easy grip ignited new quivers of awareness.

When it came time to recite her vows, Cat made the mistake of looking up. "I, Cathleen Elizabeth Calder"—his compelling gray eyes wouldn't let her look away— "take thee, Logan Andrew Echohawk . . ."

She hated the breathy quality of her voice, the suggestion of emotion in it. She blamed it on nerves and the strain of the moment. ". . . forsaking all others, till death do us part," she finished and saw the quick, hard gleam of satisfaction darken his eyes.

It was his turn now, and his voice was strong with conviction as he made his vows to her. She could almost believe that he meant every word of them.

"Will there be an exchange of rings?" Reverend Pattersby asked in a soft undertone.

"Yes." Logan produced a matching pair of plain gold bands from his suit pocket.

Cat stiffened in instant protest. More vows—she didn't want to make any more meaningless vows. Tense with anger, she went through all the motions and said all the right words, then bowed her head in prayer, relieved that it was nearly finished.

"By the power vested in me, I now pronounce you man and wife," the minister proclaimed, then added the usual encouragement, "You may kiss the bride."

Trained to observe every small, subtle shift of expressions, Logan saw the flicker of resentment in Cat's eyes before she moved to kiss him. He felt the cool impersonal brush of her closed lips and discovered a new meaning for the term *lip service.* Irritated by it, he cupped his hand behind her neck, not letting her draw back, and brought his mouth against hers with warm, nuzzling pressure.

Her lips softened under the coaxing stimulation of kiss. It was the response he'd been seeking. But he found he wanted more than that.

Before he could take the kiss deeper, the minister coughed delicately. Logan lifted his head and saw with satisfaction the dazed light in her eyes. Abruptly she turned her head from him, but not before he saw the glimmer of fear that replaced that look.

It stopped him. Fear was the last emotion he wanted to arouse in her.

During the brief, and slightly awkward, round of congratulations that followed, Logan spotted Quint, hanging back from the group. He called him forward and lifted him into his arms.

"Are we a family now?" Quint asked.

"We sure are," Logan replied.

"Is that why you kissed her?"

Cat stiffened beside him. His glance slid over her, noting the smoothness of her expression. "It's one of the reasons," Logan replied.

As soon as the license was signed and witnessed, a light supper was served in the dining room. Reverend Pattersby did full justice to the fare that was offered, which was more than Cat was able to do. To her relief, he refused an after-dinner cup of coffee, insisting that he needed to be on his way. Seizing the excuse to escape, Cat offered to accompany him to the door. The quick lift of his eyebrow advised her that Reverend Pattersby regarded it as a highly unusual thing for a bride to do. The eyebrow fell when Logan came up behind her, seconding the offer.

Together they walked him to the door. Closing it

behind him, Cat turned, sliding a glance off Logan. "At least, that's over."

He nodded a silent agreement. "Where are your suitcases? I might as well get them loaded in the truck."

"My suitcases?" she repeated, then sighed in irritation. "Don't you think a honeymoon is carrying this farce a little too far?"

"It would be, but that wasn't my intention." His gaze narrowed on her in sudden suspicion. "You haven't packed, have you?"

"Why should I?" she countered.

"Because we'll be going home shortly."

"Home," she echoed in shock. Even when she realized the meaning of his words, she resisted it. "This is home. I've already fixed up one of the guest rooms for you—"

"No."

"Why not?" Cat rushed. "What possible difference could it make where we live?"

"Isn't it obvious? I have a ranch, Cat. That means I have chores and responsibilities there. If I have to drive back and forth, plus commute to my job, there wouldn't be any time left to spend with my son. Or had you thought of that?"

"No. I just assumed—nothing was ever said—it never occurred to me we would live anywhere else."

He expelled a long sigh. "It seems we both made some wrong assumptions. We should have discussed it, I guess."

"I'll talk to Dad," she said, certain there would be a way around this. "We can arrange for one of our men to look after your—"

"No," Logan broke in, sharp and decisive. "It's my ranch and my responsibility. I don't need your father's help with it. And I'm not about to accept simply because you want to stay here—in your father's house."

"But it's my home—and Quint's home," Cat argued.

"Not anymore. Not for a year," he added, reminding her of the agreement they had made.

In the face of that, there was no argument Cat could make. "It will take me some time to pack."

"For now, just take what you and Quint will need tonight. In the morning, you can come back and pack the rest of your things."

"Very well," she accepted the logic of his suggestion.

But a half-formed fear gnawed at Cat all the way to her room. It wasn't until she saw her bed that she understood the reason for it. She felt safe here, safe from this marriage she had made. Here in this house, she would have had the distraction of family. They would have served as a buffer to keep Logan at a distance. Conversation would have been easy.

Sharing a house, just the three of them, was a whole different story. Meals, bedtimes, morning, nights, constantly in each other's company—how on earth was she going to do it?

Quint stood in the seat between them, all eyes when the pickup pulled into the ranch yard. Sunset flamed across the western sky, casting its rosy hue over the buildings and the single-story house.

"Is this your ranch?" Quint asked.

"This is it." Logan swung the pickup toward the house.

"It isn't very big, is it?"

"Not as big as your grandfather's, but it's big

enough for one man to handle—if he has some help."

Quint jumped on that. "I can help."

"I'm counting on that." Logan flashed him a smile and switched off the engine.

"Is there some work you need me to do now?" Quint followed Logan, climbing out the driver's side after him, not once glancing in Cat's direction when she opened the passenger door.

"Not tonight, but in the morning, you can help me throw some hay to the horses." He lifted the two overnight bags out of the back of the truck and handed one to Quint. Quint struggled a bit with the weight of it when he set out after Logan.

Cat trailed behind them, staring at the house. It was a homey, rambling affair, with a long front porch complete with a pair of rocking chairs, meant to be used on warm summer evenings. But compared to The Homestead, it was small. She knew it would be impossible not to be aware of someone in the next room.

Ahead of her, Quint dragged his bag up the porch steps, then stopped and looked back. "Are you coming, Mom?"

"Yes." She quickened her steps.

A hinge squeaked a loud protest when Logan opened the screen door.

"I've been meaning to oil that," Logan said, propping the door open with his body and setting the bag at his feet, then digging in his pocket for the house key.

Watching him, Quint cocked his head at a curious angle. "How come you lock it?"

Logan sent an amused look over his shoulder, then glanced at Cat as she climbed the three steps to the porch. "I lived in the city too long, I guess."

"What city?" Quint wanted to know.

"Washington, Saint Louis, but mostly New Orleans."

The tap-tapping of her heels across the porch's wooden floor masked the click of the lock's release. Logan gave the front door a push, swinging it open, then picked up the bag at his feet and took a step forward.

"You aren't going in there, are you, Sheriff?" Quint blurted, then threw a half-worried and half-uncertain look at Cat. Instantly she knew what he was thinking, and a heat started deep in the pit of her stomach and grew from there, along with a mad fluttering of her pulse.

Halted by the question, Logan frowned. "It's our home. Why wouldn't I?"

"But I thought—aren't you supposed—"

"It's all right, Quint," Cat rushed as understanding dawned in Logan's eyes.

Amused, he ran his gaze over her face, studying the tiny signs of discomfort she showed. "That's right. A groom is supposed to carry the bride over the threshold, isn't he? It's a good thing you reminded me, Quint, or I would have forgotten."

"It isn't necessary." It was a useless protest, but Cat had to make it.

"Quint thinks it is, and so do I." Turning, he set the bag inside the door, then pushed the creaking screen door wider, saying to Quint, "Care to hold the door for us?"

"Sure." He hurried to it, his bag thumping against his leg and the porch floor.

When Logan moved toward her, Cat wanted to back away, but she held her ground. With Quint looking on, she wasn't about to cause a scene. Something told her Logan knew that.

He paused beside her, his body momentarily blocking her from Quint's view. "This won't be the first time I've carried you, you know," he murmured for her ears alone.

That was the problem. She remembered too well the sensation of being cradled in his strong arms, that sense of being protected, cared for, and, most of all, safe.

His arm slid behind her back. In the next second, he was effortlessly scooping her up, catching skirt and all. Reflex had her hands reaching up to circle the muscled column of his neck, her fingers brushing the clipped ends of his hair. His head was tipped toward her. For an instant her eyes collided with the molten gray of his. She looked hurriedly away and held herself stiffly, silently denying that she enjoyed any part of this.

It took only seconds for him to maneuver her through the doorway. But they were excruciatingly long seconds for Cat. The instant he put her down, she took a quick step away from him, needing to break the contact and knit together her tattered composure.

His glance flicked coolly over her before he turned and went back onto the porch. "Come here, sport," he said to Quint. "I'll carry you over, too." He swung Quint up, bag and all, and carried him into the house. "There." He set him down, crouching beside him, a hand cupped around Quint's neck in a man's caress. "That's the way it should be done."

Quint's big smile and the absolute joy in his eyes mingled with a look of wonder when he gazed at Logan. There was little doubt that including Quint in the threshold ceremony had been the right thing to do. It was the second time Logan had made a special point to include Quint. Cat was touched by it, however reluctantly.

TWENTY

I haven't gotten around to doing any painting or fixing up inside," Logan said when Cat turned to look at her new surroundings. "I thought it would be something I could do this winter."

She took a few steps into the sparsely furnished living room, her glance skimming the cream-colored walls, bare of adornment. A fireplace stood in the center of the end wall, its carved mantelpiece and wooden front stained in walnut.

At an angle to the fireplace sat a big easy chair upholstered in a rich green and gold tweed. Finding it much too easy to picture Logan sitting in it, his long legs propped on the matching ottoman, Cat swung her glance to the long sofa, covered in a coordinating dark gold fabric.

"Look, Mom." Quint dragged his overnight bag over to an old platform rocker, the only other large piece of furniture in the room. "The sheriff has a fireplace. We can roast marshmallows in it just like at home."

"We sure can," Cat was determined that Quint would continue to regard the Triple C as his real home.

He turned earnest eyes on Logan. "I like 'em best when they're brown on the outside and all warm and gooey on the inside. I don't like 'em when they get burnt. Do you?"

"I don't know," Logan replied. "I've never roasted marshmallows."

"You haven't?" Quint couldn't have been more astonished.

"Nope." His gray eyes crinkled at the corners. "Sounds like I have a treat in store for me."

"We can fix you some, can't we, Mom? Mom knows how to do it real good."

"I'll bet she does," he agreed, his glance running soberly to her. "Would you like to see the rest of the house?"

"Please." Although she didn't really want a guided tour, Cat recognized it would be the quickest way to orient herself.

Logan took them first to the typically large and roomy ranch kitchen with its white-painted cupboards, long wooden table, and ladder-back chairs. An alcove off the dining area served as a ranch office, complete with an old rolltop desk and a metal filing cabinet.

After pointing out the kitchen's adjoining laundry and utility room with its rear door to the outside, he led them back through the living room to a hallway that branched off it. "The bathroom's down here, along with the bedrooms."

"Which one's mine?" Quint wanted to know.

"This one." Pushing open a door on the right, Logan reached inside and flipped on a wall switch.

Satisfied by the sight of a twin bed, dresser, and a corner chair, Quint then voiced his next concern, "Where do you sleep?"

"Right across the hall." Logan indicated the door on the left side.

Two sharp knocks rattled the screen door. "Any-body home?" came the hesitant call.

"Culley," Cat breathed her uncle's name, relief flooding through her, dissolving the tension that had gripped her ever since they had left The Homestead. "Yes, we're here." She went eagerly to meet him, aware that Logan followed her.

The screen door squeaked noisily when Culley opened it. Once inside, he paused and eased the door closed out of habit. Doffing his hat, he gripped it in both hands and stood uncertainly just inside.

"Hey, Uncle Culley," Quint greeted him with a child's simplistic ease. "Did you know the sheriff married my mom today? This is our new house."

"You did it, then," Culley said with a small, satis-fied nod.

"Yes." Cat unconsciously touched the wedding band on her finger.

His glance went to Quint's overnight bag sitting next to the platform rocker. "Guess you're still get-tin' settled in," he said, turning his hat in his hands.

"I was just giving them a tour through the house," Logan explained. "But it can wait, consider-ing you're our first visitor. How about some coffee?"

"Yes," Cat quickly seconded the invitation. "It won't take but a minute to put some on."

Not giving Culley a chance to refuse, she headed for the kitchen. The others followed at a slower pace. By the time they joined her, Cat had found the cof-fee in a canister and the filters in a cupboard above it.

Within minutes the coffee was brewed and poured, and all three were seated at the kitchen table, with Quint on Cat's lap. The flow of conversa-tion was natural and easy, centering on safe topics like weather and ranching. Listening to the two men exchange information on range conditions they had observed, Cat discovered she could readily imagine other nights spent like this, gathered around the kitchen table drinking coffee and talking.

Quint snuggled more comfortably against her and rested his head on her shoulder. Looking down, she saw the fight he was making to stay awake. Smiling, she smoothed the hair off his forehead.

"I think it's somebody's bedtime," she murmured near his ear.

"Not yet," Quint protested without much strength.

"Yes." She pushed her chair away from the table and stood, shifting her heavy-eyed child to ride on her hip. "Quint has decided to call it a night."

"It's been a long day," Logan observed.

"Yeah." Prompted by Cat, Quint added, "Good night, Uncle Culley. Good night, Sheriff."

They echoed his phrase. For a brief moment, Cat met Logan's glance. His eyes held a soft, warm look of love and understanding, the kind parents exchange when they see their sleepy child. It was intimate, disturbingly so.

The memory of it lingered throughout the nightly ritual of making sure Quint brushed his teeth, listening to his prayers, and tucking him into bed.

Leaving his bedroom door slightly ajar, she exited the room and flipped on the hall light. From the kitchen came the distinctive rubbing scrape of chair legs being pushed over the linoleum floor, followed by footsteps. She was halfway across the living room when Logan and her uncle appeared in the kitchen doorway.

"You aren't leaving already," Cat said on a vague note of alarm.

"It's late," Culley mumbled.

Noting the restless movement of his shoulders, Cat was reminded that her uncle had never been comfortable for long within the confines of four walls. As much as she wanted the insulation of his company, she didn't press him to stay. Instead she companionably linked arms with him.

"Why don't you have supper with us tomorrow night, Uncle Culley." Pushing through the screen door ahead of him, Cat walked onto the front porch.

"I don't know." He threw an uncertain look over his shoulder at Logan.

"We'd like to have you, wouldn't we, Logan?" she challenged when he joined them on the porch.

"Of course." His voice was smooth and very dry.

Culley slanted another look at Logan. "What time?"

"Around seven o'clock," Logan replied.

"Okay." He shoved his hat on and took his leave of them with a quick, nodding bob of his head, then cut an angle down the porch steps and headed toward the shed barn, moving with a soft-footed silence.

Cat gazed after him, tracking his progress until night's gathering shadows swallowed him. "I hadn't realized he had gotten so thin," she murmured in concern. "I've always known he doesn't cook for himself, just opens up a can, sometimes eating right out of it. But his arm felt like only bone and sinew just now."

"You don't need to justify the invitation, Cat." Logan sounded half-irritated.

It spun her around. "I wasn't justifying anything. I was making an observation."

Logan felt the sizzle in the air and knew the tension between them came from more than just anger. It hardened him. "If you say so. In any case, I agree it will probably be best for a while to have your uncle take his meals with us. It might make them less awkward for both of us until we get used to this—" He stopped, his mouth quirking in a humorless, almost bitter, line. "I don't know what to call it. That ring on your finger says you're my wife, but this isn't a marriage."

"No, it isn't." She felt something that was very much like regret, which made no sense at all. "It's a bit like having a stranger for a roommate."

The breath he expelled was heavy with irony. "We aren't strangers, either, Cat." Reaching up, he loosened the knot of his tie and unfastened the collar button on his dress shirt, a certain weariness in the gesture. "It would make it a lot easier if we were. Instead of trying to deny this physical thing between us, we'd be exploring it to see where it led."

"But that's all it is—physical."

"Are you sure?"

She ignored the swift rise of her heartbeat and unconsciously twisted the gold band around her finger. "I'm sure. You forget that I know what love is."

"Ah, yes, the boyfriend. How could I forget him." The amused disdain in his voice had her temper simmering again. "He's dead, Cat."

"That doesn't change how much I loved him," she fired back.

"Loved. Past tense," he countered smoothly. "As I recall, that night in Fort Worth you wanted to feel alive."

"And look what happened." She turned from him, folding her arms tightly across her middle.

"Yes, we have a beautiful son now." He dragged the tie from around his neck and jammed it in a jacket pocket. "Maybe you regret that night, but I don't."

"Of course not. You enjoyed yourself immensely."

"And you didn't, I suppose?" he mocked, then snapped his fingers. "That's right, I forgot—you were drunk that night and can't remember. But I can."

Without warning, without Cat even noticing the step he took to bridge the distance between them, he was inches from her. Too stunned to react, she stood there, unable to breathe, unable to move, her pulse racing.

"Everything about that night was branded in my mind." His voice was husky and thick, vibrating between anger and some other emotion. "I remember everything about it—the way you felt, the way you tasted, the way you moved against me."

She bowed her head with a small denying shake and tried to shut out the memories his words evoked. "I don't want to hear this."

"Hear what?" he taunted softly, his hands sliding onto the curve of her hips and exerting little pressure to draw her to him. "The way we fit together like we were made for each other?"

The contact with his long, muscled thighs brought her head up. She flattened her hands on his chest to keep some space between them. The intensity of his eyes blocked any other protest.

"Or"—his face drifted closer—"don't you want to hear about all the places I found where you had dabbed your perfume?" Her eyes closed of their own accord when his mouth grazed across her cheekbone to nuzzle the sensitive hollow below her ear, then came back to tease the corner of her lips, his breath warming them. But she refused to turn to them.

"Or the way you moaned when I touched you." His hand cruised experimentally up the side of her ribs to her breast, his thumb stroking the underside of it.

Cat bit back another moan, conscious of the building ache inside. Strength seeped from the muscles in her arms until her hands no longer pressed against him in resistance. She could feel the heat of his skin through his shirt and the heavy thud of his heart. She hated this needy weakness she felt, born out of a desire to feel all those sensations again.

"And I know you don't want to hear about the empty places I filled in you." His lips moved lightly over hers, forming the words as he spoke. "Or all the empty places you filled in me."

That grudging admission broke the few restraints she had left, her lips parting on an indrawn breath of surprise. His mouth was quick to close over them, revealing the hunger he felt for her.

For too long she had denied her own passions and desires, pretended that she didn't need the satisfaction that could be found in a lover's arms. But they were an instinct as basic as life, and too strong to ever be completely repressed.

When he started to break off the kiss, Cat murmured an indistinct protest, her fingers curling into his white shirt. His mouth came back before all contact was broken, this time with a heat that devoured.

It was what she wanted; Cat knew that. She wanted him as desperately as she had that night in Fort Worth. This time he was her husband. The weight of the wedding band on her finger was evidence of that. There was no reason not to know the pleasures to be had in his arms. It was absolutely natural and right.

He lifted his head, his eyes heavy-lidded, his breathing as rough and ragged as her own. "You want me now. Admit it."

There was anger in his challenge. Cat reacted to it.

"Yes," she hissed the answer and saw the quick darkening of triumph in his eyes. "You can make me want you, Logan. But you can't make me love you."

"No," he said slowly, his expression hardening. "No, I certainly can't do that."

The instant she felt the loosening of his arms, Cat

pulled away from him and moved toward the door. "If you'll excuse me, I think I'll call it a night. One way or another, it's been a very trying day." She pulled open the screen door, the *screech* of its hinge slicing across her raw nerves like chalk across a blackboard. Halfway through the door, she paused and looked back at him with a stiff little toss of her head. "I assume the room at the end of the hall is mine."

He looked at her for a long, hard second. "No," he said flatly and started forward. "It isn't."

Something in his purposeful stride had Cat stepping quickly into the house. "Then exactly which one is mine?" She continued to retreat from him when he followed her into the living room.

"Truthfully—none of them."

"Precisely what does that mean?" An ugly suspicion formed. She stopped, her hands coming to a rest on her hips. "When I agreed to this marriage, I told you I would not share your bed," she informed him, ready to do battle on that point.

"And I told you that was your choice." He took her by the arms and moved her out of his way, then walked into the hall.

"Wait a minute." Cat went after him. "Where am I supposed to sleep?"

"That's your choice." He disappeared into the bedroom across the hall from Quint's.

Cat wasn't about to follow him there. "In that case, I'll take the spare room." Passing his door, she continued down the hall.

"It's full of boxes," he said from the bedroom. "If you don't believe me, you're welcome to look for yourself."

That sounded suspiciously like the truth. Wheeling around, Cat marched back to his bedroom doorway. "Would you kindly tell me where you expect me to sleep?"

He came out carrying a pillow, a blanket, and a bedsheet. "The floor or the sofa, take your pick." Unceremoniously he dumped them in her arms.

"What?" she said, her mouth agape.

"I recommend the sofa. The floor can be a bit hard."

She stared at him. "You can't be serious."

"I'm very serious," Logan responded coolly.

Cat sputtered for an indignant moment. "You should be the one sleeping on the sofa, not me."

"Take another look at the sofa. It's about six inches too short for me, but it's about the right size for you." His mouth quirked in a cold smile. "Consider it an example of equal opportunity in action." He started to turn away, then stopped. "Don't forget to lock up before you turn in."

With that, he walked into the bedroom and shut the door. Cat stared at it, still wavering between fury and astonishment. Her first impulse was to charge in and throw the bedding at him. But that would put her in his bedroom, the last place she wanted to be.

Faced with no other satisfactory option, she strode into the living room and tossed the bedding on the sofa. In quick order, she closed the front door, locked the dead bolt, retrieved her overnight bag by the door, and disappeared into the bathroom, every movement sharp and brisk with controlled anger. Minutes later she came out, her temper still simmering, a robe of peacock blue satin hanging open over her matching nightgown, her face scrubbed clean of makeup. She set the overnight bag next to the ancient and ugly platform rocker, laid her dress and undergarments across its seat, made up her bed on the sofa, then checked Quint one last time. Leaving the hall light on for him, she turned out the rest of the lights and shrugged out of her robe, draping it over an arm of the sofa before crawling beneath the covers of her makeshift bed.

From Logan's room came the telltale creak of bedsprings. Cat gave her pillow a vicious punch and rolled onto her side.

"Some wedding night," she thought, and suddenly found herself fighting tears.

Logan's mental alarm clock went off promptly at five o'clock, as always. Dawn's pearl-gray light shone through the bedroom windows. Rolling over, he sat on the bed, stretching his shoulders in a flexing shrug in an attempt to throw off the heavy tension that continued to grip him. From childhood, he had been a light sleeper, able to come fully awake and alert in an instant. But last night had been a restless one, dogged by the knowledge that Cat—his wife—was in the living room. That thought brought back all of last night's needs and frustrations.

He pushed off the bed, all taut energy again with no release available. Crossing to the chair, Logan snatched his suit pants up and stepped into them, pulling them on over his briefs. Barefoot, he padded into the bathroom, steadfastly refusing to glance toward the living room.

A shower wasn't part of his routine first thing in the morning. That would come later, before he changed into his uniform and assumed his role as acting sheriff.

Back during the years he had lived in the city, he would have used these early morning hours to go for a ten-mile run, work out in the gym, or spend time on the shooting range. Now he spent the hours checking cattle, fixing fence, and making any needed repairs or improvements plus half a hundred other chores—seasonal or otherwise—that had to be done on the ranch.

But none of it before he had his morning coffee.

Fully dressed in boots, jeans, and a work shirt, Logan came out of the spare bedroom and headed for the kitchen. All his fine resolve not to look at Cat went up in smoke when he caught a glimpse of her out of the corner of his eye. It stopped him, turned him, and held him motionless.

She was stretched on her side, her eyes closed in sleep, her black lashes lying thick and full together, one hand clutching the blanket under her breasts. Sometime in the night she had kicked her legs free of the covers, and the satin nightgown she wore had ridden up, showing him the shapely length of her legs even as the clingy material outlined every curl and swell of her breasts.

She had a natural beauty that would arouse any man. Logan was no exception. Yet, looking at her, he found himself coming face-to-face with a cold, hard truth. He wanted more than her body. He could have her in the physical sense any time he wanted her; he had proved that to himself—and to her—last night.

No, he wanted *her*. All of her. It shook him to realize just how much he wanted that.

Pivoting on his heel, Logan walked swiftly from the room. Once in the kitchen, he went through the motions of putting on coffee.

Something pressed on her arm. Cat shifted away from it and rolled onto her stomach, drawing up a knee and coming instantly against the back of the sofa. She groaned an irritated protest at the narrow confines of her bed.

The pressure came back, this time jiggling her shoulder with gentle insistence. "Mom," Quint whispered. "Mom, I can't find my socks."

"Look in your bag," she mumbled into the pillow.

"They aren't there. Mom, I need my socks. I gotta go help the sheriff feed the horses."

The mere mention of the man who was the reason she hadn't been able to get a decent night's sleep turned Cat stubborn. "Tell the sheriff to look."

"He's already at the barn. I saw him from the window. Mom, I'm gonna be late."

An aching stiffness registered in a dozen different places as Cat levered up onto her elbows, so tired she wasn't sure she could move. "I'll get up." Untangling herself from the twisted covers, she sat up and pushed the rumpled mass of her hair away from her face. "Where's my robe?"

"Here." Quint handed it to her.

Standing, she pulled it on and absently belted it, then followed Quint to his room on legs that felt wooden. The missing socks were quickly located, jammed deep inside a cowboy boot. His eyes positively beamed with gratitude when she pulled them out.

"You found them!" He promptly sat down on the floor to put them on, then hastily tugged on his boots. Scrambling to his feet, he managed a quick, "See ya, Mom."

Then he pounded from the room at a run. By the time Cat made it to the hallway, the squeaky screen door banged shut behind him. She cast a longing glance at the sofa and knew she had to be really tired if it looked inviting. Vowing there and then that she had slept on it for the last time, she headed for the kitchen.

To her everlasting joy, she found the coffee already made. Judging by the absolute blackness of it, it had been brewed some time ago. Cat didn't mind in the least. A concentrated dose of caffeine might be just what she needed to get rid of this heavy, drugged feeling from too little sleep.

She drank the first cup standing at the sink and carried the second cup to the bathroom, stopping along the way to collect her overnight bag.

After an invigorating shower, Cat felt almost human again. She returned to the living room, folded up the blanket and bedsheet, stacked them in a pile with the pillow on top, and carried them to Logan's bedroom. Resisting the urge to see if the unmade bed was as firm and comfortable as it looked, she walked over to the straight-backed chair in the corner and dumped the bedding onto it.

As she turned away, the pillow slipped off the pile and knocked over the metal wastebasket beside the chair, spilling pink, yellow, and white flowers onto the room's slate blue carpet.

Kneeling, Cat picked up a pink daisy, its head drooping in the first stages of wilt. A faint dampness clung to its short stem. Rising, she spotted a small crystal vase sitting atop the tall bureau. Droplets of water clung to the outside edges of its inner base.

She rescued the rest of the flowers, a mix of pink and white daisies and yellow rosebuds with sprigs of baby's breath, put them in the vase, and carried it to the kitchen, filling it half-full of water. Only after she set the vase on the counter did Cat take the time to consider the significance of the dainty bouquet in Logan's bedroom. Obviously, he had bought the flowers with her in mind—no doubt as ambiance in some grand seduction scene. No doubt a little more snooping would turn up candles—maybe even a bottle of champagne.

The creaking of the screen door was preceded by the muffled clump of footsteps across the porch. Not one, but two sets, Cat realized, a quicksilver tension sliding across her nerves.

"Mom?" Quint called in a questioning voice.

"I'm in the kitchen." Instinctively she lifted a hand to her damp hair, making sure no strand had escaped from the smooth French braid before she poured herself another cup of coffee.

Quint trotted into the kitchen, bits of hay chaff dusting his hat and his clothes. "Got any juice? I'm thirsty."

"I'll see." She set the cup on the table and crossed to the refrigerator. "Did you get the horses fed?"

"Uh-huh." He dragged a chair over to the counter, then climbed onto it to get a glass out of the cupboard. "The sheriff's got a baby colt. It's all dark 'cept it's got spots on its rump. He says it's a ploosa."

"An appaloosa." Cat spied a carton of orange juice tucked behind a jug of milk.

"Yeah, an ap'loosa." He dragged the chair back to the table, the glass rolling precariously on the seat. "The sheriff says maybe when it's bigger I can ride it."

"That's nice." Juice carton in hand, Cat pushed the refrigerator door shut, and threw a quick glance toward the living room. "Where's the sheriff?"

"He went to take a shower." Quint climbed onto the chair again and sat on his knees, holding the glass while Cat filled it. "He says he'll have some juice and coffee after he cleans up." He gulped down a big swallow, then wiped his mouth across the back of his hand. "What should we name it?"

"What?"

"The colt." He looked at her with earnest gray eyes.

"That will take some thinking. A name is kinda permanent." She pulled out the chair and sat down beside him.

He frowned over that. "Not real permanent, though, 'cause you changed your name when you married the sheriff. And mine's gonna be Echohawk just like his."

"That's true." She wasn't comfortable with the turn this conversation was taking. "Are you hungry?"

"Uh-huh." His expression turned hopeful. "Can you make some pancakes?"

"I don't know if the sheriff has everything here to make them."

"Can you see? I could eat a whole stack."

Cat smiled. "It sounds like you really worked up an appetite this morning."

Nodding, he added, "And I've been up a long time, too."

"In that case," she said with a relenting sigh, "I'd better see what we can do about making pancakes."

Between the well-stocked cupboards and the refrigerator, Cat found all the necessary ingredients to make Quint's pancakes. Less than ten minutes later, bacon sizzled in the skillet while Cat rubbed a thin coating of oil over a cast-iron griddle. She turned the burner on under it, then went to the sink and washed her hands. The running water masked the even tread of Logan's footsteps. She was unaware he had entered the kitchen until she heard his voice.

"Hats off in the house, son."

Her nerves jumped. Half turning, she saw him remove Quint's hat and hook it on a corner of an adjacent chair. Logan still had the wet gleam from his recent shower, and he was dressed in his crisp tan uniform.

He glanced at her, his eyes cool, gray, and unfathomable. "Good morning."

"Morning." She turned off the faucets, shook the excess water from her hands and reached for the towel to dry them.

"Mom's cookin' pancakes and bacon," Quint told him.

"So I see."

"Do you want some?"

"She may not have fixed enough for me." Logan walked to the coffeepot and poured himself a cup, standing close enough to Cat that she caught the clean scent of soap and the woody tang of his aftershave.

"Didja, Mom?"

"There should be plenty for both of you." Nerves threatened, and she conquered them by moving to the range top to check the bacon. "Why don't you set a place at the table for him?"

"Okay." He jumped off the chair and dashed over to the silverware drawer, then reached onto the counter instead and touched the crystal vase. "How come you're keeping these dead flowers?"

The fork hovered a fraction of a second too long over the bacon slice before Cat moved it to the next. "They aren't dead, just drooping a little. I put them in fresh water to revive them."

In control again, she glanced at Logan and saw his raised eyebrow. "They looked in need of rescuing."

He said nothing to that and lifted the coffee cup to his mouth, watching her over the rim of it. "How did the sofa sleep?"

"It was definitely an experience." Her smile was pure saccharine.

Amusement gleamed in that split second before he tipped the cup and took a sip of hot coffee. Silverware clattered together as Quint dug out a knife, fork, and spoon. He pushed the drawer shut, then turned a thoughtful frown on Logan.

"How come Mom slept on the sofa? I thought moms and dads slept in the same bed."

"Not always," Cat said quickly. "Sometimes there are reasons."

"Like what?" Quint carried the silverware to the table.

She paused in the middle of pouring pancake batter on the hot griddle to throw her son a half-irritated glance. "Where are all these questions coming from? You never used to ask so many."

"The sheriff says sometimes you gotta ask questions in order to get answers."

"He said that, did he?" The batter bubbled around the edges of the first pancake as she poured the second.

"Yup."

"In that case, you can field them from now on," she told Logan with an acidly sweet look.

Amusement danced in his eyes. "I wouldn't dream of it. You do much too fine a job of it."

Not to be diverted, Quint asked again, "Like what, Mom?"

"Like snoring or reading in bed." The bacon was ready to turn.

"Do you snore, Sheriff?"

Cat jumped in before Logan could answer, "Like a freight train."

"What does that mean?" Quint frowned.

"It means he snores loud." She flipped the pancakes, then lifted the crisp bacon out of the skillet, laying it on a plate lined with a paper towel to absorb the grease.

"Are you always gonna sleep on the sofa, Mom?"

"No." That was an absolute. "There's a spare bed in the attic at The Homestead. When we go back to pack our things, I'll have the boys load it up."

"There's no need," Logan said. "I planned on driving to Miles City on Saturday and pick up a bed."

"Unless you want to experience the joy of sleeping on the sofa until then, you can save yourself the trip." Cat took the plate of bacon to the table. "Although I will be needing a dresser to put my clothes in."

"There's one in the spare bedroom." Logan pulled out a chair and sat down at the table. "I'll clean it out when I get home tonight."

"Where do you want me to put all the boxes?" She dished up the pancakes and poured batter for three more.

"I'll take care of those and set up the bed, too. You'll have your hands full just getting your things packed and moved over here today, not to mention fixing supper. Remember you invited your uncle to join us."

Actually, Cat had forgotten that, but she didn't admit it. "Here. You can start with these." She set the pancakes on the table between them. "The others will be done in a minute."

"Mom makes the best pancakes." Quint leaned over the table and forked one onto his plate.

"They are good," Logan said after he'd taken a bite.

"Surprised?" Cat gloated a little. Light and fluffy pancakes had always been one of her specialties, one she prided herself on.

"Let's just say I wouldn't have been surprised if you didn't know how to cook."

"Thanks to my mother, I do," she replied. "She enjoyed cooking and made certain that I knew my way around the kitchen."

"In that case, I'll look forward to supper tonight."

TWENTY-ONE

Cat pressed Tiny Yates and the ranch electrician Mike Garvey into service to load and transport the spare bed. She pulled into the ranch yard just as they dragged the box springs off the truck bed. Quint and her father were on hand as well, to supervise the unloading.

"Where do you want us to put this?" Tiny asked when she climbed out of the Suburban, dressed in a red University of Texas T-shirt and fashionably tattered jeans, clothing more suitable for the rigors of moving than a blouse and slacks.

"For now, we'll just put everything in the living room. I'll sort out where it all goes later." She walked to the back of the vehicle to start unloading it. "Quint, go open the door for them."

When he ran to the porch, her father came to give Cat a hand. "Let me carry that bag."

"Thanks." She gladly passed him a suitcase. "I never realized Quint had so much stuff. I hate to think how many trips we would have if we brought it all. This is worse than when I was hauling all my things back and forth to college."

"True." He ran an inspecting glance over the house. "The house looks to be in good shape."

"The house is fine." Cat dragged a box out of the back end. "It just needed another bed."

In short order, both vehicles were unloaded, the contents piled in the living room. "Do you want me to find my stuff and take it to my room, Mom?" Quint asked.

"No, I want you to go back to the ranch with Grandpa. You still have to get your saddle and gear from the tack room and make sure it's in the trailer with Molly before they bring her over."

"Grandpa can do that."

"What if I picked up the wrong one?" Chase asked, with an indulgent smile.

"You can't miss it, Grandpa. It's the smallest one."

"You'd better come with me just the same," he said. "Besides, I think your mother will make a bigger dent in this if she doesn't have you underfoot."

"I wouldn't be under her feet. I'd be in my room."

Cat caught him by the shoulders and steered him toward the door. "Go. You can unpack your things when you come back." She walked him across the porch and stopped at the steps. Head down, he plodded out to the truck.

Pausing beside her, Chase observed her half-worried look when she gazed after Quint. "You should be glad that he's looking forward to moving in here."

"I thought he'd miss the Triple C more," Cat released a long breath of disappointment. "I guess this is still an adventure to him."

"He also knows he still has his own room at The Homestead, and that he's welcome to come stay in it any time he wants."

"I guess."

Chase glanced at his watch. "It's two o'clock now. By the time we get back and get the horses loaded, we should pull in here a little after four."

"I'll watch for them," Cat promised.

She waited until they drove out of the yard before she turned back to the house. A chipped cement block propped the screen door open. As she started to shove it aside, the telephone rang in the house. Leaving the block in place, she hurried to answer it.

"Circle Six Ranch." Silence followed. Frowning, Cat tried again. "Hello. Hello?" There was a click on the line. A moment later she heard the distinctive hum of the dial tone.

Shrugging it off as a wrong number, Cat hung up the kitchen extension and went back to the living room. Her glance fell on the pile of hangered clothes draped across the platform rocker. Another stack lay on the sofa. Since it was an obvious and easy place to start, she grabbed up a handful of Quint's shirts and pants, carried them into his room, and hung them in the closet.

From there, she made a detour into the spare room to make sure its closet was empty. It wasn't. There were a dozen shirts, an equal number of jeans and slacks, three suits, and two sets of uniforms hanging on its rod.

"Aren't you the clotheshorse, taking up two closets," Cat muttered under her breath. "I can fix that."

She snatched the shirts off the rod and charged into the hall straight to his bedroom. She yanked open the closet door, determined to cram the shirts in with his other clothes.

The closet was empty.

Dumbfounded, Cat stared at the bare shelves and clothes rod, every inch wiped clean of dust. She turned slowly from it, her glance straying to the walnut-stained bureau. Crossing to it, she pulled out a drawer. Empty.

Still carrying the shirts, she went back to the spare room, skirted the neatly stacked boxes and stopped in front of the oak dresser. Almost hesitantly she opened one of the drawers and looked inside at the folded undershirts and white briefs. A second drawer held socks and two sets of thermal underwear. Sweaters and sweatshirts were in a third.

Cat didn't bother to look any farther. There could be only one reason Logan had moved all of his clothes in here—he planned to sleep in this room. Which meant he had intended for her to have the other bedroom.

She remembered the vase of flowers—and promptly sat down on the nearest box. Had the bouquet been nothing more than a thoughtful gesture on his part? More than that—why had she been so ready to think the worst? Cat shied away from the answer to that.

Very carefully, she hung his shirts back in the closet, taking pains to shake out any folds so they wouldn't end up wrinkled, then left the spare room, closing the door behind her. Still mulling over the implications of the discovery, she walked slowly back to the living room. She looked thoughtfully at her clothes, hesitated, then gathered up an armful and carried it into the bedroom she had previously regarded as Logan's.

After hanging up the clothes on hangers, Cat tackled the luggage and boxes, separating hers from Quint's and carting them to their respective rooms. Before unpacking any of them, she stopped to fix the roast for their evening meal.

In the kitchen, she opened the refrigerator door, then noticed the radio on the counter next to it and flipped it on. Ten minutes later she was standing at the sink, peeling potatoes and absently singing along with the radio.

"She ain't only purty to look at, she can sing, too."

Startled by the drawled comment, Cat whirled around. Alarm shivered through her, turning her dry-mouthed when she saw Lath Anderson lounging in the kitchen doorway, an arm idly braced against the casing, his hat tipped to the back of his head.

Recovering, she demanded, "How did you get in here?"

"The door was standing open. I took that as an invitation to come in," he said with a taunting grin. Too late Cat remembered she had left both doors propped open. "That ain't a very smart thing to do. It tends to let the flies in."

One buzzed around him. He watched it a moment, then his hand flashed, snaring it out of the air. The lightning speed of it carried a warning all of its own.

"See what I mean?" He dropped the dead fly on the floor and ran his hand down the side of his jeans in a cleaning motion.

"What is it you want here, Lath?" She had a partially peeled potato in one hand and the paring knife in the other. She tightened her hold on the knife.

"Someone told me you had married Echohawk." He sauntered into the kitchen. "But I had to see it for my own eyes. Kinda sudden, wasn't it?"

"It happens that way sometimes."

"It was one of them—your eyes meet and before you know it, you can't keep your hands off each other—was it?" His leisurely pace kept bringing him closer.

"More or less." Cat wondered whether Lath knew that he blocked her from both the living room and the side door to the utility room. She had the uneasy feeling that he did. She was suddenly furious with herself for not moving away from the sink when she first saw him, instead of allowing herself to be trapped.

His glance wandered around the kitchen. "Where's the kid?"

"With his grandfather. They should be pulling in any minute with another load of our things," Cat lied, well aware it would be a good hour or more before they returned.

Lath's eyes laughed at her, as if somehow he knew the truth. "How's he like his new daddy?"

"He likes Logan just fine. Look, I'm really busy now. Why don't you come back another time?" If she hadn't been so leery of turning her back to him, she would have resumed peeling the potatoes.

"Yeah, I see you're fixing dinner." He paused to peer into the long enamel roasting pan on the counter. "Is that Calder beef there?"

"I wouldn't know." She was curt, wanting him gone and uncertain how to accomplish it.

Lath looked past her into the sink, eyeing the raw vegetables still sitting in the colander. "Potatoes, carrots, onions. Looks like it's gonna be a real tasty meal. How does a fella go about wanglin' an invitation to supper?"

"You aren't welcome here, Lath."

Shaking his head, he feigned a hurt look, his hands hooking themselves on the hips of his low-riding jeans. "Now, that ain't a very neighborly attitude to take. An' we are neighbors, you know. I live just up the road a few miles. Ma didn't like it in town, so Rollie rented the old Simpson place."

"How nice for your mother."

"Yeah." His glance drifted down to the front of her T-shirt, his eyes stripping her. "University of Texas, huh?"

Revolted by the almost physical touch of his gaze, Cat worked to keep her breathing slow and even. "I think you should leave. Right now."

"That's a pity, 'cause I was just thinkin' about stayin'." His eyes continued their downward focus. "Is that all Echohawk gave you—just that plain gold band?" Lath gestured toward the ring with a small lift of his hand.

Cat made the mistake of glancing at her wedding ring. In a flash, his hand snaked out and plucked the potato from her gasp as easily as he had snatched the fly moments ago. Grinning, Lath tossed the potato in the air a couple times, then took a crunching bite out of the peeled end.

"I always did like raw potatoes," he said between chews. "Course, they're better with some salt on 'em."

Not trusting him, Cat retreated a step, moving sideways along the sink counter. "Get out of here, Lath." She held the knife in a low, threatening position, her fingers tightly circled around it.

"If I don't, you ain't thinkin' about cuttin' me with that puny little knife, are you? 'Cause if you are, I'll tell you right now that ain't the way you hold a knife in a fight."

"Just get out." This time she kept her eyes on him and ignored the gesturing flick of his hand.

"You aren't scared of me, are ya, little kitty-Cat." Grinning cockily, Lath moved another step closer.

Cat retreated again, then sensed the closeness of the corner area and stopped. His grin lengthened as he began tossing the potato again.

Cat had the eerie feeling he was only toying with her.

"Feeling trapped, are you?"

"Stay away from me," she warned.

"Catch." Lath flipped the potato at her face.

Instinctively she blinked and pulled back from it. In that split second, his fingers closed around the wrist of her knife hand. Before she could strike out, he twisted her arm behind her back, turning her and slamming her against the counter, bending her forward over it and pinning her there with his hips. Cat tried to kick back at him and banged her knees into the cupboards. With her free hand, she groped the air behind her, trying to grab him. But he was out of reach.

Chuckling, he increased the pressure of his hips, wanting her to feel the hard outline of his erection. "Kinda hard to fight somebody when they're behind ya, ain't it?"

"Damn you, let me go!" She fought the terror that clogged her throat, a terror that came from discovering she was utterly helpless.

"Better quit that squirming. You're getting me all excited."

Cat froze, terror striking deep, but the instant he started grinding his hips against her in a suggestive way, she grabbed at the edge of the cupboard above her head and pushed with all her strength, straining to get the needed leverage to throw him back. He simply jerked her imprisoned arm higher, drawing a pained cry from her.

He kept up the pressure until her fingers released their grip on the cupboard and fell back to the counter. Even after he eased off, her shoulder continued to throb from the wrenching. She hunched from it, battling tears.

Her reprieve was short-lived as his hand slid under her T-shirt and wormed its way around to her breasts, pushing up her bra to release them. When she tried to grab at his hand, he simply twisted her arm again.

"Oh, baby, you got a great set of jugs," Lath murmured, fondling them roughly. Revulsion rose like bile in her throat. "I'll bet Echohawk loves wallowin' in 'em at night."

"You'll go to prison for this." Cat all but spat the words.

"I could," he agreed in a smiling voice and rubbed himself against her. "But only if you talk. And you ain't the kind that would tell. As proud as you are, you'd die of shame before you'd get up on a stand and say all the things I did—especially when I get up there and tell them how you teased me, showin' me your breasts and flauntin' your body, sayin' that you wanted a little brother to go with your other bastard baby. It'd be too humiliatin' for a Calder, wouldn't it?"

Cat was all too afraid he was right, that a trial would be more degrading than her pride could stand. When she felt his fingers tugging at the snap of her jeans, she vowed he would not take her without a fight.

As she began to gather herself for it, the distinctive double click of a lever-action rifle sounded above the radio music.

"Let her go now," came the low-growled threat.

At the first sound, Lath had wheeled off of her, his grip on her wrist loosening enough that with a quick jerk, Cat was free of it. Both feet were once more on the floor. On shaky legs she staggered backward, clutching at the counter. But Lath only had eyes for the old man holding the cocked rifle on him.

"Get away from him, Cat," Culley ordered.

"Don't go doin' somethin' stupid, O'Rourke." Lath held up a cautioning hand. "You'd be shootin' an unarmed man. That's murder one."

"But you'd be dead, and that would suit me just fine." Culley's finger caressed the trigger.

"But think of the mess she'd have to clean up."

"Let him go, Culley." Cat gripped the side of the

refrigerator, unable to look at Lath, her skin still crawling from the sensation of his hands, his body.

"After what he done to you—"

"He didn't do anything," she insisted, fighting the feeling that she had been violated just the same.

"Now, you listen to the little lady," Lath urged, his eyes cool and watchful.

"You were fixin' to, weren't ya?" Culley said in an ugly snarl.

"But he didn't," Cat repeated, angry now. "Let him go. I just want him out of here. Now."

A long second dragged by. "All right, you heard her—git," Culley ordered. "And if you come 'round here again, I won't be listening to her. I'll be shooting on sight."

Lath sidled toward the door, some of his cockiness returning. "I'll remember that. And I'll remember you, old man," he added softly.

To her relief, Culley followed him out of the kitchen all the way to the front door. When she heard it close, Cat sagged onto a kitchen chair, her stomach rolling. She almost laughed when she saw the paring knife in her hand. But it was a sob that came out.

A floorboard squeaked, the only warning she had that Culley was returning. Cat struggled to pull herself together, not wanting him to see how horribly unnerved she was. Looking up, she saw him watching her with worried eyes.

"Your timing couldn't have been better." She managed a wan smile.

"I saw him snooping around outside. When he slipped in the house, I didn't figure he was up to any good." Culley paused. "Are you all right? Did he hurt you?"

"My shoulder's a little sore, that's all." A commercial came on the radio. Irritated by it, Cat got up and turned off the radio. The action made her aware of the bra riding up above her breasts. With her back to Culley, she reached under her T-shirt and pulled it down.

"You don't look all right."

"I'm fine, really," Cat insisted again, then admitted, "I'm just a little shook up. He frightened me." She rubbed her hands over her arms, still fighting that crawly, dirty sensation.

"You want me to call Logan?"

"No!" The answer was explosively quick and definite.

"You aren't figurin' on tellin' him, are you?"

"What would be the point? There's nothing he can do," Cat argued. "Anyway, it's over. Nothing happened."

"Just the same, he should know about it."

"No. He'd start asking questions, demanding details, and I don't want to talk about it. Not now. Not ever." She swung on him. "Swear to me you won't tell him, Uncle Culley."

He hesitated, plainly not liking it. "If that's the way you want it, I won't tell him what happened."

"Not a word. Not a single word. I have your promise on that?"

Culley nodded. "You have my promise."

Relief shuddered through her. Cat ran a hand over the top of her hair, her fingers snagging in the plaits of her French braid. "How could I have been so stupid to leave those doors propped open? It was dumb. So very dumb." She began to pace.

Watching her, Culley shifted his weight to the other foot. "Want me to put on some coffee?"

Cat glanced at the sink counter, remembering. "No. No, I don't want any coffee." She could still see him there. Smell him. Feel him. She bolted from the kitchen, unable to remain another second.

Culley followed her into the living room, watching as she moved about, all raw nervous energy, opening one box, looking in another, picking one up and setting it down two feet away, accomplishing nothing. It worried him.

"Maybe you should sit down, Cat."

"I can't." She kept her back to him, head down. "What time is it?"

He pulled out his pocket watch and checked. "A little after three."

"Dad will be here with Quint soon. I should take a shower and get cleaned up before they get here." Her hands moved over her body as if she was already washing it. "Will you stay, Uncle Culley?"

"Sure."

"I mean, here in the house." Her eyes clung to him in silent appeal.

"Sure, if that's what you want. But Lath's gonna know I'll be hanging around. He won't be coming back."

"Just the same, I'll feel better." Cat moved toward the hallway.

Culley waited until he heard the shower running, then went to the kitchen and picked up the phone, dialing the sheriff's office. "I need to speak to Echohawk. Tell him it's O'Rourke calling. . . . It's personal. Just put him on the phone. . . . Yeah, Logan. There's been some trouble. You better get home right away. Cat needs you. . . . I don't have no time to explain. Just get here."

He hung up, his mouth curving in satisfaction. Shifting his grip on the rifle, he walked back to the living room. From the bathroom came the sound of running water. Crossing to a front window, Culley leaned a shoulder against the casing and watched for Echohawk.

O'Rourke was on the front porch waiting for him when Logan pulled into the ranch yard. One look at the rifle cradled loosely in O'Rourke's arms had Logan piling out of the patrol car, his glance ransacking the entire area.

In three strides, he was at the steps, demanding, "What happened here? Where's Quint?"

"He's okay. He's with Calder. They'll be here in another thirty minutes or so with the kid's horse." He jerked his head toward the house. "Cat's inside. She's the one who needs you."

"Is she hurt?"

O'Rourke shook his head. "Scared."

"Why? What happened?"

His expression took on a closed look. "I gave her my word I wouldn't tell you. You'll have to ask her."

Logan's mind raced over the myriad of possibilities. But experience had taught him not to jump to any conclusions. It was better to let the facts speak for themselves. He also knew he was going to have trouble with objectivity on this one.

"Where is she?" he snapped the question at O'Rourke, simultaneously pulling open the screen door and reaching for the knob.

"Probably in the bedroom. She just got out of the shower a couple minutes ago."

That was an image Logan didn't need.

Long, ground-eating strides carried him to the hallway. Just as he reached it, Cat came around the corner, glistening wet-black hair slicked back from her face and a peacock blue robe wrapped high and tight around her. She recoiled from him with a gasping cry, color draining from her face. The fear in her eyes was closer to terror.

"You startled me," she managed shakily. "I didn't expect you home so early."

Logan gave her high marks for recovery. "Your uncle called me."

Eyes blazing with hurt and anger, she looked past

him to her uncle. "How could you do that? You gave me your word you wouldn't tell him. I trusted you!"

"You're my wife, Cat. I have a right to know."

"But nothing happened. Do you hear? Nothing happened," she insisted as Culley slipped back outside.

"I'll be the judge of that. Why don't we go over here and sit down, and you can tell me how it happened," Logan suggested, deliberately letting her believe that he knew more than he did.

"Look, I don't want to talk about it. I just want to put it out of my mind and forget that Lath was ever here."

Lath. Of all the possibilities that had occurred to him, Lath Anderson wasn't one of them. An anger, black and cold and ugly, welled up. Logan had to work to keep it from showing.

"What time was this?" Such minor details were always easier for a victim to supply. And each answer opened the gate a little more until the whole story flooded from them.

"Some time shortly after three. I'd gone in the kitchen to get the roast ready for supper—" She stopped abruptly, a hand flying to her mouth. "I forgot to put the roast in the oven. It's still sitting on the counter."

"We won't worry about supper right now." Logan placed a hand on her back, keeping its touch light and impersonal while he walked her to the big easy chair by the fireplace. "So you were in the kitchen when Lath came?"

"Yes. Look, do we have to go over all this?" As he had expected, she sank into the chair in agitation. "All he did was grab me, okay?" When Logan said nothing, she went on. "It was my fault anyway. If I hadn't left the stupid doors propped open, he wouldn't have been able to just walk in without me knowing it."

"You propped the doors open when you were carrying your things into the house, right?" Logan sat on the large ottoman, keeping his distance from her with an effort.

"Yes. It made it a lot easier than trying to open the doors with your arms full. After Dad and the boys left, I went out to close them, but the phone rang. I went to answer it. Afterward I . . . I just forgot about the doors."

"Who called?" He watched her expression.

"Nobody. Or, at least, whoever it was, hung up when they realized they had the wrong number." Cat lifted her head, a sudden thought dawning in her eyes. "You don't suppose—"

"Suppose what?"

"That it could have been Lath calling to see if I was here? He said he'd heard that we were married, but he had to see it with his own eyes. Do you think it was him?"

"It's possible. What else did he say?"

Piece by piece, Logan drew the information from her until the whole story came in a rush. Listening to it, Logan knew he had felt anger before, but nothing like this, nothing like this savage rage. Despite his attempt to maintain a dispassionate facade, some of it must have shown.

"I'm not going to press charges, Logan," Cat stated, her chin jutting at an assertive angle.

But he looked at the shimmer of tears in her green eyes. "He assaulted you, Cat."

"That won't be his story. Or have you forgotten that I had a knife? That I threatened him with it? All he has to say is that he was trying to take it away from me, that he was defending himself—not the other way around. And how can I prove differently? Look." She pushed the sleeve back on her robe, showing him her wrist and arm. "I don't have a single bruise."

"Anderson has a record—"

"Which wouldn't be admissible. And please don't suggest that Culley could testify on my behalf. You know as well as I do, they'd bring up all those years he spent under psychiatric care, and completely destroy his credibility as a witness. Not to mention what his lawyer would try to do to my reputation. No." Cat stood up. "I'm not going to file any charges. That's final."

"All right." He placed his hands on his knees and pushed to his feet, a part of him knowing too well that she was right in thinking she would be on trial as well.

A pickup truck with a horse trailer in tow rumbled into the yard. Hearing it, Cat wiped a quick hand over her eyes, wiping away any trace of tears. "That's Dad and Quint." She turned to Logan. "I don't want them to know about this. It would be pointless."

"He's your father," Logan reminded her.

"Yes, but there's nothing he can do. It would only upset him."

On that, he had to agree. There was nothing either of them could do. At least, not legally. His arm brushed against the holstered gun at his hip as he took a step toward her.

TWENTY-TWO

*T*he need to keep his distance from Cat no longer existed now that Logan had gotten the full story from her. The tight fold of her arms and the cleansing rub of her hands over them told Logan that she had yet to rid herself completely of the feel of Lath's touch. He needed to change that. For her and for himself.

"I'm sorry, Cat." His hands settled lightly, high on her arms, exerting no pressure. She stiffened in instant resistance, her eyes flashing to his face. He held them. "I meant for you to feel safe in this house."

A small, barely perceptible tremor quivered through her, taking away her stiffness. Her glance strayed to his shirtfront as she wavered, a broken look in her eyes. Recognizing that it was all the invitation she could give, Logan gently gathered her into his arms. She shuddered once, then accepted the simple comfort he offered.

"You aren't to blame for what happened, Logan. It was my fault," she murmured.

"No. There is only one person responsible for what happened, and that is Lath." His hands moved over her in slow, soothing strokes that encouraged her to relax against him, even as they worked to banish the memory of other hands. "You may have left the doors open, but that didn't give him license to assault you."

"I know." She rested her head against him, a fisted hand moving childlike near her mouth. "It's just that I . . ."

When her voice trailed off, leaving the sentence unfinished, Logan guessed at it, "You felt powerless, right?"

"Yes," she sighed the admission and stirred in his arms, the agitation rising again.

He hooked a finger under her chin, tilting it to prompt Cat to look at him. "Tonight, after Quint's in bed, I'll show you the different ways to break out of that hold."

"There's more than one?"

"Always." He watched the mix of doubt and surprise in her eyes give way to a militant light.

"Like what?"

"Like instantly going limp and sinking to the floor, forcing him to try to hold your entire weight."

"But I would be twice as vulnerable on the floor."

"Not necessarily. Your legs would be free, and a well-aimed kick could take out his knee—literally. As a defensive tactic, falling can be very effective, but it's hard to do because it goes against every instinct." He could tell that he had given her something to think about other than the attack itself. "Tonight I'll show you others." His glance strayed to her lips, seeing them part in anticipation of that. Before the thought of kissing her could take root, Logan stepped back, aware there were limits to his control. "Right now, you'd better get dressed. I'll give your father a hand unloading the horses."

Lending action to his words, he headed for the door before she could see the hard-biting hunger in his eyes. Her voice stopped him halfway across the room.

"Logan." She waited until he looked back. "You might as well know that I unpacked all my things and put them in your bedroom after I found out you had already moved all your clothes to the spare room."

"That's fine." He saw the unspoken question in her eyes and chose to ignore it.

Cat wouldn't let him. "You intended to sleep on the sofa last night, didn't you?"

"Yes."

"What changed your mind?" She studied him closely, puzzled and curious.

"I got irritated," Logan replied without emotion. "You seemed dead set on sleeping with a ghost last night. I decided I didn't want it to be in my bed."

Cat had her answer, and she didn't particularly like it. Something told her it wouldn't be Repp she thought about when she crawled into bed that night. And it wouldn't be Lath Anderson, either. Somehow Logan had managed to supplant both. On one hand, she was glad about that, but on the other . . .

"Any more questions?" Logan's raised eyebrow challenged her.

"No." She moved toward the bedroom.

"For your information," Logan began, "your uncle told me nothing about what happened. He did call me, but only to say you needed me. He refused to tell me why, claiming that he had given you his word."

Cat murmured a stunned, "Then you didn't know anything."

"No." The hard line of his mouth softened. "Getting answers from people who don't want to give them is my job, Cat. I happen to be very good at it."

"Indeed," she said in a tight voice, half-irritated

by the realization she had been tricked into telling him.

"It's better that I know, Cat. This way we can take steps to make sure you're never at any man's mercy again." But Logan knew it would be a test of his control to be in such close proximity to her.

When she made no reply to that, he continued outside. O'Rourke was on the porch, a keen, knowing look in his eyes. "I figured you could get the story out of her," he said. "Deep down, I think she wanted you to know. She was just shamed by being so helpless." He paused a beat. "Can you really teach her how to fight back?"

"No. In an actual fight, she would lose. But I can show her how to break loose and run like hell if anything like this should happen again." Assuming no weapon was involved. But Logan kept that thought to himself for now.

From the barn area came the clang and clatter of a tailgate on a stock trailer being lowered. Logan turned in that direction as a horse nickered.

"Whatcha gonna do about Anderson?" O'Rourke wanted to know.

"I plan on having a little talk with him. Unofficially, of course." He stepped off the porch and headed for the barn area.

Logan stopped by the old Simpson place the next morning on his way into town, but no one answered his knock. He listened for the sounds of anyone stirring inside the house trailer, but it was impossible to hear above the obstreperous racket of the guinea fowl.

The result was the same that evening and the next day. He didn't believe for a moment that no one was home, a suspicion that was confirmed when he saw the twitching aside of a curtain.

Finally, on the third day, Logan waited near the entrance to the Dy-Corp coal mine and followed Rollie when he left at the end of his shift. The guineas didn't distinguish between friend and foe and set up their gabbling clamor, announcing Rollie's arrival before he drove into the yard. Their din, muted by distance, brought a cool smile of satisfaction to Logan's lips.

He pulled into the old ranch yard seconds behind Rollie. His strategy was rewarded by the sight of Rollie halfway to the trailer steps and his mother at the door. Logan parked close to Rollie's truck and took the time to lock his gun and badge in the glove compartment before stepping out of the vehicle.

"You ain't welcome here. You get back in that car and get out." Bitterness and hate twisted the old woman's age-lined face.

Logan dragged his glance from her to Rollie. "Where's your brother?"

"How should I know? I just got here." Rollie wore the sullen closed-up look of a convict talking to The Man. Logan suspected it had more to do with Lath's influence than the time Rollie had spent in prison.

"Would you find him? I need to talk to him." The old woman slammed into the trailer. Logan kept half an eye on the door.

"That's your problem."

"That's not a good attitude, Rollie. Where is he?"

Rollie's smile was close to a sneer as he lifted his broad, muscled shoulders in an indifferent shrug. "You want him; you find him."

"Is that an invitation to look around?"

The flicker of alarm in Rollie's eyes was brief but unmistakable. "No, it isn't," he snapped, turning surly.

The trailer door sprang open and Emma Anderson charged out of it carrying a shotgun. She leveled it at Logan. "We got us a sign posted that says trespassers will be shot. You're trespassing and I'm tellin' you to git."

"You're making a mistake, Mrs. Anderson. I only want to *talk* to your son."

"The only thing around here that's gonna do any talkin' to you is this shotgun," she warned. "You've caused enough trouble for my boys. You ain't gonna cause them any more."

Logan pushed his hat to the back of his head. "You act like you know how to use that shotgun, Mrs. Anderson, so I'm assuming you also know that it throws a pretty wide pattern at close range like this—which means you can't shoot me without hitting Rollie. I don't think you want to do that."

The shotgun's double barrel wavered for the first time. At almost the same instant the door opened behind her and Lath stepped out of the house trailer.

"Now, Ma, you ain't behavin' very neighborly." His hand slid along the barrel, tilting it up before he gently took it from her, broke it open and removed the shells, then handed it back to her. "The sheriff's gonna think he ain't welcome here."

"He ain't," she stated.

Chuckling, Lath shook his head in amusement, his watchful gaze never leaving Logan. "My ma has always been one to speak her mind." He made a leisurely descent of the steps, knees locking on each tread. "You wanted to see me?"

"Yes." A steely coldness marked Logan's voice and his expression.

Lath sauntered toward him. A taunting smile slanted his mouth as his glance strayed to the front of his uniform. "I see you took off your badge. I guess that means this is personal," he drawled. "It couldn't be about that little social call I paid to your wife, could it?"

"You went to see that little slut?" Emma demanded in sudden fury. "I raised you better than to go sniffin' around her kind."

"Now, Ma." Lath smiled at the quick flaring of Logan's nostrils, his only outward reaction to the name-calling. "It wasn't what you're thinkin'. You run along inside, and I'll explain it all to you later. Right now, I think the sheriff wants to have a little private talk with me—man to man, so to speak. Something tells me it won't take long."

She threw a last glare at Logan, then turned on her heel and stalked into the house, the empty shotgun under her arm. Rollie stayed, a silent figure in the background.

In the interim, Lath lit a cigarette and blew a long stream of smoke into the air. "I gotta be honest, Echohawk, I didn't figure she'd tell you."

"She told me. Now I'm telling you—don't ever come within a hundred feet of my wife again."

"That's a bit harsh, don't you think?" Lath countered lazily. "I mean, is it my fault you can't keep her satisfied? She likes it from behind, you know."

Logan's expression never changed. "I'll say it only once more—don't come near my wife again."

"And if I should, what'll you do about it?" Lath challenged cockily. "Kill me? You—a man sworn to uphold the law?"

"I never said anything about killing you, Lath." His mouth curved in a smile that was deadly cold. "I even have your brother as a witness to that. How could I be responsible if you took a notion to hang yourself? Did you ever see anybody hang before? Not on an executioner's gallows with a hangman's knot to cleanly snap the neck, but with an ordinary rope tied to an ordinary beam. I heard about a man who hung himself in a jail cell once. The coroner figured that it might have taken him as much as fifteen minutes to die. Somewhere along the line he must have changed his mind because there were claw marks on his neck."

"I'm tremblin' in my boots," Lath jeered.

"That isn't what he did in his boots," Logan countered dryly, then walked to the patrol car. Opening the door, he paused with one foot inside. "Don't tangle with me unless you have a death wish, Lath."

After he drove out of the yard, Rollie dragged in a long, shaky breath and threw a worried look at his brother. "I told you going over there was a fool idea, didn't I?"

"I had to get a look at the place, see how things are laid out, didn't I?" Lath replied, unconcerned.

"Going over there is one thing, but messing around with the Calder woman is another. What the hell did you do, anyway?"

"Hey, she had a knife. I had to take it away from her."

"You must have done more than that." Rollie gave him an accusing look.

Lath shrugged. "So I copped a few feels. Let me tell you, little brother, that's one piece of tail I wouldn't mind havin' some of."

"Well, you can forget about that unless you want to die real slow," Rollie grumbled in ill temper. "And you can sure as hell forget about your brag to Ma about doing something with the kid. If anything happens over there, Echohawk'll come straight here."

"Not if we handle it right, he won't. Besides," Lath grinned, "he warned me to stay away from his wife. He didn't say anything about the kid."

"If you think he won't put two and two together

and come up with us, you're wrong," Rollie told him.

Lath was unconvinced. "Not if we lay low for a while and play it cool. He may think about us, but not seriously, and not for long."

Time passed much more swiftly than Cat thought it would. Her first days at the Circle Six were spent unpacking everything and arranging it to suit her. It was a process made longer by the time she took out to spend with Quint. Although he had always been content to entertain himself from the time he was small, Cat was concerned that he might have trouble adjusting to his new environment, a concern that proved to be groundless. If anything, he seemed happier. Which should have been a relief, but it bothered Cat that he was so quick to embrace this new life, so eager to explore every inch of it and so ready to make Logan a part of it.

"Graciously civilized" was the best way to describe her relationship with Logan after two weeks. There had been times when she was relaxed in his company, but on those occasions, someone else was invariably present, either Quint, her uncle, or some other member of her family. On the whole, Cat made it a point not to be alone with Logan. Which wasn't difficult, considering that he was away the biggest part of the day. In the evenings, after she tucked Quint into bed, she usually went to her room and read for a while or occupied herself with some household task.

The role as woman of the house was a new experience for her. At The Homestead, the responsibility had always belonged to someone else—her mother when she was alive, then Ty's first wife, Tara, and now Jessy. But here, she was in charge. With the additional work came an amazing sense of freedom. Suddenly Cat could do things the way she wanted them done, not someone else. Sometimes it was something as simple as folding the towels lengthwise first, then in half, or as major as rearranging everything in the kitchen cupboards. Without being aware of it, Cat subtly put her personal stamp throughout the house.

With Quint's help, she planted a flower border along the length of the front porch. Nearly every day, they would saddle up their horses and go for a ride. At first, it was a chance to spend time with Quint and familiarize herself with this rough, broken country that was so different from the wide, rolling grasslands of the Triple C. But as Quint's fascination with the wild landscape and his desire to explore it grew, so did hers. Out of habit, Cat would check on the condition of the range, the cattle, or the fences and pass the information on to Logan that evening.

And there was the young Appaloosa colt. Every time she turned around, Cat found Quint down at the corral trying to coax the flighty youngster to come to him. Out of concern for Quint, she began gentling the colt, teaching it to lead and getting it used to being handled, in short, making it safer for Quint to be around. Since she had always enjoyed working with young horses, the task was a pleasure of its own.

"What do you think of Raindance, Mom?" Quint climbed onto the kitchen counter and balanced on his knees to lift the plates out of the cupboard.

"Raindance?" Cat lifted the lid on the sauce pot. Steam, scented with basil and oregano, rose in an aromatic cloud as she stirred the simmering tomato and meatball mixture.

"Yeah, for the colt. We can't keep calling him

Easy Boy Easy." Balancing the plates, he climbed back onto the chair and jumped to the floor.

"Raindance sounds good. Where did you come up with that?"

"Well . . . I wanted an Indian name for him 'cause he's an Indian horse. And it looks like he's got raindrops on his rump." Quint walked around the table, setting a plate in front of each chair. "It's okay to say rump, isn't it?"

"Yes." Cat retrieved a head of lettuce from the refrigerator and took it to the sink to wash.

"The sheriff said butt isn't a nice word." Quint went to the silverware drawer.

"The sheriff's right. There are definitely better words."

The crunch of tires on gravel and the low rumble of a car engine filtered into the house. Quint snapped his head toward Cat and listened with eyes wide and mouth open, a look of excitement dawning.

"That's the sheriff!" He gave the drawer a shove and stampeded toward the door, all coltish energy. "I gotta go tell him we fed the horses."

A quicksilver tension raced through Cat, all her senses going on high alert as she rinsed the lettuce one last time and turned off the faucet. Leaving it to drain in the colander, she went to the cupboard and took down a salad bowl.

A mix of footsteps, one set slow and even and the other quick and light, thudded across the porch. The squeaking of the screen door signaled their entrance into the house. A tremble skidded up her spine when she heard the low, rich timbre of Logan's voice.

Cat chalked it up to nerves and this awkward marriage that had them living together for Quint's benefit. She consoled herself with the knowledge that it would be twice as unnatural if she weren't aware of Logan as a man, a virilely attractive man. If there were times when she longed to be held and touched, such urges were perfectly natural, too. Probably even healthy. But that didn't mean she wanted to give in to them.

Except for that first night, their wedding night, Logan hadn't shown any interest in her as anything other than Quint's mother. Even that night when he had shown her the various ways she could escape an attacker's hold, his attitude and touch had been purely instructional. Which was precisely the way she wanted it, Cat reminded herself and ignored the funny ache inside.

Footsteps approached the kitchen, and she busied herself patting dry the head of lettuce, her pulse rushing a little as it always did when Logan was around.

"Something smells good." Logan walked to the stove, lifted the lid on the sauce pot and inhaled the fragrant steam. "Spaghetti and meatballs. Looks like we're going Italian tonight."

"Yeah, Mom makes the best spaghetti. It's even better than SpaghettiOs, 'cept she doesn't make the Os," Quint added.

"That's a shame." A smile was in Logan's voice.

"She can't find the Os at the store," Quint explained. "She's looked and looked. Haven't you, Mom?"

"That's right," Cat agreed, too aware of Logan moving to the counter area where she was working.

He opened a cupboard door and took out a cup, slanting her a sideways look. "Quint tells me you fed the horses already. I don't expect you to take care of the house, look after him, and do ranch chores as well. I hope you know that."

Uncomfortable and half-irritated that he should be so thoughtful and considerate, Cat dug her fingers into the head of lettuce and tore out a chunk. "I had been working with the colt. Since I was already at the barn, it seemed logical to go ahead and feed the horses. It didn't require that much effort."

"Maybe not. Anyway, thanks for doing it." The warmth in his voice was genuine, and much too unsettling.

"No problem." She was cool to the point of being brusque. Out of the corner of her eye, she saw his mouth tighten.

"I thought of a name for the colt," Quint put in. "It's a good one, too."

"Let me guess," Logan said. "You're going to call him Lollapaloosa."

Logan's suggestion was so unexpected and whimsical that Cat couldn't keep a laugh from bubbling out. She struggled to smother it, even though this wasn't the first time Logan's sense of humor had taken her by surprise.

Just for a moment, amusement danced in both their eyes. The guarded look was gone from her expression. She was open to him, warm and vibrant and beautiful. Desire crawled through Logan with an enveloping heat. Then Quint spoke up, reclaiming his attention.

"Lollap'loosa," he stumbled over the name, a deep frown knitting his forehead. "What's that mean?"

"It means the colt is unique, the best there is," Logan explained.

"Is it an Indian name?"

"I'm afraid not." Logan carried his cup over to the table.

"The colt needs an Indian name," Quint said with a decisive nod, then proceeded to tell him the one he liked and explained at length how he had come up with it, finishing with, "What do you think? Do you like Raindance, too?"

"I think it fits him perfectly," Logan agreed. "He certainly does a lot of dancing around when you put a halter on him."

"Not anymore. Mom's got him leading real good. But he used to, didn't he?" Quint said, pleased to find another reason for choosing the name.

"He sure did." Logan drank the last of the coffee in his cup and took it back to the counter, glancing at Cat. "Do I have time to change before dinner's ready?"

"Easily," she answered without looking at him. "I won't be cooking the spaghetti until Uncle Culley gets here."

"I'm gonna put on a clean shirt," Quint announced. "Mine's dirty."

Cat started to suggest that he finish setting the table first, but the words died on her tongue when she saw Quint trailing Logan, doing his best to copy Logan's long, unhurried stride. The image of father and son couldn't have been stronger. For some reason it cut deep.

She stood for a long minute, listening to Quint's steady run of chatter fade to the other end of the house, then shook aside the vague melancholy and finished setting the table before putting the water on to boil in anticipation of her uncle's arrival.

Conversation lagged at the supper table that evening. Cat had quickly exhausted her supply of mundane topics and wondered if she was the only one who felt the strain of this silence. She glanced at Quint, noting the way he idly toyed with his chopped-up bits of spaghetti.

"You're awfully quiet tonight, Quint." A few weeks ago Cat wouldn't have found that at all unusual. Since moving here, he had become much more talkative. It was something that had happened so gradually that Cat was only now realizing it—and how much she had come to rely on him to keep the table conversation going.

"I been thinking." He wore his serious face.

"About what?" Logan glanced at him, amused and curious.

"Well . . ." Quint laid his fork down and gazed intently at Logan, "I was just thinking that I'm really glad you found us, Dad."

It was the first time Quint had ever called him that. Cat didn't know if she was more shocked by that or the breathtaking look of love that shone in Logan's eyes.

"I'm glad I did, too, Quint," he replied with husky sincerity.

A beautiful, beaming smile lit Quint's whole face. Cat stared at it for a numbed instant, then pushed to her feet, turning from the table. "I forgot to put fresh coffee on." Her voice shook almost as much as her hands.

Her appetite was gone. She could hardly wait for the meal to be over. But her attempt to shoo everyone from the kitchen failed when Culley insisted on helping with the dishes. In the end, Cat didn't have the energy to argue and consoled herself with the knowledge that Culley wouldn't expect much in the way of conversation.

Working in a companionable silence, she dipped the first dinner plate in the rinse water and set it on the drainboard rack, then immersed her hand in the soapy dishwater to wash the next one. Culley picked up the plate and began wiping it dry.

"It's natural for a kid to love his father, Cat."

Instinctively tensing, she managed a relatively even, "I know that."

"You looked like your heart had got torn out of your chest."

"That's ridiculous." She felt her skin heat.

"You thought it was safe to love the kid, didn't you?" He set the dried plate on a clean section of the counter.

"I don't know what you're talking about." Cat rubbed vigorously at the already clean plate.

"I got a feeling you've been playing it safe just about ever since your mother was killed. I can't say that as a fact, 'cause I was pretty tore up myself back then."

Determined to change the subject, she said, "Remind me to tell Logan that Dad called today. He wants us to come over for dinner on Sunday."

"Now that I think about it," Culley took the plate from her before Cat could place it in the rack, "I was kinda like you after Maggie died. I figured as long as I didn't let myself care too deep about anybody, I wouldn't be hurt that bad again. Then you started coming around, reaching out and needing someone because you didn't have anyone to turn to, not with Calder laying in the hospital and your brother suddenly finding himself holding the reins to the ranch. You looked so much like Maggie that it hurt sometimes, but it helped, too. And I knew she'd want me to look out for you. So I reached back. You were family. I guess you're more like me than Maggie."

Cat shook her head at his rambling discourse. "You aren't making any sense, Uncle Culley."

He frowned. "I guess I'm not saying it plain."

"It doesn't matter." She threw him a quick smile, her tension showing.

"Things aren't working out between you and Logan, are they?"

"Everything's fine."

Culley grunted his doubt. "I could tell you liked kissing him that time. I thought he was safe enough for you."

The plate slipped from her fingers and splashed into the rinse water. "When did you see me kissing him?"

"That night at The Homestead after those cattle were found dead."

That seemed like a lifetime ago. "You shouldn't be spying on people, Uncle Culley." Cat rescued the plate and jammed it in the rack.

He responded with a small, negligent movement of his shoulders. "I guess I thought Logan was like the Taylor boy."

"How can you say that? I loved Repp." In quick order, she washed the last two plates and started on the silverware.

"You sure were sweet on him," Culley agreed, then paused in his wiping and stared thoughtfully into the middle distance. "I don't know, I guess I'm comparing you to Maggie again. When she cared for somebody she did it with her whole heart. There was no holding back with her, even when she knew she'd get hurt. Calder hurt her more than once."

He eyed her astutely. "You weren't that way with Repp, or you never would have let him keep putting you off when you wanted to get married. And you gotta admit he wasn't all that eager about it, either. It kinda makes you think that he might have been awed by the idea of marrying a Calder—maybe even worried that you'd find out he couldn't measure up."

Why had Repp dragged his feet about marrying her? And why had she been so quick to believe that he was trying to do what was noble and honorable? Had she argued that strongly against waiting? Or had she simply gone through the motions of objecting?

Cat couldn't remember. The memories were all too fuzzy now, blurred vignettes of horseback rides, slow dancing, and passionate kisses. But she couldn't recall the intensity of the hunger or the heat, not with the sharp, disturbing clarity that etched every detail of the night she spent with Logan.

Which meant absolutely nothing.

"I loved Repp," Cat repeated with force.

Culley nodded in a show of approval. "You hang on to that. It's a kind of protection that'll keep you from letting yourself care about anyone else."

"I don't do that." But the denial came too late. Doubt had already set in.

TWENTY-THREE

Always a light sleeper, Logan couldn't have said what initially woke him. Eyes open, he remained on his side, fully alert and listening.

There was a whisper of movement in the hallway, the faintest rustle of cotton brushing cotton. His bedroom door was open a crack, letting in a sliver of light from the hallway. A small shadow blocked the lower part of it. Then the door inched open a little more. Quint slipped through and stood, staring at the bed.

Logan made a show of waking up and levered himself onto an elbow. "Quint. Having trouble sleeping?"

"You don't snore." He walked to the bed. "I been listening."

"You have?" Logan hid a smile.

"Uh-huh. Do you think I should tell Mom?"

"I don't think so." He glanced at the digital clock on the bedside table. Its green numbers read 1:16. "It's after one in the morning. I'm sure she's sleeping, which is what you should be doing."

"I know." Quint nodded and heaved a big sigh.

"Aren't you tired?"

"Kinda."

Smiling, Logan pulled the covers aside. "Why don't you hop in bed with me for a while. Then when you get really tired, I'll take you back to your own bed."

"Okay." He climbed into bed and stretched out facing Logan, a hand propping his head up. "You aren't wearing pajamas. Don't you have any?"

"No."

"You should tell Mom. She'll get you some."

"I'll keep that in mind."

"What happened to your shoulder?" Small fingers touched the reddened area of newly healed flesh.

"A scar."

"How'd you get it?"

Logan hesitated, trying to decide how much to tell him. "I got shot," he said, reasoning that Quint had seen him in uniform nearly every day and had already asked some questions about the gun Logan carried.

His eyes got big. "By a bad guy?"

"Yup."

"Did you catch him?"

"We sure did."

"Does it hurt a lot to get shot?"

"It hurt an awful, awful lot," Logan stressed.

"Did you have to go to the hospital?"

"Yup, and the doctors had to operate to get the bullet out."

"Were you there a real long time like my grandpa was when he got hurt?"

"I was there a long time, but probably not as long as your grandpa."

"Do you think I could be a sheriff when I grow up?"

"I think you can be anything you want to be—a sheriff, an astronaut, or a cowboy in a rodeo."

Of all the things Logan had imagined doing with a son, this middle-of-the-night conversation wasn't one of them. Yet lying there, talking with his son, and listening to him prattle on a dozen different subjects, this was easily one of the most enjoyable things he had ever done. He was sorry when he saw Quint's eyes growing heavy. He waited, watching as Quint nodded off. Only then did Logan gather him up and carry Quint to his own room.

Cradling a child in his arms was a new sensation. It moved him in some deep, bonding way Logan didn't understand. Slow to relinquish the moment, he laid Quint on the twin bed and took his time pulling the covers around him. A little self-conscious, he brushed a kiss on Quint's forehead and straightened away from the bed.

There were too many emotions, too many desires running too close to the surface when Logan came out of Quint's room and collided with Cat. Automatically he reached out to steady her even as her hands moved to clutch at him.

"Quint? Is he—"

"He's sleeping. I just tucked him back into bed." A dozen different impressions registered at once—the drowsy, only half-awake look of her eyes, the bareness of her shoulders and neck, and the full contact with her satin-draped body. It all worked into him and through him.

"I thought I heard— Did he have a bad dream?"

"No." Logan smiled. "He discovered I don't snore. He wanted to wake you up, but I told him I didn't think that was a good idea." Looking at her, all he could think was that this stunning woman was the mother of his child, easily the most amazing gift he had ever received. "Thank you, Cat, for giving me such a beautiful son."

But it wasn't his murmured words that held Cat

motionless. It was the incredible love shining in his eyes. It filled her vision, dazzling her even as his mouth moved over hers in a warm and fiercely tender kiss. She had no time to collect her scattered defenses—no time to even remember that she should.

The pressure eased until his lips were barely brushing hers, evoking an ache that was gnawing and sweet. "I probably should have told you that before." The tips of his fingers caressed her cheek. Her lashes fluttered down, then lifted again when he raised his head to gaze at her through heavily lidded eyes. "I'd like you to give me more children. Maybe a little girl next time. One with gorgeous green eyes like yours."

She couldn't seem to get her breath as his eyes darkened with undisguised hunger. Something inside leaped at the thought of a child, a little girl. It sent her pulse racing.

"Once I thought it would be enough to have you in my bed." His thumb stroked her lower lip, setting all its sensitive nerve ends to tingling. "But it isn't enough, Cat. Not nearly enough. I wish to God I knew how to get him out of your mind."

Perhaps it was the lingering effects of a sound sleep or the distraction of Logan's closeness that addled her thinking. But there was only one other "him" on her mind, and that was Quint. It made no sense that Logan would be talking about him.

"Who?" Cat whispered in confusion.

Before she could remember, an exultant sound came from his throat. His mouth came crushing down. The fire was instant. At that moment, with her head spinning and her body humming, it no longer mattered to Cat that it was Logan who ignited this blaze. No one else ever had, not as completely as this.

When she melted against him, Logan swept her up and took the three strides that carried them into the bedroom that had once been his, then hers, and now was one he was determined to make theirs. His fingers curled into the slick material of her nightgown and pulled the gown up around her arms as he let her feet settle onto the floor.

"Let's get rid of this," he said in a voice raw with the need to feel skin against skin.

Giving her no time to object, he dragged it over her head and slung it away. He heard her quivering gasp and saw her startled eyes, then his gaze traveled downward.

"My God, you're beautiful, Cat," he declared in a fervent whisper.

Uncertainty flickered in her eyes when he started to reach for her. Logan saw it and knew he could erase it. But he also knew he couldn't stand any regrets or recriminations later. When she made a move toward him, he seized her shoulders and kept her away.

"Damn it, Cat, tell me you're awake," he ordered roughly. "Tell me you aren't sleepwalking through some dream of him."

But Cat knew what he was really demanding—make sure it's me you want, not a stand-in for Repp. She wanted Logan. It frightened her how much she wanted him. She knew the deeper the love, the deeper the grief would be.

She wasn't emotionally safe with Logan. Subconsciously Cat had known that all along. She had already lost too many people she had loved. Something told her losing Logan could be a more devastating loss than all the rest.

And the risk was there, much too vividly before her.

Her fingertips traced the area of raised flesh on his chest. Cat had seen too many of the scars from her father's injuries and numerous surgeries not to recognize that the redness of Logan's indicated it was fairly recent.

"You were shot, weren't you?" she guessed.

"Yes." His answer was clipped and impatient. "Cat—"

She shuddered uncontrollably at the closeness of the scar to his heart. Fear told her to use Repp's name and push him away before she was hurt again. But pride made her lift her head and face the truth. "It terrifies me to want you this much, Logan. If—"

But Logan had heard all he needed to hear—his name. Any other words were meaningless now. He had a much more elemental form of communication in mind, the kind that used his hands, his lips, and his body. He was stunned to find in her arms a need that matched his own.

The raw urgency of it drove them both onto the bed, turning them wild as they hungrily sought all the pleasure to be found between a man and a woman. Time stood still, without a yesterday or tomorrow—only now, together.

There was no patience, no gentleness. This was a hunger that had waited six years to be sated, and now could wait no longer, driving each of them relentlessly, ruthlessly, with its desperate, urgent demands. But there never seemed to be enough.

As wave after wave of awesome pleasure swept through her, Cat suddenly understood that one moment would never be enough to satisfy her desire for this man. It would take a lifetime of moments—and more.

Surrounded by Logan's warm, earthy smell, the firm pressure of his arm holding her close to him, Cat lay with her head on his shoulder, a place that seemed to be reserved just for her. Both her breathing and her pulse were far from steady yet. She could tell that Logan's weren't, either. Somehow that made all the inner tremblings easier to accept.

Tilting her head to look at him, she felt her breath take a funny little hitch at the possessive light in his eyes. She liked the way he looked at her. She liked everything about him, then immediately discarded the word. *Like* was much too tame a word to describe the things she was feeling.

"I don't understand how I could possibly be in love with you when I know almost nothing about you." She marveled that such a thing could happen, then realized. "That isn't quite true, is it? I know very few details of your life, but I do know a great deal about the man you are."

If Logan had asked her to elaborate, Cat would have found it difficult to explain. Yet she only had to remember the times she had seen him with Quint—the patience he'd shown, the genuine interest and affection, the incidents of gentle but firm discipline and boyish playfulness—the calm way he had faced down her father and the bouquet of flowers she'd found in the bedroom, his clever questioning that had drawn the full story from her about Lath's assault, his insistence that she wasn't to blame and the subsequent lessons on ways to protect herself, giving her a sense of empowerment rather than making some extravagant manly vow to protect her. If she thought about it, Cat knew she could come up with more examples that would illustrate the knowledge she had gleaned about the kind of man he was—strong, intelligent, competent, sensitive, dependable, caring, patient, understanding, and determined.

Cat also knew she had deliberately not asked any questions about his past. It had been a defense mechanism, a way to convince herself Logan was a stranger. It was time to correct that.

"You told Quint you worked for the government?"

Logan was slow to answer. He was too shaken by her easy declaration of love. Love was a word too many women used to justify going to bed with a man. He was stunned by how much he wanted to believe her.

"The Treasury Department, ATF." Idly he rubbed his hand along the smooth curve of her waist, remembering how roughly he had taken her. But as tender as his feelings were inside, they were also that fierce and primative.

"Is that where you got this?"

He felt her fingertips brush against the scar. "Yes." He caught her hand and raised it to his lips.

"What happened?" She levered herself up, more of her body gliding onto him. The dim light from the hall filtered through the open door and mingled with the moonlight that came through the windows, touching her face and showing him the deep concern etched in her expressive green eyes.

"I was on a joint raid after a paramilitary group who were trading in guns and drugs. Somebody tipped them off. They were waiting for us. My partner was killed in the first exchange." It had never been an easy thing to talk about. Logan discovered it was harder now because he knew how close he had come to dying without ever seeing his son—without ever seeing Cat again.

"Weren't you wearing a vest?"

His mouth crooked with cynical humor. "Vests are only bulletproof if the other guy is using legal ammunition. That's why four men went down that day before we got them."

Mixed in with the look of horror, Logan saw the

flaring of outrage in her eyes. He wasn't all that surprised when he thought about it. Cat was essentially a fighter. In that way, they were very much alike. It pleased him to know that. But there was much about Cat that pleased him. He wanted her to know that, but action came easier to him than words.

With a fluid, sideways turn of his body, he rolled her onto her back and dipped his head to take a tasting sip of her lips. She made a contented sound and snuggled against him, a hand coming up to caress the side of his face.

"The shooting, is that why you decided to quit?" Her thumb moved across his lips in a slow stroke.

"Not really." His hand skimmed over her waist to the rounded swell of a breast. "But I spent a lot of time just lying around thinking while I was recovering—enough time to take a good long look at myself. I didn't like what I saw."

"Why?"

"Because I was fast becoming too hardened, too cold, too cynical, trusting no one and believing in nothing. If you had seen me—even as little as a year ago—you would never have walked up to me in a bar. You would have taken one look at me and turned away."

Cat smiled. "I find that hard to believe."

"Believe it." The sudden edge to his voice warned her that Logan was far from a tamed man.

"Why did you come to Blue Moon?"

"I knew I had to get as far away from the cities as I could. I had some money saved, enough to buy a small ranch if the price was right. I also knew I'd have to be very lucky to make it without an outside income. Which is when I decided to get a job as a deputy sheriff. After living in the South for so long, I wanted to get back to the Plains. I looked around the Dakotas first, but there were too many . . . unpleasant memories. I heard about the opening here, and I'd been here before—"

"When?"

"A few years ago." He was deliberately vague. "Before you and I met."

"Really. What brought you here?"

"I was trying to get a lead on a man suspected of selling illegal firearms." Logan wasn't about to mention Lath by name and have his memory intrude on this. "I asked my questions and left the next day. But I remembered the bigness of the sky and the scarcity of people. Unlike the rest of Montana, the land prices around here were reasonable. The celebrity and big-money types prefer more spectacular scenery, I guess. After I got the job, I started dickering to buy the Circle Six. The rest you know."

"Yes." She smoothed a hand over his chest in an exploring fashion. "What about your family?"

"Other than the odd cousin or two, I don't have any." Seeking to distract her, he nuzzled at the corner of her mouth. "I don't remember you talking this much before. I guess Quint gets it from you."

She laughed against his lips, then gave them a quick kiss. "That's because I spent most of my time avoiding you. Now I want to know everything about you."

"But you don't have to learn it all now." He nibbled his way from her mouth to her throat. "We have plenty of time."

"We don't know that. Nobody knows that," she said with a telling throb in her voice. Convinced she was thinking of Repp and angered that she had, Logan lifted his head and saw the fiercely needy light that burned in her eyes—for him. Everything smoothed out as she cupped a hand to his face. "I can't bear the thought of anything happening to you, Logan. I love you too much now."

There was that word again. Again, he dodged it. "Nothing's going to happen to me—unless you talk me to death."

"You know what I meant." She feigned exasperation, then turned serious again. "I don't want to lose you."

"You aren't going to lose me. You and I are going to grow old together and spend our evenings out there rocking on our front porch." Logan paused, turning thoughtful and tender. "I guess that's what love is—wanting to grow old with someone and watch her hair turn silver and the wrinkles line her face, loving every one of them because each is a memory of the days, months, and years you've shared with her." A long slow smile curved his lips. "I have a feeling when I'm ninety, I'll still be chasing you around those rocking chairs."

"And I promise I'll slow down so you can catch me."

"Ah, but will you stop talking?" he mocked and covered her mouth with his to make sure she did just that.

This time when he made love to her, it was with none of the urgency of before. It was long and slow and tender.

He loved her. It still had the power to shake him to know exactly how much he loved her. She wrapped her legs around him when he slid between them. His mouth traveled over her while he moved deeply inside her with slow, steady strokes. Each time she shuddered, a new pleasure rippled through him, and he glimpsed the glory a man and woman could know together.

Logan stirred, conscious first of a wall of heat pressed against him. Then he breathed in the familiar fragrance of the shampoo Cat used and remembered with a sudden rush of feeling. Opening his eyes, he shifted away from her, careful not to disturb her, then frowned in surprise at the sunlight pouring into the bedroom. He threw a quick glance at the clock on the nightstand. It was after six in the morning. His mental alarm clock had failed him for the first time. Hardly surprising, considering all the strenuous nighttime activity, he thought with a rather smugly satisfied smile.

"Good morning." The whispered greeting came from the doorway.

Logan sat bolt upright, his startled gaze locking on Quint, standing just inside the room, still dressed in his pajamas. "Good morning," Logan echoed the soft tone, unable to remember feeling more awkward and uncomfortable than he did at that moment. "Your mom's still asleep."

Quint nodded, then smiled. "I guess you told her you don't snore."

"I did." Hastily Logan checked to make certain Cat was fully covered, then remembered his shorts were somewhere on the floor, probably not too far from Cat's nightgown.

"I'll bet she was glad about that."

"I think she was. Why don't you run and get dressed and you can help me with morning chores?"

"Okay." Quint turned to leave, then hesitated. "Mom might get worried if she can't find me."

"Wha'?" Cat lifted her head and peered over her shoulder toward the door. "Quint. It can't be morning already." She rolled onto her back, levering herself up on her elbows. As the covers started to slip a little too low, Logan pressed her shoulder back onto the bed.

"Careful," he warned.

Her eyes sprang open as her cheeks took on a

rather beautiful color. Logan grinned when she clutched at the sheet.

"Quint's going to get dressed and help me with chores. Is that all right with you?" he asked.

"It's fine, yes. You go right ahead, Quint," she said in a rush.

"Okay." He glanced again at Logan. "You're gonna get dressed now, aren't ya?"

"I'm right behind you." He swung his legs off the side of the bed, careful to keep the sheet tucked around his middle. "Want to have a race to see who can get dressed the fastest?"

"I bet I'll beat you." Quint grinned and ran for his bedroom.

Logan didn't waste time locating his shorts and pulling them on. Cat lay in bed watching him with an all-too-contented look, much too beautiful and tousled. Walking over to her, he leaned down and gave her a long, thorough kiss.

"Good morning," he said.

"Good morning," she sighed.

He kissed her lightly again, then lifted his head a couple inches, eyes twinkling. "Remind me to get a lock for that door while I'm in town today."

The corners of her mouth deepened. "And you wanted to have another child."

"Correction—*more children*."

Cat raised an eyebrow. "How many is more?"

"However many you and the Good Lord bless us with." He grinned. A drawer slammed in Quint's bedroom. Logan glanced briefly over his shoulder. "It sounds like I'd better get a move on if I expect to make a decent showing in this race."

She wrapped her hands around his neck and dragged him down for another long kiss that started his pulse hammering in his neck. "The race," she reminded him, impish laughter dancing in her eyes.

"I wouldn't want him to beat you too badly—at least, not until you get a lock for the door."

"Witch," he murmured, then planted a quick, hard kiss on her lips before pushing off the bed and leaving her to fetch his clothes from the spare room.

Understanding at last what bliss felt like, Cat snuggled back under the covers and savored this bottomless contentment she felt inside.

During the next two days Cat was amazed by how easily they went from being two people sharing the same house, careful to give the other plenty of space, to a man and wife doing things together and doing their best to take up the same space every chance they had. With Quint around, that wasn't often.

With her hat pulled low to block the sun's strong and slanting rays, Cat held one end of the board while Logan hammered the other end to a corral post. Quint stood to one side of Logan, ready to hand him the next nail. Cat smiled when she considered that even something as simple as replacing a rotting board had become a family affair.

How had it happened? she wondered. When had it changed from physical attraction to love? Why hadn't she recognized it before that night? Abruptly she threw away all the questions. The how, when, and why of it didn't matter. This was love, deeply rooted and in full flower.

Finished with his side, Logan moved to her end. She shifted position to make room for him and held the board until he had the first nail hammered in place. She stepped back to watch when he took a second nail from Quint.

After he was done, Logan gave the board a hard shake to test its solidness, then nodded in satisfaction. "That should do it." He tipped his head toward Quint. "Take a look at that. I think we did a good job, don't you?"

"We sure did," Quint agreed. "Do we got another board to fix?"

"Nope. They all look sturdy enough to hold a tall boy or a stout horse," he replied, then glanced at Cat. "Which reminds me—a rancher over by Lewiston has a pair of draft horses for sale—Clydesdales. I was planning on taking a look at them on Saturday. Would you and Quint like to ride along? We could make a day of it."

"It sounds great, but—what do you want with a draft horse team?" Cat asked, a little puzzled.

"What's a draft horse?" Quint wanted to know.

"It's like the kind you see pulling the wagon in the beer commercials," Logan answered his question first, then hers. "I don't have enough acres in hay to warrant the cost of a tractor—even a used one. Horses will be practical and economical. It may take a little more time to mow and windrow and load it, but I kinda like the idea of doing it the old way."

She pretended to give his argument careful thought. "The upkeep on them would be cheaper. They certainly won't be as noisy as a tractor, either."

"My thinking exactly." He smiled, then turned a little serious. "You may as well know now that you married a man without any great ambition to build the next ranching empire. I don't want the Circle Six to get so large that I can't work it myself. I want to pull my own calves and mend my own fences. I don't want to pay somebody to do the work for me. I'm not saying the other way is wrong; it just isn't right for me. This keeps me sane, gives me the balance I need to—"

"You don't have to explain," Cat told him, touched that he seemed concerned about her reaction to this, as if it might somehow affect her opinion of him. If anything, it reinforced the feeling that Logan was a man who didn't feel the need to prove anything to anyone, not even himself. At the same time, she was certain she had never met anyone more capable of stepping in and taking charge of a ranch the size of the Triple C.

"I'm not explaining exactly," he said with a trace of impatience at the interruption. "I'm not saying we'll be poor, either. We'll make a good living here. It's just that I don't want you thinking that someday we'll be building us a great big house to live in."

Hiding a smile, Cat turned to look at their home. "No, but I do think it might need to be larger."

"Why? We have plenty of room."

Shrugging, she said, "You're the one who said you wanted more children."

He stared at her for a stunned second, then threw back his head and laughed.

The two draft horses, Jake and Angel, were all Quint wanted to talk about when they went to The Homestead for dinner on Sunday. "You should see them, Grandpa. They're really big," Quint declared with emphasis. "And they're tall, too. About as tall as this room."

Chase glanced at the dining room's ten-foot ceiling and contained his skepticism. "That's really tall."

"Yeah, and Dad's got harnesses for 'em to hitch 'em to things," he stumbled a bit over the new terms, but it was his use of the word "dad" that had Chase glancing at his son-in-law, only to have his eye drawn to Cat, noting the glow in her eyes when she looked at Logan.

"What's that thing you put over their heads, Dad?"

"A collar," Logan supplied.

"You should see how big it is, Grandpa. If you try to put it on me, it falls to the ground—without even touching me."

"You are pretty skinny," Ty observed.

"Yeah, but it's gigantic." Quint made a big circle of his arms to show him.

"I think it's time you did less talking and more eating," Cat suggested.

Obligingly Quint picked up his fork and scooped it into his mashed potatoes. Chase filled the silence he left. "What do you have in the way of horse-drawn implements, Logan?"

"Right now, just a hayrack. I've got a line on a mower. I thought I'd check it out this next week."

"We still have a sledge and an old buck rake stored in shed three," Jessy recalled.

"Now that you mention it, we do." Chase nodded. "I remember dragging all that stuff in there. I couldn't have been much more than fourteen or fifteen."

"Any idea about what kind of shape they're in?" Logan asked. "I might be interested in buying them from you."

"They were in working condition when we put them in there," Chase replied. "After dinner, you and Ty can take a look at them. If you're still interested, I'll make them a wedding present to you."

When Logan started to say something, Cat laid a silencing hand on his arm. "Thank you, Dad. It's the best gift you could give us."

Logan was clearly amused by her quick assertion. "I have the feeling your daughter thought I might object. I don't. I accept it as a wedding gift." Somewhere within his answer was the inference that he wouldn't be so quick to accept future "gifts."

Chase nodded. "I'm glad we agree on that."

"What's a buck rake?" Quint frowned.

"It gathers up hay," Logan explained.

"How?"

"It's easier to show you than to tell you. As soon as you finish eating, we'll go look at it."

When the meal was over, Ty, Logan, and Quint did just that while Cat stayed to help Jessy with the dishes. Chase pitched in, carrying a stack of dessert plates to the kitchen, then lingered to have another cup of coffee, his glance running over Cat in quiet speculation, noting the new vibrancy, the shining ease.

"I guess I don't have to ask how you and Logan are getting along," he remarked.

A little startled, she stopped, then laughed softly. "No, you don't." She paused and looked thoughtfully at the kitchen with its dark cherry cupboards and huge, brick-fronted fireplace, a room that was as big and solid and lived-in as the rest of the house. "It's funny, but I thought I would never be happy living anywhere else but right here. But I am."

"It shows," Jessy told her with an approving smile.

"I guess it does." Cat was glad that it did, and proud, too. Sighing, she admitted, "I'm so happy it scares me sometimes. In a way, it's like waiting for a shoe to drop."

"Don't borrow trouble, Cat." Chase was sharp with her. "It'll find you soon enough. When it does, it won't be when or from where you expect it."

"I know." But his words only reinforced the feeling that a menacing black cloud loomed on the horizon.

PART 5

Danger now surrounds you.
There's nowhere that you can hide.
Fighting back is your only answer.
Go armed with that bold Calder pride.

TWENTY-FOUR

A dusting of stars threw their silver sparkle across the dark sky as night settled over the rugged and broken country of the Circle Six. The smell of wildness came from those tangled hills, carried on the wind's cool breath.

Comfortably cradled on Logan's lap, Cat felt only the heat radiating from his body as they shared one of the rocking chairs on the front porch. Quint was in his room, sound asleep, giving them some rare time to themselves.

"Dad's flying to Miles City at the end of the week to attend a livestock association meeting." Cat idly ran her fingers through Logan's hair, disturbing its smoothness. "I thought I might ride along, and do some shopping, maybe pick up a couple of chairs for the living room and get rid of that old platform rocker."

He drew his head back, raising one eyebrow. "What's wrong with the rocker?"

Cat looked him straight in the eye. "It's ugly."

"It's a little nicked and worn."

"A little?" she scoffed.

"All right, more than a little. Just the same, you'd better hold off replacing it for a while. After buying the mower, we can't really afford to get anything else right now." He rubbed a hand over the curve of her hip.

"That's not a problem." She kissed the corner of his mouth. "I'll buy it myself. I do have some money of my own."

"Good. You can save it to pay for our kids to go to college."

This time it was Cat who drew back to look at him, more amused than annoyed by his attitude. "For your information, Logan, I happen to have more than enough money in my trust fund to do just that. There is absolutely no reason not to use the income from it to buy some of the things we need."

"And there is absolutely no reason you can't wait a couple months until we can afford it." His tone of voice was just a little too firm for her liking.

"Let me see if I have this straight." Falsely calm, she sat upright. "It's all right for me to buy something as long as it's with your money."

"That isn't what I said."

"That's what it sounded like to me." Eluding the hands that tried to hold her, Cat swung off his lap and moved away.

"There is nothing wrong with that rocker, Cat. It's solid and well-built." He stood up.

She wheeled to face him. "It's ugly."

"Then throw a damned blanket over it."

"Now, wouldn't that look lovely."

Reining in his anger, Logan strove for patience. "Cat, I don't want to get into a fight over this."

"That's too bad, because it's exactly what we're going to do." She folded her arms high and tight across her breasts.

"Damn it, I didn't marry you for your money."

"Well, you've got it. In case it hasn't sunk in yet, when you married Cat Calder, you didn't get just me—you got my family, my friends, and my money. You can't take what you want and throw the rest away."

"I'm not throwing it away."

"It's the same thing."

"No, it isn't."

"You want me, but you don't want anything to do with my money. Therefore, you don't want me to have anything to do with it, either. Don't you know how archaic that sounds?"

"I wouldn't call it that," he said tightly.

Cat widened her eyes. "Oh? What would you call it? A little too much pride, maybe?"

"Look who's talking about pride," Logan countered as the sharp jangle of the telephone cut across his words. "I'll get that," he muttered, spinning on his heel and striding into the house.

In less than three minutes, he was back, his hat pushed squarely on his head and car keys in his hand. "There's a grass fire ten miles south of Blue Moon. The wind's whipping it straight toward town. I don't know when I'll be back."

The news pushed aside their unresolved argument. "A fire. Logan, I—" She took a step toward him.

He turned, catching her by the arms. "Buy the damned chair. Buy fifty chairs if that's what you want."

"You're too late. I've already decided to look at samples of upholstery fabric, maybe try my hand at refinishing the wooden arms on the platform chair. There really isn't anything wrong with the way it's constructed."

"It's just ugly." His smile was quick and warm.

"Very ugly. But I am buying the fabric to recover it—maybe even a coffee table," Cat warned.

"I can live with that," he told her. "But I'm not sure I could live without you." He kissed her once, lightly, thought about kissing her again, but it was difficult enough stopping with one. He ran down the steps to the patrol car.

Cat watched until the headlights stabbed into the darkness of the ranch lane. Looking to the southeast, she noticed a black smudge staining the starred sky, possibly smoke from the fire. But the ranch was too far away for any glow from the flames to be seen. It seemed an odd time of year to have a prairie fire. The spring rains had been scarce, but Cat hadn't realized conditions had gotten that dry.

With a slightly confused sigh, she went back inside the house and turned a critical eye on the platform rocker, trying to visualize it covered in different colors and patterns. For a few moments, she toyed wickedly with the idea of lacquering the wooden arm a vivid scarlet and upholstering the rest of it in royal purple, with hot orange accents. Logan might not like it so well then.

Ideas about redoing it floated through her mind even after she picked up a Michener epic she had started a couple weeks ago. It was almost midnight before Cat put the book down and accepted that Logan wouldn't be home any time soon. She reached up to turn out the lamp. The instant her fingers touched the knob, the lights went out—both the one in the hallway and the overhead light in the living room.

"Great," Cat muttered to herself.

The fuse box, she knew, was in the utility room. The location of the spare fuses was another matter entirely. Moving cautiously across the pitch black room, Cat groped her way toward the kitchen. She flipped the wall switch for the kitchen light, only to find it wouldn't come on, either.

Then it hit her. The tall outside yard light was out

as well. That's why it was so black. Had the fire caused a power failure? Changing directions, Cat felt her way to the front door and looked out, half expecting to see the red glow of flames in the distance.

There was nothing, not even the smell of smoke in the air. Frowning, she scanned the yard, faintly suffused by pale starlight. Something moved along the lane. Cat stared into the pooled shadows, half-convinced she had imagined it.

She froze as a dark figure moved out of the blackness onto open ground where the dim light of the stars could outline him. A second figure joined him, both running toward the house with a hunched-over stealth. She couldn't see their faces, then she realized why—something dark covered them.

Logan's advice came back to her, the advice he had given her the night he had shown her various ways to break an attacker's hold. "When you get loose, you run. Don't try to fight. Don't grab something and try to hit him with it. You run—and you run like hell."

Cat lingered only long enough to close and lock the door, then raced to Quint's room and snatched him out of bed. He protested sleepily, then sagged against her. As she reached the living room, a flashlight beam played over the front of the house. Taking a chance, Cat tightened her hold on Quint and ran across the intervening space to the kitchen, almost knocking over a chair before reaching the door to the utility room. She paused long enough to check the phone. As she expected, the line was dead.

After the jostling from the run, Quint was awake. "Mom, where—"

"Sssh." She pressed a hand to his mouth and whispered, "There's two men outside, trying to break into the house. We're going to sneak out before they can catch us. Okay?"

"Where's Dad?" he whispered back.

"He had to leave." Cat glanced out the back door. Seeing nothing, she slipped out as quietly as she could, and eased the door shut.

The instant her foot left the last step, she broke into a run and didn't slow down until she reached the stand of firs twenty feet from the house. Needles brushed her face as she pushed her way between the outreaching branches of two trees.

She had no idea whether they had been seen. She couldn't hear anything but the frantic pounding of her own heart. Already her arms ached from holding Quint, but she knew she didn't dare put him down. Without shoes, he'd never be able to run over the rough ground. There was no choice; she had to carry him.

Run, she thought again. But where? And how? Both vehicles—hers and Logan's—were parked in front of the house. If she tried to reach them, there was too much risk of being seen.

A snort and a shuffling of hooves came from the corral. Cat briefly considered saddling their horses, but that meant going into the barn, trying to find the tack in the dark. It would take too much time. Then she remembered Molly. Dear, sweet, reliable Molly. A halter and a lead rope were all she needed with that gentle, biddable mare. And both were just inside the rear barn door within easy reach.

Kneeling, she whispered to Quint, "Climb on my back."

While he did, Cat measured the distance to the barn area and chose a route that gave them the most concealment. When Quint's skinny arms and legs were securely clamped around her, she set out at a jogging trot.

Her fingers closed around the halter and lead rope with the first groping try. She threw a glance toward the house as a spear of light flashed over the back of it, then winked off. Fighting panic, she took a quick steadying breath and moved quietly among the horses.

The bay mare, as always, was easy to catch. Holding the lead rope looped around Molly's neck, Cat led the horse out of the corral and halted deep in the barn's soot-black shadows. There, she transferred Quint to Molly's back, then buckled on the halter.

"Where are we going, Mom?" Quint whispered.

"To Uncle Culley's." She vaulted up behind him, centered herself on the mare's back, then one-reined the horse into the darkness beyond the barn, confident she could find her way to Shamrock, thanks to the rides she and Quint had taken, exploring their new surroundings.

"Where the hell are they?" Rollie crawled into the van's passenger side, the black ski mask muffling his voice. He yanked it off.

"How should I know?" Lath snapped in frustration, his own mask already lying between them on the seat. He gunned the motor and the van shot out from the concealing motte of trees onto the ranch lane.

"It doesn't make sense," Rollie declared, still feeling the pump of adrenaline. "They weren't at the fire with Echohawk. We would have seen them. And the pickup and Suburban were both parked in front of the house. They had to be there."

"They weren't, damn it. We went through that whole house, closet by closet." Nearing the intersection with the highway, Lath flipped on the headlights.

"I know." Rollie wadded the knit mask into a ball

and started to jam it into the pocket of his dark navy windbreaker, then stopped and felt inside the pocket. His heart froze, then started pounding wildly. He made a frantic search of his other pockets and swore bitterly. "Turn around, Lath. We gotta go back."

"Why? What's wrong?" He let up on the accelerator, slowing the van.

"The ransom note, it's gone. It must have slipped out of my pocket back there."

"Are you sure?"

"Would I be telling you to go back if I wasn't?" Rollie used anger to cloak the sick feeling in his stomach.

Lath started to swing onto the shoulder of the highway, then changed his mind and stepped on the gas. "Forget it."

"Forget it? Are you crazy?"

"It might take too long to find, and we need to get this van back before your coal-mining buddy finds out we borrowed it. Besides," Lath grinned, "I kinda like the idea of Echohawk finding it."

Rollie stared at him. "You are crazy."

"Think about it. You know he's gonna go straight to Calder with it. And you know Calder will start sweatin', knowin' that somebody was trying to kidnap his grandson. Think how much sweeter it's gonna be when we do steal the kid."

"But the note."

"What about it? The FBI can run it through their crime lab from now until forever and never trace it to us. Hell, the paper and glue are the kind every kid uses in school, and you know damned well I was wearing gloves when I lifted them from your friend's house. I had on gloves every time I handled 'em. The same with the newspapers."

Rollie gave that heavy thought. "Echohawk is still gonna look at us."

"You forget—we've been fighting that grass fire," Lath reminded him with a wickedly smug look. "And even if he sics the FBI on us, they can comb our place from one end to the other and not come up with anything. That's why I made sure we burned everything we used and dumped the ashes in the river."

"That's right." Rollie breathed a little easier remembering that.

"Why, we'll be so clean, they won't even look at us when we snatch the kid for real," he said, then laughed. "Don't you know Calder's gonna go wild waitin' for a ransom call that we ain't never gonna make. That's what's gonna fool 'em. They're gonna think this is all about money."

"In a way, it's kind of a shame not to take it," Rollie mused. "You know Calder'll come up with it."

Lath gave him a sideways look of scorn. "You're crazy if you think Calder never saw that movie *Big Jake*. That money would get us caught for sure. And I don't figure on anybody ever knowin' that we had anything to do with the kid disappearin'."

"I guess you're right."

"Hell, I know I'm right."

The plan seemed foolproof, even to Rollie. Only one thing still bothered him. Other than some vague talk about keeping the kid stashed in the root cellar until the heat died down, then maybe hauling him down to Mexico or Central America and dumping him in some remote village, Lath hadn't said what they were going to do with him. Rollie knew the smart thing would probably be to kill the kid. The thought made him squeamish. Stealing the kid was one thing, but killing him was another.

But getting rid of the body could be an even bigger problem. He convinced himself that Lath knew that. As long as they kept the kid blindfolded, he could never identify them, which meant they could dump him off anywhere, anytime. He was sure Lath knew that, too.

Cat searched the rearing blackness ahead of them. They had to be close to Shamrock's headquarters. They had to be. Quint was half-asleep in front of her, his weight sagging against her encircling arm while the mare's head bobbed rhythmically with the pace of her quick-striding walk.

An instant later Cat recognized the solid black shape of the barn's hipped roof jutting against the night sky. Relief trembled through her.

"We're almost there," she murmured to Quint.

A shrill neigh rang out, sharp with query. The mare nickered an answer and broke into a rocking lope, ears pricked in the direction of one of her own kind. Starlight frosted the edges of a board fence. The mare slowed before they reached it. Other hooves pounded to meet them, the sound preceding a collection of snorts and curious whickers as a trio of horses poked their heads over the fence to check out the newcomers.

When the mare stopped, Cat slid to the ground, keeping one hand on Quint until she could lift him off the horse. With Quint once again balanced against her hip, she stepped to the mare's head. A bright light sprang out of the darkness, blinding her.

"Hold it right there," a familiar voice barked as she threw up a hand to protect her eyes from the glare. Instantly the light swung away. "Cat! What are you doing here?"

"Uncle Culley, you don't know how glad I am to see you." A sigh rippled from her in a sudden release of tension. As succinctly as possible, she told him about the two men and her escape from the house, explaining that Logan had been called away to the fire. "I need to call him."

"The power went out about a half hour or so ago." He unbuckled the halter and turned the mare loose in the corral with his horses. There was a flurry of squeals and flying hooves as a new pecking order was established. "The phone should still work, though. Let's go see."

With his flashlight to guide them, they made their way to the house. She laid Quint on the living room couch and tried the phone. It worked. Jenna Grabowski, who usually worked the day shift, had been called in to man the phones at the sheriff's office. As Cat had expected, Logan was somewhere on the fire line, and unavailable at that moment. She told Jenna what had happened and where she was. Jenna promised to pass the information to Logan as soon as she could track him down.

By the time Cat had hung up, Culley had dug out the old kerosene lamp, lit it, and set it on the kitchen table. The bright glow of it filled the small room and banished the dancing shadows to the far corners. Cat wandered over to a chair and briefly gripped the back of it. In silence, Culley watched the way she reached up and raked fingers through her hair, dragging it back from her face. It was a habit she had whenever she was nervous. Culley doubted that she even knew she did it.

He got an old jelly glass out of the cupboards and rummaged through the shelves until he found the bottle of whiskey he kept on hand for cold winter nights. He poured some in the glass, added a splash of water and some ice cubes, then took it to her.

She looked at it and shook her head. "No thanks."

"You're strung out like a high-tension wire. Drink it." He pushed it into her hand.

She took a small sip of it, shuddered, and

wrapped both hands around the glass. "Utility men wouldn't wear ski masks. In winter, maybe, but not at this time of the year."

"What are you talking about?" Culley frowned.

Her shoulders moved in a vague shrug. "I was just thinking that maybe the men I saw were with the utility company—that maybe I panicked for no reason. But I didn't. They had something black over their heads, like ski masks."

"You did the right thing coming here."

The phone rang. She whirled toward it, the diluted whiskey sloshing in the glass. Before Culley could answer the phone, she snatched the receiver off the cradle. "Shamrock—"

"Cat, it's me. Jenna gave me your message." Logan's voice traveled through her. It calmed her, steadied her. "Tell me again what happened."

For the third time, she repeated the story, careful not to leave out anything.

When she finished, Logan made no comment and asked instead, "How's Quint?"

"He's fine. In fact, he's sound asleep on the couch." She glanced into the living room. "We're both fine."

"Good. Jenna called the utility company. The outage had already been reported. They think a transformer blew. They have a repair crew rolling now. You stay with O'Rourke. I'm on my way to our place to check things out."

"Be careful, Logan." She clutched the phone a little tighter.

"You can count on it."

Cat heard the smile in his voice—and something else that had the solid ring of competence. This time, after she hung up the phone, she sat down in one of the kitchen chairs, relaxing a little and taking another sip of the whiskey drink.

"That was Logan," she told her uncle, unnecessarily.

"I figured." He nodded.

Roughly an hour later Logan called back. "They were already gone by the time I got here," he said. "But I found where they jimmied open a window. So far I haven't discovered anything missing."

"Thank God," Cat murmured.

"I'll probably be here a while longer yet, and I was afraid you might start worrying if you didn't hear from me."

"I would have." She smiled into the phone.

"That's what I thought. In the meantime, plan on spending the rest of the night at O'Rourke's. I'll grab some clothes for you and Quint and bring them with me when I come."

"Don't forget to bring toothbrushes and a comb. Quint's in his pajamas, so he'll need a full set of clothes—and his boots."

"I'll get them. Is O'Rourke there with you?"

"Yes?" The surprised lilt of her voice turned the answer into a question.

Logan ignored it. "Let me talk to him a minute." During the pause that followed, he heard Cat's muffled voice relaying his request to her uncle. When he came on the line, Logan wasted no time coming to the point. "I don't want Cat to know yet, O'Rourke, but this was a kidnapping attempt. They were after Quint." Logan stared at the ransom note, sealed in an evidence bag on the seat of the patrol car. Rage warred with the cold, hard knot in his stomach.

Quick on the uptake, O'Rourke said, "Don't you be worrying about her. Cat's fine. It kinda shook her a little, but she's made of strong stuff."

"I may be worrying for nothing, but you keep a sharp lookout just the same."

"You can count on it. What're you gonna do?"

"Look around some more. I've already called the FBI. They'll have agents here in the morning. Tell Cat to get some sleep if she can."

"I will."

Logan hit the disconnect switch on the mobile phone, then paused. He still had one more call to make—to Chase Calder. For the next few days at least, he wanted Quint and Cat installed at the Triple C, where they would be safer.

Nerves. Cat showed them as she raked fingers through her hair whipping it into place. But she had control of them, too, Logan observed with a touch of pride. That showed as well.

"Are you certain there were only two men, Mrs. Echohawk?" The question came from Matt Russell, the younger of the two agents. He sat in one of the den's tall-backed chairs that usually faced the room's massive desk. It was angled now toward the leather couch where Cat was seated.

"No, I am not certain." Impatience surfaced in her voice. The question was another variation of a previous one as the agent went over the same ground from a different direction. Logan was familiar with the routine. He also knew that rewording a question sometimes elicited vital bits of information. "But I only saw two men," Cat said again, then paused and released a heavy sigh. "In all honesty, I can't swear they were even men. They were just two dark figures."

"Do you recall if both 'figures' were approximately the same height and build?"

"I don't recall anything about them. I have no idea whether they were tall or fat, thin or short. I wish I could give you a better description, but—

when I realized the starlight wasn't casting any sheen on their faces, that their heads were covered by some kind of ski mask, I knew I had to grab Quint and get out of there. I'm sorry. I know I'm not being very helpful." Sighing again, Cat reached for the insulated coffeepot to refill her cup.

"On the contrary, you're being very helpful," Agent Russell assured her.

Temper flashed in her green eyes. "I know better, Agent Russell. Please don't humor me." She snapped open the lid to the coffeepot and tipped its spout over her cup. Only a trickle of coffee came out. Annoyed, she set the pot back on the serving tray and shot a quick look at her father. "Dad, would you ask Audrey to bring some more coffee?"

Chase sat behind his desk, a silent, impassive figure all through the lengthy questioning of his daughter. At Logan's request, he had asked no questions of Cat when they arrived at the ranch early this morning, which meant he was hearing many of the details for the first time.

"I'll get it," Ty spoke, moving away from the fireplace before Chase could reach for his cane.

The empty coffeepot in hand, Ty crossed to the double doors and pushed one open. A telephone jangled in another part of the house, the strident sound intruding into the quiet of the den. The extension on the desk remained silent, its bell switched off.

Earlier in the morning, the press had gotten wind of the attempted kidnapping of—as they were putting it—the heir to the Calder empire. The telephones at both the sheriff's office and the Triple C hadn't stopped ringing since. Two reporters had already been politely escorted off the ranch, and Logan had posted a deputy at the entrance to the Circle Six to keep the media away. It was only a matter of time before the television crews arrived, and they would have to contend with helicopters buzzing overhead.

As soon as the door closed behind Ty, Russell resumed his questioning. "What made you feel so strongly that you had to get away?"

"Logan said to run—"

"How was he able to tell you that?" The second agent, an older man by the name of George Markus, turned from the window where he'd been standing, his sharp gaze locking on Cat. "The telephone line to the house had been cut."

"I didn't mean he told me that night. It was before then . . . after—"

Catching the hesitation in her voice, Logan stepped in to explain, "My wife was assaulted a few weeks ago. Afterward, I showed her a few self-defense tactics and stressed as strongly as I could that the best defense was to run."

"This is that Lath Anderson you were telling us about?" Markus asked, seeking clarification.

"Yes."

Chase rocked forward in his big chair, the movement drawing Cat's glance. "I guess I should have mentioned it to you, Dad, but—nothing happened. I wasn't hurt. He just had me trapped and I couldn't get away. Then Uncle Culley came and—it was all over. He left. I—" Breaking off the sentence, she swung to Logan. "You don't think it could have been Lath and his brother I saw?"

"I don't know, Cat. I did see both of them last night, working alongside the other volunteers fighting the grass fire. But I couldn't swear that they were there the whole time."

"We'll check that out." Agent Markus thumbed an antacid tablet from the roll in his hand and popped it in his mouth.

Ty came back with the coffee. After filling Cat's

cup, Logan poured one for himself, then offered it to the agents. Both men shook their heads, and Markus turned back to the window.

After the agents were satisfied they had gleaned every grain of information from her about the actual kidnapping attempt itself, they asked the usual questions of everyone: Had they noticed anything suspicious the last few days? Seen anyone hanging around? Received any strange or unusual phone calls? What about enemies, disgruntled employees, anyone holding a grudge, recent hirings, recent firings, arrests, convictions?

From outside came the drone of a motor, overridden by the distinctive chop of helicopter blades. "A television crew getting some aerial footage of the ranch," Markus remarked from his post at the window. Glancing sideways, he looked at Chase. "This is one time, Mr. Calder, when publicity can be an ally. If the spotlight is big enough and bright enough, it can scare them off completely." He held up a hand, as if expecting a protest. "I'm not saying we aren't going to do everything we can to catch these guys. But what we don't want is for them to make another try for your grandson."

Logan nodded. "You or Ty need to draft a formal statement, call a press conference and read it to them, show them a solid family front. Maybe offer a reward."

"Not here on the ranch," Chase stated. "I don't want camera crews and photographers crawling around here."

"I was going to suggest that you hold it on the steps of the sheriff's office," Logan replied. "I prefer that the media regard the Triple C a fortress. They can fly over it, but they can't get into it."

"That's a good idea," Markus agreed. "Believe me, the kidnappers will get the message."

"Consider it done." Chase reached for the telephone. "I'll call Stumpy right now, and have him make sure every road gate leading onto the Triple C is closed and men stationed at them."

But Logan knew that was just the beginning. The press conference alone would require precise planning for it to come off without a hitch. Which meant more work for him. Fatigue tugged at his muscles. He ran a hand over his jaw, feeling the rasp of whiskers. He needed a shave and a shower, a change of clothes, some sleep, and a few hours with Cat and Quint. But he didn't think he'd get the time for any of that.

On the late evening newscast that night, the attempted kidnapping was the lead story on all three stations. Sitting on the living room sofa, with Logan's arm a warm weight around her shoulders, Cat watched with pride when her father's image came on the screen. He made a commanding figure in his suede jacket and dark Stetson, age lines giving his raw-boned face a craggy strength. His voice, when he spoke, resonated with authority and conviction. Ty stood at his side, a younger, taller version of his father, stamped with all the same features and characteristics.

"Good job, Dad," Cat said when the image on the screen switched to aerial footage of the Triple C headquarters.

"The fifty-thousand-dollar reward should start the phones ringing," Logan added.

"In a related story," the newscaster said, "fire investigators have determined the wildfire that threatened the town of Blue Moon last night was deliberately set. There is speculation it may have been started by the kidnappers as a diversion. Calder's son-in-law, Acting Sheriff Logan Echohawk, was called to the fire, leaving his wife and son alone at their ranch. Cynthia Tate has more on that story. Cynthia."

"Do you think they could have started it, Logan?" Jessy sat on the arm of Ty's chair, watching when they switched to a shot of a willowy redhead, a fire-blackened prairie filling the background. "Would the kidnappers have had time to start the fire and knock out the transformer, too?"

"It's possible." Logan's hand rubbed the point of Cat's shoulder in an absent caress.

"Logan, that's you," Cat murmured in surprise when a shot of him came on the screen. "You didn't tell me you'd been interviewed."

"I wouldn't call it that," he began.

She shushed him and sat forward to listen, studying his face on the screen. Beard stubble shadowed his jaw and accented the hollows of his cheeks. There were hints of weariness and lack of sleep around his eyes. At the same time, there was a sense of alertness and bottomless energy.

When the reporter asked him about the possible connection between the kidnapping and the arson, his response was a simple but firm, "I can't comment on an ongoing investigation."

"What about the reports that your wife collapsed after last night's ordeal, that she is heavily sedated and under a doctor's care?"

He leveled cool gray eyes on the reporter. "My wife is a Calder, and Calders are cool under pressure. A little night riding isn't about to shake her."

"Then she's all right?"

"My wife is fine. My wife and son are both fine."

Moved by the way he had chosen to defend her, Cat settled back against him. "That was a beautiful thing to say."

"I couldn't have said it better myself," Chase agreed.

"It was the truth," Logan said, his eyes smiling down on her. "You never lost your head. Our son is upstairs asleep because of what you did. You're quite a woman, Cathleen Calder Echohawk."

"Thanks to you." Cat looked at him with proud love.

"I have to agree with my sister," Ty said. "There was a time when Cat would have tried to fight them off."

"Let's hope the day never comes when she's forced into that situation." Logan's voice was much too serious; it sent a little chill shivering up her spine.

When the station went to a commercial, Ty picked up the remote and flipped through the channels. "Ty, go back." Jessy pressed a hand on his shoulder, urgency in her voice. He switched to the previous channel. "Look." Jessy pointed to the television. "It's Lath Anderson."

His hat was pushed to the back of his head, the sun full on his face with Sally's restaurant and bar visible in the background. ". . . whoever tried to snatch that kid was a fool. Ask anybody here—" he waved a hand toward the small crowd gathered outside the building—"and they'll tell you, no matter what else you might think about him, Chase Calder is the original Big Jake. You ain't gonna get anything from him but a whole heap of trouble."

"Let's hope the kidnappers hear that," Jessy murmured.

Logan knew the sound bite was the kind of catchy comment the rest of the media would pick up—one that could prove to be an effective deterrent. Yet he was bothered by the cocky way Lath looked directly into the camera and winked.

* * *

"My brother, the television star." Rollie thumped Lath on the back.

"That oughta throw Echohawk and those FBI boys off the scent." He got up from the kitchen table and walked over to switch off the portable television set on the counter. Delighted with himself, he laughed and shook his head. "Now I ask you—who's gonna really believe those nasty kidnappers would make another try for the kid after I just told 'em Calder might not come up with the ransom money? Nobody. Absolutely nobody."

"That's true, but I don't know what good that will do us as long as they hole up at the Triple C with the kid. Did you see all those men they had guarding the place?" Rollie asked. "It looked like a damned fort."

A loud harrumph came from Emma. "I knew you'd get cold feet." She glanced with scorn at her youngest.

"I don't have cold feet," Rollie insisted, reddening. "I'm just smart enough to see that we haven't got a chance at the kid as long as he stays in that house."

"You're just scared to go up against Calder." Rising from her chair, she began gathering up the dirty cake plates. "That man as good as sent you to prison, and look at you—trembling at the mere thought of walking into his house. Lath's clearly the only one with guts in this family."

"You saw all those men guarding the place," Rollie protested.

"You'd better take another look at those men." She swiped at the cake crumbs on the table, using a corner of her apron. "Those were nothing but cowboys. Calder was just putting on a show for your benefit. He can't keep 'em standing around there much more than a week before he'll have to put 'em back to work. Then what've ya got?"

She faced him, one hand on her hip in challenge. She was waiting for an answer, but Rollie had no idea what it should be.

"I don't know." He shot a look at Lath, trying to see if he knew. But Lath watched their mother with a rapt and curious attention.

She sniffed her disgust. "Use your eyes. You got a big house sitting off by itself, all white and proud and important-looking. There's nobody living within shouting distance of it. Don't you know it'd kill Calder if you snatched the boy right from under his nose?"

Chuckling, Lath came up behind her and gave her a big hug, smacking a kiss on her cheek. "Ma, you are a jewel. You're right as rain. That house is about as isolated as you can get."

Rollie couldn't believe what he was hearing. "But look at how big that thing is," he argued. "How are we supposed to find the kid? We can't go searching through the whole place."

"You don't have to. All the bedrooms is upstairs, and there ain't but six of them," Emma stated. "Somebody told me once that Calder's got the big one in the southeast corner. And I'd guess the family would have the other bedrooms that faced the front so they could look out and gloat over all they own."

"You see, little brother," Lath said, grinning. "It ain't as impossible as it sounds. You just gotta think." He tapped his head.

"Maybe," he conceded. "But logic tells me that there's only two of us and a whole lot more of them."

"You only got two people to worry about," his mother stated. "Echohawk and that crazy O'Rourke, if he's hanging around. Those two'll be the ones who'll react the quickest. You get rid of them, and you'll only have the Calders to deal with. This time, though," she added, "you better make sure that tramp isn't slipping out the back door with the kid."

"You can count on that, Ma," Lath promised.

TWENTY-FIVE

Outside Quint's bedroom window, rose light flooded the ranch buildings of the Triple C headquarters, strengthening to a rawer red along the sky's western rim. Finished with his prayers, Quint clambered into bed and waited for Cat to draw the covers around him.

"Why can't I stay up till Dad comes? I'm not tired." The weariness in his eyes told Cat otherwise.

"Maybe you're not, but it's already past your bedtime."

He gave an adultlike sigh. "I know, but—where is Dad?"

"He had to go feed the horses and check the stock." Cat sat on the edge of the bed and smoothed the hair off his forehead.

"When are we gonna go home, Mom?"

The longing in his voice tugged at her. "Soon. Maybe in a few days."

"Raindance is gonna forget me."

"It's only been two weeks. I don't think Raindance will forget you that quickly." Two weeks. In some ways, it seemed much longer than that.

"He could, though," Quint insisted.

"But he hasn't."

"Don't you want to go home, Mom?"

"Yes. Very much," Cat answered truthfully, surprised that she felt it so strongly.

She loved The Homestead and the Triple C as deeply as she always had, but this wasn't her home anymore. Her home was the Circle Six, with Logan and Quint. It wasn't something she could easily explain, not even to herself.

"Mom, I don't think I can go to sleep."

"Why don't you try closing your eyes?" she suggested.

"It won't work."

"Try." Bending, Cat tapped his nose and gave him a goodnight kiss.

By the time she reached the door, his eyes were already drifting shut. She left the door standing slightly ajar and went downstairs to wait for Logan.

A nearly full moon had begun its climb into the night sky when headlight beams flashed across The Homestead's front windows, signaling Logan's return. Cat met him on the porch and went straight into his arms, greeting him with a long, welcoming kiss.

"You must have been reading my mind," Logan murmured against her lips. "I've been thinking about kissing you for the last ten miles."

"I've been thinking about it longer than that." Cat locked her hands behind his neck and added suggestively, "Among other things."

He slanted a hard, quick kiss across her lips. "Hold that thought until after I've had a shower." He reached up to pull her hands from around his neck.

"Yes, I noticed you're wearing every rancher's favorite cologne—Eau de Manure." She let him draw her hands down between them.

"A cow got stuck in the mud. I had to dig her part way out before I could pull her free. I hosed the worst of it off before I left."

"How are things at the ranch?" Cat wasn't ready to go inside yet.

"Fine."

"Quint wants to know when we're going to move back. So do I."

"I don't know. Maybe next week."

"Why not tomorrow?" She saw the refusal forming in his expression and quickly reasoned, "Everything is almost back to normal. The media pulled out last week and the FBI two days ago. You don't honestly believe we're in any kind of danger or you wouldn't have told Dad he could take his men off guard duty and let them go back to their regular work. So why do we have to wait until next week?"

"Blackmore reports back next week," Logan explained. "When he takes over as sheriff, I'll have regular hours again. I'll be able to spend more time at home, especially in the evenings. I won't feel comfortable leaving you and Quint alone at night, not for a while. And that's not the right frame of mind to have when you go out on a call."

Cat understood his reasoning. She didn't like it, but she understood it. "All right," she gave in, with a sigh. "Next week."

Beer in hand, Lath strolled over to the jukebox and glanced over the selections. Rollie adjusted his angle on the cue ball and took aim on the seven ball near the corner pocket. Drawing the pool cue back, he let it fly. There was a crack and a rumble followed by the solid thud of the seven ball falling into the pocket.

"What was that noise?" Lath turned from the

jukebox, a heavy frown on his face.

"*That* was the seven ball." Rollie moved around the pool table, his eye measuring the best angle on the eight ball. "You might as well get your money out now, Lath. This game is mine."

"No, I heard something else." Still frowning, he looked toward the front windows, his head cocked at a listening attitude.

"You aren't going to break my concentration playing that old diversion game," Rollie told him and bent over the table. "Eight ball, side pocket."

"It's no game. I swear I heard something." Lath came back to the pool table.

"Then maybe you should go check it out." Rollie did a practice stroke.

"I forgot—how much was the bet?"

"Ten dollars. You can lay it right there by the chalk." Rollie nodded to it.

"I thought it was five."

"It was ten and you know it." A sharp tap sent the cue ball rolling forward. It clipped the edge of the black eight ball, tumbling it into the side pocket. Grinning, Rollie turned to his brother, rubbing his thumb across his fingers in a "gimme" gesture. "Pay up."

As Lath reluctantly dug in his pocket, the restaurant door flew open. "Call the police," somebody shouted. "A tanker rig just flipped over on the highway. It's blockin' both lanes."

"Come on. Let's go have a look." Lath headed for the door.

Rollie went after him. "You owe me ten dollars, Lath."

"Forget about the damn money," he muttered and pushed Rollie out the door ahead of him. "This could be what we've been waiting for."

Outside, Lath wasted no time getting more information. As soon as he confirmed the accident had ruptured the tank, spilling some kind of chemical on the highway, he grabbed Rollie and shoved him toward the pickup.

"This is it," Lath said. "We're going tonight."

Rollie's stomach gave a nervous little jump, right before a kind of excitement kicked in. He didn't have to ask where they were going; he knew.

Logan got the call shortly after he stepped out of the shower. Cat watched him dress. A selfish side of her wanted to interfere with the process, spend a little time exploring that smooth ripple of muscle. But she had been born a Calder; duty was something she understood.

"You did say Blackmore would be back next week?" she said when he retrieved his gun from the closet's top shelf.

"Yes. Why?" He glanced up while he strapped it on.

"Because this isn't the way I envisioned the night ending."

"Me either." The glow of desire was in his eyes when he crossed the room and gathered her to him, his mouth coming down with a hungry need.

"Maybe you could wake me up when you get back," she murmured, breathing in the fresh, light hint of soap on his skin.

"Maybe I will." He skimmed his lips over her cheek before he drew back.

Cat saw the hesitation, the flicker of concern in his eyes. "You get that chemical spill cleaned up, and don't worry about us. We'll be fine."

With a small smile, he touched a finger to her cheek and left.

"That damned moon is like a spotlight." Rollie hunched over the van's steering wheel, peering up at it.

"It'll make it easier to run without lights." Busy attaching the silencer to his automatic, Lath glanced up long enough to see they were almost to the end of the lane. The highway was just ahead. "Turn right. We'll go to O'Rourke's first."

"O'Rourke's?" Rollie shot him a surprised look.

"Yeah. If he's there, we'll take him out. If he isn't, then we gotta worry about him bein' somewhere around the Calder house."

On that sobering thought, Rollie fell silent. It wasn't hard to figure out why Lath hadn't said anything about O'Rourke before now. He thought Rollie would chicken out. Truthfully, Rollie felt a little sick at the moment—and a whole lot scared. He saw the logic in it, just as he'd seen the logic of carrying guns in case they had to shoot their way out. But killing someone that way seemed more like an accident and less like murder.

He clung to the hope O'Rourke wouldn't be home, knowing it was stupid, knowing that it could mean the old man might be at the Triple C, that he could screw up the whole works.

A half mile from the Shamrock ranch yard, Lath told him to kill the engine and let the van coast. It rolled to a stop about a hundred feet short of the house. No lights showed from its windows.

"It doesn't look like he's there," Rollie whispered.

"I'll take a look." Lath pulled on his ski mask, adjusted it, then zipped up his jacket.

All the bulbs had been removed from the van's interior lights before they left the Simpson place. The door latch clicked under Lath's hand. Then he was outside the van, the moonlight glinting on the automatic's metal silencer.

Nervous, Rollie chewed at the inside of his lip, watching while Lath darted into the shadows of the nearest trees. Almost the instant he melded into the darkness, a door slammed. Rollie jumped at the sound and broke into a cold sweat.

A second later, he saw O'Rourke's thin shape moving across the moonlit ranch yard, a rifle loosely carried in his swinging hand. He scanned the shadows under the trees, searching for Lath.

"O'Rourke!" The ski mask partially muffled the barked call.

The old man swung in a half crouch, then jerked as if he'd been punched in the stomach and crumpled to the ground. Rollie hadn't heard anything but the crunch of gravel under O'Rourke's boot. Lath came out of the shadows near the yard and approached the man on the ground with caution. Pausing, he looked down on him, took aim and fired again.

Swearing bitterly, Rollie looked away, fighting tears and a churning nausea. He didn't say a word when Lath climbed into the passenger seat.

"Let's go. Let's go!" Lath ripped off the mask, sounding breathless and high all at the same time.

There was no turning back now. If there had been a chance before, there was none now. Recognizing that, Rollie started the engine, a cold anger welling inside.

Back on the highway again, they followed it for a short distance, then turned onto a side road that took them to the Triple C's seldom-used north gate. The last time they'd tried to snatch the kid, Rollie had been a bundle of nerves. This time he felt nothing. It was as if everything inside him had turned to ice. Hot ice.

He drove straight to the big house and parked behind it, out of sight. In silence, he donned the ski mask and pulled on a pair of thin leather gloves while Lath did the same.

"Got the tape?" Lath asked.

Nodding, Rollie patted the bulge in his jacket's zipped pocket. Lath jammed a clip in the second automatic, its silencer already attached, and passed it to Rollie, then gathered up his own. At a signaling nod from Lath, he slipped out of the van. Quickly they found the breaker switch and cut the telephone line.

The back door was locked, but the massive front door wasn't. They stepped inside and closed it carefully behind them. A pulsating silence greeted them, heavy and thick. Lath snapped on his penlight. It lanced the darkness, touched on the rounded back of a sofa in an area directly ahead of them before Lath switched it off.

The living room. According to their mother, the staircase emptied into it. Their rubber-soled sneakers made only a whisper of sound as they crossed the room to the staircase. Lath went first. Rollie followed, wincing when a board creaked under his weight.

At the top of the steps, they paused to listen. But all was quiet. Concentrating on the front section of the house, Lath streaked the penlight over the room doors. One was open a crack. Rollie pointed to it. When he was a kid, his mother had always left the door to his room ajar like that.

Lath nodded, and Rollie wondered if he remembered the same thing. He waited, fingers flexing around the trigger guard, while Lath went to check it out. Within seconds, Lath was motioning him to follow.

It was the kid's room. Rollie couldn't believe their luck. Moonlight flooded through the windows, spreading to the boy lying on his stomach. Rollie handed Lath his gun and quickly got the tape out of his pocket, tore off a wide strip of it and moved to the bed.

The kid mumbled a sleepy protest when Rollie turned him over, but he didn't wake up, not until

Rollie slapped the tape over his mouth. He grabbed the slender arms that came up to fight him off, held them easily in one hand and wrapped the tape tightly around them, then went to work on the wildly kicking legs.

Even in sleep, Cat's hearing was tuned to any sound coming from her son's bedroom, however faint. She raised up, propping an elbow under her, and struggled to throw off the heaviness of sleep. A muted thump came from Quint's room.

Pushing aside the covers, she swung out of bed and reached to turn on the lamp. The knob clicked under her fingers, but no light came on. Alarm shot through her, jolting her fully awake. Fighting panic, Cat picked up the telephone. The line was dead.

Her blood went cold.

She shot off the bed and out of the room, surprising two dark-clad figures near the stairs. One had a wiggling bundle under his arm. It was Quint.

Cat threw herself at them, screaming, "No, you can't take him! Let him go!"

In her haste to reach Quint, she ran into the first man as he wheeled toward her. With a backward shove of his arm, he hurled her away with a force that slammed her against the wall. Stunned by the impact, Cat stumbled to her knees.

Ty came out of his bedroom. "Hold it—"

There was a loud, spitting sound. At almost the same instant Cat saw Ty spin back into the door and crash to the floor.

"Go, go, go," an urgent voice whispered.

Feet clumped down the stairs in rapid flight as Cat struggled to her feet, a hand automatically touching the back of her head where the throbbing pain was centered. She started toward the top of the steps, but her father caught her.

"Stay back," he ordered. "They have guns."

"They took Quint."

"Oh, my God, Ty," Jessy murmured from the far doorway, then called, "He's been shot."

"I'm coming." Chase released Cat to go to his son. "How bad is it?"

"I'm not sure," Jessy answered. "It's his shoulder. I can feel where the bullet came out the top of it."

". . . okay," Ty mumbled.

Cat ran back into her bedroom, grabbed a pair of tennis shoes from the closet and raced for the stairs.

"Cat, where are you going?" her father demanded.

"The lines are dead. There's a mobile phone in the truck."

She flew down the steps and heard a door shut somewhere in the house. The path through the living room was ingrained in her memory. She crossed it without checking her headlong pace. At the front door, Cat paused long enough to push a foot into one of the shoes, then hopped onto the front porch while tugging on the other one.

The rumbling growl of an engine starting up momentarily froze her.

It came from behind the house. The kidnappers. It had to be the kidnappers.

Cat ran to a pillar and flattened herself against it as a van came barreling around the corner of the house, its lights off. She watched to see which direction it went. When it turned onto the north road, she ran to the pickup.

The interior light flashed on when Cat opened the door on the driver's side. She snatched the keys off the floor mat and scrambled behind the wheel, driven by only one thought—she had to find out where they were taking Quint.

Hurrying, she inserted the key in the ignition and

started the truck. She reached for the headlight switch, then pulled her hand back. She had been born and raised on this ranch. Cat knew its roads better than whoever had taken Quint. Gunning the motor, she reversed away from the house and sped after the van.

The lights atop the patrol car flashed their eye-jarring cadence, throwing their jerky glare across the Shamrock ranch yard. Logan spotted the dark, wet glisten of a blood trail that led straight to the house. The hand that had been on the butt of his .45 now drew it.

"Stay alert, Garcia," he told the deputy with him. "It could be a trap."

Moving parallel to the trail, they followed it to the front stoop and flanked the door. Logan checked to make sure the stocky deputy was ready, then burst onto the porch and into the darkened house, Garcia on his heels. High-powered flashlight beams raked the interior. Then Logan hit the wall switch, flooding the living room with light.

A scratching sound came from the kitchen. At a nod from Logan, the two men moved toward it with caution. The beam picked out O'Rourke's body on the floor, the back of his shirt soaked with blood. The telephone was near him, his fingertips touching the beeping receiver off the hook.

Logan flipped on the light switch, motioned for Garcia to check the rest of the house, then went to the motionless body, sidestepping the blood smears on the floor. Crouching beside him, Logan pressed two fingers to O'Rourke's carotid artery and found a pulse. It was on the thready side, but it was there.

"Hang on, O'Rourke. Hang on." Logan holstered

his gun and ripped open O'Rourke's shirt, exposing two bullet wounds. One appeared to be an exit wound, while the second was an entrance wound, an apparent kill shot, intended to finish off the old man.

Garcia returned to the kitchen. "We're clear." His dark eyes focused on O'Rourke.

"He's alive," Logan told him. "Grab some towels. We need to get a compression bandage going and slow down this bleeding."

"How the hell did he drag himself all the way in here, shot up like that?" The deputy moved to the cupboard, pulling out drawers.

"Sheer force of will." Logan picked up the receiver on the old rotary dial phone and depressed the cradle's disconnect button, silencing the irritating beep. A soft moan came from O'Rourke as his fingers moved in a feeble effort to reach the phone. Logan bent close to his face. "O'Rourke, are you with me? Can you hear me?" Lashes fluttered and lifted, showing him glazed and unfocused green eyes. "Who did this, O'Rourke? Who shot you?"

". . . don' know . . ." The words were barely louder than a breath.

". . . mas' . . ."

"He had on a mask?" Like the kidnappers. The connection in Logan's mind was instant.

Eyes closed in confirmation. "Yeah . . . Ca' . . . alone . . . sorry . . ." The last faded into a long feathering breath.

There was a perceptible slumping of his body. Seeing it, Logan thought they had lost him. But, no, the pulse was still there. Gathering up the phone, Logan straightened and moved out of Garcia's way, then silently cursed the slowness of the rotary dial. He wouldn't let himself think about the mask yet.

"Jenna, it's Echohawk," he said the instant her voice came on the line.

"Logan. Thank God, I—"

"O'Rourke's alive—barely. Get an ambulance out here double quick. Alert the air-evac while you're at it."

"Right away. I've been trying to reach you on the radio," she rushed. "Your wife called—two men in a van took your son. Ty Calder was shot. I've got paramedics headed there now."

"When was this?"

"I'm not sure. She called a few minutes ago." She paused a beat. "Logan, she's following them. She called me from the mobile phone in the ranch pickup."

"Give me the number." His mouth tasted tinny and dry. She read it off to him. He hung up and dialed the number with sharp, impatient strokes. When Cat answered on the second ring, Logan wasted no time.

"Cat, where are you?"

"Logan. Thank God it's you." He heard her voice waver, heard it steady. "I'm on the main north road, almost to the gate. The van is less than a mile ahead of me, heading for the highway. They took Quint. I tried to stop them—"

"I know, I know—"

"It must be the same two men, Logan. They wore ski masks and cut the phone line just like before. They shot Ty in the shoulder. I don't know how bad he is."

"Listen to me, Cat—"

She broke in again. "Logan, they're turning east on the highway. They're turning east! They're in a dark-colored van. I don't know what the make is. And I haven't been able to get close enough to get a license number."

"Cat, pull over. Do you hear me? Pull over," he ordered harshly. "I'm only a few minutes away, and the highway south of town is blocked. They can't go anywhere."

"But they could turn onto a side road," she argued.

"Damn it, pull over and stay where you are. I'll find them. Don't follow them any farther."

"Logan, I'm almost sure they don't know I'm behind them. My lights aren't on and—They're slowing down. Logan, they're slowing down."

"Stay back. For God's sake—"

"Oh, my God," she murmured.

"What is it? What's happening?"

"They're turning off, Logan." Her voice sounded strange. "They're turning into the old Simpson place. That's where Lath Anderson lives."

"I'll handle it from here, Cat," he spoke carefully and clearly. "You just stay right where you are and wait until I get there."

"Logan, hurry. He's got Quint."

"I'll take care of—" He heard a click on the other end. "Cat? Cat?" She had hung up. He swore viciously.

About a mile from the head of the rutted lane, Cat swung the pickup onto a section of grassy shoulder and killed the engine. Common sense told her not to go any farther; she didn't know how long the driveway was. Logan was right, she decided. She should wait until he got there.

Cat rolled down the window and listened for the wail of a siren. There was nothing. It was impossible; she couldn't just sit there. She had to go look, see where they were, maybe find out what they had done with Quint.

When she started to climb out of the truck, her

legs became tangled in her long nightgown. Stretching across the seat, Cat rummaged through the glove compartment and found a razor-edged box cutter. Using its sharpness, she sliced through the side seam and started ripping, shortening the nightgown to mid thigh.

Unimpeded, Cat stepped to the ground, noticed a denim jacket stuffed behind the cab seat, and pulled it out. It looked like one of Ty's. Knowing it would be miles too big, she put it on and rolled back the sleeves, hesitated, then picked up the box cutter and stuffed it in a side pocket. It was a weapon of sorts, the only one she had. After her last experience with Lath, Cat knew better than to rely on it. Just the same, she felt better having it.

After a quick scan of the lane behind her, she took off, running alongside the rutted track, following it as it led her toward the old Simpson ranch yard. At the first glimmer of light ahead, Cat slowed and ducked into the trees, her breath coming quick and fast, her heart pounding.

The sudden, harsh gabbling of guinea fowl momentarily froze her near a tree trunk. Through the trees she could see the lights of a house trailer. An angry mutter came from somewhere nearby. She crept forward with caution.

". . . worry too much, little brother." Lath's voice; Cat recognized that cocky drawl instantly. Rage rose up like bitter bile in her throat. "In the first place, ain't nobody gonna come here lookin' for him. Even if they did, you aren't gonna hear a peep out of him. That sleepin' pill will knock him out in five minutes flat. And they'll never find him in there otherwise."

Where was "in there"? Cat stole a look, glad of the denim jacket's dull blue color that hid the paleness of her bare shoulders and the satin sheen of her nightgown. The two men were walking toward the trailer, coming from a hillside area off to the left. Both were dressed in ordinary jeans and plaid shirts, the ski masks and gloves gone.

Rollie mumbled something.

"Hell, I'll just stick those guns in the next shipment. If they ever surface again, it'll be somewhere in Texas," Lath replied with a strut in his voice. "I tell ya, I got this all figured out. Ma's got a whole bottle of them pills. We can keep the kid doped up for a couple weeks if we have to." He thumped Rollie on the back. "Wouldn't you love to see Calder's face about now?"

Laughing, he opened the trailer door. Cat ducked low behind the brush as light poured through the opening. Then the door closed, muting the voices, leaving only the occasional gabble of the still-uneasy guinea hens.

What were they doing over by that hillside? Cat wondered. Could that be where they had hidden Quint? She didn't see anything that looked like a building, just trees and some brush.

"Nobody will find him," Lath had bragged.

Maybe she could, if she got there before the sleeping pill knocked Quint out.

TWENTY-SIX

"Dammit, Cat, why couldn't you have waited?" Logan clutched the torn swatch of satin from her nightgown. He looked in the direction of the Simpson place, his mind registering the odd noises coming from the pickup's cooling engine. He was only scant minutes behind her.

"She can't be far ahead of us," Garcia echoed Logan's thoughts.

"I know." His fingers curled into the slick cloth an instant before he tossed it back onto the seat. "Wait here for our backup. I'll see if I can find her—and get her out of there." Logan checked his watch. "With or without her, I'll be back in ten minutes. The state troopers should be here by then, and we'll move in."

"Right."

Logan set off at a loping run.

An old root cellar. Cat stared at the weathered door that lay flush with the hillside slope. This had to be where they had hidden Quint. Hugging the shadows, she crept closer to it, darting wary looks at the trailer.

The door lifted with barely a sound. She slipped inside and carefully lowered it shut. Blackness swallowed her, total and absolute. She battled back the surge of panic and reminded herself that she didn't see either man carrying a flashlight. Somewhere, there had to be a light. She felt along the walls, encountered a string and pulled it. She heard the *snick* of a chain a split second before a single, bare bulb came on with blinding brightness.

Eyes narrowed against its glare, Cat looked around the cellar and saw nothing but shelves, a stockpile of canning jars, some empty and some filled. There was no sign of Quint. Her heart sank. She had been certain he would be here. But where? Where could they have hidden him when it was all so open and empty?

Taking a chance, she called in a loud whisper, "Quint, it's Mom. Are you in here? If you can hear me, make some kind of noise."

Cat held her breath, listening. Two seconds later, she heard a faint thump. She took a hesitant step forward, not sure where it came from.

"Do it again, Quint."

There was a second thump, a little louder. Glass jars rattled on an end wall shelf. He was behind that wall, Cat realized. Somewhere there had to be a door. She tugged at the middle shelf, felt it give a little, heard the rubbing of wood against wood and pulled harder. With a groaning scrape, it swung toward her, almost the whole wall.

She saw Quint lying in the narrow space behind it, his mouth, hands, and legs taped. Swallowing a sob, Cat rushed to him and yanked the tape off his mouth, then dug the box-cutter out of the jacket pocket and went to work on the tape binding his wrists. Quint turned his head and spit, then spit again. "They tried to make me swallow a pill," he told her, gray eyes blazing. "Yuck, it's all stuck on my tongue." He screwed up his face at the taste of it.

"Use your pajamas to wipe it off." As soon as his hands were free, Cat moved to his ankles. "Your dad's on his way here. We've got to find him. Okay?"

"What if those men come back?" Quint sounded as worried as she felt.

"We've got to get out of here before they do." She rubbed his legs and arms hard just in case the tape had cut off the circulation to them, and resisted the urge to hug him to her. There would be plenty of time for holding him and hugging him once they were safely away from here. Cat stood him up and turned. "Get on my back. We'll do this just like we did before."

He climbed on and wrapped his arms around her neck. "Are we going to ride Molly again?"

"Not this time, honey. This time we'll have to run until we find Dad. Hang on tight now."

Outside, the guineas set up another racket. Cat stopped halfway to the slanted door, fear striking deep in the pit of her stomach when she heard a voice muttering.

"Damned noisy birds. Don't you know that I'm the one that buys your damned feed."

"It's them, Mom." Quint whispered near her ear.

Cat swung him off her back. "You hide right there by that door. When he comes in, I'm going to talk to him so he won't see you. You run outside as soon as you can—and you run that way." She pointed in the direction of the highway. "Don't wait for Mom. You run as fast as you can."

He nodded, his eyes big.

She could hear footsteps now. "Hide, quick," she whispered and pushed him toward the side of the door.

As soon as he was hugged against the edge of it, Cat pulled the string, switching off the overhead light. She backed up a couple of steps and bumped against the shelf door. Hearing the clink of jars, she reached around until her fingers touched smooth glass. As she eased the jar off the shelf, the slanted door was raised up. A moonlit sky showed the bulky silhouette in the opening. Cat knew she had only seconds before he turned on the light and saw her. She prayed she could distract him long enough for Quint to get away.

His hand reached for the string. Cat heard the slide of the chain and closed her eyes against that first blinding glare. It flashed against her eyelids.

"What the hell—" Rollie stared at her in open-mouthed shock, then took an angry step forward.

Cat threw the jar at his head. "Run, Quint! Run!" She grabbed for another jar, her heart soaring at the sight of Quint darting into the open doorway.

Rollie looked back in time to see him scamper outside. He charged after him, bellowing, "Lath! Get out here! The kid's loose!"

Cat ran after him and jumped on Rollie's back, hammering at his head with the second jar. A door slammed. With an angry roar, Rollie threw her off. She landed hard and struggled to get up. She had one short glimpse of her barefoot, pajama-clad son running as fast as he could over the rough ground. But a little boy's 'fast' wasn't fast at all. Rollie could catch him easily, and he had already started after him.

"You fool, get her!" Lath yelled. "She's the one that can get us the death penalty. Here." He threw something to Rollie. Cat saw the flash of moonlight reflecting on metal and knew it was a gun. "I'll grab the kid."

In those seconds while Rollie caught the gun, shifted it into his grip and turned toward Cat, she scrambled to her feet and raced for the tree-covered hillside five yards away. Footsteps pounded after her. As she ducked behind the first tree, Cat heard that sharp crack of sound. Bark chips flew. She ran to the next tree.

"Throw down your weapon, Anderson!"

Logan. Cat swung toward the sound of his voice. Lath let loose with his automatic, raking the brushy edge of the clearing with a spray of bullets. At almost the same time, a skinny pajama-clad boy scurried into the concealing brush.

"Keep running, Quint. Keep running," she whispered.

Twigs snapped not far from her location. Cat instantly changed directions to lead Rollie away from Quint. But it was Logan she was worried about, conscious of the silence that had followed Lath's gun burst.

Logan melted back into the trees, away from the yard, placing each foot carefully and angling to intercept Quint. Once he had his son out of harm's way, he could concentrate on Cat.

Somewhere Lath moved along the tree edge. Once in a while, Logan could hear a faint rustling. The trailer door opened a crack, letting out a sliver of light. "Lath," a woman's voice called softly. "Did you get him?"

"No," came the answer far off to Logan's right. "But stay inside. I'll let you know when it's safe."

The heel of his foot touched a rock. Logan shifted silently off it, then picked it up and hurled it as far as he could to the right, where the voice had been.

It landed with a thud, drawing another spate of

bullets. Logan used the masking noise to sprint closer to where Quint should be. He spotted him just ahead, running awkwardly in his bare feet, the moonlight picking up the paleness of his light-patterned pajamas.

"Quint," he whispered.

The boy stopped and turned his tear-streaked face toward him. "Dad," he sniffled, his face crumpling.

Logan scooped him under his arm and angled back toward the ranch lane and the waiting patrol car. Seconds after he intersected the rutted tracks, he heard footsteps running toward him, coins jangling in a pocket.

"Garcia," he called out softly.

The stocky deputy puffed to a stop. "Logan, thank God. I heard gunfire."

"Is our backup here?"

"Not yet."

"Take Quint back to the patrol car." He handed him into Garcia's arms.

"Dad, no."

"I've got to go get your mom."

When he made his way back to the ranchyard, Logan saw that all the lights had been turned out inside the trailer. He scanned the area, trying to locate Lath's position, sweat beading along his upper lip.

A partially muffled outcry came from high on the hillslope, followed by scuffling sounds. Abandoning caution, Logan broke toward it, fully aware that Cat was a bigger threat to the Andersons alive than she was dead.

Gunfire exploded again, bullets chopping the brush directly ahead of him. Logan skidded to a stop, going to the ground in a feet-first slide as a shower of leaves and branches rained on him.

Gathering his legs under him, he sprang into a

crouching run, making for the nearest tree, snapping off three shots as he went. His shoulder hit the solidness of the trunk and immediately he dived behind a boulder an instant before another spray of bullets chewed the tree bark.

The shooting had driven the guinea fowl from the house yard. Their disturbed racket now came from somewhere near the old ranch buildings. Under their covering noise, he scooted back to another tree and stood up behind it, taking off his hat to peer around it and locate Lath's position.

Something moved in the shadows near the trailer steps. Logan shifted to another tree for a better look. Suddenly there was Lath vaulting onto the wooden stoop and yanking the door open.

Above the boom of a shotgun, a voice yelled, "You ain't takin' my boys!"

The blast blew Lath back against the railing. Logan briefly closed his eyes against the anguished scream that followed, then he looked to the hillside, his fingers tightening around the .45. Cat was up there somewhere.

With the gun pointed straight at her head, Cat didn't move. The sharp rock digging through the denim sleeve into her elbow didn't register, nor the trickle of blood from her scraped knee. The piney smell of resin was all around her. There was a sharpness and a clarity to every sight and sound that gave all of it a feeling of unreality.

But that gun was very real. Cat forced her eyes to look beyond the muzzle's deadly maw at Rollie. Anger and regret warred in his expression.

"Why? Why did you have to follow us?" The gun shook with his tightly bit words.

Hope sprang. If he truly wanted to kill her, he

would have already pulled the trigger. "Don't do this, Rollie." Her voice sounded thin. She worked to strengthen it. "It will only make things worse for you."

"It can't get any worse."

Cat heard the sob in his voice. "Yes, it can. Rollie, I can testify for you. I—"

"You wouldn't before!" he raged. "Vengeance, that's what you wanted. Now I'm getting mine."

His voice was low and ugly, hard purpose ridging the set of his jaw as he looked down the barrel of the gun. "Rollie—"

An explosive blast reverberated through the night. Cat flinched, thinking he had fired, but he was spinning away. A keening wail came from the house yard. Rollie took a step toward it, his whole body tense, listening.

Seizing her chance, Cat was on her hands and knees in a flash and scrambling away even as his voice rang out, "Ma? Ma!" Then the rattle of stones alerted him to her escape. "Come back here, you little bitch." He lunged after her.

Her foot slipped on a rock. She stumbled. His fingers closed around a handful of denim, pulling her back. With a wild, twisting shrug, Cat was out of the over-sized jacket. Before she had taken two scrambling steps, he grabbed her hair and yanked her back, a muscled arm banding itself across her throat in a chokehold. Her hands came up to pull at it and release the pressure.

"Let her go, Rollie."

Cat instantly stopped struggling at the sound of Logan's voice, relief soaring through her when she saw his dark shape near a tree, his outstretched arms braced in a shooting stance. It crashed at the cold feel of the gun muzzle pressed against her temple.

"Drop the gun, Echohawk. Drop it or she dies."

Logan never changed his stance. "You're no killer, Rollie. We both know that. Now, give it up. It's over."

"It isn't over yet. Lath—"

"Lath is dead."

"You're lying." A tiny mewling sound came from Rollie's throat. "Get away from that tree. Step out here where I can see your face."

Cat gasped at the sudden, hard jab of the gun against her temple, then bit down on her lip to stifle any further cry. With frightened eyes, she watched Logan move with slow, deliberate steps into the moonlight, keeping his gun still pointed at Rollie.

"He's dead," Logan repeated. "Now drop the gun. It's over."

The muzzle eased back from her head. Testing its closeness, Cat turned slightly, felt it and felt the movement eliminating some of the pressure against her throat. If she could turn her head all the way to the side, if he took the gun away, Cat was certain she could duck out from under his arm.

"Ma?" Rollie said in a kind of question.

"She's crying over your brother. She won't want to lose both her sons tonight. Drop the gun, Rollie."

"You did it, didn't you?" Anger trembled in his voice. "You killed my brother!"

Out of the corner of her eye, Cat saw the barrel of the gun swing toward Logan. She didn't remember anything; she didn't remember twisting her head out from under Rollie's arm, only the gun centering on Logan. She didn't remember dropping to the ground to be out of Logan's line of fire, only the explosions coming one on top of the other.

She didn't remember screaming, only the sight of Logan falling in that sharp limp way that told her he'd been hit.

Sobbing, Cat ran to him.

The pain, he couldn't breathe. Eyes closed, Logan felt himself rise, then fall back again. A whisper of perfume came to him. The fragrance of it made him open his eyes and make sure it was real.

But Cat was with him. She sat on the hard, dusty ground and she had taken his head onto her lap and her hands now tugged at his shirt. She looked down, her eyes a shimmering green. This close to her, Logan noticed the length of her lashes, the curve of her cheek, and the grimly determined set to her mouth, something willful and steel-proud about her expression. Her breasts were against his head so that he felt the quick and frantic beat of her heart.

"Logan, please don't die," she said with a sob in her voice. "I love you too much. Please."

"No." He had to fight for the breath to speak, his mouth curving in a weak smile as he tried to get out the words. "I'm . . . okay. The vest . . ." He slid a hand up his stomach and fingered the hole in his shirt. "No . . . blood, Cat."

He heard her gasp, then her lips came down, hot and firm on him. A tear fell onto his cheek. His hand came up, fingers touching her face, feeling the other tears that were there. She caught it and pressed it to her face, eyes closing in happiness.

"When you fell, I thought—" She couldn't finish it.

"Close range like that . . . the bullet packs . . . a wallop." Logan tried to sit up, but every muscle in his chest protested the attempt. He looked at the man lying on the ground. "Rollie?"

"I think he's dead." She glanced briefly at the body.

"Help me up," he said with a grimace. "Quint will be worried."

"He found you?" Propping and lifting, Cat got him to his feet.

"More or less." He leaned on her, his mouth crooking in a small smile that sent her heart tripping over itself.

Emotions trembled through her—relief, fear, love—most of all, love. He was safe, and Quint was safe. At the moment, nothing else mattered. Cat wrapped both arms around him, content to simply hold him and feel his solidness and strength.

Below them, Logan saw Garcia and the long-awaited backup moving in, approaching the house trailer and the sobbing woman with caution. The ordeal was over. There would be time enough later to count up the toll—and to tell Cat about her uncle.

But right now, Logan wanted only one thing—to hold both his wife and his son in his arms.

The future is before you,
The ones you love at your side.
You'll walk this land together
And you'll do it with Calder pride.